BITTER PARADISE

THE DR. ZOL SZABO
MEDICAL MYSTERY SERIES

Tainted
Tampered
Up in Smoke
Beneath the Wake
Bitter Paradise

ROSS PENNIE

BITTER PARADISE

A Dr. Zol Szabo Medical Mystery

Published by ECW Press
665 Gerrard Street East
Toronto, Ontario, Canada M4M 1Y2
416-694-3348 / info@ecwpress.com

LIBRARY AND ARCHIVES CANADA
CATALOGUING IN PUBLICATION

Title: Bitter paradise : a Dr. Zol Szabo medical mystery /
Ross Pennie.

Names: Pennie, Ross, 1952- author.

Identifiers: Canadiana (print) 20200158015
Canadiana (ebook) 20200158031

ISBN 978-1-77041-465-5 (softcover)
ISBN 978-1-77305-474-2 (PDF)
ISBN 978-1-77305-473-5 (ePUB)

Classification: LCC PS8631.E565 B58 2020
DDC C813/.6—dc23

Cover design: Eric Mohr, Made by Emblem
Author photo: IPC Canada Photo Services
Printing: Marquis   5   4   3   2   1

The publication of *Bitter Paradise* has been generously supported by the Canada Council for the Arts which
last year invested $153 million to bring the arts to Canadians throughout the country and is funded in part by
the Government of Canada. *Nous remercions le Conseil des arts du Canada de son soutien. L'an dernier, le Conseil
a investi 153 millions de dollars pour mettre de l'art dans la vie des Canadiennes et des Canadiens de tout le pays.
Ce livre est financé en partie par le gouvernement du Canada.* We acknowledge the support of the Ontario Arts
Council (OAC), an agency of the Government of Ontario, which last year funded 1,737 individual artists and
1,095 organizations in 223 communities across Ontario for a total of $52.1 million. We also acknowledge the
contribution of the Government of Ontario through the Ontario Book Publishing Tax Credit, and through
Ontario Creates for the marketing of this book.

ONTARIO ARTS COUNCIL
CONSEIL DES ARTS DE L'ONTARIO
an Ontario government agency
un organisme du gouvernement de l'Ontario

Canada Council   Conseil des Arts
for the Arts   du Canada

Canada

PRINTED AND BOUND IN CANADA

MIX
Paper from
responsible sources
FSC® C103567

CHAPTER 1

Hosam ended the call, and from the back of the shop Max watched him scowl into some dark, malignant place. It was like the man was staring into a black hole — maybe Monocerotis or Cygnus X-1 — in a remote sector of the universe. Behind him, the dusky red spatters on the front door looked almost dry. But the splotches on the picture window still glistened.

"What did he say?" Max called, trying but failing to suppress the shivers. "Is h—" His voice cracked, and all that came out was a frog's croak. At fourteen, that happened way too often. He cleared his throat with a short cough and tried again. "Is he coming?"

Hosam seemed incapable of hearing, his mind stuck in another galaxy. But his left thumb was visible in this one, and it was stroking his thick black moustache. His comb and scissors were here too, poking from the pocket of his blood-soaked apron. The front-desk phone was tight in his fist, and there was no missing Marwan's blood clotted on the keypad.

"Hosam?"

After a while, he put down the phone and rubbed the back of his neck, staining it with more of Marwan's blood. He steadied himself against the desk and jerked his head as if tumbling out of a bad dream. His deep-set eyes, usually a light greyish-blue, had turned as black as the muzzles on Max's second-favourite *Fortnite* weapon, the double barrel shotgun.

Eventually, Hosam blinked. "Yes, Max. Your father, he says he is coming."

"Right now?"

"Inshallah."

Inshallah, that was for sure. And though Max never went to church, he hoped God or Allah, or both together, were pulling hard on whatever strings it took to get his dad here fast.

Max turned to Travis sitting beside him in the row of chairs set against the back wall for customers waiting for a haircut. Max raised the edge of the damp facecloth he'd been pressing against his forehead. "How . . . how is it?"

Travis leaned in and lifted the cloth for a good look. Squinting into the wound, he whispered, "The bleeding's stopped. Well, mostly. And I don't think I see any bone or brain tissue."

"Geez," Max said.

Travis pressed the makeshift dressing back into place. "You were out of it for a few seconds after you hit your head. I'm betting you cracked your skull."

"Thanks a lot, Trav. That makes me feel so much better."

A master blogger and Snapchatter, Max's best bud and video game squadmate was sometimes given to exaggerating details for the sake of his audience and his ratings. Hosam had examined the gash with a more professional eye a few minutes earlier. He'd said Max was going to need only a few stitches and he should keep pressure on the wound. He'd mentioned nothing about visible brain tissue or a fractured skull. But he had said Max would have to come back another day for his haircut. He'd finished Trav's moments before Marwan's attackers had rushed in, so Trav's low fade was already done.

Sitting next to Travis was Marwan's twenty-something client. He was rubbing his face with one of Hosam's damp cloths and struggling to appear calm and manly. But it was impossible to look even close to cool when your high fade was barely halfway done and blood from your barber's arteries was sprayed across your cheeks. The warm towels that Hosam had draped over their shoulders were supposed to help the three of them relax and stop shivering. But the only thing Max needed right now was the sight of his dad walking through the front door.

Ibrahim, the shop's head barber, had been standing at a display case in the back half of the shop immediately before, during, and after the attack. He'd been stocking the shelves with grooming stuff and trying way too hard to act as if nothing was happening. And now, his hands were shaking more than ever as he arranged and rearranged the tubes, bottles, and jars. He seemed to think that rows of perfectly aligned hair products might compensate for the horrific spectacle of his shop's junior barber splayed on the floor, his blood splattered in every direction.

Kneeling in the middle of the shop beside their gear, and still working on Marwan, were the two paramedics who'd been there for what seemed like ages but was probably only a few minutes. Max had no idea whether the young barber was dead or alive. Marwan's blood, in streaks and dark pools, was splotched across the floor, the walls, the arms of his barber chair. His now bloody-cheeked client had been in that chair not twenty minutes earlier when the two men in black hoodies rushed in. One of them, built like a super-tall wrestler, wore a WWE bandana to hide his face. He grabbed Marwan and pinned his arms behind his back. The other guy — skinny frame, tanned skin, long nose — shouted some sort of warning meant for everyone in the shop. Max didn't understand the words but recognized the language. He heard it here often.

The skinny guy spat in Marwan's face then set his jaw and whipped out something from beneath his shirt. At first, Max couldn't see what it was, but when the guy raised it high above his head, he saw the naked blade of a mean-looking bowie knife. Skinny Guy's eyes were on fire as the polished steel flashed for everyone to see.

The man lowered the knife, held it directly in front of Marwan's face, and muttered something it didn't take a linguist to know was menacing. The degree of terror bursting through Marwan's pores was something Max had never witnessed before, not even in the gruesomest scenes in Trav's extensive slasher-movie library. Marwan blinked at the spit gumming his eyes and nodded eagerly as if pledging to obey any warning his assailants might deliver from now until eternity.

Skinny Guy smirked then took a long, admiring look at his weapon. He raised an eyebrow and ran a finger the full length of the blade. Three times, he smiled and adjusted his stance, his black Chuck Taylor high tops squealing against the floor. Then, as quick as a samurai, he slashed Marwan's left arm above the elbow. Before the helpless barber could even wince, Skinny Guy crisscrossed Marwan's chest with the blade. Marwan screamed, and blood welled through the rips in his polo shirt, turning it from electric blue to magenta.

When the knife went for Marwan's neck, Max's breakfast launched itself into his gullet. The acidic mess of Cheerios and OJ burned his throat, but he managed to force it down again. His eyes were another matter. They refused to let him watch any more of this. His lids screwed themselves into light-tight mode while his hands put vice grips on his chair.

He'd read somewhere that silence could be deafening, especially when you had your eyes closed. With Marwan's screams snuffed by the bowie knife, a terrorizing stillness descended like a suffocating blanket.

After what felt like an ice age, a sickening drip, drip, drip invaded the silence.

Clothing rustled.

Something thudded to the floor.

High tops squealed as they strode across the room.

Max's heartbeat slammed into overdrive. The attackers must be closing in. They were choosing their next victim before picking off the witnesses one by one. Suddenly, sitting with your eyes closed was infinitely scarier than not knowing what was happening.

He forced his eyes open and willed them to focus. All he could see of the assailants was the backs of their hoodies. They weren't eyeing further victims but hightailing it through the front door. Marwan was on his back, next to his chair, motionless except for the twin arcs that throbbed from his carotids like maniacal firehoses.

The coppery smell of all that blood hung in the air along with the reek of the intruders' chewing tobacco. Max had friends who chawed because they thought it was cool. Right now, the familiar stink was the furthest from cool it could possibly be.

The moment the men were out the door, Hosam reacted as fast as a combat medic in a video game. He grabbed a stack of towels then cut off Marwan's shirt with his scissors. After a quick look at the wounds, he whipped off his belt and tightened it around Marwan's half-severed arm. While he was staunching the blood with the towels and the tourniquet, he told Ibrahim to call 911. He had to remind Ibrahim a minute later because the head barber, still clutching his shampoo bottles, seemed suddenly frightened of his own telephone.

No one in the shop, except for poor Marwan, had made eye contact with the attackers. No one had said a word to them. Now that Max had a chance to think about it, he wondered if the skinny slasher was the guy called Ghazwan who'd worked briefly at the shop a few months back. He'd never cut Max's hair, nor Trav's, but had spent most of his time sweeping the floor. He hadn't smiled and had never said a word in English. As far as Max could tell, Ghazwan spoke only Arabic. The other barbers spoke it too. Hosam had taught Max a few Arabic phrases such as *Good morning*, *Thanks a lot*, *I'm hungry*, and *Inshallah*, which seemed to fit pretty well every occasion.

And now, as another round of sirens wailed from close range, the boys looked at each other and braced for a second set of uniformed responders. A blaze of red and blue flashed from a roof rack. Tires screeched. Rubber smoke rose in the air. Two officers rushed in with their guns drawn and told everyone to freeze.

Ibrahim looked like was going to fill his pants. He put up his hands.

"They gone," he told the police, his knees shaking. "The men, they run away."

One of the paramedics looked up and told the cops, "Yeah, the premises are clear. The suspects were gone by the time we arrived." He jerked his head towards Marwan. "This guy's the only victim. Alive, but vitals unstable. Everyone else is mostly just shook up."

"What about those kids back there with blood on their faces?" said one of the officers. His blond hair was buzzed ultra short, and he was glaring at Max, Travis, and the half-shorn guy beside them as if they were a criminal gang. He motioned to his dark-haired partner to stand guard by the door then headed toward the boys, avoiding the thickest patches of blood on the floor. Travis whispered that the click of his boot heels sounded like the Foley work in a low-budget zombie movie.

Blond Cop set his eyes on Travis, giving him the Stare of the Ignorant. Travis had a purple birthmark that covered the left half his face. There was no denying its conspicuous nature or that from a distance it did look like dried blood. Although it was kind of ugly until you stopped noticing it, Max reckoned that only ignorant people stared at it quizzically, as if Travis was too stupid to know what they were thinking.

The officer holstered his gun, and Hosam stepped forward. He had removed his bloodied apron and wiped his face, but fine spatter still dotted his forehead and cheeks. "This boy," he explained, tipping his head toward Travis, "his face, the angels touched it at . . . at time of birth." A hint of the nice-guy warmth had returned to Hosam's eyes, and they were looking closer to their normal grey-blue. But Max could tell from the strain in Hosam's voice that the cop was making the cool-headed barber super nervous. "The medical term is . . . is port-wine nevus."

"Huh?" said the cop, ignoring Hosam's extended hand. A thin scar glowed red under his chin. Max could see the veins bulging on the sides of his scalp.

"Birthmark," Hosam told him. "Not . . . not injury."

The cop pointed at Max with a gesture that made Max feel like a wad of gum stuck to the sole of his regulation steel-toes. "What about this kid?"

"Slipped. His forehead, he hit it on the washbasin. Simple scalp laceration. Superficial to the aponeurosis. In need of sutures for the closure of the skin. Also, the boy might be suffering slight concussion."

Max was grateful that Hosam hadn't gone any further into the embarrassingly klutzy way he'd gashed his forehead. He'd tripped while running for cover when the paramedics were at the door, afraid they were the attackers coming back for another round of slash and run. He'd reached forward to steady himself against the basin but lost his grip. His left arm had always been sketchy — weak, short, and skinny. Max knew the proper terms: spastic, contracted, and hypoplastic. At the time of his birth, he'd suffered a stroke. *Yeah,* he often told the curious, *newborn babies can get them too.*

"That's your professional opinion, is it?" Blond Cop said. "What are you, some kind of *medical* barber?" He snorted, and his half-grin morphed into a sneer.

Hosam straightened his shoulders. "In my country, I am a trauma surgeon." He pulled at the collar of his polo shirt. "Much experienced with war wounds." He looked down and added, "Too much experienced."

The officer made a show of casually looking around to take in the pools of blood, the hyperfocused paramedics loading Marwan onto their stretcher, the terrified head barber now talking to the other cop. "Well, you're not *in* the old country," he told Hosam. "In *this* country, we make sure injured parties get checked out properly. At a hospital. Where they —"

"Are having real doctors?" Hosam interrupted.

The officer's sneer stiffened. "You got that right."

The door opened and Max could barely let himself believe that the slim, six-foot-plus figure filling the opening was his dad, Dr. Zoltan Szabo. His father looked aghast, and his face had turned as grey as his suit. The psychedelic flashes from the cop car parked outside, and the blood sprayed across the shop's gigantic mirror, did make the place look like a scene from *The Rocky Horror Picture Show*. There was no missing the tears in his dad's eyes when he caught sight of Max waving from the back of the shop. Max had seen that same look on his father's face when everyone had thought — mistakingly — that Max had been bitten by a giant, poisonous monitor lizard on Komodo island. That was last November during their trip to Indonesia. Dad's awesomest coworker — and now fiancée — Natasha Sharma, had been sharing the adventure with them. Travis too. Travis covered the story of Max's Komodo dragon near-miss quite nicely on his blog. And posted dozens of photos of the four of them with the dragons on Facebook, Instagram, and Snapchat. Max had to admit he'd enjoyed that brief bit of internet fame.

His dad rushed past the cops before they had a chance to stop him. He crouched in front of Max, grabbed his shoulders, and gave him a long hug. "Oh my God, Max. Can you talk? Are you all right? Is that blood caked on your eyebrow? What's under that cloth?"

Once his father finally let him go, Max briefly lifted the improvised dressing. "I'm okay, Dad. It just stings a little."

"Someone attacked you?"

"I fell."

Zol looked puzzled and searched the room with his gaze.

"Against the sink, Dad."

Zol turned to Travis, who was posting on his phone and watching the paramedics wheel Marwan to the ambulance. Max knew that everyone at school was going to lap this up, big time. Too big, maybe.

"And how are you, son?" Zol asked. "You okay?"

Travis nodded, raising his eyebrows the way he often did. And as always, he didn't make a sound. He never uttered any actual words to anyone except in private to Max and his mom. His dad died when he was little, and though Travis liked Zol a lot, he could never speak to him. No one knew what restricted Trav's use of audible speech, but the doctors said he had a bona fide medical condition called selective mutism. At school, he earned top marks without saying a word to anyone.

Blond Cop dismissed Hosam with a flick of his hand and started interrogating Max's father as if he had no right to be in what was now a crime scene.

But Max had never seen his dad intimidated, and he knew it wasn't going to happen now. His father had had plenty of practice dealing with cops, politicians, hostile reporters, and angry mobs. He always said it was his job to settle people's fears by calmly convincing them to face difficult situations with more logic than emotion. As the specialist in charge of the region's public health service, Dr. Zol Szabo closed restaurants serving rotten meat, caught pharmacists selling counterfeit drugs, and led a team investigating epidemics as scary as flesh-eating streptococci. Once, he busted a factory worker who was infecting people on his shift with condiments laced with typhoid bacteria. Max couldn't imagine committing such an indignity to Miracle Whip! At the moment, Dad and Natasha were chasing an outbreak of polio that showed no sign of letting up. The cases kept on coming. As Max understood it, the epidemic was a big deal because doctors around here hadn't seen a case of polio in more than sixty years. The kicker was, the vaccine everyone received when they were little didn't work against this new kind of polio. And this was one nasty disease. Zol had told Max that when the germ found its way into the spinal cord, it could paralyze a person from head to toe for weeks or months, even forever.

Once the cop had run out of questions, he told Zol that Max and Travis could go. He'd noted their names and contact details and said that someone from headquarters at Hamilton City Police Service might be in touch. Zol reassured the cop he was driving the boys straight to Emergency.

Before leaving the shop, Zol clapped an arm around Hosam's shoulder and pressed firmly. "Thanks for taking such good care of the boys, Hosam. You're the best." Zol ran a hand through his hair. Max was surprised to see his father's cheeks redden a little. "And I don't just mean at cutting hair."

"It was nothing, doctor," Hosam said. There was almost no light in his eyes.

"No, I mean it. I'm incredibly grateful to you."

Hosam gave a faint smile and handed Zol a clean cloth to take with them.

As the boys followed Zol to the front door, they edged past the dark-haired cop, who was still grilling Ibrahim. Max looked back and saw Hosam standing motionless at his sink, the sweat pouring off his chin. It was obvious he was straining to hear every word his nervous-looking boss was saying to the cop. As the door started to close behind the boys, Max heard Ibrahim swear to the cop that he had never seen either of the suspects before and had no idea who they were.

Travis and Max looked at each other. If it was true the slasher was Ghazwan, why was Ibrahim misleading the officer? Was he more afraid of ratting on a former employee than bullshitting the police?

CHAPTER 2

"I'll get to it, Mummyji."

Natasha's mother phoned her health-unit office every weekday morning at eleven thirty and fretted over the same subject. It took an effort to limit the calls to ten minutes. Today, she'd have to end it at three.

"You keep saying that, Tasha. But when are you actually going to do it? Time is of the essence."

"There's heaps of time." To be fair, June 30th was approaching pretty quickly, and there were tons of details still needing attention. But for now, her mind was riveted not on her wedding but on the outbreak of poliomyelitis that had spilled out of North Hamilton two weeks ago. Eight cases of polio across the city so far: two dead, two recovering at home, four still in hospital — three of them paralyzed from the neck down and on life support. That's what poliomyelitis did to you: it gave you fever and flu-like symptoms, then killed the muscle-controlling cells in your spinal cord. Polio left you paralyzed but awake with your mind intact, letting you feel every bit of the horror. She watched the wall clock's second hand sweep its relentless advance. Every minute that passed without her team of epidemic investigators finding and eliminating the source of the virus was another minute the next victim could become infected. And they would have to live, or die, with the consequences.

"Are you out of your mind, daughter of mine? There are only fifty-seven days left until your wedding, and today is half over. Dinesh Ramsay is no magician. He cannot be designing and producing three wedding outfits for you at the wave of a wand. I insist you telephone today to make your appointment."

Her mother would have a fit if she knew Natasha had already picked out her wedding saree from an online website. She'd found the perfect garment in bridal scarlet at an excellent price on *Indianweddingsarees.com*. The saree's fabrics were Bemberg and Georgette — silky to the touch but not the authentic, overly pricey silk her mother would be counting on. But who was wearing it anyway? The Mumbai manufacturer guaranteed delivery by international courier within five days, so there was plenty of time to finalize the online transaction.

"I don't need three outfits. One saree and one going-away dress will be fine."

"Do not be ridiculous. Three is absolute minimum you will require. A saree for the service — while exquisite, it should suggest innocence, even if that is no longer the case."

"Mother!"

"Next, a lehenga for the reception. It must be nothing short of sensational. Skirt must flare and positively dazzle when you dance with your father. And for the going away, salwar kameez is only choice — modest from distance, but of highest quality on close inspection. And everyone *will* be watching. Especially the Patels and the Shankars."

Her mother's acquisitive friends could gawk all they wanted. Natasha had already warned her parents that she and Zol were keeping things simple. A maximum of one hundred guests instead of the thousand her mother had in mind. The same bridal saree for the marriage service and the reception immediately following it.

No need to make a spectacle of herself by carrying out an elaborate change of outfits. She hadn't decided whether to go with a salwar kameez or a cocktail dress as her going-away outfit. What image did she want to leave with the guests as she started her new life with Zol and Max? The modern but demure Indian-ancestry housewife or the confident international professional? (No contest there.) She'd thought about the crisp white blouse and killer jeans that drove Zol wild when she wore them with her Jimmy Choo latticework stilettos. No, those would not be for going away. The blouse, jeans, and heels would make up the third outfit, the one only Zol would see. Though, she wasn't sure about the jeans; she'd have to try them on to be sure they still fit.

"And what about Zoltan? What has he done about his sherwani and turban? His height makes him difficult to fit, so he cannot be leaving it until last minute."

"He'll be wearing a business suit." Zol would look ridiculous in brocade and a turban. Her mother was still pretending to herself that Natasha was marrying a Punjabi, not a Hungarian. It was the only way Mummyji could bring herself to accept the marriage. Her father had the greatest respect for Zol — as a man and as a fellow physician — and had told Natasha she'd made an excellent choice in a husband. In a quiet moment away from her mother, he had asked her how confident she was in taking on a teenager as a stepson. Natasha had no difficulty in reassuring him on that score. She loved Max as if he were her own. And she had no doubts about him loving her too. His occasional outbursts of temper, mostly about the hours he and Travis spent playing video games in their computer room, were only ever directed at Zol.

"And what about that hairdresser of yours? What has she decided? Will it be extensions or a wig?"

"She's thinking about it."

"She will have to do great deal more than think, especially with *your* hair." Her mother had been appalled when Natasha transformed her long, traditional tresses into a pixie cut a few years back. Mummyji mentioned it almost every time they talked. "For that small head of yours, wig will have to be specially ordered. And that takes —"

"Time. Yes, Mummyji. I know. And speaking of time, I have to go."

She'd barely put down the phone when it rang again. Call display told her it was Zol. On his mobile. He'd be calling from his car on his way to Cathcart Street Elementary. The school's principal, Mrs. Simon, was about to lose it completely. She'd been haranguing Zol every day this week. And using local TV newscasts to tearfully lobby her board and its superintendent to close the schools until the polio epidemic was brought under control. Short and petite, Muriel Simon oozed vulnerability and embodied the fears of the entire city. Zol had emphasized the panic that would ensue if every school in the district shut its doors. What would follow? Daycare centres? Libraries? Banks? Supermarkets?

Natasha conceded it was hard to blame the woman for losing her nerve. The epidemic's first three cases came from her school. Two pupils and a teacher's aide. The pupils were recovering, but the aide had died while on life support in the intensive care unit at Caledonian University Medical Centre. And earlier this week, twelve of Mrs. Simon's students had presented with flu-like symptoms. They were being tested for the strange little virus that had shown up in the stools of the hospitalized cases. How many would test positive was anyone's guess.

"Tasha, it's me."

"Bracing yourself for Mrs. Simon?"

"On my way to Emerg at Caledonian. With Max."

A chill gripped her heart. She closed her eyes and was barely able to get out the words: "Is it . . . fever and headache?"

"Just a forehead laceration. At the barbershop. He's fine but it's going to need stitches."

She opened her eyes. "What happened?"

"A couple of lunatics rushed in and sliced up one of the young barbers." She heard a catch in his voice that he covered with a cough. "Right in front of Max and Travis, for God's sake."

"Oh my God, Zol. At that Arabic-speaking shop they like?"

"Yeah, Paradise Barbers. Max ran for cover and slipped — cut his head. Could have been a lot worse for him. It's still touch and go for the barber."

She closed her eyes and twisted the fly-away curls at the nape of her neck. A cold shiver passed across her shoulder blades. "Who —" She glanced at the clock. "I'll call Cathcart Elementary and cancel your meeting."

"No, it's too important. You go."

"You're sure?"

"Take a taxi. Parking down there may be tricky."

"But . . ." Natasha had a million other things to do. Any calls she didn't get done this afternoon would have to wait until offices reopened on Monday. The prospect of more time wasted made her feel physically ill. "You sure?"

"You're the hawk-eyed one. I would've dealt only with the politics. I can see you turning up some crucial piece of evidence down there. It's your forte."

She ignored the compliment, though she couldn't deny how wonderful it was he always had her back. That their marriage was going to complicate, or even terminate, their working relationship niggled at the back of her mind like grit in an oyster. Leaving this job for a position elsewhere was something she wasn't prepared to contemplate. Not now, anyway. "What am I going to say to her?"

"Don't worry, she'll do most of the talking."

In her experience, school principals were good at that. And from what Natasha had seen of Muriel Simon on TV, the woman was particularly gifted.

"Today's a PA day," Zol continued. "With no kids at the school and the teachers offsite, you can have a good look through the place. And then hear Mrs. Simon out. Make her feel supported. If she feels she's out there alone in North Hamilton, knee-deep in polio, she'll close down her school no matter what anyone has to say about it. And then the shit will really hit the fan."

"Hi Max," she called, knowing he'd be listening to every word on the minivan's speakerphone. He was fascinated by the details of his dad's investigations and had become the polio epidemic's unofficial silent partner. "So sorry about your head." She was far more sorry about what must have been those terrifying minutes of the knife attack. She'd talk to Max in person about it this evening. He still seemed to like their bedtime chats, though they'd become shorter and later now that he was approaching high school. And he usually had one eye on his phone. "Uncle Hamish will make sure they take good care of you."

"We're not jumping the queue, Tasha," Zol said. "Even if Hamish offers to arrange it."

Zol would be careful not to ask for expedited care from any of the city's cash-strapped hospitals. It wouldn't look good for the director of the Health Unit to use his doctor friends to bypass the notorious eight-hour waits in Emerg. Especially during the current polio crisis. More than ever, concerned citizens were scrutinizing the health-care system with a cynical microscope.

"Hi, Tasha," Max said. "I'll be fine. Trav is here too. He says hello."

They said their goodbyes, and she hung up the phone. She'd almost rather be getting stitches in her forehead than making a trip to the principal's office and facing the feisty Mrs. Simon.

CHAPTER 3

"Here, drink this," Hosam told Ibrahim, extending a steaming mug to him across their table at the Paramount Restaurant. "My mother cured everything with lemon, ginger, and turmeric."

It was a relief to be speaking Arabic after their shattering morning. Years of private English lessons as a teenager had given Hosam reasonable confidence talking sports, weather, and weekend plans with his barbershop clients, but conversing with Dr. Szabo and the police in the aftermath of today's attack had demanded a higher level of proficiency. The concentration had left him exhausted.

Ibrahim's face was ashen. The police had taken the keys to Paradise Barbers and secured the shop with yellow crime-scene tape. They had refused to estimate how long business would be suspended.

Ibrahim's grilling by the officers had been measured and respectful. Compared to the brutality of Hosam's own interrogation by the Syrian secret police back home in Damascus, Ibrahim's chat with Hamilton's men in uniform had been a gentle stroll along a sunny Mediterranean promenade.

It was three years ago now that a powerful IED exploded in the lobby of the city-council building in Aleppo, Hosam's hometown and Syria's largest city. The blast, only blocks from his hospital, rumbled through his operating theatre at about eleven o'clock one morning. Dusty tiles dropped from the ceiling while he did his damnedest to save the mangled arm of the young woman on the operating table. She had been injured during a mortar attack on the Al-Madina Souq, the city's famous market.

In the ensuing weeks, the Syrian secret police, under the direction of the country's dictator-president, Bashar al-Assad, decided Hosam's family was responsible for the bombing. Late one night, the Mukhabarat tore Hosam from his bed. They blindfolded him, threw him into the back of a truck, and drove him to an overcrowded prison. There, they put their violent squeeze on him — boots, batons, chains, a cattle prod. He endured weeks shackled in a living hell until his hospital's chief administrator rescued him with a wad of bills stuffed in an envelope. Later, the Mukhabarat extracted a false confession from Hosam's cousin, an accountant with no political leanings. The mild-mannered father of four was never seen again. After that, Hosam's entire family was marked by al-Assad's regime, determined to incarcerate perceived opponents on falsified charges. Hosam's only choice had been to flee the country with his wife and son via the sometimes porous border with Turkey.

Ibrahim's flight from his bombed-out Christian enclave in Iraq a decade earlier had probably occurred under similar circumstances, but the two men had never traded stories. There was an unwritten rule that such tales did not get shared. It could turn out that your esteemed colleague in Canada had been allied with your sworn enemy back in the Middle East.

Ibrahim's lips quivered as he sipped his turmeric tea. The prospect of a formal interview in Hamilton's central police station was scaring him almost shitless.

Hosam had suggested that he and Ibrahim come to the Paramount to debrief, knowing the lunch crowd would be gone. He had hoped the restaurant's famous hummus, falafel, and fattoush would provide the comfort of the familiar. But as he looked around, he realized the place had been a bad choice for a frank discussion. It was full of ears and eyes from back home. They should have gone for Thai or Chinese.

Ibrahim took another sip of the tea and swallowed hard. "I don't know when they're going to give me the keys back. It's going to take some work to make that blood disappear."

"They have companies that specialize in that sort of thing. Your insurance will cover it."

"Insurance? You must be dreaming." Ibrahim set his mug on the table and cleared his throat. "Look, Hosam, if we stay closed for more than a few days, we'll start losing our clients to other shops. Business will get slow. And . . ." He shrugged and raised his palms to show that the consequences were beyond his control.

Hosam pictured himself spending full days on his ass at the shop and bringing home a near-empty wallet. He had to face it — no matter how quickly the shop reopened, some clients were going to jump ship the moment they got word of the knifing. He was proud of the diversity of his clientele — he did not cut only Muslim hair. But an incident like this was bound to bring out people's hidden prejudices.

Ibrahim looked around, checking for prying ears. "I'm worried about Mr. Smith. He's picky about that weekly Friday appointment of his."

"Will the shop not be cleaned up and reopened by then?"

"That gives us only seven days. It's crucial we look after him on time or he'll find another shop. Mr. Smith is loyal, but I've seen him flare up in seconds and explode like a Scud missile."

"Can he not skip a week? It is only a haircut."

Ibrahim's face hardened. "You know he gets more than a simple haircut."

Mr. Smith's needs were anything but simple. His appointments lasted an hour and a half. Sometimes longer.

Ibrahim toyed with his mug. "Our Mr. Smith exerts a certain influence among his associates." He leaned into the table and added, "More than you might think."

"Are you saying that if Mr. Smith leaves, many of our other clients will too?"

"That's part of it."

Hosam had no idea what other sorts of influence Ibrahim was implying, but he knew this was neither the time or place to ask him directly.

Ibrahim finished his tea then studied the dregs at the bottom of the mug. Was he reading the leaves? And if so, what was he seeing? "Our problem right now," Ibrahim said, "is Ghazwan. I knew he was bad news from the moment the boss told me to hire him. As a barber, he wasn't worth a dog's ass."

Ghazwan had stopped working at Paradise Barbers shortly after Hosam started there, so they barely knew each other. But when Hosam saw it was Ghazwan slashing Marwan with the bowie knife, it was all he could do to keep it together. *Violation* was an overused word these days. But that was exactly how he felt — violated by a countryman and former colleague.

A shiver pierced Hosam's shoulders. "The guy must be into some pretty nasty stuff."

"Unpleasant enough," Ibrahim admitted.

"And reckless. Carrying out such a brutal knifing in public? No mask or disguise? That was crazy."

Ibrahim nodded. "Out of his mind, over-the-top crazy. And slashing Marwan's throat? Mother of God, the boss must be furious. He would never have ordered that type of hit. I could understand a warning cut on Marwan's arm. But not cold-blooded murder in front of witnesses. Ghazwan is done for. The Caliph will see to it. No doubt about it."

Hosam felt the familiar boulder roll in the pit of his stomach. He thought he had left that ominous rock behind seven months ago when he and Leila and Omar had boarded the aircraft in Istanbul bound for Toronto. "You are saying Marwan's knifing was *ordered*?"

Ibrahim raised his eyebrows. "But Ghazwan went overboard. The big man must be pissed about getting so much attention from the cops. After all, the Caliph is first and foremost a businessman. I'm sure he only wanted to send us a little warning."

Hosam gulped down some tea, but it did nothing to alleviate the dread crammed into his belly. *"Us?"*

"Everyone at the shop. The Caliph wants us to remember that he owns Paradise Barbers, that we work for him, that we do what he says. He gave me a clean job."

"Meaning?"

Ibrahim picked a falafel from this plate, studied it, then set it down. It looked tired and stale. Last week's fare. "I . . . I look after the place and provide him with the cover he needs — a place for his money and his guys to look legit. To . . . you know, hide in plain sight."

Hosam felt a flicker of understanding. "You mean, you help him launder the proceeds from his other . . . business endeavours?"

There was little ambiguity in Ibrahim's shrug. The look on the man's face was enough to explain the recent purchase of titanium haircutting shears for every barber in the shop — each a five-hundred-dollar "gift" from "a grateful boss." In reality, they were strings-attached tokens from the elusive Syrian everyone referred to as the Caliph.

Hosam churned his tabbouleh with his fork. His suspicions of money laundering confirmed, there was no way he could stomach any more of his salad. "You have met the Caliph?"

"Oh no. No one sees him. Everyone deals only with his messengers. Rumour has it he's missing an eye and stays hidden so he doesn't appear vulnerable. But I think that's a bullshit story. When you're ordering rough guys around, it pays to create a little mystique."

"By rough guys, you mean kids like Marwan who do extra jobs for —"

Ibrahim raised his hand and looked around again. "Marwan wanted out. No more dirty jobs." His face crumpled. "He has been dating a Canadian girl. And he likes being a barber."

"And so?"

Ibrahim grabbed a napkin and dabbed the sweat on his brow. "The Caliph knows that if he lets you go, eventually you will squeal. Especially if, like Marwan, you belonged to the wrong faction back home."

Over a couple of beers, Marwan had broken the unwritten rule and confided to Hosam that at the start of the Syrian civil war he had belonged to the since-disbanded Farouq Brigades. A ragtag rebel group with allegiance to no one, the Brigades had created havoc inside the country. Marwan's rebellious involvement, no matter how idealistic, had marked him as a government target. His parents insisted he leave the country before he was arrested, tortured, and executed by President Bashar al-Assad's henchmen.

After a few more beers, Marwan had told Hosam that he was being coerced into doing increasingly disagreeable favours for the Caliph. According to Marwan, the Caliph had been active with the al-Nusra Front, a Syrian civil war faction whose kidnapping, torture, and summary executions of Syrian civilians were legendary. Any reference to al-Nusra made Hosam's palms run with sweat. If any of what Marwan said was true, Hosam could only imagine the lies a brute like the Caliph had concocted to win himself asylum in Canada.

Ghazwan had given Hosam a pointed looked as he wiped the bloodied bowie knife on Marwan's chair. That look was now making sense: with Marwan out of commission, the Caliph was likely to contact Hosam with a "request" for a job. At first, it might be couched as an innocent favour. But any relationship Hosam would have with the Caliph would end in a prison or a morgue.

His chances of requalifying as a surgeon and practising in Canada were about to vaporize in a cloud of smoke. The Caliph was poised to smash his dreams into smithereens. The al-Nusra bomb that had exploded through the roof of his parents' house in Aleppo had done the same. Warlords like the Caliph had left nothing of his mom, his dad, or his sweet, eight-year-old Farah to commit to sacred ground.

Hosam's mouth filled with bile.

CHAPTER 4

By three thirty that Friday afternoon, Zol figured if he didn't get fifteen minutes alone — just fifteen little minutes — he was going to explode. He pictured the mess: blood, guts, and neurons spattered over every square centimetre of his new office. And what a pity. He'd worked so hard for the promotion that came with the picture window, the bleached birch panelling, and the orthopedic chair that was perfect for his long, achy back. He shuddered as he sensed his dad shaking his head and muttering from his workshop in the sky. Even in the Hereafter, Dad's accent was undiminished: "I always was tell you, Zoltan. Be careful what you wishing for."

At least he'd got Max squared away. The Emerg staff had Max's skull X-rayed and his forehead stitched within two hours of their arrival. And now, he and Travis were "chilling" at home. They were debriefing in the best way they knew how: playing an absorbing game of *Fortnite* on Max's PlayStation 4. Zol offered to spend a fatherly afternoon deconstructing the barbershop trauma with the boys, but they made it clear they'd rather be in the company of the heroes and villains of *Battle Royale*. He wondered whether he should arrange to have them talk to a counsellor about this incident or wait and see if they had nightmares or flashbacks.

He figured watchful waiting would be best for now. Both kids were nothing if not resilient. Was there a better quality a father could foster in a son facing the future challenges of climate change, massive refugee migration, and unpredictable populist politicians? Well yes, a heavy dose of compassion was also essential. Was he was modelling that well enough for Max? Tasha certainly was. He could feel himself smiling in spite of himself. It took little imagination for him to conjure the sandalwood-scented warmth of her beneath the goose-down duvet she'd given him as a pre-wedding gift.

He pulled open the bottom drawer of his desk. From underneath his treasured copy of Sir William Osler's *The Principles and Practice of Medicine* — an 1899 edition bound in brown leather and worn at the edges — he fished out his briar wood pipe, tobacco pouch, and brushed brass Zippo. Sir William would have appreciated the hiding place. The great physician had indulged. A lot. A good pipeful helped him think, he'd insisted. And allowed him to keep his head, weigh the evidence, and help others see reason, the prerequisites of any medical man facing a crisis.

Shoving his smoking stuff into his suit jacket pockets, Zol glared at the phone on the desk. Paperwork had almost buried it. Daring the cursed thing to ring before he made his escape, he strode to the coat rack by the door and grabbed his hat — a black Stetson he'd bought at the Calgary airport last summer. He and Max had flown out west to Alberta. And had a blast doing their single-father-early-teenage-son thing at the Stampede and the Badlands. Was that only ten months ago? It felt a helluva lot longer. And in a safer time.

He looped a cotton scarf around his neck to counter the chilly May winds that had superseded this year's overheated April. He tugged the Stetson's brim as low over his forehead as it would it go and headed for the back stairs. Anyone who wanted a piece of him would have to wait fifteen minutes.

He walked across Concession Street and opened the rear door of the Nitty Gritty Café. Without stepping inside, he knocked

three times and waved a greeting to the barista. Then he walked
to the grassy vacant lot conveniently adjacent to the café's non-
smoking patio and sat at the beaten-up table he'd found at a flea
market. Here, the leafy limestone Niagara Escarpment sliced its
way through the city only steps away, its rocky precipice protected by a fence. Hamilton's downtown core, lakeside suburbs,
and rusting steelworks were spread below him like a 3D map. On
the horizon to the left, Toronto's over-priced condos and cocky
CN Tower flashed in the crisp sunshine. To the right, the Falls at
Niagara thundered unseen and unheard in the far distance.

Marcus, the café's ginger-bearded owner and barista, wasted
no time in bringing Zol his usual to the makeshift patio. A large
double latte. Guatemalan beans. An extra splash of cream, no sugar.
Marcus had been particularly attentive lately. He understood Zol's
heavy burden in the face of the city's first polio epidemic in sixty-
four years. So far, two deaths and three cases of total-body paralysis.
Dozens of emotional stories had been flooding the *Hamilton
Spectator* and the TV news, many of them chastising Zol for not
ending the crisis as soon as it started.

He pulled his pipe, pouch, and lighter from his jacket and set
them on the table beside the steaming mug. Provincial laws said
you couldn't smoke on café patios but made no reference to vacant
lots. He'd taken up smoking only a month ago, though he'd had a
lot of experience with tobacco. As a boy, he'd learned the knack of
packing his father's after-dinner pipe exactly the way Dad liked it.
Tobacco had to be sprinkled, not dumped, into a pipe's chamber.
And it had to be tamped to the proper density. If you pressed
too hard, the pipe wouldn't draw. Too lightly, and the tobacco
would burn too quickly — all flame and no smoke. The novelty
of preparing his dad's pipe without being allowed more than an
occasional puff himself wore off by the time he became a teenager.
But it was a skill he'd mastered and retained. Like setting acres of
tobacco leaves on wooden laths and hefting them into the drying
kilns on his parents' tobacco farm, an hour's drive south of the city.
One long, stifling summer after another.

Feeling the bite of the afternoon's burgeoning cold front, he tugged his scarf tighter around his neck then flicked open his Zippo. He waved the lighter's flame in a circular motion over the tamped tobacco and took short puffs on the pipe. A few strands glowed, swelled, and unravelled in the short-lived flame of the customary "charring light."

He pressed the blackened strands gently with his finger and applied the Zippo's flame a second time. A few puffs later, he was basking in the sensuousness of the smoke. The sun winked at him from the mirrored surface of Lake Ontario on the far side of the city, and an orchestral version of "Rêverie" by Claude Debussy filled his brain with its glorious, sinuous melody. He sat back, breathed deeply, and let his late mother's favourite musical piece waft through him without the benefit of a PA system, a radio, or any other device. His neurologist had an explanation for this tech-free phenomenon: post-concussion synesthesia. A blow to the head a few years back had crossed a bunch of wires in his brain. He'd slipped on a patch of ice, bashed his head on the sidewalk, and woken up in a hospital bed with a new set of pathways linking his sense of smell to his hearing. Strong scents conjured musical sound bites so vivid they sounded like the real thing. Cumin summoned Miley Cyrus, cardamon brought on k.d. lang. The sensation happened less frequently now than it used to. Céline Dion had finally stopped bellowing "My Heart Will Go On" every time he brewed a pot of coffee.

As the orchestra played in his head, he realized he hadn't felt this relaxed in weeks. Had someone spiked his pouch with marijuana? For a moment, he wondered if Tasha, tired of his recent moodiness, had slipped him some weed. Like him, his fiancée supported Parliament's move to get recreational pot use out in the open by legalizing it. But as public health professionals, Zol and Tasha knew that weed was going to preoccupy their working lives for years to come. On the home front, getting stoned wasn't for either of them. He was content with numbing his brain with pipe tobacco and a single malt Scotch. Tasha usually stuck to white wine. As for fourteen-year-old Max, Zol was almost certain he hadn't yet tried dope. Although . . . perhaps he was just an earnest dad who was kidding himself.

The Debussy lasted longer than his usual crossed-wire snippets of synesthesia, and by the time the piece had finished he'd smoked his pipe down to the dottle. As he was about to clear the spent tobacco from the chamber, his cellphone chirped. It was a call from a number he didn't recognize. He ignored it and tapped the pipe against the ashtray. The chirping stopped then restarted a moment later. The same local number lit the screen. Still, he ignored it, frustration and resentment intruding on his tenuous state of tobacco-induced contentment. Whoever it was should bloody well have the courtesy to stop calling and leave a voicemail.

The phone rang a third time. Same number. As he reached for the power-off button, curiosity overtook him and he stabbed the bright green icon. "Szabo here."

"Darling. I was afraid you'd never pick up."

"Tasha? Where are you? Are you okay?"

"I'm in the principal's office."

"Don't you have your cell?"

"Long story. Mrs. Simon just collapsed at her desk. She looks awful. I called 911. I need you to come down here."

"Me?" He hadn't touched a patient in years. "The paramedics will take care of her. I'd just be in the way."

"You have to see what I found."

"What?"

"Zol, you have to see this for yourself."

She'd hit pay dirt at the elementary school? "Tell me, Tasha. What is it?"

"Bring N-95 masks, gloves, Tyvek coveralls, and shoe covers. Everything's in the tall cupboard in my office."

"Give me a hint?"

She paused for a moment, then told him, "Think Central America. And I'm not talking honeymoon."

CHAPTER 5

Zol pulled into the parking lot inside the grounds of Cathcart Street Elementary School. He'd expected to see the ambulance dispatched for Mrs. Simon, but the only vehicle in sight was a grey Ford Taurus hugging the chain-link fence at the rear of the lot. Hamilton's first responders were either particularly efficient today or dangerously slow. He hoped it was the former.

It struck him that the school — three storeys of dusty-rose brick, green aluminum siding, and sleek windows — was the most well-kept building in Beasley. The otherwise exhausted-looking neighbourhood, sandwiched between the lake and the city's downtown office blocks, was a community of potholed streets, crumbling sidewalks, and scruffy houses. Almost every place needed fresh paint and major yardwork. On the way in, he'd passed the Good Shepherd Food Bank, the Salvation Army centre for the homeless, and rows of subsidized townhouses.

As he opened the rear door of his minivan to retrieve the personal protective gear Tasha had asked for, a Saab 9-3 pulled cautiously through the opening in the fence. Behind the wheel was an anxious-looking Dr. Hamish Wakefield, Zol's best friend. A specialist in infectious diseases, and an assistant professor at Caledonian University's medical school, Hamish had a serious case of obsessive compulsion. More a character trait than an illness, his compulsions manifested most acutely at the car wash. Until recently, Hamish's Saab got sprayed and buffed at least half a dozen times a week, especially in the winter. Not even the Swedes had been able to formulate a paint that could stand such a beating. But since his beau, Al Mesic, had come into Hamish's life, the frequency of the car wash visits had tapered dramatically. Today, the car looked brand new. Either he'd traded his old one in for another of the same year and model, or he'd had it repainted. Hamish was colourblind and would have no idea that his precious vehicle was now the blue-grey hue of a stinky blue cheese, something he detested. He hated the idea of eating mould, no matter how exotic or expensive a form it took.

Hamish straightened his tie in the rearview mirror and ran a hand across his always-perfect blond flattop. It seemed that fussing with his hair took Hamish's mind off his diminutive stature. Poor guy was only five-foot-three. Zol had him beaten by almost a foot. No one ever said it, but they did sort of look like that magician duo from Las Vegas, Penn & Teller.

Hamish got out of the car and locked the doors. He clicked the fob four more times as he looked around him. It wasn't just his obsessions that were making him anxious. The Saab had been stolen in this part of town once before. Of course, he'd had it professionally fumigated after the police returned it to him more or less untouched.

"Thanks for coming so quickly, Hamish."

"Anything more from Natasha? I hope this isn't going to be a waste of time."

"Whatever it is, she wants us to see it for ourselves."

"I'm not counting on any breakthroughs."

"As Professor Romero used to say, 'It behooves us to keep the eyes wide —'"

Hamish rolled his eyes as he completed the dictum, "'— and the mind open.' Yes, I know."

A decade ago, they'd shared four years of medical school at the University of Toronto. There was no denying that Hamish's success as a genius clinician at a tertiary-care hospital — and Zol's advancement as a public health physician — owed a lot to Dr. Romero's pithy tidbits.

Zol shifted the box of protective gear in his arms and closed the rear door of his dusty, aged Toyota. When they reached the school's main door, Zol motioned for Hamish to push the buzzer. "Tasha says she'll let us in. They keep the doors locked."

A minute later, Tasha greeted them with her warm smile and radiant dark eyes, and a hint of sandalwood perfume. As always, her presence made him feel a glow deep inside.

Her eyes clouded as she bit her lip. "You just missed the paramedics."

"Was she breathing on her own?" Hamish asked.

Tasha nodded. "Didn't need CPR, thankfully."

Zol let the door close behind them. "What did they say?"

"Not much. They seemed satisfied with her vitals and the reading on their blood oxygen thing."

"Where did they take her?" Hamish asked.

"Caledonian."

"Good," Hamish said. "I'll check her out when I get back."

Tasha glanced approvingly at the box in Zol's arms and led them down the hall and into the closest classroom. Zol set the box on a tiny desk at the back of the room, the last in a row of identical desks with attached chairs. A pervasive sense of déjà vu consumed him. As the tallest kid among his peers, he always sat at the back of the class. Today, the smell of crayons, chalk, and sweaty sneakers had Paul McCartney singing a dozen bars of "Blackbird" inside his head.

Tasha, always quick to sense Zol's episodes of synesthesia, gave him a moment while she rummaged through the box. "Before we go any further," she said, "we better put this stuff on."

Once they'd put on the white hooded Tyvek coveralls and

donned shoe covers and vinyl gloves, Tasha led them along an ordinary-looking school hallway to a closed door.

She held up three N-95 masks.

Hamish first tightened the hood of his coverall around his head and tied the drawstring in a neat bow. Then he placed a mask over his nose and mouth and felt around the edges several times to be sure that the fit was absolutely snug. Zol and Tasha did the same with their gear, but with less gusto. Both of them found the claustrophobic feel of an N-95 almost intolerable.

Tasha opened the door and stepped inside. A hoarse voice said, "Come in. Don't be shy."

Zol's heart skipped a beat.

Hamish's eyes looked like dinner plates. He turned to Zol and gestured toward Tasha. "You said she was the only one here."

"Be careful. He bites," said another voice.

Zol looked at Tasha. Her eyes crinkled into a smile.

And then Zol saw the cage. It was sitting on a table by the window on the far side of the classroom.

Hamish saw it too. "They're alive?"

"Very much so," Tasha told him.

"What are they?" Hamish said. "Some kind of parrot?"

"Yellow-naped Amazons," she said. "Pancho and Pedro."

"Don't they contravene some sort of school-board regulation?" Hamish said.

"Apparently not," Zol said, stepping closer to the cage, his gloved hands clasped behind his back.

Inside a barred enclosure almost a metre cubed, two green parrots with prominent beaks were perched on a tree branch. They looked like identical twins bobbing their heads in unison. Each was about the size of a crow. But much prettier. Most of their feathers were the iridescent green of a Granny Smith apple. The tops and backs of their heads shimmered a bright lemon yellow. Their eyes — shiny black pupils surrounded by slim circles of orange — gave the birds a studious air. They resembled a pair of old-world professors, garbed in green robes with yellow hoods, passing judgement on the world around them.

Tasha approached the teacher's desk at the front of the classroom and pressed a button beside a mug bristling with pencils. The ring of an old-fashioned telephone echoed through the room.

"Mother, it's for you," came a voice from the cage.

"Hurry up," said the other bird.

"Impressive, eh?" Tasha said.

"They are cute," Zol admitted. "But how can they be responsible for our polio cases?"

"Mrs. Simon's husband is a vet," Tasha said. "Pancho and Pedro are rescue parrots. Their elderly owner died and a neighbour brought them to Dr. Simon's veterinary office."

"Their owner died of polio?" Zol asked.

"Not that we know of," Tasha said. "Her obituary in the *Spectator* says she died suddenly and has been cremated. Mrs. Simon showed it to me in her office."

Hamish drew closer to the cage and peered into it, a pensive look in his eyes. "How long have they been here?"

"About a month," Tasha said.

"Hmm," Hamish said. "Our first polio case was a pupil from this school, right?"

Tasha had the line-by-line details of the eight polio cases firmly in her head. "That's correct."

"And presented with weakness of both legs two weeks ago?" Hamish asked.

Tasha's eyes went skyward as she recalled the date. "Sixteen days ago," she said. "And a second case from this school a day later, and another two days after that."

"The first two are pupils?" Zol said. "And the third was a teachers' assistant?"

"An unpaid volunteer," Tasha said, "who had hoped to re-certify as a fully qualified teacher."

"Re-certify?" Zol asked. "Is there something dodgy in her record we should know about?"

She shook her head. "Ms. Asante was from West Africa. To be certified as a teacher here, she had to upgrade the credentials she'd earned in Ghana. Mrs. Simon said that would have been a long road for her."

Hamish scratched his nose through the mask. "The timing is intriguing."

"That's what bothered Mrs. Simon. She found out from her husband only this morning that the lady who owned the parrots died unexpectedly."

Zol's mask was getting itchier by the minute. And it was damn hard to talk through it, let alone breathe. "But surely, parrots don't carry poliovirus? It's strictly a human pathogen."

"That's right," Hamish said. "But the cause of our epidemic isn't poliovirus."

"What?" Zol and Tasha said simultaneously.

For the past two and a half weeks, the identity of the virus responsible for their cluster of polio cases had been a puzzle. The presenting signs and symptoms of the illness resembled those reported during the last North American epidemic back in the 1950s. But the virus causing the current outbreak had been impossible to identify. Like traditional poliovirus, the current virus was particularly small. Detectable only by examination of victims' stools with an electron microscope. The local virologists had not seen anything like it and had been unable to assign it an identity. Samples of all manner of body fluids from the affected patients had been sent to Canada's version of Atlanta's CDC, located in Winnipeg. But there hadn't been so much as a peep out of the country's best microbiologic boffins in two long weeks.

"Don't look at me like that, Zol" Hamish said. "I haven't been holding anything back. The email from Winnipeg arrived less than five minutes before you called me to come down here. I thought it best to tell you in person."

Zol felt the calming pressure of Tasha's hand on his arm. "So . . . what did Winnipeg have to say?"

"They're calling it a parvovirus."

"Parvo?" said Tasha. "That's what puppies get."

"*And* humans," Hamish said. "It manifests most commonly as Fifth Disease in little kids."

"Fever and . . . and red cheeks that look like they've been slapped," Zol said, proud to have dug those details out of his memory.

Hamish raised his right forefinger as if making a point with a student. "And a red rash that looks like lace."

"But Fifth Disease is a far cry from our polio cases," Zol said. "It's one of the milder infections *every* kid gets. I remember Max having it when he was a toddler."

"A far cry from our polio," croaked one of the parrots. It bobbed its head up and down as if quite pleased with itself.

Hamish frowned at the bird. "There are dozens of sub-families and genera of parvoviruses. Winnipeg is calling ours Parvo-W until they find a match with one that's been previously characterized."

Tasha looked mildly puzzled. "If the offending agent is parvovirus, not poliovirus, do we still have a polio epidemic on our hands? Or do we need a new name for the illness?"

"Polio is short for poliomyelitis," Hamish explained in his inimitable tone, "which simply means inflammation of the spinal cord's grey matter. The identity of the offending virus doesn't change the name of the illness."

Tasha squeezed Zol's arm again and threw him a conspiratorial look with her eyes. "Okay then. We'll continue to call it polio in our press reports."

Zol gestured towards the cage. "Can parvoviruses infect birds?"

"Certainly," Hamish said. "And cats and pigs." His eyes began to sparkle with the exotic factoid he was about to share. "And funnily enough . . . even crickets and starfish."

Below her mask, Tasha's throat was aglow in poppy-red blotches. "Oh my God. You'd better see what's down the hall."

CHAPTER 6

Zol followed Tasha and Hamish out of the classroom and into the hallway. He ripped off his mask and threw back the hood as soon as the door shut behind him. Hamish, too, loosened his suit then wiped his sweaty face with a polka-dot handkerchief. Tasha, her mask dangling around her neck, looked as fresh as ever.

"Give us five, okay, Tasha," Zol said, eyeing the water fountain down the hall. "I need a drink."

"Forget the fountain," Hamish told him. "We're not eating or drinking a thing in this building."

"But —"

Hamish narrowed his eyes. "Come on, Zol, everything inside this school is a potential biohazard. You know that perfectly well. The only thing we're going to consume in here is air." He mopped his face again and took a deep breath. "And that's only because we have no other choice."

Zol caught Tasha's knowing smile. Hamish's approach to life and work was often pedantic. But he was so often right about so many things that they'd agreed long ago they had to forgive — and celebrate — their friend's eccentricities.

They suited up again without the benefit of a drink and let Tasha guide them into a classroom two doors down from the one they'd been in.

"Something's bubbling in here," Hamish said, "and it's not a kettle."

Tasha pointed to a large glass tank at the back of the room. It was three-quarters full of water and seemed to be glowing from the inside. A steady stream of bubbles was breaking the surface.

"I had one of these as a kid," Hamish said, his eyes brightening for the second time. He turned to Tasha. "Fresh or salt?"

She hesitated for a moment. "Um . . . I'm not sure."

"Must be salt," Hamish said, his mask-covered nose almost touching the tank. "As in seawater." He pointed to what looked like a massive white flower waving its petals at the bottom of the aquarium. "That's an anemone holding court with its colony of clownfish."

"Nemo?" Tasha said.

Hamish waved his hands dismissively. "If you must. Nemo and his pals survive only in seawater."

"When was this aquarium installed, Tasha?" Zol asked.

"Several years ago. Mrs. Simon couldn't remember exactly when."

"Hmm," Hamish said. "It looks well established. Lots of inter-dependent species." He pulled his mask off his face and threw back his hood. "We don't need these in here."

Tasha put her gloved hand on Hamish's forearm. "The starfish are new."

"How new?" Hamish said, pulling up his mask and hood.

"About a month. Mrs. Simon told me a pet store donated two of them. She said the kids love their bright colour. They're called orange bat stars."

Zol didn't like the look of the fine spray coming off the breaking bubbles. He adjusted his mask and stepped back. "Hamish, a few minutes ago you mentioned parvovirus and starfish in the same breath. Should we be worried?"

Hamish wasn't taking his eyes off the tank. "Maybe." Something other than Nemo was engrossing him. "About a year ago I read a fascinating story in *National Geographic*. A newly recognized parvovirus has been killing millions of starfish."

"Where?" Zol asked.

"Along the West Coast, from Mexico up into B.C."

Zol looked at Tasha. "We have to get Winnipeg to test them ASAP." A dark thought struck him. "And find out what pet store they came from." He pictured parvovirus-infected starfish lurking in families' aquariums throughout the city. Was that how the epidemic had extended its reach from the city centre to the outer suburbs? Was ground zero not this school but the pet store?

"Winnipeg will be awfully surprised," Hamish said. "I don't imagine they often get starfish."

"We'll have to talk to them first," Zol said, wondering silently what the protocol might be for shipping starfish, potentially infected with a deadly virus, halfway across the country.

"And if these starfish do test positive for our Parvovirus-W?" Tasha said.

"That's easy," Hamish said, backing away from the tank. "We'll find ourselves in the middle of the biggest public health circus we've faced since that mad cow debacle. Remember that guy? He was one crazed butcher."

Zol could never forget *that* Dumpster fire. And this one had the makings of something even worse.

CHAPTER 7

Hosam strode the eight short blocks from his regular bus stop at King and James to the tiny, two-bedroom townhouse that was now their home. The irony was, it was an end unit with a garage for cars they might never afford. A double-car affair, the garage was attached on the left.

Before putting the key into the front-door lock, Hosam took a good look around. None of Leila's clients was hanging around the garage's side entrance. No one was sitting in the battered Honda Civic across the street. The street was empty except for a middle-aged woman hefting a bag from the Beer Store farther up the street at the traffic light on Barton. He had been watching since alighting from the bus but had seen no sign of anyone following him. It seemed he was in the clear. For now. But the Caliph would know where he lived. Ibrahim would have told him. He would have had no choice.

He turned the key, slipped inside, and breathed in the comforting aroma of cumin, coriander, and sesame. He refused to let today's events and Ibrahim's tacit revelations get him down. After everything they had been through, Leila and Omar needed him to be strong. And positive. Even if he had to fake it.

He was getting used to taking the Route 34 Upper Paradise bus to and from the barbershop on Mohawk Road West. He was even getting used to working there and taking direction from an Iraqi Christian with only four years of schooling. In Aleppo, as the chief surgeon at a well-respected hospital, he'd had a chauffeur and an E-Class Mercedes. Once the civil war hit, many roads became impassable and the chauffeur fled to the relative safety of the countryside. He had expected to wake up one day and find his hospital replaced by a pile of rubble, his colleagues dead. The government and the rebel groups targeted hospitals with the same cynical dictum: When you murdered a surgeon, you killed the hundred wounded soldiers he could have patched together.

Hosam set his lunchbox on the kitchen table, grabbed a can of Moosehead lager from the refrigerator, and climbed the stairs leading to the home's two small bedrooms. He and Leila had the larger one, of course. And the three of them shared the single bathroom. But more important than anything else, the bedrooms were safe. A bomb was not going to drop through the roof. A thug was not going to throw a Molotov cocktail through the window. And despite Hosam's ongoing nightmares to the contrary, the police were not going to roust him at gunpoint in the middle of the night. It had taken a long time to get used to the quiet here in Beasley. No mortar fire, no rocket-propelled grenades, no low-flying fighter jets. Just the occasional young guy roaring down the street on his Harley, overdosed on the androgens he bought from the guy running an informal boxing gym in his garage in the next block.

"Hello, son," he said, as he opened Omar's bedroom door. "I came home early. Going to do a little studying."

The lanky fifteen-year-old lifted a dark eyebrow, gave a quick wave, and returned his attention to his laptop. His face gave no acknowledgement that it was unusual for his father to be home this early from work. But it was a relief to see the hints of sparkle returning to Omar's eyes after so many months of despair.

When he was not at school, Omar was in his room with the door closed. He wanted a lock for it, but Hosam told him definitely not. The boy was almost always at his desk, headphones covering his ears, a microphone at his lips, and his laptop opened in front of him.

The gear was not for his studies but for *Fortnite*, the interactive online game he played to the point of obsession. The game's saving grace was the wonder it was doing for Omar's self-confidence and his English. Or, at least the kind of English spoken by Canadian teenagers amongst themselves. At first, Hosam and Leila had worried their son was spending far too much time gaming. But they had to admit, he had become less sullen lately. Perhaps the online comradeship fostered by *Fortnite* was coaxing him out of his shell. He had encased himself in a carapace the moment the family traded their villa in Aleppo for a refugee shack in southern Turkey. Lately, he had befriended a couple of boys his age online, fellow *Fortnite* players. One boy's mother was said to be a chaplain, the other boy's father a government official. If the boys were telling the truth about their parents, Hosam was prepared to keep an open mind about *Fortnite*. As long as Omar made a solid effort on his schoolwork. He glanced at the below-knee prosthesis lying on Omar's bed and felt a spark of the anger that lurked, day and night, below the surface of his psyche. His cheeks burned. No version of *Call of Duty*, or anything like it, would ever be allowed in this house. Wargame videos were far too real, too close to what had destroyed Omar's lower leg, their cherished Farah, and their happy lives in Aleppo.

He stepped into the other bedroom and closed the door. After several gulps of the lager, he pulled his earplugs from the drawer and stuffed them into his ears. While the Beasley neighbourhood was surprisingly quiet, the interior of their townhouse was often bedevilled by the brain-piercing screech of Leila's equipment. It bored through the flimsy wall between the garage and the kitchen five and a half workdays a week. Leila and her various part-time helpers took only Saturday afternoons and Sundays off. A friend had helped Hosam with the plumbing, and they had purchased the supplies, tools, and equipment Leila needed on eBay for a reasonable sum and no questions asked. He had hated to see her pawn the diamond ring that celebrated their tenth anniversary. But she said the equipment was a good investment and she knew she would earn the ring back.

What she was doing was not strictly legal. Well, it was and it was not. It was a question of paperwork, not Leila's skill. She was providing a desperately needed service at a reasonable cost. What could be wrong with that? Her growing list of grateful clients was proof enough of the quality and value of her work. She could not be expected to sit around wasting her skills when they were so much in demand.

Besides, Leila's income was going to allow them to put together the four thousand dollars the authorities charged to determine his suitability to practise surgery in Canada. If they accepted his degree from the University of Aleppo, and if he came up with their exorbitant fee, they would let him sit their three-day Medical Council of Canada Qualifying Exam, the MCCQE. It was an especially tough exam for a doctor fifteen years out of medical school. It demanded answers to comprehensive questions about a host of conditions a busy surgeon had not thought about in a decade: cystic fibrosis, mucopolysaccharidosis, leptospirosis, hemochromatosis, trypanosomiasis, leishmaniasis, hypochondriasis, thalassemia, myxedema, polycythemia, chikungunya, fragile X, maple syrup urine disease. If he passed the exam, they might give him a chance to prove himself on a team of carefully supervised junior surgeons.

He considered himself a surgeon to the core, and surgeons belonged in the operating theatre. He was going to do whatever it took, hurdle by hurdle, to return to the sacred table under the bright lights. He opened his $180 copy of *Toronto Notes*, the entire curriculum of the University of Toronto's medical school reduced to a nutshell. It was one highly concentrated nut. He turned to the chapter entitled "The Essentials of Essential Hypertension: Pathophysiology, Investigation, and Management."

Minutes later, or perhaps it was an hour, he felt a hand on his shoulder and a dark presence by his side. His heart stopped. His stomach dropped. His throat closed. He couldn't breathe. For a moment, the world went black.

"Father, it's okay. It's just me." The touch of the hand on his shoulder, he realized, was tentative rather than angry.

The lights came back on, but his head was still spinning. "Son of a dog, Omar." He yanked out his earplugs and took several slow breaths. "I was sure you had come to kill me."

"Sorry, Father." The boy held a large sandwich in his hand. It smelled of garlic and tahini.

"I have told you before —"

"Didn't you hear the doorbell?"

Hosam held up his earplugs. "I was concentrating."

"Someone slipped a note through the mail slot. I found it on the carpet."

"Something from the Church People?" Hosam's gaze shot in the direction of Leila's room. It was quiet. Omar must have given his mother the warning knock when he heard the doorbell.

The family's resettlement as refugees was being sponsored by a local Christian church, First New Canaan Baptist. A committee of always-smiling volunteers had procured and furnished the townhouse and was paying the rent for the first year. It was extremely generous and well-meaning. And intrusive. From time to time, a volunteer or two appeared at the front door unannounced *just to be sure everything is okay*. The Church People wished to inspect their investment and find out more about the strange family who were born and raised so close to their Holy Land. After all, one of their key Bible stories took place centuries ago on the road to Damascus, a place the Church People were hearing so many terrible things about on their television news. Hosam and Leila, deeply grateful for the Church People's generosity, did their best to present a welcoming face when they dropped by. Omar usually stayed in his room.

But it would be a disaster if they started asking questions about the noise coming from the garage. Hosam and Omar were always quick to give Leila the warning knock at the first sign of a smiling volunteer. On the door leading to the garage from the kitchen,

Hosam had mounted a plaque that said *Prayer Room* غرفة الصلاة. The sign worked better than any lock at keeping out the curious. Canadians, he had come to realize, were extremely paranoid about offending Muslim immigrants by intruding on their religious rituals. The mysterious, backward-reading Arabic cursive added to the taboo. It didn't matter that the Khousas never visited a mosque, or read the Qur'an, or said any prayers. Millions throughout Syria had done all three without fail, and look where it had brought them.

At each visit, the Christian volunteers were patronizingly complimentary about the family's fluency in English and how well the three of them were *adjusting to your new lives in Canada, the new Land of Canaan*. Some of them were disconcerted that Leila did not wear the hijab and that Hosam kept a few cans of Moosehead in the refrigerator. When you did not fit their Muslim stereotype, even the most benevolent souls could prove more than a little confused. And judgemental.

"Definitely not from the Church People," Omar said.

He dug into the back pocket of his blue jeans and brought out a crinkled, letter-sized envelope. Across the front, in thick black ink, it said *Hosam Khousa, Father of Omar, Husband of Leila*. The script was roughly scrawled Arabic.

Hosam felt the blood drain from his face. "Did you see who it was?"

"Um . . . I got a quick look at his back, that's all. Then he took off. A small Toyota." Omar swallowed a large bite from his sandwich. "But I did see the bowie knife on his belt. Are those things legal here?"

CHAPTER 8

"But Tasha, I have your favourites ready."

"I know, Mummyji, but we just can't make it. Not tonight. Not after what Max, Zol, and Travis went through today. Zol and the boys need to veg quietly at home."

"Never mind them. You're still a single woman. You come. You have to eat sometime."

Her mother had a point. The three guys would be fine on their own. And more comfortable at home. It would have been a tense meal with her parents. She pictured her father desperately engaging in small talk to draw attention from the disapproving looks clouding her mother's face. The only time Mummyji had met Travis, she hadn't been charitable in her opinion of his mutism. Still, Travis would have joined them. With his mother away on a three-month Canadian Forces training course on preventing suicide amongst its ranks, he was staying with Zol and Max. The arrangement felt completely natural. Even when the Reverend Colonel Andersen was at home, the boys were almost inseparable.

"Okay, Mummyji, give me a couple more hours."

"Everything will be cold by then," said the woman who was never satisfied, no matter how much you gave in to her.

Natasha wanted to remind her that murgh dopiaza, dum gobi, and cho chori heated up beautifully in the microwave. But there was no point in wasting her breath. Mummyji was adamant that *proper* Indian cooking could only be accomplished over a gas flame using traditional pots and utensils. It wasn't that Mummyji was afraid of the microwave. She used it to heat up Dad's mac & cheese and Scottish oatmeal.

Natasha returned her cellphone to her purse and walked through the wide, automatic doorway into Petz Haven. She'd never been in one of these pet megastores before and was amazed at its size — larger than her favourite supermarket and much brighter. There were four such outlets in Greater Hamilton. Companion animals were obviously as big a business as children. Or bigger. Mrs. Simon said they purchased their fish, starfish, and supplies exclusively at Petz Haven. The owner grew up in the Beasley neighbourhood and gave the school a generous discount. A phone call to the branch on Upper Wentworth Street revealed that only one of their stores sold fish and aquariums. It was this one, on Queenston Road.

After a long search of the aisles for an employee who might help her, Natasha found a tired-looking woman with salt-and-pepper hair tied in a ponytail. Her navy apron showed the store's logo in letters too large to miss. She was hefting jumbo bags of dog food from a cart onto a display.

At Natasha's approach, the woman wiped her large hands on her apron. "Can I help?"

"I'm looking for the store manager."

The woman chuckled without smiling and wiped the sweat off her forehead with the back of her hand. "At this time on a Friday night, that would be me. The only one here over eighteen." The name badge pinned to her apron said *Terry*.

"I'm wondering about your starfish."

"You wanna buy one?"

"Not exactly."

Terry looked like she'd heard that response many times before and pointed to the rear of the store. "The fish and sea creatures are in aisle thirty-two." She patted the walkie-talkie clipped to her apron. "You got questions, get one of the girls at the cash to call me."

"I'd prefer we looked at the starfish together."

Terry pushed a stray strand of dull hair off her face and gestured to the almost-full cart. "I'm kind of busy here. You wanna watch the sea life in our aquariums, help yourself. We're open till nine. But I tell you, starfish are kind of boring. Don't move much."

Natasha pulled one of her health-unit business cards from her purse. It listed her title as *Field Epidemiologist*. No one ever knew what that meant, but the Hamilton-Lakeshore Public Health Unit logo was usually impressive enough.

The woman glanced at the card then pulled her glasses from her apron and read it more carefully. "From the Health Unit, eh? Somebody do something wrong? With the starfish?" She took a step back and held up a hand. "Look, I'm here only part-time. Evenings and weekends."

"No one's done anything wrong. I'm not here as an inspector. I just have a few questions about the starfish." Natasha never used the words *epidemic* or *quarantine* when she was looking for information; they put people off by making them think of the bubonic plague. And she was afraid if she mentioned *polio*, Terry would be scared into silence, no matter how world-weary she seemed. Natasha used the stock phrase that rarely alarmed and usually opened doors: "We're working on a small project at the Health Unit."

"A project on starfish at . . ." The woman checked her watch then looked Natasha up and down. "At seven o'clock on a Friday night?" Her voice sounded skeptical, but her eyes showed she was intrigued. "Okay. Let's have a look at them." She gestured at the heavily laden shelves surrounding them like the loot in Aladdin's cave. "There's more than enough dog chow on display in this place, anyways."

Terry parked her cart at the end of an aisle and the two of them walked to the rear of the store. Against the back wall, dozens of brightly lit aquariums were bubbling away. From a distance, the wall was a mass of small, colourful fish, some swimming, some darting, some resting.

Terry stopped in front of one aquarium that was much larger than the others. Natasha recognized a sea anemone and its clown-fish, and thought of Hamish. "This one is seawater, isn't it."

"Yep. Most of the smaller tanks, though, are freshwater. Your guppies, your tetras, your mollies. A few freshwater snails."

Inside the tank, Natasha could only see two starfish, both bright orange. One seemed to be prying a live clam open with its long arms and tiny suckers. "You have only these two starfish in stock?"

"We introduce newcomers into this tank one at a time," Terry said. "Everything has to be kept in balance. It's our show aquarium, and it took us a long time to get it perfect." She beckoned to Natasha to follow her. "Starfish are more aggressive than you'd think. They're carnivores."

At the end of the line of aquariums was another large tank. It was bubbling like the others but was dimly lit. Nothing appeared to be moving inside it.

"We keep the new starfish in here."

Natasha pressed closer to the glass. When her eyes adjusted to the dim lighting, she could see orange starfish throughout the inside of the tank. Many were stuck to the glass walls, revealing their white bellies and tiny feet, or whatever the undersides of starfish were called.

"Did these arrive together?"

"Same batch. We take delivery every few months. Takes a while to sell them all. As I said, people don't find them exciting." A glint of humour flashed in her eyes. "Though if you were a live seashell, you'd be terrified."

Natasha tried to smile, but her shoulders shuddered. "When did you get these?"

Terry shrugged and looked into the distance. "Exactly?" She shook her head. "Can't remember."

"Can you find out?"

"Maybe Monday, when the back office opens. I don't have the key, and Mr. Petz is away this weekend. Las Vegas. He loves his baccarat."

"This is kind of important," Natasha told her, trying not to sound desperate. "Are you sure you can't remember?"

"Well," Terry said, twisting her ponytail and gazing upwards again. "It was the Monday or Tuesday of . . . of a long weekend. Yes, that's right. They were shipped on a Tuesday and supposed to arrive on a Saturday at the latest. But they got delayed in transit because of the holiday. The boss, Mr. Petz, was furious. He was sure every one of them would be dead by the time they got here."

Natasha took out her phone and studied the calendar app. "The last stat holiday was . . . Easter. Good Friday. Does that sound —"

"That's it," said Terry. "It *was* Easter weekend. I worked that Saturday when the boss was having his hissy fit. But I had the Sunday off, for a change. The grandkids came over and smeared chocolate bunnies all over my good sofa."

Natasha checked the calendar again. If Terry's memory was correct, these starfish arrived four and a half weeks ago. Mrs. Simon said the new starfish had been at her school for about a month. The timing worked.

"Do you know where this batch came from?"

"Mexico. Cabo San Lucas. I know that for sure. Mr. Petz made umpteen calls to some office there, trying to locate the shipment." Terry laughed. "His Spanish is nonexistent and Easter is a big deal in Mexico. He couldn't get hold of anyone in charge. No one knew anything." She laughed again and wiped a tear from her cheek.

With Terry now in a good mood at her boss's expense, it was time to break it to her: the starfish had to be quarantined immediately. They needed to be taken to a back room and left strictly undisturbed. Natasha would put on her Tyvek suit, mask, and gloves and retrieve four or five starfish from the tank. She had a small container in her car that met the standards for shipping hazardous materials. She'd already phoned the Winnipeg lab and convinced them to bring someone in on the weekend to test the starfish for parvovirus. They'd thought she was crazy until she reminded them of the time she'd convinced them to follow her hunch about orf virus, milking goats at a petting zoo, and a kindergarten full of kids with a nasty rash.

She'd have to get the starfish to Winnipeg by overnight courier. The timing was tight but doable. The courier's eastern hub was close by, at Hamilton Airport. If she worked fast and drove the starfish to YHM herself, she'd just make tonight's nine o'clock deadline.

But before she had a chance to pull the heavy and order the starfish into quarantine, Terry's smile morphed into a suspicious frown. "Are these guys making people sick?"

Natasha didn't know what to say. The truth was, she had no idea. Weird things happened in the medical field. And in her profession, you had to follow every lead until you came across the unexpected nugget that solved the case. But a polio outbreak arising from starfish imported from Mexico sounded truly far-fetched. One for the books. But stranger things had happened. She, Zol, and Hamish had once cracked a case of high school students poisoned by herbal chewing gum imported online from China.

Terry looked Natasha straight in the eye. "You don't need to answer. It's written on your face." She pulled a pen from her apron pocket and clicked it nervously. "There's a girl who comes after school and cleans the tanks. I sent her home today. I called her an Uber as soon as she got here. She looked awful — flushed and feverish, complained of a terrible headache, and the back of her neck seemed to be bothering her. She kept on rubbing it."

Natasha felt sick. Terry had just described polio's early symptoms so vividly that it was as if she'd memorized the textbook. "Did she clean the starfish tank?" Natasha asked her.

"Of course. She does *all* the tanks."

"Can you give me her name and address?"

"I know only her first name. Jamila. She goes to Sir John A. Macdonald High School. Nice girl. Polite. Speaks with an accent. Gorgeous long eyelashes and covers her hair with that scarf thing."

"A hijab?"

"Is that what you call it? Goes with her religion, she told me."

"What about her last name? And her phone or address?"

Terry shook her head. "No idea. And, as I said, the office is locked until Monday."

"I need to speak to her this evening. Might the girls at the cash know her name?"

"You've got to be kidding. Those dimwits barely know how to spell their *own* names."

Terry paused, then fished her cellphone out of the back pocket of her jeans. "Jamila called me. On my cell. A couple of days ago. Said she was very sorry but she'd be fifteen minutes late. Held up at a doctor's appointment." Terry smiled and shook her head, remembering. "Poor sweetheart. Let me see if I've still got her number in my recent calls list."

CHAPTER 9

As Travis headed from the kitchen to the recycling bin in the garage with the empty pizza boxes, Zol caught Max eyeing the computer-room door. Like a husky straining to get back into the Iditarod, Max was anxious to return to their game. But hadn't he had enough *Fortnite* for one day?

Duh, of course not.

"Let's the three of us play a few hands of gin rummy," Zol said, bracing for eye rolls.

"Geez," Max said, patting his pants pocket for his cellphone. The thing was strictly off limits during meals and had beeped several times while they'd been gorging on pepperoni, mozzarella, and marinara. "Do we have to?"

"Come on, it'll be fun." Like a father-son car ride, a father-son game of cards could be the perfect time for a candid talk. An opportunity for meaningful conversation that arose as if out of nowhere. A time for spontaneous dialogue that flowed naturally, came from the heart, and aired important issues — like what it felt like to watch someone get stabbed to death at close range and be terrified you'd be next. It was all over the news and the

Twitterverse, so the boys were well aware: the assistant barber had died of his injuries.

"But we promised Omar this would be just a short break."

"Who's Omar?"

"Just a kid our age."

"He plays *Fortnite*?"

Max made the face that said the answer was obvious.

Zol rubbed at a kink in his neck. Was "Omar" in actual fact a teenager? Or was he some pervert pretending to be one? Did *his* father worry he was spending too much time playing *Fortnite*? Or did the boy live in a home where the parents were out most of the time — working multiple jobs to make ends meet, or gambling, or cruising the bars until closing time?

"You're sure he is who he says he is?"

"He sent us a selfie. And a picture of his —"

Max's eyes flashed and his mouth snapped shut as Travis came back from the garage. The boys exchanged a look.

"A picture of what, guys?" Zol asked.

Travis wiped his lips with the back of his hand and looked at his sneakers.

"Nothing important," Max said flatly then turned and pointed to the cupboard where they kept the playing cards. "You're right, Dad, we should play gin rummy."

Omar had shown the boys something of interest, but Zol knew it was going to be a long time before he found out what it was. And the way teenaged boys operated, he probably never would.

They played the gin rummy one-on-one, taking turns as the dealer. Travis never lost a hand. Perhaps staying mute allowed the brain to concentrate on other tasks such as keeping a keen eye on every card. Zol tried to ease the conversation toward the barbershop with a complimentary comment about Hosam, Max's regular barber. The man had kept his cool and administered advanced first aid with the skill of a battle medic. Max didn't bite. And because he was showing no signs of brooding about the morning's events, Zol left it at that.

During Zol's second turn as the dealer, his phone rang. When he saw it was Tasha, he answered it on the second ring. "Hi, darling. Where are you?"

"Are the boys okay?"

"I think Travis prefers Hawaiian pizza to curried chicken, so they're fine. We're playing gin rummy."

"You're kidding. The PlayStation's on the fritz?"

"A little bonding, that's all." Zol turned to the boys and threw them a wink. "Right, guys?"

Max scowled at his cards as his lips tightened in a suppressed grin. He'd been enjoying the game in spite of himself. "Whatever."

Travis, bless him, gave Zol a full smile that looked sincere.

"Where are you, Tasha? Still at the pet store?"

"In the car. On my way to the airport. With the starfish."

"The courier is going to accept them?"

"I think so. They said as long as I had them in the approved containers, they'd take them tonight."

"Well done. Are there any left in the pet store we have to worry about?"

"Two or three dozen."

"Shit! You're kidding. What are we going to do about them?"

"It's okay. I put most of them in a back room with strict orders that no one goes near them. Starfish can go a few days without being fed, so they'll be okay."

"What do you mean *most* of the starfish?"

"There are two in the store's massive, showcase aquarium. The tank is far too heavy for anyone to move it. They'd have to empty it first."

"Geez, we can't have them doing that." Zol pictured parvovirus contaminating the entire Petz Haven megastore. When Max was little, Zol used to take him to watch the fish and other creatures in that tank. It was a fascinating and free Saturday morning outing. The place was always teeming with families.

"The night manager helped me isolate it from the public with a wall we constructed of jumbo dog-chow bags."

"Clever."

"I left her several sets of coveralls, masks, and gloves with strict instructions that anyone feeding the fish in that tank should wear them."

The crick in Zol's neck was bothering him again. Hunching over the cards had made it worse. "Did Winnipeg say how long it would be before we can expect some results?"

"It may be fairly quick. They're working on a project involving sea-creature viruses in Canadian waters. Something to do with those dead starfish Hamish told us about. I gather they've got a grant from Fisheries and Oceans Canada."

"Did they tell you anything more about the Parvo-W they isolated from our human specimens?"

"It doesn't match any of the viruses they've ever recovered from fish, starfish, or other sea-dwelling invertebrates."

"So they think we're totally off base with our starfish theory?"

"I'd say they were skeptical. But interested enough to be cooperative."

"The money from Fisheries and Oceans might have helped a bit, too."

"But it's safe to say we won't be getting any results for a few days at least."

A few days was too long for an infected aquarium to be sitting in a busy public space. "Do you think we should close the store now?"

"The owner is away in Las Vegas for the weekend. He never takes his phone to the gaming tables, so it'll be difficult to contact him."

Zol needed a moment to think. It was hard to make the best decision in the face of so much uncertainty. And the problem was, the best decision was often only visible in luminous hindsight. "At this point, the starfish are only an unsupported hunch. And given what Winnipeg told you about our Parvo-W, we're probably way off track with the aquariums. I say we cross our fingers that no one interferes with the tanks, and we let the store stay open."

"Cross our fingers, yeah." Tasha paused and exhaled a lungful of air. "Except . . ."

"Except what?"

"Well, there's this girl. Jamila Khateb. She's a high school student and cleans the fish tanks. Part-time."

"What about her?"

"The manager sent her home sick today. Fever, headache, stiff neck. Apparently, she looked awful."

The mushrooms, bacon, and mozzarella churned in Zol's stomach. "Sounds like meningitis or —"

"Early polio? I called the family. They live in Beasley. Same neighbourhood as Cathcart Elementary."

Beasley was looking more and more like ground zero. But how could that be? The Petz Haven store was across town from Beasley, and its customers came from every corner of the city. Geographically and scientifically, it was a stretch to imagine starfish as the source of parvovirus and the resulting poliomyelitis.

"Jamila was confused when I got her on the phone," Tasha continued. "The only other person in the house who spoke English was her nine-year-old brother. I explained that I was calling an ambulance for his sister because she needed to go to the hospital right away."

"The paramedics should be warned to wear their protective gear."

"Already done. And I left word they need to take her to Caledonian."

As the city's only university-affiliated acute medical facility, all the polio cases were being cared for at Caledonian Medical Centre. The staff there were on a steep learning curve. Most of them weren't alive when polio last traumatized the country, six decades ago.

"I'm having second thoughts about letting the store open its doors tomorrow." He looked at his watch. "What time do they close tonight?"

"In less than an hour. Nine o'clock."

"Good. I'll get Hamish to have a look at the girl when she gets to Emerg. Jamila Khattar, you said?"

"Khateb," she corrected and spelled it out.

"Got it. Unless Hamish is certain she doesn't have polio, I'll get the cops to seal the place before opening time tomorrow." He pictured the circus that would ensue: one angry pet-store owner, a gaggle of volatile reporters, and a zillion curious animal lovers.

A dark cloud descended as he rubbed the back of his neck. Had Tasha's trip to Petz Haven exposed *her* to the parvovirus? He shoved that thought into the black hole at the back of his brain. There were a lot of demons and bugbears in there. The trick was to keep them captive and not let any of them escape.

CHAPTER 10

"Dad!" Max called from the computer room after they'd put the cards away. "The doorbell?"

"Yeah, I'll get it." Zol shut the dishwasher and pressed start.

As he approached the front door, he could see Hamish standing on the outside steps. It wasn't a surprise. Except for Travis and Jehovah's Witness canvassers, Hamish was the only person who showed up unannounced.

He shuddered as he stepped into the hall and set his loafers side by side on the mat. His ruddy cheeks said he was steamed up about something, but Zol dared not ask. He was sure to be treated to the dramatic details sooner or later. "Your phone went straight to voicemail, so I thought I'd see if I could catch you here."

"What's up?"

"They called me from Emerg. About another polio case they want me to see."

"A young girl? High school student? Family doesn't speak much English?"

Hamish looked briefly puzzled but pressed on with his own agenda. "No, a young guy. Mid-twenties."

"Shit!"

"No kidding, eh? There's no end to them."

"What's his story?" Zol asked.

"Fever and headache for a couple of days, maybe longer. The Emerg doc said the guy was cagey with the details. Anyway, the family got worried when he was unable to climb the stairs to his bedroom."

"And that started when?"

"Today."

"Early paralysis?"

"Looks like it. The Emerg doc says she found significant muscle weakness and diminished tendon reflexes in both legs. The arms are still okay. And he's breathing fine — oxygen saturation is 97%."

Zol pictured the small finger clip that measured a patient's blood oxygen level and expressed it on a monitor as a saturation percentage. Anything over 95% was good. "Are they working him up? I mean, for polio?"

Hamish nodded. "CT of the head and a spinal tap are in the works. They may have some results by the time we get there."

"We?"

"Yes, I want you to come with me."

"You're sure?" Zol felt guilty at the thought of abandoning the boys, especially today. But there was no denying that the noises coming from the computer room were nothing if not enthusiastic. By now, those congenial few hands of gin rummy had been completely forgotten. Zol could stay out the entire night, it seemed, and the boys would neither notice nor care. Which, when he thought about it, wasn't a bad thing. Resilience did deserve to be fostered.

Hamish stroked his flattop with his palm. "I hear our guy's got quite the family entourage. Maybe you can get some helpful clues out of them while I'm assessing him."

Family groups made Hamish nervous. When tasked with a clinical problem, he was best with patients one-on-one. "A double-pronged approach, then?"

Hamish looked pleased. "Exactly. I'll drive."

Hamish always drove.

Twenty minutes later, they were striding through the Emergency entrance at Caledonian University Medical Centre. Before the heavy doors had closed behind them, the department's evening charge nurse hailed the much-respected Dr. Hamish Wakefield with a wave of her clipboard. Dressed in blue scrubs and white sneakers, the woman was taller than Hamish, her bearing every bit as confident. Blond, spare, and unadorned, she looked like she'd been designed at an IKEA studio. Her piercing green eyes had seen everything, and her thin, unpainted lips looked more suited to giving orders than praise.

"Evening, Dr. Wakefield," she said, then turned to Zol. "Dr. Szabo, I presume." She cracked a sly smile and lowered her voice. "I've been seeing too much of you on TV these days." Then, realizing her unintended double-entendre, she blushed and said, "I mean . . . well, just a lot of your face."

Zol chuckled at the witticism and her discomfort. "*Altogether* too much exposure, I'm afraid."

Her eyes flashed briefly, then her chin dipped as she became decidedly sober. "I guess you gentlemen know we've got two suspected polio cases on this shift?"

Hamish looked surprised. "What are you saying, Cheryl? No one told me anything about a second case." The guy hated surprises. They were neither neat nor orderly, and they were impossible to control.

"Sorry, Hamish," Zol said, touching his friend's arm. "I should have told you."

The truth was, Zol hadn't had the chance. From the moment he'd backed his Saab out of Zol's driveway, Hamish had talked non-stop about the *catastrophic* flood in his lovingly renovated kitchen. Hamish and Al were restoring — in exacting detail — their nineteenth-century house in a gentrified corner of Hamilton's North End. The property overlooked the lake and the yacht club. Al discovered the *deluge* when he arrived home today after work. He was now dealing with the mess and the *extortionist* on-call plumber.

"Tasha had to call an ambulance," Zol explained, "for a girl with suggestive symptoms. She's a high school student."

"Exactly how suggestive?" Hamish asked.

"I'm not sure." Zol dug into his pocket for the Post-it Note with the details. "Her name is Jamila Khateb." He turned to Cheryl. "Is she here yet?"

Cheryl checked her clipboard. "Yes. We have her in isolation. Room Three. I'm organizing a brain CT and a spinal tap." She looked around to be certain no one was within earshot then turned to Hamish. "Dr. Wakefield, there was a little altercation with the family of the young man we called you to see." She glanced again at her clipboard. "Bhavjeet Singh Malik."

"What sort of altercation?"

"He's visiting from Pakistan and has no medical insurance. His uncle falsely presented another family member's Ontario Health Card to Daphne, our registration clerk. You must know Daphne. She's a smart woman with . . . with a distinctive appearance."

Hamish swept his hand along the length of his left arm. "She has a giant crocodile tattooed from her shoulder to her wrist?"

Cheryl offered a sardonic grin. "It's a *dragon*, doctor. Anyway, Daphne noticed that the insurance card photo shows a young man with a tiger's head tattoo on his neck." She pointed to the side of her neck, and the grin disappeared. "The patient, whose real name is Bhavjeet Singh Malik, has no such tattoo. We called them out on their deceit, and the uncle made a loud fuss for a while before he calmed down."

"Thanks for the heads up, Cheryl," Hamish said as he guided Zol around a corner and into a quiet hallway. "We may be in for quite a ride with this lot."

"That's okay. I always tell myself we're here to serve the public and —"

"Celebrate our diversity. I know. But I hate it when people try to scam our system."

As Hamish was about to push open a door marked male locker

room, Zol led him back a few paces. He lowered his voice. "I forgot to ask you about the school principal, Mrs. Simon."

"They're keeping her in the coronary care unit overnight. She's had a couple of spells like this before. They think she must have triple S. As in sick sinus syndrome." Hamish paused and searched Zol's face for any sign he had an inkling of what he was talking about.

Zol had more than a damned inkling. He was a real doctor, not a paper-pushing bureaucrat. "You mean episodes of extremely slow heart rate caused by a defect in the heart's built-in pacemaker, the sinoatrial node? During such an episode, the blood pressure drops like a stone and the person can collapse in a syncopal attack. You mean *that* triple S?"

Hamish had the good grace to study his fingernails for a tiny moment of self-reproach then said, "They're going to insert a temporary pacemaker through her jugular sometime tomorrow."

"Thank God it's not polio. Oh, there's one more thing . . . The girl who Tasha called the ambulance for this evening, she works at Petz Haven."

"The pet store? Do they have aquariums?"

"Sure do."

"No . . . Did she handle any starfish?"

"Cleaned their tanks."

"Are we onto something?"

"Dunno." Zol looked at his watch. "But some of those starfish should be winging their way to Winnipeg any minute now. Tasha's taking care of it."

Hamish gave an approving nod and headed toward the locker room. "We'd better get rocking. But first, I need to ditch my street clothes for a set of scrubs."

"Say, Hamish, may I come in with you and eyeball these patients?"

Hamish hesitated. "You have privileges here, right? I mean —"

"It's okay. Yes, I am legit." Zol tapped himself on the chest. "Your Chief Medical Officer of Health has privileges at *all* your local hospitals." He flashed his eyebrows. "One of the special perks of the job."

A few minutes later, they were dressed in their protective gear and shuffling toward Bhavjeet Singh Malik's isolation room. In addition to disposable gowns over their scrubs, they had vinyl gloves on their hands, shoe covers on their feet, caps on their heads, and suffocating N-95 masks on their faces.

Zol felt decidedly silly in the getup. They were now into the third week of the epidemic and hadn't seen a single case of polio-myelitis transmitted from a known case to a household member. If the polio patients weren't passing their disease on to their closest loved ones, medical personnel probably weren't at risk from them either. Going the whole nine yards with protective gear was over-kill. The only protection the staff needed was a good dose of soap and water.

The worst part of the getup was the N-95 mask. It made it damned hard to breathe and awkward to establish rapport with patients and families. As Hamish opened the door to Bhavjeet's sparsely furnished isolation room, Zol ripped off his mask.

CHAPTER 11

At nine twenty on that cool but clear Friday evening, following the Caliph's detailed instructions in the envelope Omar had found dropped through the mail slot, Hosam put on a dark jacket over his dark shirt and dark jeans. He checked to be sure he had his gloves, also dark, then opened the front door. Behind him, Leila was sobbing in the kitchen. Alone. She had refused to have a neighbour lady come and sit with her while he was gone. Omar was upstairs in his bed, the covers pulled up to his neck and a heavy-metal band blasting so loudly it was escaping through his earphones and audible downstairs.

The streetlamps along this section of the street had burned out months ago, or maybe it was years. It was too dark to see whether anyone was lurking in the shadows or in the decrepit Honda across the street. According to the locals, that car hadn't moved in half a decade. How much did it matter, anyway, if someone was waiting to pounce with a fist or a knife? Unless he wanted Leila and Omar to suffer terribly at the hands of a Syrian mob here in Hamilton, he had no option but to do as the Caliph commanded.

He closed the door behind him and strode northward the two minutes to the traffic light at Barton Street. There, he turned right at the Beer Store. In front of him loomed a modern-day fortress armed with searchlights and automatic rifles: the Hamilton-Wentworth Detention Centre. The thought of that jail lurking at the end of his street gave him the shivers during the day. Standing in front of it in the dark conjured the tortures he'd endured in Damascus at the hands of the Mukhabarat. Was that exactly what the Caliph had in mind, a vivid reminder of those horrors? Did the man want him to stand here alone in the dark contemplating the terrors that beset those who didn't do exactly as they were told?

As directed, he waited at the bus stop. The bright glow of the Beer Store, the only business open at this hour, provided a measure of comfort. He could take refuge inside if a menacing figure showed up before the next Route 2 Barton arrived. The instructions said to expect a bus shortly after nine thirty.

Dinnertime had been an emotional hurricane. Neither he nor Leila could contemplate food in any form, and Omar would not leave his room. Late in the afternoon, after finding the envelope, Omar had made the rounds of the social media sites he had neglected while playing *Fortnite*. He was soon bombarded with photos and stories of the barbershop attack and was the first to learn that Marwan had died of his wounds. He tore from his bedroom and shouted at Hosam over and over and over, until his vocal cords gave out: *You broke your promise. You broke your promise. You promised we'd be safe here. But they know where you work, and they're going to get us. All of us. Just like that barber. They always do.*

Hosam's throat had tightened at the news. He had tried to blink away the tears as he pictured Marwan exsanguinating on the barbershop floor. Merde! He had been such a decent young man. Always quick to do more than his share around the shop.

He realized, now, he should have interrupted Omar's computer game. He should have calmly told his son about the attack at the shop and provided fatherly reassurance. But he had not been able to do it. Not when Omar was finally engaged with a simpatico group of friends his age.

During the relentless bombardment of Aleppo, and for many

months thereafter, they had each withdrawn into themselves. These days, Omar was still in partial retreat. His distress made that clear. In Aleppo, Hosam had coped by working day and night in the operating theatre. Admittedly, he had spent far too little time with his family. That changed in Turkey. Crammed together in the refugee camp, they had scrounged for food, space, and dignity. Hosam's well-thumbed copy of *Toronto Notes* now replaced the theatre; his bedroom desk was now the operating table. Cramming for his crack at the MCCQE was a distraction as absorbing as a full day of challenging surgery. Chasing a dream made you selfish, he knew that. But if you achieved that dream, would you not be a better man? Would your family prosper? He could only hope.

He had told Leila about this morning's barbershop attack the moment she finished her workday. And after that, he showed her the note from the Caliph. He had wanted to shield her from the threats, but he knew better. If they were going to survive this, she had to know everything. A professional herself, and never one for hysterics, Leila sat quietly at the kitchen table, her mouth contorted, her cheeks flooded with tears, her shoulders heaving in never-ending sobs. It was like living those final weeks in Aleppo all over again.

Three years ago, when Syria's not-so-secret Mukhabarat police arrived from Damascus to cart Hosam off to President Bashar al-Assad's notorious prison, Hosam had been terrified. Leila too. But they did have an inkling of what was in store for him. They had heard stories of prisoners doused with water, electrocuted, and hung from the ceiling by their wrists. But tonight, waiting for a city bus in peaceful, law-abiding Canada, Hosam had no idea what his fate would be at the end of the thirty-minute ride along Barton Street. Somehow, this was worse.

How distasteful was the job that awaited him? If he survived this one, how many others would there be until the Caliph deemed him out of favour? And then what?

For the moment, all he knew was that someone would be waiting at a Tim Hortons coffee shop on Barton Street, one block past the route's final stop at the Bell Manor loop. And if Hosam did not want Leila and Omar to end up like Marwan, he had to be there at ten o'clock, dressed in black.

When the Route 2 Barton arrived, he climbed aboard. He tapped his transit card and held his breath. Would it trigger the proper beep? If the transit card didn't work, he would have to pay in cash. Sufficient fare with no change given. But all he had was a ten-dollar bill. If he gave the driver the full ten dollars now, he would never get home.

Relief! The card beeped and let him ride. The driver gave him a quick glance but said nothing. As he walked into the aisle, he could see five riders. Three teens were huddled in the rear, two perky girls and a boy with a passable *Peaky Blinders* undercut fade and effeminately sculpted eyebrows. They were giggling over something on their phones. Two middle-aged men, nondescript, were sitting separately and halfway back. Their eyes were closed. Hosam took a seat within earshot of the driver, a forty-something woman with spiky hair faded to a number one at the sides and back, and enormous thighs. Bus drivers did a lot of sitting.

By the time the driver announced the end of the line at the Bell Manor loop, Hosam was the only passenger left on the bus. As he descended, he could see the bright signs of a Tim Hortons coffee shop up ahead. It was on his side of Barton Street and only a few paces beyond the next intersection.

The three-minute walk felt like an eternity. He took several deep breaths to slow his heart rate. It did not work. His chest still pounded. How would he recognize the guy he was supposed to meet? What if he missed the man, and the Caliph took it out on Leila and Omar? He would never forgive himself. The note mentioned nothing more than the Route 2 city bus, a Tim Hortons at this location, and ten o'clock. He told himself to relax, the contact would probably have swarthy skin like his own, dark hair without any grey, and mutter a brief greeting in Arabic. And, if the contact was one of the Caliph's al-Nusra buddies from back home, he would have a full beard. He was probably not going to miss him.

Hosam had been standing on the sidewalk in front of the Tim's for less than a minute when a black, full-size Lincoln SUV in mint condition pulled to a stop beside him. The front passenger window dropped down. The sole occupant was a woman his age with huge dark eyes, glistening red lips, and blond hair showing dark roots like Madonna's. The hair was so long, he realized, it went down to her waist. "Quick," she said, "get in."

"Sorry, ma'am. I . . . I cannot. I'm waiting for . . . for a friend." He looked from side to side and felt himself blush. He had been approached by hookers before, but never by one driving her own luxury tank. And not for a good many years.

"Seriously," she said, "put on your gloves and get the *F* in." She had switched to Arabic. "This is a no-stopping zone, and I can't afford to attract attention." He could not place the accent, but there was no missing the anxiety scrawled across her face as she glanced at her rearview mirror. "You're Hosam. From the barbershop. I'm supposed to pick you up. For God's sake, jump in."

He yanked the door open with his gloved right hand and slipped in beside her.

CHAPTER 12

When Zol and Hamish walked into Bhavjeet Singh Malik's isolation room in Caledonian's Emergency Department, the first thing Zol sensed was the testosterone. Two men as tall as Zol, even taller in their turbans, were standing at the patient's bedside. Their skin was light brown, their shoulders broad, and their beards thick and well groomed. They had to be a father and his mid-twenties son. The tiger's head tattoo on the side of the younger man's neck was impossible to miss.

Their masks and gowns lay discarded in the biohazard bin. Zol could feel why. The heat in the room was oppressive. He tossed his mask in there too.

The youth in the bed — late teens, frightened eyes, black turban — was awake, lying on his back, and shivering beneath the sheets. A blanket was pulled up to his sparsely bearded chin. Such shivers in a hot room said the young man had a fever.

Before anyone had a chance to introduce themselves, the older man strode forward from the bed and said sharply, "Doctors, you must tell me what is wrong with my nephew." His enormous brown belly threatened to burst through the buttons of his gaping shirt. "Why is he so poorly walking?" His deep blue turban wavered with the shaking of his head as his anxious eyes flipped back and forth between Zol and Hamish. Pools of sweat glistened above his eyebrows.

"That's what Dr. Szabo and I are here to find out," Hamish said. He glanced at Zol, caught the absence of his mask, and pulled his off. "I'm Dr. Wakefield, the infection specialist." He didn't offer his hand.

"Specialist?" said the uncle. "My brother is specialist also. Cardiologist."

"Here in Hamilton?" Hamish asked.

The man bobbed his head in that unique South Asian way that could be difficult to decipher. "Lahore."

Hamish addressed the patient without further comment to the uncle. It became clear that the young fellow was drowsy, could speak only a little English, and his uncle and cousin would need to translate.

Zol found it painful to watch poor Hamish trying to pull the patient's story out of the three men, only two of whom were fully awake. The cousin volunteered almost nothing and the uncle interrupted incessantly. Neither showed any interest in providing answers to questions such as did anyone among their friends and relatives have a similar illness, exactly what medicines had Bhavjeet taken, how had he been occupying his time, did he have any hobbies, what local sights had he visited, and what was his occupation back home.

The hard facts were that Bhavjeet was visiting Hamilton from Pakistan and staying with his paternal uncle, the man in the blue turban. Also living in the townhouse were the uncle's wife and adult son, the fellow with the tiger tattoo. They claimed to be in good health. Bhavjeet was nineteen years old and had been perfectly well until three days earlier when he began shivering and complaining of a headache. Since then, he'd eaten little, developed a sore neck, and hadn't wanted to leave his bed. Today, after the family had coaxed him downstairs to try eating a little snack, he couldn't walk back up again and had fallen to the floor. They'd called 911. As Hamish tried to tease out whether this was an illness acquired overseas or in Canada, the uncle was cagey about the date of Bhavjeet's arrival from Pakistan. Zol took that to mean that the young man had probably outstayed his six-month visitor visa. If his symptoms were the result of an infection, he had almost certainly acquired it in Canada.

Zol caught Hamish's eye and then asked the men, "Do you know anyone who has an aquarium?" When only puzzled looks came back in reply, he rephrased his question and mimed a fish tank with his hands and arms. "I mean, a glass tank that you fill with water and keep tropical fish in." He held up a thumb and forefinger to show he was talking about little fish, not mackerel or tuna. The puzzled looks persisted.

Hamish shook his head, satisfied that this group had no idea what Zol was talking about. "Have any of you ever visited a pet store called Petz Haven?"

Uncle made a face. "We are not liking dogs or cats."

Hamish turned to Bhavjeet. "Are you certain you have never been to a store called Petz Haven?" Bhavjeet looked beseechingly at his uncle who translated the question and the answer. "He is too busy for shopping."

"Well then," Hamish asked, "Do you keep birds? Perhaps a parrot or a macaw?"

Uncle waved a giant, dismissive hand. "You are asking are we crazy, keeping birds in the house?"

Hamish shrugged Uncle an apology and approached the patient's right side. He pulled the sheets and blanket down to Bhavjeet's waist and motioned for Zol to stand close and look over his shoulder. Slipping the young man's arms out of the flimsy blue hospital gown, Hamish carefully inspected the skin on his upper body — chest, arms, belly, and back. Zol could see no rashes, wounds, or lesions. Hamish palpated for swollen glands in the neck and armpits and seemed to find none. He cradled the back of the teenager's head in his hands and pulled gently upwards. The poor fellow grimaced, and his neck muscles tightened visibly on both sides. Such painful neck stiffness was definitely not normal. Hamish listened without comment to the chest, using the stethoscope provided on the counter beside the sink. When he palpated the slender abdomen with the palm and fingertips of his right hand, Bhavjeet gave no indication of discomfort.

After helping the patient don the gown again, he palpated the groin for enlarged lymph nodes and examined the legs for skin lesions and swollen joints. None found. Next, he tested the power in the young man's upper limbs. Perhaps a little weakness there. The lower limbs were another story. The muscles were abnormally floppy and decidedly weak. Bhavjeet could barely lift his heels a centimetre off the bed. The tendon reflexes at the elbows were present but diminished from what would normally be expected in a teenager. At the knees and ankles, there was no response to Hamish's tendon-hammer taps. Bhavjeet's sensory function in his arms and legs seemed to be preserved: with his eyes closed, he could tell when Hamish stroked his skin with a bit of paper towel, and he could accurately say whether Hamish moved his big toe upward or downward. When Hamish stroked the bottom of his feet with the pointed end of the hammer, Bhavjeet's face showed he didn't like it, but his toes didn't move. The toes of a person with a healthy nervous system would have curled downward.

Hamish took the flashlight from the counter and tested Bhavjeet's eye and facial movements. They were normal. He gestured to a box of wooden tongue depressors on the counter, and Zol handed him one. "Open your mouth, please," Hamish said, "and stick out your tongue."

It was obvious it had been days since Bhavjeet had last brushed his teeth. And even a non-dentist could see he had several cavities that needed attention.

Hamish held the flashlight's beam over the lower left molars. "Those are sutures," he said, his tone indignant. "Black silk." He turned to Uncle. "You didn't tell me he'd recently been to the dentist." He removed the tongue depressor from Bhavjeet's mouth and mimed a tooth extraction. "When did you have that tooth pulled?"

Bhavjeet looked at Uncle and shrugged. Either he was too drowsy to remember or had been cautioned not to say.

Zol hoped a less indignant tone might shed some light on the story. "Uncle, did your nephew have a bad toothache recently?" Zol mimed pain and swelling around his left cheek. "Perhaps a nasty infection? Did a dentist have to remove a tooth?"

Uncle looked up from his shoes and said, "I take him to my dentist. No can fix. Have to take two teeth."

"A dentist here in Hamilton?"

Uncle said, "Of course, doctor." He wiped the sweat from his forehead with his beefy hand and made no further comment.

"And when was that, sir?" Zol asked him.

"Um . . . last week. Wednesday or Thursday."

By the looks of Bhavjeet's teeth, he'd neglected them his whole life. Dentists were probably as expensive in Pakistan as they were in Canada and beyond the reach of ordinary people without dental insurance. Uncle would have paid for the extractions out of his own pocket — unless he'd successfully scammed his dental plan by passing Bhavjeet off as his son.

Hamish completed his examination by taking hold of Bhavjeet's hands and studying them carefully — the backs, the palms, the fingertips. "Look at this," he said to Zol, pointing to the grit under the fingernails and the dark stains in the palmar creases.

Still holding Bhavjeet's hands, he turned to Uncle. "Tell me, is it the Petro-Valu gas bar on Upper James that you own, or is it the one on Longwood Road?"

Uncle looked like he'd seen a phantom with psychic powers. His eyes grew huge and he took two steps backwards toward the door. "Um . . . um . . . Longwood Road!"

"Longwood, eh? I thought so. You have the best gas prices in the city. And you do quick oil changes too." Hamish made a point of studying Bhavjeet's palms for another long moment then placed them on the young man's belly. He smiled as he slowly pulled the sheets and blanket up to Bhavjeet's chin. "I always like to support family-run businesses, don't you, Dr. Szabo?"

While Uncle, now tongue-tied, pondered Hamish's pointed comments, Zol explained that he and Dr. Wakefield needed to go check on Bhavjeet's lab test results.

"Bhavjeet, I take it your parents are still in Pakistan?" Hamish said, reaching for the door handle.

When the youth nodded a clear affirmative, Zol added, "If Auntie is out in the waiting room, perhaps she'd like to come and join us. In say, fifteen minutes?"

CHAPTER 13

The blonde caught Hosam taking in her perfume as he fastened his seatbelt. She frowned. "You can smell it, can't you? It's that strong, eh?" Her Arabic was fluent enough, but she wasn't a native speaker. And she certainly was not Syrian.

"It is a lovely scent," he told her.

Leila used to wear the pink scent by Chanel. Coco Mademoiselle. He used to buy it every year for her birthday. She had to leave the last bottle behind in Aleppo, unopened. More important things out-competed it for space in the single suitcase they each were allowed on their late-night escape into Turkey. Some barbarian rebel fighter had probably found the handsome glass container on Leila's side of their abandoned bathroom, sniffed it, and brought it home to his mother or sister. Most of those guys did not have steady girl-friends. They were too rough and too much on the move. When they wanted sex, they took it by force, then shot the girl before she could complain.

"Shit," said the blonde. "I was not supposed to stink up this car."

"It is not your vehicle?"

"Of course not. It's borrowed." The look on her face suggested she was using the term loosely.

It was best to play dumb. He had no idea who this woman was. She could be the Caliph's girlfriend sent to test the loyalty of a new recruit. "Borrowed from a friend who is allergic to perfume?"

"Shit, no! From the valet parking lot at YYZ. We have an associate who's a car jockey there."

"Where?"

She shook her head as if frustrated at dealing with an idiot. "Toronto Pearson Airport. *Everyone* who's been in Canada for five minutes knows what YYZ is.

"I guess I have a lot to learn."

"Just do not make a mess. And no vaping or smoking. I have to return it before morning in perfect condition."

"I am a surgeon, I do not smoke. I have had to cut cancer out of too many throats and lungs."

"They told me you were a barber."

"That, as well." He could have told her the two professions had been one and the same for hundreds of years, and that he had started cutting his friends' hair when he was a teenager. But the less he said the better.

As they continued eastward along Barton Street, she was watching her speed. He waited for her to explain where they were headed and what he was expected to do, but she was saying nothing about any plans. It was clear the Caliph wanted him as unsettled and submissive as possible.

"I heard you had a bad morning," she said, her eyes still firmly on the road. "You know, at the shop."

"You could say that."

"Well, the boss is sorry. And . . . well, steps have been taken."

What sort of steps? Was Ghazwan now a lifeless corpse tied to a pile of bricks at the bottom of the lake? *Merde!*

The city and streetlamps were petering out. Barton Street was leading them into the darkness of the countryside, and it had been a while since they had seen another vehicle travelling in either direction.

"They, um . . . told you *my* name." His mouth was so dry he could hardly speak. "What is . . . what is yours?"

She hesitated then said, "They said you should call me Farah."

His eyes quickly flooded with tears, and there was no point in trying to hide them. She might as well have stabbed him through the heart.

"What?" she said.

"The bastards! They knew that name would upset me."

"I just do what I'm told." She flipped a bottle-blonde strand into place behind her ear then glanced nervously at both side mirrors. "What do you mean?"

"That was my daughter's name." He forced himself to say it out loud. "Farah."

"Was?" The woman's eyes darkened. "What happened?"

"A mortar bomb. Our second-last night in Aleppo. If only . . ."

She looked ashamed. "I'm sorry. I never would have . . . Was she little?"

"She had just turned eight."

The woman gave his arm a squeeze then returned both hands to the steering wheel. "Call me . . . call me Saramin."

If this woman was working for the Caliph, there was a softer side to the gangster's operation. It would not hurt to exploit it by learning more about her. If he was going to keep his head, he had to get his mind off his family. "Your accent," he said. "I have been trying to pinpoint it."

"And you don't have a clue."

"May I guess?"

"A hundred guesses and you'll never get it."

"Northern Iraq? From the mountains?"

She made a face. "God, no. You think I'm Kurdish or Yazidi? Their Arabic is horrendous. And their manners!"

"Sorry, I did not mean it as an insult."

"Enough with your foolish guesses. My family is from Damascus."

She could not expect him to believe such a story. Not with *that* accent.

Seeing the doubt on his face, she tilted her head and smiled. "My grandfather immigrated from Syria to Saint Lucia after World War Two."

"Saint Lucia?" He had to think for a moment. "You mean, the West Indies? The Caribbean Sea?"

Using her arms and upper body, she pretended to dance. "Yo' got dat right, mon." She stopped abruptly and became serious again. "Syria was a bad place for Christians after the French left in 1945."

"You are Christian?"

"Who knows anymore?"

"My late grandfather was French. A baker from Brittany."

"That explains the blue eyes."

In this light, she would not be able to tell what colour his eyes were. Someone must have told her about the blue-eyed Arab who worked in the barbershop. It was disconcerting to be talked about even when you did everything you could to keep your head down.

"You speak French?" she asked.

He had lost most of the language after his grandfather died and left no one in the family Hosam could speak it with. He did remember some of the swear words the lively old man had seasoned his speech with. Hosam told himself he used them in honour of Grandpapa André.

"Un p'tit peu," he told her.

"Just a little, eh? We had the French in Saint Lucia on and off for two hundred years. We got taught some of their language in school. A friggin' waste of time."

"Have you been back home recently?"

Her eyes narrowed and her lips tightened in a frosty red line. He had touched a nerve. "Enough," she said. "We're getting to the tricky part. Shut up and let me do my job."

When they reached the termination of Barton Street, she turned right at the stop sign onto Fifty Road. Soon, the roadway narrowed and they started a steep ascent of a forested ridge looming ahead of them. Saramin hunched over the steering wheel, her right foot alternating between the accelerator and the brake. The Lincoln's massive engine revved and purred beneath its hood. After several alarmingly tight switchback turns that could hardly contain the massive vehicle, he realized where they were. They were climbing the Niagara Escarpment, the famous formation that gave its name to the region.

The forest, black and menacing on both sides, crowded the barely adequate roadway. Was she going to cast him into this lonely wilderness of trees and gullies? He told himself to calm down. He had given the Caliph no reason to harm him. And as a corpse, he would be of no value to anyone. Still, his heart raced and his palms sweated inside the gloves.

When they reached the summit, the road flattened and the encroaching forest gave way to the expansive darkness of wide, featureless terrain. Saramin relaxed her iron-fisted grip on the wheel and sat straighter in her seat. She pressed the accelerator to the floor. After a kilometre of dead-straight blacktop, he could see the road was about to end at a T-junction beyond which there was nothing but a light-consuming void. They could be anywhere: Syria's Badia Desert, Arabia's Empty Quarter, a dark-matter star. Saramin reined the heavy vehicle to a stop and removed a phone from her inside jacket pocket. She flashed him a warning to keep his hands off the mobile then studied the navigation app on the screen. She must have been told not to risk making an incriminating record of their journey by activating the vehicle's built-in navigation system. Together, they peered through the windscreen at the rickety sign that identified the crossroad. He could just make it out in the indirect glow of the headlamps: Mountain Road East.

"Okay," she said, "this is us." She hit the gas pedal and turned left.

Less than a minute later, they came to what appeared to be a large, unpaved parking lot with a substantial building on its far side. There were no lights illuminating anything anywhere. Not even a sliver of moon. As Saramin applied the brakes and turned right into the lot, Hosam could see a large cross towering above a steeply pitched roof. A sign at the front of the property partially revealed itself in a flash of the headlamps. He could not catch every word, but the last two said *Baptist Church.*

It seemed a remote location for a Christian church. On his daily bus rides to and from work along Route 34, he saw dozens of churches in various shapes, sizes, and degrees of ostentation. It seemed strange for the faithful to drive far into the country when there were many churches convenient to the heart and suburbs of the city. Perhaps it had something to do with cheap land. Or maybe these people had strange worship practices they preferred to conduct well away from prying eyes. By the size of the parking lot, this church had a substantial membership. A *congregation,* he reminded himself, was what his sponsors at First New Canaan called themselves.

But merde, what was he doing here in a stolen, mint-condition, extra-long Lincoln Navigator that smelled strongly of expensive perfume?

Saramin parked behind the church in a spot well hidden from the road. Hosam heard a car door open and close. A second door opened and a vehicle's interior light came on. He could see it was a truck, a pickup with an extended box. A medical colleague used to have a Toyota Tundra much like it for hauling gear around his hobby farm near the Mediterranean, southwest of Aleppo. Hosam could not let himself imagine the sorry condition of the farm and the handsome truck these days. He had heard that the colleague had been kidnapped for ransom, his left thumb delivered to his wife on ice as proof of life.

The pickup's front passenger door closed, the light went off, and footsteps crunched against the gravel.

Saramin lowered her window and hailed the two approaching figures, both of them with stubbled faces blackened by paint or charcoal. In the glow of the Navigator's vast instrument panel, Hosam could see only four eyes and a lot of crooked teeth.

"I brought you a helper," she told them in Arabic. "I hear he's good with tools." She checked her watch. "You have three hours until moonrise."

The shorter man, who had been standing by the truck on the driver's side, told her, "Enough time for two trips, then." It was obvious his mother tongue was Syrian Arabic. His accent was straight from the city of Homs.

"The boss wants at least three trips to the yard tonight," she told them. "So don't mess around."

The man shrugged and produced a small flashlight. "How strong and fast is your boy?" He blinded Hosam with his torch while he took a good look at him. "Hey, you'd better have a strong back."

Hosam nodded. Two years in the refugee camp shifting cases of bottled water and burlap sacs of Thai rice had given him strong arms and, yes, a strong back.

The man dipped his beam away from Hosam's eyes and pulled a small object from his pocket. "Here," he said, tossing it. "Put this on."

"Careful," Saramin hissed. "That stuff stains."

The man shrugged off the warning as Hosam caught the projectile. It was a tube of face paint. Jet black.

Over the next couple of hours, Hosam and the man from Homs filled the truck and the Lincoln with several loads of what must have been thousands of dollars of copper sheeting. The church was in the process of having its asphalt roof replaced with a brand new copper one. The supplies could only have been delivered recently. The shiny metal shingles were still stacked on their wooden pallets where they showed no signs of weathering.

The other guy — tall, super muscular, and reeking of the same chewing-tobacco stench that had accompanied Marwan's assailants into the shop this morning — spent his time at the top of a ladder. He was so monosyllabic that Hosam could not tell what part of the Middle East he was from. His job was to remove the church's copper flashing, eavestroughs, and downspouts with a crowbar and hacksaw. He worked with an LED headlamp strapped to his forehead, his practised hands proof he had stripped buildings numerous times before. Neither man said more than a dozen words, although the taller guy did a lot of spitting onto the ground. When he wiped his mouth with what looked like the same dark WWE bandana Marwan's silent attacker had worn this morning, Hosam nearly swooned and took care not to come even close to looking the guy in the face.

The short man from Homs barked occasional instructions and aimed his flashlight at whatever bundle of shingles he wanted Hosam to lift. Hosam learned nothing of either men's stories and could not figure out whether they were willing partners in the Caliph's operation or, like himself, were working under some private threat.

Almost three hours later, Hosam was too exhausted to ruminate any further over the crime they had been committing. He closed the Lincoln's rear door while the other two secured the cover on the pickup's cargo box for a final time. They had already made two trips in both vehicles from the church to a scrapyard on the lower side of the Escarpment. The place was conveniently obscured by a high wall topped with shiny razor wire.

Saramin, who had spent hours sitting in the Lincoln reading magazines and fiddling with her phone, now called to him through her open window, "Here! Don't forget. You know the drill." She handed him four baby wipes and added, "Remember, I've got a plastic bag for you to put the dirty ones in so you don't —"

"I understand."

He *did* understand Saramin's fussing about the face paint. Traces of it on the upholstery might arouse suspicion among the owners when they reclaimed their cars from Toronto Airport's valet parking service. If anyone spotted new stains or smudges inside their vehicles, the Caliph's nice little jig would be up. He would no longer have unlimited access to a fleet of wheels invisible to the police. The cars and trucks the Caliph quietly "borrowed" had not been reported stolen, so no one was on the lookout for them. Furthermore, CCTV surveillance cameras would not have recorded them making previous deliveries to the Caliph's scrapyard, which sooner or later would be under suspicion of receiving stolen property.

The scheme was ingenious, but distastefully crooked. He was not sure what had his heart pounding fastest: his fear of getting jailed and deported for thievery; his dread of the Caliph's reprisals if he did not cooperate; his revulsion at working alongside a sadistic murderer; or his guilt at stealing from the decent citizens of the fair-minded country that was providing sanctuary to his family.

As they turned away from the ravaged building for the last time, he received a shock that filled him with more shame than he could remember. The Lincoln's headlamps lit the complete inscription at the front of the church: *Welcome to First New Canaan Baptist Church, A Caring Community.*

The heist he had committed was particularly cruel. Not only had he stolen expensive copper shingles and trim from his benefactors, but he had violated the dignity of their house of worship. Leila would insist on knowing the details of his experience tonight. He could describe the tough-as-nails woman with hair down to her waist, but he could never tell Leila about the crime he had committed against their Church People.

CHAPTER 14

After leaving Bhavjeet's room, Zol pulled up a chair beside Hamish at one of several workstations in the Emergency Department's central hub. Hamish brought the boy's electronic record onto the computer screen in front of them.

Zol pointed to the house address on the top line. "Violet Drive? Where's that?"

Hamish opened Google Maps on his phone and typed in the name of the street. "Stoney Creek. Look, it's few minutes' walk from those starfish in the Petz Haven on Queenston Road. But nowhere near our school in Beasley."

"And the uncle's gas bar on Longwood Road is a long way from all three places."

Hamish shrugged off their disappointment at the lack of obvious connections and returned his attention to the computer. "His basic blood work's okay." He clicked on an icon that brought up Bhavjeet's chest X-ray. After they'd studied it together for half a minute, Hamish said, "I don't know why they ordered this, but it looks okay to me. You agree?"

Zol pointed to the top segments of each lung. "No scarring or infiltrates in the apices?"

"I don't see any. So, despite his South Asian provenance —"

"No evidence of TB, past or present."

"Not bad," Hamish said. "Now let's look at the results from the spinal tap." He clicked on a different icon.

"I'm getting to know what to expect if it's polio," Zol said. "Okay if I try my hand at interpreting the results?"

"Be my guest."

"So, starting with the cell count: only five reds."

"A nice clean tap."

"And 350 whites." Zol knew that cerebrospinal fluid obtained from a spinal tap should have no more than ten white blood cells per cubic millimetre. Bhavjeet's fluid had 340 cells too many. "That's up, but well less than a thousand or two. So not suggestive of a bacterial infection."

"Agreed."

"And the cells are 85% lymphocytes and 15% neutrophils. That rules out bacterial meningitis."

"I never say never in this business. But we didn't think he had a bacterial infection anyway. He's not sick enough. Well, not yet."

As Zol was acutely aware, if Bhavjeet did have poliomyelitis, he could become seriously ill in a matter of a day or two. Paralysis could set in, and it could last anything from a few days to forever. Or, if he was lucky, he could escape the paralysis and go home in a week.

"What do you think of the CSF protein and glucose results?" Hamish asked.

"Normal glucose. Protein is up just a tad."

"Your verdict, Doctor Szabo?"

"Given the history, the signs you elicited on physical exam, these lab results, and the fact we've seen eight cases in the past two weeks, it's got to be poliomyelitis."

Hamish rested his chin on his hands. "Our Parvovirus-W at work. Poor devil."

"Does he need the CT scan of his head?"

Hamish gave the screen three taps. "There. Cancelled. We have our diagnosis, so we can safely spare the uncle *that* expense, at least."

Zol pictured the hospital bills that lay ahead for this family. A couple of weeks of intensive-care treatment could bankrupt them. And if Bhavjeet remained a quadriplegic for the rest of his life, what would become of him? A young guy with an expired tourist visa and no means of support was in a tough spot. The immigration people would be on his case sooner or later. But at least the province's government health service knew better than to try to get blood from a stone.

Hamish closed Bhavjeet's record and straightened in his chair. "Will you go back in and explain everything to them? Tell them what the lad can expect over the next few days?" He paused then added, "You're better with this sort of people than I am."

"Just what sort of people *are* they, Hamish?"

"Well . . . you know . . ."

In the general hubbub of the department, no one seemed to be listening. Zol kept his voice down anyway. "You mean brown people from the *subcontinent*?"

"I didn't mean —"

"You didn't mean to say that I must understand three somewhat cagey Sikh gas jockeys from Pakistan because I'm marrying Tasha?"

"Well . . . um."

"Yes, *um*. My marrying into Natasha Sharma's Indian Hindu family doesn't make me a cultural expert on everyone from South Asia. Not any more than your having a Muslim lover from Bosnia makes you an expert on the sex lives of subsistence farmers in the Balkan States."

Hamish let out a long, dramatic sigh and shook his head. "My relationship with Al isn't just about the sex, you know. It's a lot deeper than that. Hell's bells! Why do you heteros always think gay men care only about screwing and decorating?"

Zol held up his hands and crossed his index fingers in front of him. "Truce! Truce! I'm sorry, Hamish. I overreacted." With his wedding approaching and Tasha's mother still not warming to him, Zol knew he was overly sensitive to having certain buttons pushed. "Look, let's not get hung up on stupid stereotyping. You're my best friend, for God's sake."

Hamish's entire head turned cardinal red. Throat, cheeks, and scalp. Several moments went by before he spoke. "Seriously?"

"Of course, *seriously.*"

Hamish wasn't the sort of guy who had ever cultivated friends. The loner streak in him was strong. Having a best friend who wasn't your lover was clearly a revelation to him. And when Zol allowed himself to think about it, he knew he was much the same himself.

Hamish said nothing in reply, though Zol could see the wheels were turning.

"And, yes," Zol said, "I will go back and explain everything to Bhavjeet and his family. If the auntie is there too, at least one person in the room will remember a kernel of what they need to know."

Hamish smiled. And then he touched Zol's arm. He'd never done that before.

Almost an hour later, back in his street clothes, Zol found Hamish at the computer.

"How did your guys take the news?" Hamish asked.

Zol couldn't remember being this exhausted or emotionally tapped out. "A bomb went off as soon as I told them we're calling it poliomyelitis."

"What do you mean?"

"I tried to break it to them gently, but as soon as I said the P-word, the auntie's eyes rolled back and she sank to the floor. Thank God, she didn't hit her head."

"A vasovagal?"

"Yeah, a dead faint. I clocked her pulse as low as forty before it recovered. Her husband and son helped me get her feet in the air, and she came around pretty quickly. But then, oh my God . . ."

"What?"

"The auntie and the uncle started wailing."

"I hate that."

"And they haven't stopped. The charge nurse, Cheryl, heard the ruckus and came in to help. She paged the social worker. Until he arrived, I did my empathetic best to get Auntie and Uncle to calm themselves and listen to a modicum of reason. The social worker is doing his best to help them see that there's always hope, but they're not buying it. In their minds, they've got Bhavjeet already cremated or buried, or both."

"What's behind the fuss?"

"Sad family tales back in Punjab. We forget how difficult life is for so many people in that part of the world. It's like we imagine them living on a different planet." Except, Zol mused, we share the same one with them, and that made it sadder.

"And exactly what does this have to do with our patient and his poliomyelitis?"

"The family relationships are a little tricky, so bear with me. Bhavjeet's auntie, the one who fainted, had an uncle and a brother who developed polio as children. They were left with withered, badly deformed legs and became the subject of ridicule. As the family put it, they were shunned as cripples with no prospects for marriage or education. The uncle died begging on the streets. The brother ekes out a living selling trinkets at the railway station in Lahore."

Hamish had gone quiet and looked more pensive than usual. "Lahore, that's in Pakistan, right?"

"A huge city in Punjab Province. Not that far from the border with India."

"I suppose I don't need to remind you that Pakistan is one of only three countries in the world where the poliovirus has not been eradicated. Has Bhavjeet been immunized?"

"You're thinking he could have *real* polio, not Parvo-W? Classic polio brought in by a recent visitor from Pakistan?"

"It's possible. We didn't get a straight answer when we asked if anyone had recently visited them from back home."

"What's the incubation period of classic polio?"

"As opposed to our very own Parvo-W variety?"

Hamish did a quick Google search and the answer flashed on the screen: seven to twenty-one days. "There you are," he said. "We need to find out if they've had any visitors directly from Pakistan within the past three weeks. If not, the answer is simple and immediate — Bhavjeet has *our* Parvo-W, not *their* classic polio."

"But either way," Zol said, "his spinal fluid is going to be tested for viruses, right?"

Hamish tapped a few strokes on the keyboard and hit enter. "It's in the works. Whatever he's got, we'll find it."

"But I can't help thinking," Zol said, "here's poor Bhavjeet, presumably safe and sound in Canada where few people alive can remember our country's last scourge of epidemic polio. And then, he gets caught in a wave of something that's just as bad and looks identical to —"

"But is completely different . . . I guess they call that irony."

"This family has been suffering under the shame of the disease for decades. I could feel it pressing against me like an evil force. The more they talked about the auntie's crippled brother, the more the shame oozed from their pores like a bad smell. I think they feel tremendous guilt about leaving him behind when they emigrated."

Hamish scratched the ginger stubble on his chin. "What did Kurt Vonnegut's guy, Billy Pilgrim, say in *Slaughterhouse-Five*? You know, when bad things kept happening?"

He paused then answered his own question:

"So it goes. So it goes."

CHAPTER 15

By the time Natasha let herself into Zol's place on Scenic Drive that Friday night, it was almost eleven thirty. It had been a long day, and more so for Zol and the boys, who would still be reeling from the horrendous events at Paradise Barbers. Her tummy was filled with more than enough of her mother's murgh dopiaza and dum gobi. It had been after ten o'clock when she'd arrived at her parents' for supper. Her father was in bed asleep, and Mummyji was dressed in her nightclothes, too tired to start any arguments about missed meals and wedding details. She watched Natasha eat every mouthful of the dinner, looking for the merest hints of perceived imperfections. Despite the exhausting day, Natasha performed well under the boundless scrutiny, and they parted on good terms. As she left, Mummyji retired upstairs to read. She was working her way through the public library's collection of Scandinavian noir. She'd mostly given up on bridal magazines.

Natasha locked the front door behind her and called Zol's name from the entrance hall. There was no direct answer from her betrothed (she loved how he laughed when she called him that), but she received an indirect reply from his pipe. The power of love continued to surprise her. Who would have thought she'd learn to savour the aroma of premium-brand pipe tobacco?

She slipped off her shoes and followed the cedary scent into the sunroom, her favourite place in the house. She'd helped Zol do it up in uplifting yellows and blues and added a kilim rug with tangerine accents. Facing north, the sunroom overlooked the Niagara Escarpment's breathtaking brow as it sliced across the bottom of the garden. Zol never closed the curtains, so the room offered a wide-open view of the night sky. Sometimes you could see the moon admiring itself in the vast, black sheen of Lake Ontario. There was no moon yet tonight, but perhaps it would put on a show a little later. For now, the lights of downtown and the lower city made for a handsome spectacle in their own right.

She found Zol asleep in his favourite leather armchair. Left to him by his father, the thing was a brown, scaly monster in desperate need of rehab. When Zol had asked her to redecorate the house, he said she should transform the entire place from *his* home to *their* home. He'd given her free rein. Except for the chair. It had to stay, and it couldn't be sissified.

He sensed her presence and awoke with a start. He extended his arms in a long, sleepy stretch. "Oh . . . Hi . . . Is that my darling bride-to-be? Did I fall asleep for a second?" He squinted at the ashtray beside him and seemed relieved that the ash and dottle were exactly where they should be; he hadn't dropped his smouldering pipe onto the carpet when he'd nodded off.

Before he had a chance to stand up, she bent down and kissed him on the lips. "You were dozing for more than a second, my dear betrothed." Delighting in his smile, she took his hand and helped him out of the chair. "Where are the boys?"

"In Max's room, I suppose. Snapchatting with their friends." He looked at his watch. "I told them lights out by eleven thirty. They need their sleep. It's been quite the day."

"How's Max's forehead?"

Zol laughed. "I think he's mostly forgotten about it."

Max seemed to take everything in his stride, even more so than his coolheaded father. "Let's say a proper goodnight to the boys." She felt bad about not seeing them since this morning's horrors in the barbershop. "And after that, you can tell me about your exploits with Hamish in Emerg."

"You've been speaking to him?"

"Wedding stuff you don't need to know about," she said. "We didn't talk for long. He was preoccupied."

"Oh, yes, the flood. How bad is it?"

"The repairs are going to cost a bundle."

"We did have a fascinating time in Emerg. He's turning me into a proper clinician. Two tricky cases in one night."

Upstairs, they found the boys' bedroom doors closed and no light seeping into the hall beneath either one.

Zol beamed a satisfied smile. "Looks like it's all quiet on the Western Front."

"Poor guys, they must be exhausted," she said. "You're sure Max's forehead's okay?"

Still beaming, he told her not to worry and led the way to the bedroom.

She'd repainted the walls a heritage shade of rich blue and energized the room with a perfect apple red in the curtains, duvet cover, and upholstered chair. The two of them dropped their clothes on the chair, brushed their teeth in the overly masculine bathroom, and slid between the sheets. She couldn't imagine obscuring the delicious sensation of skin on skin by ever wearing pyjamas or a nightie again.

She nestled into the warmth of Zol's chest and torso, then said, "So . . . you saw my girl, Jamila? And another patient?"

"Hamish assessed her while I was breaking the diagnosis to the other family. I had the auntie, the uncle, the cousin, and of course, the patient, Bhavjeet Singh Malik. The uncle had called 911 when they realized Bhavjeet was too weak to climb the stairs."

"Bhavjeet? Sounds Punjabi. Are they Indian or Pakistani?"

"Pakistani. The uncle operates the Petro-Valu gas bar on Longwood Road. Bhavjeet is here as a visitor. He's just nineteen. His parents are still back in Lahore."

"Do we add Bhavjeet to our list? Is he polio case number ten?"

Zol cleared his throat. "Hamish was worried, at first, that it was *classic* polio. Imported directly from the sustained outbreak in Pakistan."

"No, really?" She knew it *was* a possibility, given the polio situation west of the Indus River.

"But no, Bhavjeet has been in Canada for several months. That's way beyond classic polio's incubation period. And, if the family is telling the truth, none of them have been in contact with any recent arrivals from Pakistan." Zol let out a long sigh and gave her a play by play of the auntie's vasovagal attack and the family's hysterics when he'd brought up the P-word. She had no trouble picturing the scene. She had family members who might react the same way. No wonder Zol looked so exhausted.

"Were you able to link Bhavjeet with either Petz Haven or Cathcart Street School?"

Zol explained how the family had denied such connections, and their gas bar and townhouse were a long way from the school. But it did remain possible that Bhavjeet had paid a few visits to the Petz Haven, only a short walk from Auntie and Uncle's home.

"Well," Natasha said, "an outing to a pet store could make a nice diversion for a bored teenager left alone after the other members of the household have gone to work."

"Except, by the looks of Bhavjeet's hands, he wasn't staying home alone watching Netflix. Hamish and I are pretty sure Uncle had him rotating tires and doing oil changes at the family's service station."

"An under-the-table arrangement?"

"If he's here as a visitor, it would be."

She ran her pumice-softened heel along Zol's shin and felt his shoulders relaxing. "When you think about it, it *is* too much of a stretch to imagine him handling the starfish or putting his hands in the tanks at Petz Haven." Zol's heartbeat was quickening against her back. "Where does Auntie work?"

"A garment factory of some sort. Out in Stoney Creek." She reached up and stroked Zol's earlobe. "What did Hamish have to say about Jamila? Does he think she's our tenth case of polio?"

He kissed the top of her head. "I had to make that call to the cops. By now, they'll have that Queenston Road Petz Haven sealed tighter than tight with their yellow tape."

"Oh dear. I feel so bad for her. She sounds like a well-motivated kid. How sick did she look?"

"If we weren't up to our necks in polio, you'd think she had a regular case of viral meningitis with some cerebral involvement. West Nile or Powassan or maybe herpes simplex. She had a fever, headache, stiff neck, confusion. Hamish spent a long time examining her limbs."

She smiled, picturing Hamish scrutinizing the tiniest of details.

"He's convinced that the girl's muscles are too floppy for anything but polio. Her tendon reflexes are completely absent — not even a flicker."

"Pretty typical, then. She's slipping into the paralytic stage?"

"That's what Hamish said, especially when we reviewed the results of her spinal tap."

"And how did *that* family take the news?"

"Hamish insisted I come in with him when we briefed them."

"No surprise there."

"He stayed cool as anything."

She knew Hamish's lack of upset meant the family hadn't made a scene or asked dozens of questions. The guy wasn't good at questions. His brilliant but longwinded answers often upped his pedantic factor, which put people off. She often thought he needed a minder — someone like Zol who was equally smart and a whiz at gracefully toning him down.

"The mother and father didn't turn a hair when Hamish mentioned polio," Zol said. "But then, they understood little of what we said. They're a family of four, refugees from the civil war in Syria. Here less than a year."

She wondered how you translated *poliomyelitis* into Arabic. "Could they speak *any* English?"

"Only the nine-year-old brother could converse with us — well, more or less. Certainly not the parents. And Jamila wasn't making any sense. I think the mom and dad finally understood that their daughter was being admitted with some kind of infection. They were stoic the entire time."

"Or just numb?"

"Anyone from Syria has been through a helluva lot in the past seven years. A week ago, the father started mowing lawns for a landscaper. And the mother is cooking meals in what sounds like a refugee women's lunch cooperative. They meet on Wednesdays in a church, somewhere in the North End."

"Oh dear," Natasha said.

"What?"

"Jamila's mother is cooking meals for public consumption?"

"Well, I guess so. What's wrong with . . . ?"

"I hope I hear a penny dropping," she said.

"Shit! But we've seen no transmission between friends or within families. Hamish says this Parvo-W is behaving more like hepatitis C virus than classic poliovirus. It persists on environmental surfaces, but person-to-person transmission requires a special set of circumstances."

Hepatitis C's *special set of circumstances* included contaminated blood transfusions and heroin needles, which didn't apply to any of the three polio cases at Cathcart School. She'd verified that already. But until they discovered what was unique to Parvo-W, every mode of transmission was on the table. "But we haven't absolutely ruled out foodborne transmission. Not yet, anyway."

Zol drew a diminishing circle on her tummy with his fingertips. "Okay then, you're going to make a visit to that women's cooperative." His fingertips moved up toward her unusually sensitive nipples. "But all of that can wait."

CHAPTER 16

Max had a run of bad dreams featuring blood gushing out of fire-hoses, hunting knives whirling through the air, and eyeballs staring from beneath black hoods. Each time a dream woke him up, he told himself it had been more gory than scary and gore never bothered him. He'd watched tons of operations on YouTube and had practically memorized the illustrations in his dad's copy of *Gray's Anatomy*.

He got up early, about seven thirty, even though it was Saturday. He couldn't sleep any longer because his head was aching. And it hurt when he touched the Band-Aid above his left eye. Travis heard him in the bathroom having a pee and shaking a couple of Tylenols out of the bottle. The two of them threw on some clothes and went down to the kitchen.

Before entertaining any notion of putting breakfast together, Travis made Max walk a straight line, heel to toe. Next, he grabbed Max's right wrist and pushed and pulled on his arm to test its strength. After that, Dr. Travis told Max to do some deep knee bends, walk on his heels, walk on his toes, and put his feet together and stand with his ankles touching. Travis was happy that even with his eyes closed Max kept his balance. Using the flashlight from his bedside table, Travis checked Max's pupils then told him to keep his chin still and follow the light with his eyes.

"You're good," Travis said confidently when he'd finished. "You passed the same tests my neurologist does on me twice a year." He chuckled and pointed to the huge bruise around Max's left eye. "Except for that shiner." Trav's eyes strayed to the door leading to the basement. "I didn't test your reflexes. I should get a hammer from your dad's workshop. You know, for completeness' sake."

"Forgeddaboutit," Max told him. He looked at the clock. It was almost eight. "You hungry?"

"You ever see me not?"

"Banana pancakes?"

"Deal." Travis reached into a top cupboard above the counter and removed the electric frying pan.

Max handed him two bananas. "You mash these up with a fork. I'll get out the Bisquick."

"The what?"

"You'll see." Max pulled the box of Bisquick out of the baking cupboard and showed it to Travis. "Dad says he wants a shipping container full of this if he's ever exiled to a desert island. You can make anything with it."

"Including KFC?"

"Something pretty close."

"And pizza?"

"You have to add yeast."

"We should try it sometime."

"Dad's taking Tasha out tonight. Somewhere nice for dinner. We can make a couple of pizzas for ourselves."

"Deal. If they flop, we can always order in. You got the yeast?"

"In this house? You need to ask?"

"I forgot." Travis pulled a silly face, made air quotes with his fingers, and said, "*My dad used to be the chef to the stars.*"

"I never said that. I just said that when he was young he was a chef in a restaurant where lots of Shakespearean actors used to hang out after their shows."

"Yeah, yeah. He made risotto for Romeo and jambalaya for Juliet."

"For shit's sake, Trav, how come I get all your lip and —"

"Nobody else gets anything?" He shrugged and looked at his bare feet. "You're just lucky, I guess."

They never discussed Trav's selective mutism. It wasn't an issue between them, so there was no need to talk about it. They bantered constantly when they were alone. But Travis had been staying with the Szabos for a month already and was planning on staying for at least two more. Max was finding it increasingly embarrassing that the guy never said a word to Dad or Tasha. Not even a quick *thank you* under his breath.

Max waved his sketchy arm to catch Trav's eye and said, "You mean I'm lucky the two of us crawled out from under the same toadstool?" Max punched Trav's shoulder with his good fist then opened the fridge for the eggs and milk. "Now, get back to those bananas."

Travis threw Max a military salute and said, "You got it, KB."

Only Travis and their buddies from *Fortnite* ever called Max by that handle. It was a secret between the two boys that showed Trav's prowess as a history buff. KB was short for Kaiser Bill, Queen Victoria's grandson who became Kaiser Wilhelm II, the Emperor of Germany. According to Travis, Kaiser Bill lost World War One for the Germans and was a nasty prick who nobody liked. But the guy had guts to spare — he'd been born with a withered left arm and grew up to be a commanding soldier-emperor. He was always pictured riding a tall horse.

Max's headache disappeared after four plates of pancakes. Travis pronounced it was the perfectly executed banana component that brought the batter so close to perfection.

"Yeah, yeah. Do you want any more?"

Travis patted his belly and let out a burp. "I'm stuffed."

They both heard a dinging sound echoing from upstairs and looked at the clock.

"It's not even nine," Travis said. "Why is someone inboxing you at this hour?"

"You clean up, and I'll check."

Travis shrugged as if he didn't care who was Facebook messaging Max so early on a Saturday morning. But the speed at which he whipped around the kitchen told Max he was just as curious as he was.

It was Omar, from their *Fortnite* squad. They played with him three or four times a week, and he always got his fair share of kills because he was quick on his feet and didn't hide or hang back. His specialty was outsmarting timid opponents with the bludgeon. He'd once confided that the reason he loved playing *Fortnite* so much was that in real life he was no good at running. His left foot was fake and fit poorly. He'd lost his real leg below the knee when a bomb exploded in a market in his hometown.

His in-game name — his IGN — was RUBBLE MAN. He said he picked it because there was nothing left of his neighbourhood back in Syria but a pile of rubble. Max preferred to call him by his real name when they were messaging outside of *Fortnite*.

hello KB. i worrie. no sleep.

What's wrong, Omar?

inbox me only from now on.

no voice calls. okay?

No problem. Messaging only. I got it.

thanks.

Where are you?

bedroom. door open. parents downstairs. can hear everything.

What's wrong?

mother crying. not werk today.

Travis, now reading over Max's shoulder, was up from the kitchen and up to speed on the thread. The boys groaned at Omar's slow typing speed but cut him plenty of slack because he'd only been writing English seriously for a few months. His mother tongue was Arabic. Max was a bit slow at typing too, but his right hand was adept enough at double duty. His dad said that was because the right hand got his brain's full attention.

> *Did your parents have a fight? Is your mother hurt?*

no fighting. just angry talk.
no one hurt.

> *So why are you worried about your dad?*

u watch tv news?

> *Sometimes.*

last night?

> *No.*

u hear about barbershop?

> *You mean the one on Upper Paradise where they had a knifing?*

my father, he was there. I
see blood on his clothes.

"Holy crap!" Travis said, then covered his mouth and shut Max's door. "His dad must be that big guy, the wrestler type who pinned Marwan's arms while Ghazwan . . . Oh my God, Omar's dad's an accessory to murder."

Max felt close to shitting his pants but took a deep breath and kept typing.

> *OMG! Your dad, what did he do?*

he help. now i scared for
him.

"No shit!" said Travis, pacing behind Max and pointing to the laptop's screen. "See? His dad has to be one of the murderers, and Omar's scared of the cops coming after him."

All Max could do was keep typing and hope that Omar's dad was one of the barbers, not the assailants.

> *What's your father's name?*

u not tell anyone?

> *Never.*

promise? on grandmother
grave?

> *Promise.*

sorry. father coming. wait.

Travis looked like he was going to toss his pancakes. "What do we do now? If his dad sees this message string on Omar's . . . he's gonna . . ."

Max pointed at the screen. "Omar hasn't signed off. You taught him how to blank the screen, remember?"

"So we wait, or what?"

"Go brush your teeth."

Travis loved brushing his teeth. He had four different brands of toothpaste and used them in rotation. Something about the buzz of the electric toothbrush calmed him down. Because he was mute, everyone thought Travis was a passive, boring guy. Max saw his dark side of the moon, which wasn't dark in the least. Just hidden.

Two minutes later, Travis was back in Max's room. He smelled like spearmint. A second later, Omar returned.

KB? u still there?

> *Here.*

father bring me breakfast.
gone now.

"What kind of murderer delivers breakfast to his son in his bedroom the day after slitting a guy's throat?" Travis said. "He sounds like some weird dude."

Max shrugged and kept typing.

> *Are you okay? I mean, did your father see our string?*

no problem.

> *You were going to tell me his name.*

why u care?

> *We care about you. We want you to be safe.*

we?!!!! who is WE?

> *Just me and Trav.*

you mean TRAVMAN from our fortnite squad? he got 100 dubs?

> *It's 107 wins. But yes, that's him. He says hi.*

hi TRAVMAN. why you at KB house so early? r u brothers?

Max looked at Travis. What should he say? Max knew what he *wanted* to say.

"Tell him the truth," Travis said, elbowing Max in the ribs. "We're bros."

Max gave Travis a thumbs-up and went back to the keyboard.

> *Yeah. Travman is my bro.*

who is older?

> *Trav. By one year.*

same promise? grandmother grave?

> *Same.*

```
okay . . . i tell you.
my father. he is hosam. he
is working as barber in that
shop.
```

Travis thumped his forehead with the heel of his palm. "That's a relief."

"Oh my God," said Max. "Hosam told us he had a boy about our age. I remember when he went to the Salvation Army thrift store and bought a used laptop for him."

"Got an incredible deal on a passable Acer," Travis said. "It even has a camera."

```
KB?
                                        Still here.
u guys know LION-NADS,
from FN?
```

The boys nodded in unison. Sure, they'd played against a *Fortnite* player whose IGN was Lion-Nads. He was a pro who'd logged almost two thousand dubs, which was a good nineteen hundred more than either of them. They had no idea what his real name was or what city he lived in.

```
                        Yeah, we know who he is. Aggressive
                        dude. Averages thirty kills a game.
he is from back home.
i saw him at my father
barbershop before they fire
him.
now he making big trouble.
                        Trouble? How?
deliver bad messages to my
father from syrian warlord.
```

"This is too much," Travis said. "Omar's talking Syrian warlords? The guy's been playing way too much *Fortnite*."

"Come on, Trav," Max said. "We did see Marwan murdered right in front of us. And he was Syrian, same as Hosam. Omar's not making this up."

> *LION-NADS brought your dad a message? How?*

two times. envelopes to our
house. afternoon yesterday
and today morning.
they say wicked things in
arabic. bad things gonna
happen.

> *You mean the envelopes contained threatening messages?*

wait. i check google translate.
yes. threatening. my father
have to do certain things
or the warlord gonna send
men to kill us. me and my
mother. like happen to
marwan. like happen to
people in syria.

> *You read these messages yourself?*

yes. but father does not
know i open envelopes.

> *And you're sure the guy who sent them is a warlord?*

i hear my parents talk.
sounds like warlord from
aleppo. thats my city in syria.
they call him the caliph.

> *Doesn't sound good, Omar.*

very very bad. my father
promised canada not have
such bad guys!!!
he lied to me. what a piss-
off.

Travis tapped Max on the shoulder. "A guy, his IGN is Lion-Nads, and he used to work at our barbershop? Must be Leo. Remember him? He got fired because he gave such lousy haircuts and was rude to the customers."

Max knew Travis had nailed it. But a Syrian gangster who played *Fortnite* against teenagers and made dozens of kills every time? That was beyond weird.

"So Leo shows up at Hosam's house with written death threats from his boss," Travis continued, "after Ghazwan, one of his ex-barber buds, knifes Marwan to death in broad daylight?"

"We don't know for sure the slasher was Ghazwan. Maybe he just looked like him."

"Oh, yeah. It was Ghazwan. I'm almost sure of it."

Max wiped his sweaty hand against his knee. It felt like his laptop had become a wormhole, a path into *real* danger. This wasn't the exhilarating danger of *Fortnite* that everyone knew was fake. "Come on, Trav. *Almost sure* isn't good enough when you're talking about a murder suspect. It all happened so fast we didn't get much of a look at the guy's face."

"I got a pretty good look."

"Enough to identify him to the cops?"

Travis made a face, then studied his sneakers and retied the laces. "So, what do we do?"

"We gotta think. Plan a strategy. This isn't the sort of thing we can handle on the fly."

"We should tell your dad."

"He's not a cop, Trav. What do you propose we tell him?"

"That Hosam, his personal barber, is in deep trouble with a bunch of Syrian gangsters. And like I told you yesterday — but you didn't want to hear it — we have to tell him we have a good idea of who one of Marwan's murderers is."

"So, we give Ghazwan's name to my dad and the cops, and we end up dead or in Witness Protection. Is that what you want?"

"You're exaggerating. Those things only happen on TV."

"Trav, get real. If we rat on Ghazwan, his boss the warlord will be on us in a flash. We'll have to hide — you, me, and Dad. Tasha will never marry Dad if he's in Witness Protection. I'll lose my only chance at getting a mom who actually lives with us. You'll never see your mom again. And . . ."

"And what?"

"You and me, we're kind of distinctive. Sooner or later, someone in a shopping mall at the other end of the country is gonna notice us. And . . ." Max beamed his stare straight into Trav's dilating pupils. "Do I have to spell it out?"

KB?

Max wiped his right hand with a Kleenex then let his thumb and fingers hover over the keyboard. He felt like a sapper approaching an undetonated bomb. He needed to type his reply with as few keystrokes as possible and get him and Trav out of there. He wasn't going to bother with the SHIFT key.

KB?
answer PLEASE.

> *heavy stuff, omar. gotta keep r heads. me and trav wanna keep u safe.*
> *lotsa thinking to do. inbox u later, k?*

u gonna help?

> *do r best.*

inshallah.

> *inshallah, you bet. bye.*

Max shut the laptop and let out a sigh that morphed into a long moan. Travis crossed the room and grabbed one of Max's best t-shirts from a drawer then mopped his cheeks with it. Max told him he'd better sit down before he fainted. His face was so white his port-wine birthmark had practically disappeared.

CHAPTER 17

At seven o'clock on Saturday morning, Hosam gave up trying to sleep. Saramin had dropped him at the Beer Store sometime after two. His mind had been racing with guilt, anger, and fear ever since. Not in his wildest dreams had he expected Canada to resemble the Syria he had left behind. But it had happened again: the moment life seemed to be humming along pretty nicely, it kicked you in the gut.

He took a shower then shaved with the only object he possessed from his life in Aleppo, his chrome-plated Solingen safety razor, a sixteenth birthday present from his father. The shave made him feel a bit fresher, but yesterday's events weighed on his shoulders like a surgeon's lead-lined X-ray vest.

Leila was still in bed, curled under the covers. He could not tell whether she was sleeping or hiding. She had done a lot of both during these past few years.

He dressed quickly and quietly and set off for James Street North, five short blocks away. The barbershop would be closed today and for a good few more. He would not be working his usual weekend shift from ten until six, but he could still try to enjoy the Saturday morning routine he had come to count on. He wished he had put on a scarf, for a heavy cover of low cloud had moved in sometime early this morning. The accompanying sharp wind made the air feel even colder than it had last night. The entire month of April had been comfortably warm, but here it was the first week of May and the weather had turned cold already. Had summer come and gone that quickly in this unpredictable country?

Of course, he told himself, long stretches of warmth and heat did not make a place a paradise. Look at Syria. Since the French had pulled out in 1945, the country had been in a state of almost continuous political turmoil. Embedded in the chaos, however, was a legacy from les Français that could only be called exquisite: the crusty baguettes, flaky croissants, and tangy lemon tarts crafted at his grandfather's Patisserie Chez André in Aleppo. During the good years, it had been Hosam's routine to collect, for the family's Saturday breakfast, a dozen oven-fresh croissants from Nabil, Grandpapa André's young successor. No matter how many hours Hosam might have spent in the operating theatre the night before, he rarely missed an early Saturday bakery run. Sadly, the trips ended when the civil war descended and Nabil disappeared. The missing croissants became symbolic of many untold losses and deprivations.

One day, while Hosam was scouting the neighbourhood around their new home in Hamilton, he found a small but authentic French bakery on James Street North. How wonderful it had been to walk through a bake-shop door for the first time in years and breathe in those wonderfully yeasty aromas reminiscent of happy family times. He had lost his daughter, his surgical practice, his villa, and his car, but in that moment he had regained a cherished Saturday tradition inspired by his late grandfather's devotion to his craft.

Today, he paid for six croissants with part of the one hundred dollars in small bills that Saramin had thrust upon him when she dropped him outside the Beer Store. He did not want to take the tainted cash because it magnified his guilt, but she had made it clear that he had no choice. And there was no point in pissing her off.

When he returned to the townhouse, he found a tearful Leila at the kitchen table. She was clutching an envelope. It looked identical to yesterday's, but that one he had already ripped into pieces and tossed in the garbage.

Like the previous envelope, its flap was unsealed. The Caliph was taunting the household by making it easy for everyone in the family to see for themselves the plainly worded threats.

"Did you read it?"

"I found it on the mat at the front door when I came down to put the kettle on."

His throat tightened. "Did Omar see it?"

"I do not think so."

"Merde, I hope not."

She handed it to him. "You will find it contains similar threats and another assignment."

"When?"

"Monday night."

"Putain! So soon?"

"Are you going to tell me what they made you do last night?"

"You do not want to know."

She stood up and checked the staircase around the corner in case Omar was eavesdropping. When she returned, she whispered, "Habibi, I have to know. Did they make you kill someone? Or force you to bury a body? I saw the mud from your shoes on the mat. Allah have mercy on us! Please tell me. What were you doing last night in the pitch dark?"

He took her hand. "No bodies, Habibi. And no violence. It was thievery, plain and simple." As she pressed his hand in both of hers, he felt more guilty than ever that the thievery had been neither plain *nor* simple.

"Did you meet the Caliph?"

"Nobody meets him."

He stroked her cheek with his left hand and took back his right. He removed the note from the envelope and read the rough scrawl. It gave instructions to meet at eleven thirty on Monday night in front of a McDonald's on Mohawk Road East. He should allow twenty minutes to walk from his house to the McNab city bus terminal and board Route 23 Upper Gage from Platform 5 at eleven.

He stuffed the envelope in his pocket and set about making the coffee. He did not ask Leila if she wanted any. He prepared it the way she liked it, placed a croissant on each of two plates, and hoped she would accept the sustenance. They both needed it.

On those cheery Saturday mornings in Aleppo, they had always had their croissants with honey from a local farm.

"Do we have any honey?" he asked.

"Like everything in this country, it is too expensive."

One of the first shocks that had hit them in Canada was the exorbitant price of food. For what they spent on a week's groceries in Hamilton they could have had six weeks of good eating in Aleppo. Before the war, that is. Now, Aleppo had no functioning supermarkets, and most of the independent market traders had fled. "Fine, Love. I will enjoy mine plain."

He pulled apart his croissant and watched its extravagant, buttery flakes scatter onto the table. Leaving her plate untouched, she looked blankly at the wall and sipped her coffee without comment. He had not seen her this defeated since Turkey, since those terrible weeks after Farah's death.

"How many clients do you have this morning?"

"I cannot face them, Hosam. Not today. I rebooked and told my helper not to come."

He finished his pastry and took a croissant upstairs to Omar on a tray with a cup of sweet black coffee. As he opened the door, the boy rushed to greet him with a guilty look on his face. As he set the tray beside Omar's open laptop, he noted that though the screen was blank the device radiated a telltale warmth. Why, he wondered, was his son communicating with friends so early on a Saturday morning? Would they not still be asleep?

Downstairs, he kissed Leila goodbye and told her he needed a walk. She knew an hour of fast walking often cleared his head. He had done a lot of walking during those two years in Turkey. The endorphins had kept him sane. And alive.

He found himself first at his workday bus stop at the intersection of King and James. One more block, and he was at McNab city terminal. If he followed the Caliph's orders, he would be boarding here from Platform 5 on Monday night. Some thirty metres ahead, a Route 21 Caledonian U was loading passengers from Platform 7. The posted route map showed that bus meandering through the upper city above the Escarpment and terminating at Caledonian University's Medical Centre on Mud Street at Winterberry Drive.

Filled with longing for what he had lost, he strode to Platform 7 and jumped aboard. He tapped his transit card on the electronic reader next to the driver and found a seat.

Knowing it would be a fairly long trip, he pulled out his copy of Omar Khayyam's *Rubáiyát*. Edward FitzGerald's translation from the original Persian was the first bit of poetry Hosam's English tutor had assigned him to read those many years ago. The individual words were simple and their meaning superficially clear. But underneath, the poet's message was intriguing and complex. Omar Khayyam was not generally appreciated, or condoned, by most Arabic speakers. But Hosam's secular, largely Mosque-free upbringing blended well with the *Rubáiyát's* philosophy: carpe diem because life on Earth is all there is. Don't expect a heaven or a paradise.

He read several of his favourite quatrains and concentrated on memorizing two or three more. Anything to take his mind off yesterday's barbarities. The poetic imagery so absorbed him that the end of the route arrived before he realized it, and the driver shouted at him to get off. Hosam dropped the Persian poet back into his bag, raced down the steps, and strode away from the bus and toward the large red-and-white sign that said Emergency/Urgence.

He found a seat in the Emergency Department's crowded waiting room and felt instantly comforted by the familiar bustle. He breathed in the unique hospital amalgam of blood and body fluids tinged with the no-nonsense odour of germicide. He watched the human dramas unfolding: parents with tearful children, worried wives with grim-faced husbands, middle-aged women fussing over their elderly fathers. He recognized the scenarios, imagined the symptoms, speculated on the diagnoses, and predicted the interventions. He ached to be knee-deep in the fray.

Frustration overwhelmed him, and after the better part of an hour he couldn't take the ache any longer. Other people were wearing *his* scrubs. Other doctors were putting *his* patients' lives back together. Why was he torturing himself? Was this an act of penance for the treachery he had perpetrated last night? Or was his subconscious at work, secretly strengthening his resolve to pass the devilish MCCQE and get back to the business of healing? The Caliph be damned.

As he stood, desperate to head for the exit, he spotted a familiar sight. In the farthest corner of the waiting room, a youngish couple — the woman wearing a hijab and a long skirt, the man dark-haired and unshaven — were huddled together. A young boy was asleep across their laps. Were they waiting for the doctor to see the lad, or were they awaiting news of another family member undergoing assessment in one of the treatment rooms? The parents' eyes had the vacant look of two people hopelessly lost in the hubbub of an alien landscape conducted in a tongue of which they did not understand a word.

At first, he thought the trio seemed familiar because they resembled almost any family from back home. But when the father caught Hosam looking at him, the man's face brightened and Hosam realized they recognized each other from the neighbourhood. Not from Hosam's old neighbourhood in Aleppo but from their new one in Beasley.

As Hosam walked over to the couple, the parents roused the boy and quickly lifted him off their laps. They leaned forward on their toes, the mother's head partly bowed, their eyes beseeching. It was as if he had found them lost in the desert and he was holding the first vessel of water they had seen in days.

Hosam extended his hand to the father and greeted him in Arabic: "As-salaam alaikum."

"Wa-alaikum salaam," the parents responded in unison.

Tears welled in the woman's eyes.

The husband beamed with relief. "We are so very happy to see you," he said. "We do not know what is happening. We have been in this place the entire night, and they have not found us anyone who speaks our language."

"That is a poor show. They should have tried harder. But I would be pleased to act as your interpreter."

"Yes, yes," said the man, his whole body nodding along with his head.

"You need to give them your permission," Hosam cautioned, "but I can help you arrange that."

"Most certainly," said the husband, still nodding vigorously. He pointed toward the registration clerk sitting at a desk behind a glass panel. "Tell her the doctor must come and speak to you."

"We will ask for one of the nurses, first. The doctor may be too busy to come for some time."

Hosam invited them to sit down and introduced himself by name, first and last. He did not mention his former title.

"Oh, we know who you are, Doctor," said the father. "The famous surgeon from Aleppo."

"No, no. *Please*, I was never famous. And in this place, I am just Hosam, a helpful neighbour. Now, remind me, you are . . . ?"

"Khateb," said the husband. He pointed to himself and then to his wife. "Fadi and Rima."

"Ah, yes. Of course." They had met and chatted briefly on a previous occasion, although Hosam couldn't remember exactly when or where. He did remember that Fadi had worked as an auto mechanic in the city of Hama. That was before Bashar al-Assad's government forces destroyed much of the city in the process of driving out the ragtag rebel forces that had occupied it.

Hosam gestured to the lad who was clinging to his mother. "Is this fellow the patient?"

"No, no," Fadi said. "Achraf is tired but not sick." Fadi pointed to the door leading to the clinical areas beyond the waiting room.

"It is our daughter. She is in there. A private room." His face tightened. "Where you must wear a gown, a mask, and gloves."

"Her name is Jamila, and she is only seventeen years old," said the mother, wiping more tears from her cheeks. "We do not know what is . . . what is wrong with her."

Fadi shook his head and stared at the floor. "It was a mistake to let her take that job."

"What job is that?"

"At a pet store," Fadi said. "Cleaning fish."

Rima touched her husband's forearm. "Jamila does not clean the fish, Doctor. She cleans the tanks where they keep the fish. And it is good that she earns the extra money. She is saving for a laptop computer and also helping us with the grocery bills."

Hosam wondered what diseases you could get from fish tanks. Some sort of diarrhea, perhaps. It did not sound too serious, and if the diagnosis *was* gastroenteritis, it made sense to keep the girl in isolation.

Before speaking with a nurse on the family's behalf, he needed to hear the parents' version of their daughter's illness. They quickly told him how she had been well until yesterday morning when she complained of a headache. Hours later, she developed a sore neck and Rima noticed the girl was feverish. Ultimately, she became confused. This was not the story of simple gastroenteritis. It sounded more like meningitis, an infection of the membranes covering the brain. It was a serious diagnosis, and common enough among teenagers.

He was about to approach the registration clerk and present himself as the Khateb's interpreter when a siren began wailing inside the building. A red strobe light flashed behind the clerk and a woman's voice came over the PA system: "Code Blue, Emergency Department, Isolation Room Three. Repeat, Code Blue, Isolation Three."

The Khatebs could not understand much English, but they understood sirens and flashing red lights. They gaped at the ceiling in stunned silence as if it were about to collapse. Fadi pushed Achraf under their chairs.

"What room is Jamila in?" Hosam asked.

The parents came up blank. But little Achraf poked his head out and held up three fingers.

"Are you sure, son?" Hosam said.

The boy nodded shyly, bit his lip, and drew the Arabic number three in the air.

CHAPTER 18

For sixty excruciating minutes, Hosam sat in the waiting room with Fadi, Rima, and young Achraf. Four times, he approached the registration clerk for news of Jamila. Each time, he was told, "Take a seat, sir, and someone will be with you shortly." And each time, he made certain to keep his hands in his pockets with his fists balled, his fingernails biting into his palms. He couldn't afford to show any signs of what his *Toronto Notes* study guide termed *microaggression* in the chapter on Physician Behaviours. The MCCQE website stressed the importance of a satisfactory score in professional ethics and deportment. He did his level best to keep the annoyance off his face, the contempt out of his voice, and his hands lower than his waist. If he wasn't careful, a security guard would be summoned to give him a sharp warning. And if he demonstrated anything close to what Canadians liked to call a *meltdown*, no matter how justifiable, he would be escorted off the premises and the Khatebs would not have a chance.

When his patience finally ran out, he stood by the electronically controlled door leading to the department's inner sanctum and waited for a professional to come by with their keycard. After a few minutes, a stressed-looking nurse, mid-thirties, dressed in pink scrubs and white running shoes, approached the door. She had her keycard at the ready. He accosted her with the largest smile and most confident English he could muster and recited the pitch he had memorized: "Excuse me, I am Doctor Khousa visiting from . . . from Sudbury. They called a Code Blue an hour ago on my niece, Jamila Khateb. We are hearing nothing since. My poor sister, she is out of her mind with worrying. She has no English, and her husband has but a few words. We would be most grateful if you could find out what is happening so that I can explain it to them."

"What was the name, again?"

"Jamila Khateb. She is from —"

"Jamila? I haven't got a clue who that person is." It seemed the local guidelines of deportment allowed the nurses to give stern looks and answer in a curt tone of voice. "What room's she in?"

He had the answer ready. "Isolation Three."

"I'm not working that corridor." She paused and looked at her keycard, anxious to be on her way. Then something clicked in her mind and she looked up. "A Code Blue? How old is the patient?"

"Seventeen."

Her shock was unmistakable. Code Blues on seventeen-year-old girls were a rarity in this place. This was not a war zone.

"We heard it announced." He pointed to the ceiling. "Over your system."

"I'm sure someone will be out to talk to you shortly."

Struggling to keep his facial expression neutral, Hosam made a point of looking at his watch. "That is what they told us an hour ago."

"An hour? Goodness. What was your name again?"

He told her.

"Are you a family doctor up there in Sudbury?"

The world over, doors that were closed to others were often opened to surgeons. With so much at stake and so little to lose, he had to give it a try. "A general surgeon."

"And they haven't told you anything?"

"Nothing."

The nurse swiped her card in the lock and pulled on the door. "Dr. Khousa, please wait right here. I promise, I'll be right back."

Ten minutes later, a slim young woman came through the door. She was dressed much like the nurse and wore a stethoscope around her neck. Her thick, chestnut hair was pulled into a neat ponytail. The lines around her eyes suggested she was rarely favoured with a full night of uninterrupted sleep. The name badge on her scrubs said Dr. S. Manning.

She extended her right hand. "You're Jamila's next of kin?"

Hosam pointed to Fadi and Rima huddled in their far corner of the waiting room. "Those are her parents. They have asked me to interpret for them."

"And you're her uncle?"

"A member of her extended family." They were Syrian, they were refugees, they were neighbours. Yes, they were family.

"I see. I suppose you heard the Code Blue?"

"Is she still alive?"

"It was a respiratory arrest. Not cardiac. I intubated her, and now she's on a ventilator. Vitals are stable."

"Is it . . . is it meningococcemia? No one has mentioned a purpuric rash, but the parents told me she —"

"No, doctor. It's not sepsis. And it's not bacterial meningitis." She leaned toward his ear and whispered, "Our infection specialist says the clinical picture and CSF results point almost certainly to . . . well, I'm sure you've been hearing about the outbreak on the news."

Hosam cupped his hand over his mouth to stop himself announcing the diagnosis to the entire waiting room. "Polio?"

The doctor's face muscles relaxed into a calm solemnity. Amid the frenzies of her job, she hadn't lost her capacity for empathy. "I'm afraid so."

"When can the parents see her?"

She pointed vaguely behind her. "A portable chest X-ray is being taken at the moment. As soon as that's done, the nurse will come and get you."

"All of us?"

"You'll have to put on gowns, gloves, and masks." She paused while she sized up Jamila's family clutched together and watching hopefully from across the room. "Is there anyone who can stay with the little boy?"

"Sorry, no."

A different nurse, not the one from before, raced up to the doctor and tapped her arm. "Dr. Manning, Room Five, the BP is dropping again."

She closed her eyes for a brief moment then shook her head. "Geez, I thought we were on top of it. Turn the saline up full blast, order six units of plasma, and I'll be there in a minute." She turned to Hosam. "The nurse, Breanne, told me you're a surgeon. You can explain the ventilator to the parents, right?" She paused, and a guilty look came across her eyes. "Tell them I'm sorry about her tooth. I . . ."

Hosam gave her an understanding smile and raised his eyebrows. "You chipped a tooth in your hurry to intubate and get her breathing again?" He could picture the scene: Jamila's lips and tongue turning darker blue by the second, her heart rate falling, her eyes rolling up into her head. "She was probably frighteningly cyanosed. Do not worry about it."

"You understand, then?"

He'd chipped teeth on a number of occasions when the situation was frantic, the anesthetist was otherwise occupied, and speed was critical. "Some of these Syrian refugees haven't seen a dentist in seven years. Their teeth are in terrible shape. Soft as butter."

She put out her hand and gave his a firm shake, colleague to colleague. What he saw in her eyes was neither judgement nor pity. It was their shared humanity.

"Before you go," he asked her, "can you tell me what you have planned for her?"

"She'll be taken upstairs to the ICU. That is . . . whenever they have a bed ready."

"And after that?"

She shrugged and a sad smile took over her face. "It's a waiting game. This polio business has put us on a steep learning curve. We're still only at the bottom of it."

"It is quite a challenge, I am sure."

"I hate to think what it was like in the early 1950s. Thousands of cases a year, and they didn't have a clue where the virus was coming from. My grandparents had friends who . . ." She stopped. They both knew that further details would be neither helpful nor hopeful.

The news reports had been clear. A forgotten disease was making a deadly revival. And his haircutting client, Dr. Szabo, could not say why it was happening or who would be next.

He held the door as the doctor strode back into the fray. It seemed her unnamed patient was going in and out of shock. An uncontrolled bleeder, perhaps? At least you couldn't blame it on a mortar bomb.

CHAPTER 19

"I know you're upset, Mr. Petz," Zol told the pet-store owner over the phone on Monday morning. "And I would be too if I were in your shoes. But it won't be for much longer."

Petz was still in Las Vegas and not happy about being disturbed. "It'll be *your* fault when the SPCA sends their lynch mob to collect my head on a platter."

The man was overreacting. After Zol had closed Petz Haven to the public for undisclosed public health issues on Friday night, he had made sure that the store's custodial staff had been afforded full access to the premises throughout the weekend. "One of your employees — Terry, is it? — has been working with my team and the security company to make sure your furred and feathered friends have been properly fed and their cages cleaned."

"For God's sake man, we don't keep our companion animals in cages. They are housed in customized enclosures."

"As I said, we expect to get the lab test results back on the starfish later today, or tomorrow at the latest."

"I'll be bankrupt by then."

Zol had a strong urge to call the man's bluff and mention the significant coin he must have been dropping at the baccarat tables over the weekend. But Zol chose the professional approach that would keep him his job. "I can assure you, sir, our colleagues in Winnipeg are working as fast as they can."

There was a rap on Zol's office door, and Tasha rushed in, her laptop tucked under her arm. She had a computer printout in her other hand and was waving it triumphantly. "Good news!"

Zol pressed the phone's mouthpiece into his palm. "From Winnipeg?"

"With a big fat zero on the starfish."

He lifted his palm from the phone. "Mr. Petz, are you still there?"

"Of course, I'm still here. Where do you think —"

"The results have just come in from Winnipeg. I'm going to put you on hold for a minute while I have a look at them. Please don't go away."

"I'm not —"

Zol hit the hold button and set the receiver on his desk. Tasha returned his exasperated smile. She'd heard plenty from Mr. Petz on Saturday, again yesterday, and first thing this morning. "So," he said, "what have you got?"

"They performed their DNA amplification tests on the starfish I sent them. Every one of them came up negative."

"How did they manage to work so fast?"

"They knew to hone in on Parvo-W from the word go. When you know exactly what you're looking for," she said, clicking her fingers, "DNA testing is a snap." She shot him a sly smile. "Well, more or less."

With no Parvo-W in any of the starfish, the creatures had nothing to do with the epidemic. But were they infected with anything else that could be a public health hazard? Zol wondered. "What about that other parvovirus Hamish was telling us about? The one that's killing so many starfish along the West Coast. Were the Petz Haven starfish infected with that?"

"Negative as well. Again, Winnipeg knew what they were looking for. They've been helping Fisheries and Oceans track that epidemic strain as it moves through our coastal starfish populations."

"I can tell Mr. Petz his are perfectly healthy?"

"Well," she said, "the ones he has left in the store, yes. Those I sent to Winnipeg . . ."

"What do you mean?"

"They made the ultimate sacrifice and won't be making the return journey, poor things."

One of the many things Zol loved about Tasha was the way she made him chuckle, especially when she wasn't doing it on purpose. "I don't think he'll care about that." He pointed to the empty chair beside his desk. "Have a seat while I give him the good news and send him back to his gaming tables."

"Mrs. Simon will be relieved."

"She gambles too?"

Tasha threw him her *Earth to Zol* look.

"Oh yeah. I forgot about Mrs. Simon's aquarium at Cathcart Elementary. Her starfish are also in the clear?"

"And so are Pancho and Pedro."

"Oh my God, you didn't courier her parrots —"

She rolled her eyes then shook her head. "Just samples of their feces."

"Oh yeah. But we'll have to tell her about the missing starfish."

Zol took Mr. Petz off hold and gave him the good news. They agreed that Zol would call off the police and the security company, and Mr. Petz would give instructions to his employees about re-opening the store. As they ended their conversation, there was, of course, no congenial *Thanks, Dr. Szabo, for doing your best to safeguard the health of our community under trying circumstances and mounting pressure from the public.*

Zol put down the phone. "Okay, my bride-to-be," he said, inhaling the joyful notes of her sandalwood scent. "We're back to square one."

"I think it would help to make a fresh review of the ten cases we have so far. It's been a few days since we looked at them as a group."

"I guess it's worth a try." The two new cases from the weekend might point them to something they'd overlooked.

Zol saw epidemiology as a game of commonalities. When you were seeking the source of your epidemic, you looked for the thing or things the victims shared in common. When parasite-infested raspberries on a wedding cake had caused thirty cases of crippling diarrhea, the commonalities that solved the case were attending that wedding and eating that cake. But life was always throwing curveballs. A straightforward investigation often got derailed by misconstrued perceptions, poor memories, overlooked details, and the fact that some people were hardwired to lie to conscientious government officials.

"While you're getting your ducks in order," he suggested, picking up the phone again, "I'll tell the police and the private security company they can cancel their guards at Petz Haven."

A few minutes later, Tasha had Zol's wall-mounted flatscreen mirroring her laptop.

"Okay," she said, pressing a small remote controller she held in her hand. "Here are our cases in the order they presented."

1. Boy, age 11, born El Salvador, Grade 7 Cathcart School in Beasley neighbourhood, in Canada 4 years, Recovered

2. Girl, age 10, born Haiti, Grade 6 Cathcart School in Beasley, in Canada 1 year, Outpatient Physiotherapy

3. Woman, age 38, born Ghana, Teacher's aide Cathcart School, lived in Limeridge neighbourhood, in Canada 3 years, Deceased

4. Woman, age 27, born Philippines, Nanny, lives in Dundas, in Canada 4 years, on Mechanical Ventilator in ICU

5. Woman, age 30, born Philippines, Nanny, lives in Dundas, in Canada 2 years, Stable condition on hospital ward

6. Man, age 56, born Canada (Caucasian), Retired labourer, lives in Beasley, in Canada entire life, on Mechanical Ventilator in ICU

7. Man, age 34, born Canada (Caucasian), Janitor, lived in Limeridge, in Canada entire life, Deceased

8. Man, age 63, born Canada (Caucasian), Laid-off menswear salesman, lives in Dundas, in Canada entire life, on Mechanical Ventilator in ICU

9. Man, age 19, born Pakistan, Visitor (Gas Station Attendant?), lives in Stoney Creek, in Canada about 6 months, Acute stage of illness

10. Girl, age 17, born Syria, Student Sir John A. Macdonald HS, lives in Beasley, in Canada <1 year, on Mechanical Ventilator in ICU

"And here I've grouped their demographic characteristics." She clicked the remote and a another data table appeared.

DEMOGRAPHIC CHARACTERISTICS OF POLIO CASES	
Gender:	5 male, 5 female
Age (yrs):	10, 11, 17, 19, 27, 30, 34, 38, 56, 63
Ethnicity:	Caucasian 3, Filipino 2, South Asian 1, El Salvadorian 1, Haitian 1, Ghanaian 1, Syrian 1
Hamilton Address:	Beasley 4, Stoney Creek 1, Dundas 3, Limeridge 2
Yrs in Canada:	0.5, <1, 1, 2, 3, 4, 4, 34, 56, 63
Occupation:	Student 3, Nanny 2, Gas Station 1, Teachers' aide 1, Ex-salesman 1, Janitor 1, Retired 1
Outcomes:	Still ventilated 4, Deceased 2, Recovered 2, Acute phase 1, Stable 1

Their cases were all over the map, demographically speaking. What, Zol wondered, could an eleven-year-old boy from El Salvador have in common with a retired labourer or a mid-sixties menswear salesman?

After giving Zol a chance to study the table, Tasha aimed her pointer at the flatscreen and circled the home addresses and occupations with the laser.

"There seemed to be some clusters here that I didn't notice before, so I made a new chart while you were on the phone with the police."

"Great! Let's have a look."

"I put them on a separate slide." She pressed the clicker and up came her new chart.

CLUSTERS OF POLIOMYELITIS CASES IN GREATER HAMILTON	
Living in <u>Beasley</u> neighbourhood:	1 Boy, 2 Girls, 1 Retired man
Attending school in <u>Beasley</u>:	1 Boy, 1 Girl, 1 Teachers' aide
Living <u>Limeridge</u> neighbourhood:	1 Janitor, 1 Teachers' aide
Working at <u>Limeridge</u> Mall:	1 Janitor, 1 Ex-salesman
Living in <u>Dundas</u>:	2 Nannies, 1 Ex-salesman
Family's gas bar near <u>Dundas</u>:	1 Young Man, "Visitor"/Mechanic

The data in Tasha's table was so clearly displayed that it didn't take him long to see her point. It was also a bit unsettling that it had taken this long to appreciate what had been staring at them all along. That was the thing about connections — they were only obvious when someone pointed them out to you. Their polio cases had strong connections to only three areas of the city: Beasley, Dundas, and Limeridge.

"It looks like the virus is spreading by . . ."

"Word-of-mouth?" Tasha suggested.

"But that's impossible."

"Unless . . ." She paused for a moment. "What if people are inadvertently coming in contact with Parvo-W because it's hidden in some person, place, or thing they're *hearing* about by word-of-mouth?"

"You mean they're being recommended — coerced, maybe? — to go somewhere, do something, or purchase something that happens to be contaminated with Parvo-W?"

Zol studied the data again with their new hypothesis in mind. "How about this?" he said. "The janitor at Limeridge Mall talks to the salesman who worked at the mall's major department store until it went bankrupt earlier this year. The laid-off salesman, now with plenty of time on his hands, chats with one of the nannies when he runs into her near his home in Dundas. She tells the other nanny who also lives in Dundas and is a member of the same Filipino community."

Tasha's eyes were sparkling with renewed enthusiasm "And what if the janitor also tells the teacher's aide who lives near his apartment? And then she tells the two kids at her school."

"Or their parents, anyway."

Tasha flipped through the data-crammed binder she assembled for each investigation. "The janitor and the teacher's aide live, um . . . yes . . . in adjacent apartment blocks on Mohawk Road. We need to talk to them again."

Zol pointed to the flatscreen. "Except . . . go back two slides?" She pressed her clicker twice. "See? Cases number three and seven? The teacher's aide and the janitor? They're dead."

Tasha looked crushed for a moment, then returned to the binder and flipped a few pages. "And they lived alone, both of them. The teacher' aide and the janitor. Nuts."

"What about the laid-off salesman?" Zol asked as they scrutinized the slide together.

"Case number eight. He's still in the ICU. On a ventilator."

"Does he have family we can interview again?"

She consulted her bible. "Divorced and living alone." She closed the binder and tapped her pen on its bright blue cover. "Do you think the virus's source is associated with something shameful or illegal?"

"Why do you say that?"

"I know there've been language barriers with most of these families, but still, we didn't pick up so much as a hint of what the source could be when we interviewed them."

"You think they're purposely covering it up?"

She shrugged. "Could be."

"How significant is it that only three out of the ten are white?"

She shot him a teasing look. "Are you saying brown people are more likely to lie?"

"Very funny. But look, everyone on the list seems vulnerable in some way. Half of them are refugees or immigrants here four years or less. How many of the cases speak English as a first language?"

"Only the three white guys and perhaps the woman from Ghana."

"At least two of the white men were vulnerable. One lost his job and his pension in the department-store bankruptcy. The other worked part-time at minimum wage."

Tasha was staring at her binder. "There are no doctors, lawyers, or accountants in here. I give you that."

They both knew that viruses couldn't distinguish between the hot shots and the underprivileged. But whatever was spreading this one was preying on the vulnerable. Exactly how was it doing it? If they figured that out, they might get to the bottom of the outbreak.

There was a firm knock at the door, but whoever it was didn't walk in. Tasha raised her eyebrows and then opened the door.

Standing there with a smug grin on his face was the Health Unit's front-desk receptionist, a slim young man named Jesse. He had perfect manners, a fine head for detail, a facility with numbers, a sharp wit, and an excessive need for praise. His duties included sorting out everything at the Health Unit that had to do with IT. He acknowledged Tasha with a brief nod and then beamed a huge smile across the room at Zol.

"Excuse me, Dr. Zed, but this just arrived from Winnipeg via the confidential email account. I knew you'd want to see it immediately, so I decrypted it and printed it out. No one else has seen it."

He pranced into the room and handed the printout directly to Zol. The smirk on his face said, *For your eyes only, Boss.*

"Thanks, Jesse. Good thinking."

The young man's eyes were twinkling as brightly as his earrings. "Always glad to be of service, Dr. Zed. Please let me know if there is anything else I can do to help." He spun on one heel and slipped out the door, closing it behind him.

"I think he's gunning for a wedding invitation," Zol said.

"Then he's making eyes at the wrong person. Dr. Zed, my eye."

Zol read the printout, a preliminary report from the lab in Winnipeg. The facts were simple, but making sense of them was tricky.

"Something you can share?" Tasha asked.

Zol rubbed his eyes. "Our first nine polio cases have tested positive for antibodies to Zika virus. In their blood and spinal-fluid samples. Results on the two cases from the weekend will be ready tomorrow."

"Good God! Zika? That's weird. What kind of antibodies? IgG or IgM?"

"Both. But stronger on the IgM." They both knew that high levels of IgM signalled recent infection — within the past few weeks.

"Did they use PCR to test for the virus itself, or did the lab find only the antibodies?"

Tasha was right to be skeptical. Antibodies were viral footprints, not the microbes themselves. Like footprints everywhere, one microbe's antibody could be confused with another's. For these results to be absolutely convincing, the lab needed to prove that the Zika virus itself was in the victims' blood or spinal fluid, not just some cross-reacting antibody left by another microbe.

There was a second reason to be skeptical about Zika. It was a tropical virus spread by a tropical Aedes mosquito. You'd never expect to see an outbreak in this country because Canada was too cold to support the required Aedes species.

He studied the page again. "They're setting up the Zika PCRs right away," he told her. "We should expect results tomorrow after-noon. Only then will we know for sure what we've got."

"Every case simultaneously infected with two rare viruses? What does this mean?"

For a while, he couldn't take his eyes off the printout. Then some-thing clicked at the back of his brain and he googled "Geographic range of Aedes albopictus mosquitoes" on his computer. Together, they read the third hit listed.

Bingo! He'd remembered correctly. There *had* been sightings of a winter-hardy Aedes species as far north as New York State. They were Aedes albopictus, known as Asian Tigers because they came originally from Asia and sported black and white stripes. They were aggressive biters that preferred human settlements over untamed wilderness. They'd been introduced into the U.S. in shipments of used tires imported from Japan. The rubber provided insulation and protection for the mosquitoes' eggs. When the imported tires were left out in the rain, the eggs hatched into larvae and matured into adults. Sometimes, these aggressive newcomers carried Zika virus.

"This means I start with my friend Dr. Polgar at the Niagara Health Unit," he said. "Even on a misty day, she can see New York State from her office on the other side of the Falls. And I know she's been on the lookout for those Asian Tigers."

CHAPTER 20

"Hi, Szabo," said Stephanie Polgar. "Good to hear from you. What can I do for you?"

On the telephone, the voice of Zol's counterpart at the Niagara Regional Health Unit was low and mellow. Almost a decade ago, that voice had done a mean interpretation of Elvis's "Are You Lonesome Tonight" and had belonged to Dr. *Stephen* Polgar.

During their four years of public health training together, Zol and Polgar had enjoyed an easy camaraderie built on the similarity of their ages and their heritage. Their parents were born in Budapest and had fled to Canada as political refugees during the short-lived Hungarian revolution of 1956. Polgar had been a congenial beer-drinking buddy with a sympathetic ear when Francine ran off to her ashram in India. Max was only one year old at the time. As it turned out, Francine did her guys a huge favour by leaving them; she was suited neither to motherhood nor an organized routine, and life with her would have been loveless, traumatic, and chaotic. When things had gone sour at home, Polgar's friendship got Zol through it.

Last year at a conference in Toronto, Zol was startled by a tall woman who sidled up to him and said, "How's it going, Szabo?" In the context of the high heels, the shoulder-length hair, the sizeable breasts, and the glistening red lips, the familiar voice floored him. When the voice told him, "My name's Stephanie, and I'll give you a second to pick your jaw off the floor before someone tramples it," Zol wanted to sink through the carpet.

It took a couple of days of sitting with *Stephanie* Polgar at the conference for Zol to begin to adjust to her physical persona. The longer the two of them talked shop and reminisced about the old days, the more Zol accepted the whole package.

Today, Zol got down to business. "We've had some developments in our polio epidemic."

Stephanie sucked in a breath. "You mean it's spread outside your region?"

"So far, no. The Ministry has every health unit on the lookout, but we're the only ones who continue to be blessed. Have you seen anything suspicious?"

"One neuro case that turned out to be Guillain–Barré. But that's it. You've got a fresh lead, haven't you? I can hear it in your voice."

"A couple of leads. Which is why I called you."

"Moi, good buddy? What do you need from *me*?"

Zol explained that Winnipeg had found Parvo-W virus and anti-Zika antibodies in samples of blood and spinal fluid taken from his polio cases.

"Zika, eh?" Stephanie said. "Are they going to run PCRs on the spinal fluids?"

Stephanie knew her stuff. "We've been promised results for sometime tomorrow," he told her.

"And meanwhile, you're thinking maybe I've been hiding Zika infections acquired on my turf? Cases I didn't report to the Ministry?"

"Of course not, but —"

"It's okay, Szabo. I understand. You're grasping at straws. But I can assure you we've had no locally acquired Zika in Niagara. At least . . ." She paused, then added, "none that we know about."

"Do I hear a *but* in there, Stee . . . Stephanie?"

She ignored the slip. "Three local seniors did pick up Zika in the Dominican Republic a few months ago. On winter holiday packages to Punta Cana. Didn't turn out to be anything serious. Just mild fever and a rash."

Stephanie cleared her throat then paused as if debating with herself. She had more to say, but the phone line went quiet. Zol didn't fill the silence. Hoping for something juicy, he held his breath.

Finally, she let out a long sigh that sounded like capitulation. "All right," she said, "I do have something for you. It's going to be formally announced by the Ministry later this week. I've been sworn to secrecy, so you can't say anything until —"

"Oh, my God! What do you have?"

"Calm yourself, buddy."

"Sorry."

"Well . . . we do have a few Aedes albopictus. Right here in River City."

Tasha was going to be astounded. Even Hamish was going to be impressed. "Asian Tigers have crossed the border?"

"In the interest of political correctness, they've dropped the *Asian* from the name. If you can't manage Aedes albopictus, call them Aedes Tigers."

"How did you find them?"

"I've got an excellent mosquito surveillance team. They caught them in their traps. Never found them here before, of course."

The first documentation of Aedes albopictus anywhere in the Great White North was a huge deal. And perhaps a giant piece in his polio puzzle. "At the Falls?"

"No, downriver. In the northeast corner of our region. At a little place called Virgil. You've probably stopped there for peaches and tomatoes on the way to Niagara-on-the-Lake."

Zol knew the popular hamlet well. It was surrounded by orchards, fruit stands, and show case vineyards. From May to October, the area was flooded with wine enthusiasts, foodies, high-end shoppers, and drama-festival patrons. Under the right conditions, Aedes mosquitoes transmitted not just Zika, but dengue, yellow fever, and chikungunya, any of which could be lethal. Shit!

"You think tourists brought the Aedes Tigers over the border with them?" Zol asked. "From New York State?"

"Unlikely. Our tourist season has barely started. But I don't mind telling you, those Aedes albopictus buzzing next door have been worrying me for some time. We only have the Niagara River dividing us from the U.S., and it's pretty narrow in places."

"Were any of the Tigers carrying human pathogens?"

"That's the million-dollar question, eh?"

"You've sent them off for testing?"

"I wanted to send them directly to Winnipeg, but the Ministry insisted I follow their time-wasting protocol."

There was no point in hiding his disgust. "Don't tell me you sent your Aedes Tigers to the Provincial Lab in Toronto?"

"Yeah, I know. It's the least efficient lab on the damned continent. But your favourite boss, and mine, Elliott York, is hoping to make the public-health discovery of the decade. His personal cred would skyrocket if revealed that a tropical disease or two had hitchhiked into his jurisdiction."

Elliott York was a well-known grandstander. He wouldn't want the guys and gals over there in the frozen wilds of Winnipeg, Manitoba, to be the first ones to tell the world that tropical viruses were now residing here in dreamy Ontario. York would be positively salivating at the chance to announce that a deadly disease or two was poised to ride on mosquitoes' wings into the rest of the country. Any press release from his office would suggest that he, Dr. Elliott York, had discovered the whole infected Aedes Tiger thing singlehandedly.

"If the Tigers were not brought in by tourists, do you have any theories on how they got here?" Zol asked.

"Like you, Szabo, we're following up a few leads."

"Any hints? Imported rubber tires, maybe?"

"How about letting a girl and her team have a crack at the puzzle first? Before the hotshots come knocking."

"I get it."

"We'll keep each other posted, okay? I'll let you know if our Tigers are infected with Zika, and you can tell me if any of your polios have been enjoying the delights of Niagara-on-the-Lake . . . Deal?"

"Deal. And, uh . . . *Steph.* Thanks a lot, eh?"

CHAPTER 21

At school on Monday, still distressed beneath the weight of Friday's travesty against Marwan, Max felt that he and Travis had turned into celebrities in a sick kind of way. Many of their classmates had seen Trav's blog post over the weekend — he'd made it as respectful of Marwan's dignity as he could — and some of them had read Saturday's front-page shocker in the *Hamilton Spectator*. It was head-lined: Deadly Slashing Hits Upper Paradise Barbershop.

At lunchtime, kids crowded around their table in the cafeteria and asked what seemed a zillion stupid questions. Two doofuses wanted to know if Travis had any wicked forensic-type photos of the blood-spattered victim. *Yeah, right*, thought Max, fighting back the tears, *we took pictures of Marwan's final gory minutes so we could remember the kid, not much older than us, who used to joke around and bring us Cokes while we were waiting to have our hair cut*. It was a relief when the bell rang to signal the start of afternoon classes.

By the time the school day was over, and they'd trudged the fif-teen minutes home, Max felt as sweaty as Bo Dallas and Zack Ryder after a couple of rounds in the ring. April had set a heat record in Southern Ontario, the first week of May had turned unseasonably cold, and today it had turned stifling again. Like most of the other kids at their school, Max understood that global warming really was a thing, even though some days were too cold and wet to do much outside. In science class, their teacher talked about how it was going to be a bumper year for mosquitoes, cicadas, and gypsy moths.

Travis tore into the fridge and pulled out the OJ while Max set out two glasses. In Trav's house, they never drank it straight from the carton. His mom was strict about that. So Travis poured, and they both guzzled. Max's dad said he wished he'd bought shares in a Florida orange grove before Travis came to stay.

Max's laptop dinged in his backpack. It had picked up the house wifi, and his Facebook Messenger was now live after almost seven hours of silence. Their school made the kids keep their phone notifications off while they were on the premises, and none of them had the password to the school's wifi for use on their own devices. Max had heard some parents complaining that the policy was draconian. Other parents, like Dad and Trav's mom, thought it was spot on.

Max finished his OJ and opened his laptop while Travis guzzled a second glass of Florida sunshine.

hello KB. i worry again.

> *Yeah, Omar? What's wrong?*

TRAVMAN is there?

> *He says hello.*

no school for me today.

> *Are you sick?*

father does not want me to
get paralyzed.

> *Sorry. Don't understand.*

girl down the street. name
jamila. my father visit her at
hospital emergency on
saturday. she got the polio
they talking about on tv.

> *Oh. How bad is she?*

on machine because
paralyzed.

> *You mean a breathing machine, a
> mechanical ventilator?*

i guess.

> *Sounds serious. I'm sorry. Is she a
> friend of yours?*

sort of. she okay about my leg.
she from syria. hama city.

> *Is that near where you come from?*

less than 2 hours in my
father e-class.

Travis jumped around the kitchen, upended a chair, and nearly
knocked over the juice carton.

"Hosam used to have an E-class Merc?" Travis said. "Incredible!
But now the poor guy has to take the bus to work. I saw him getting off once. At the stop on Upper Paradise near the barbershop."
Travis pointed to the keyboard. "Ask him what engine it had. The
two-litre four or the twin-turbo V6? I bet it was the V6."

> *My dad says we shouldn't obsess
> about the polio. We're probably
> not going to get it.*

but i sit beside jamila on
the bus.

> *Don't you walk to school? Sir John
> A Macdonald, right?*

school trip. niagara falls.

> *When was that?*

one month ago. maybe less.
i forget.

> *And you sat beside her on the bus
> trip? Both ways?*

i know i am gonna get the
polio from jamila.
and then i am gonna die.

> *Omar. Stay calm. My dad says you*
> *can't get this polio from just*
> *sitting beside someone who has it.*

Travis tugged at Max's shirt. "But maybe he kissed her, or even
...Ask him."

> *Did you kiss her?*

no!!! she wear hijab. and too
old to be gf. she is 17.

> *I'm sure you'll be fine, Omar. But*
> *if you do start feeling sick, let me*
> *know.*
> *My dad will take care of you.*

but KB, your father is not a
doctor. u tell me he werk
for goverment.

> *He's a doctor who works for the*
> *government. Sort of like a detective.*
> *And he's in charge of investigating*
> *the polio and stopping it from*
> *making more people sick.*

he know lots about the polio?
he can help jamila?

> *I'll talk to him about it.*

but KB. very important. do
not tell him my name or
my father name. u
remember? grandmother
grave?

> *No names. We promise.*

good. i trust you.

Travis pulled at Max's shirt again. "Ask him if those guys are still bothering his dad?"

The two of them had argued a lot about what to do about Lion-Nads and the guy whose name could be Ghazwan but they weren't sure. They'd only managed to square that they had no idea how to deal with murderers, gangsters, and warlords beyond the realms of *Fortnite*. After what they'd witnessed in the barbershop on Friday, they more or less agreed (Max more, Travis less) that they'd better take a back seat on this one for the time being. It was one thing to be brave and daring while playing video games, but this situation was real, and the less they said about it to anyone, the better. Providing Omar with a pair of friendlies to chat with on Facebook was probably the best they could offer and still keep themselves out of Witness Protection. Or worse.

KB

> *Yes.*

one more thing. very
serious.

> *Okay.*

my father out walking
yesterday. i search his
bedroom for more notes
from Lion-Nads and warlord.

> *Did you find any?*

no. something worse.

> *What?*

You promise not to tell?

> *Of course.*

really promise?

> *Yes, Omar, we both promise.*

okay . . . inside one sock i
find drugs with needle and
syringe.
i look up on google.

drugs used for execution.

lethal injection.

Omar, you can't be serious.

i send photos.

Half a minute later, three photos pinged into Max's inbox. He could see they were of three different vials containing medications in liquid form. Each one was full and hadn't been opened. In the photos, the lettering on the labels was too tiny for the boys to read, so Travis reached over and blew up the images until they filled the screen. The barcodes on the vials said *Pharmacy Services, CUMC Hamilton*. Both of them had made plenty of visits to that place: Caledonian University Medical Centre.

Travis retrieved his laptop from his backpack and set it beside Max's on the kitchen table. "You spell out the drug names," he said. "And I'll Google them."

The first drug was midazolam. Max spelled it out loud. Travis typed it into Google on his keyboard.

Travis picked the Wikipedia entry from the first page of hits, and they read it together. Wiki explained that midazolam was a sedative given to ease the discomfort of mechanical ventilation. It could also be used in surgical anesthesia and to treat epileptic seizures.

The next vial was labelled *Succinylcholine*. Its Wikipedia entry said it caused rapid-onset, short-duration muscle paralysis and was mostly used to facilitate endotracheal intubation and mechanical ventilation.

"Endotracheal intubation?" Travis said. "What's that?"

"That's where they put a tube in your windpipe to help you breathe."

"Oh, yeah. Like on those YouTube channels you like so much."

"Hey . . . you watch them often enough too."

Travis was too intent on their research to argue. "What does the third vial say?"

"Rocuronium." Max spelled it, and Travis brought up a page that outlined the attributes of the drug in detail.

"Another paralyzing drug," Travis said. "Its effects last much longer than the other one. About forty-five minutes."

"And here it is again," Max said. "*Facilitation of endotracheal intubation and mechanical ventilation.*"

Max was a faster reader than Travis, who had a fine appreciation for nuances and read slowly to catch them. "Keep reading," Max told him.

After a moment, Travis said, "Bingo! Midazolam and rocuronium are in the lethal-injection cocktail used for executions. Just like Omar said. That's way cool!"

The details Wikipedia divulged were spellbinding: most government-sanctioned lethal injections were performed with a pharmaceutical triple whammy. The first drug, midazolam, made the condemned go more or less unconscious. The second drug, rocuronium, stopped their breathing. A third drug, potassium chloride, arrested their heart. "Game, set, and match," Max said, then was suddenly appalled at how easy it was to kill someone that way. "Sorry. That was kind of an asshole thing to say."

Travis shrugged and pointed to his screen. "You could kill someone with the rocuronium by itself, eh?"

"A nasty way to go. The victim would be fully conscious and desperate for breath until they finally passed out from lack of oxygen."

Travis had that look their science teacher called *pensive* when they were pondering a particularly meaty question. "They'd know exactly what was happening and feel themselves asphyxiating. Talk about a horror show!"

After that terrifying notion had well and truly sunk in, Max said, "What is our favourite barber doing with a powerful sedative and two drugs that can kill you within minutes?"

Travis, Mr. Nuance, was developing a theory. Max could see it in his eyes.

"Omar said his dad visited this Jamila girl in an ER on Saturday," Travis said. "That must have been at CUMC because all the polio cases are going there, right?"

"That's what my dad told me."

"So . . . Jamila is paralyzed from the polio. Which means she has to be on a mechanical ventilator to stay alive. That means she was given at least a couple of these drugs when they performed the endotracheal intubation so they could —"

"— hook her up to the ventilator. I get it."

"So . . . Hosam goes in to visit Jamila soon after that's done . . . and he sees the vials on the . . . what-do-they-call-it?"

"The crash cart."

"So he sees the drugs sitting on the cart, scoops them up when no one is looking, and slips them into his pocket."

Trav's birthmark was on fire. The other half of his face had turned green.

Or maybe the green was Max's imagination working overtime because that's how *he* was feeling. His tongue was so dry he could hardly talk. He reached across the table for more OJ, but Travis had finished the carton.

Max coaxed the last few drops from the bottom of his glass. "So, what's Hosam going to do with his executioner's cocktail?"

Travis shrugged. "Go after warlords?"

KB? you still there?
you get the photos yet?

Holy crap! What could they possibly say to Omar that would make the guy feel any better?

CHAPTER 22

By the time Hosam found himself standing at the McNab Street bus terminal at almost eleven o'clock on that surprisingly hot Monday evening, his guts felt like the inside of Vesuvius. With Leila working long hours and Omar in his bedroom glued to his laptop, he had passed much of the day alone. Too distraught to study, he had watched hours of mindless television in the living room but could not remember a thing he had seen.

He had convinced Leila not to cancel her appointments. She was better working than fretting all day about the Caliph and the polio circulating far too close to home. And they needed the money now that the barbershop was a fenced-off crime scene. He could not quench the fear that the sensational attack was going to drive away most of his and Ibrahim's clients. The Syrian war, a complex game of failed alliances and outright betrayals, had shown him that loyalty was a rare commodity.

Earlier, on the telephone, Ibrahim had been agitated but still holding it together. He explained that this morning he had been summoned to the police station downtown and kept waiting alone in a stuffy room for over an hour. When the homicide detective assigned to the case finally arrived, he had grilled him with the same few questions over and over.

"Did you give him Ghazwan's name?" Hosam asked him.

"And sign my death warrant?"

"Do you think they have any idea about the Caliph?"

"Like everyone else, they think you Syrians are cuddly little refugees who know their place and never give any trouble."

"Maybe, but that will not last long," Hosam told him, picturing what he had been up to on Friday night.

"The detective was more interested in our involvement with the Italian mob."

"Seriously? That is strange."

"I had nothing to give him, of course. And he could see I was telling the truth. After a while, he and his assistant lost interest. I don't think they're going to call you in."

"Alhamdulillah! That is a relief."

"The police were impressed when I told them you were a trauma surgeon awaiting your re-certification papers. And that you'd worked in a war zone and saved so many lives it was impossible to count them."

"A shameless exaggeration, but thanks for that," Hosam had said as they ended their call. "I owe you one, my friend."

But now, as Hosam sweated inside his dark clothing and waited for the bus to arrive, Omar's health loomed as a worry bigger than anything involving the barbershop. The boy had spent hours sitting next to that girl, Jamila, on their school trip to Niagara. The doctor in Hosam reckoned that Omar was safe because the excursion was a good three weeks in the past, well outside the period of contagiousness for most infections. But the parent in him worried that Dr. Szabo and Co. had no idea what was causing the polio epidemic. Jamila could have been spewing its unknown contagious agent for weeks before she began to show signs of fever, headache, and paralysis. And if Jamila had polio, how many other students at their school were walking time bombs? How many were silently spreading the disease to their classmates while on the verge of developing paralysis themselves? No, Omar was not going back into that high school until Hosam was sure it was safe. Until then, Omar could improve his English by chatting with his friends on social media and playing *Fortnite*.

He glanced again at his watch, the seven-dollar Casio he had bought from a shady Kurdish merchant in Gaziantep's central bazaar. His Omega Seamaster had been stolen from him at knifepoint on one of Gaziantep's busiest streets in the middle of the day. Syrian refugees were soft targets in Turkey, especially amid the bustle of its larger cities. Everyone looked the other way when petty thieves brought out their knives.

The Caliph's instructions said to catch the Number 23 Upper Gage at eleven o'clock and be waiting at the appointed McDonald's at eleven thirty. Eleven ten came and went and there was still no sign of the bus. Had the schedule changed? Had he missed the bus by a few minutes? He looked around for someone to ask. The place was deserted. Not a single soul was waiting at any of the platforms. Merde! The bus service must have shut down for the night. Life was so much easier, dammit, when you had your own car. Just as he was about to give up and trudge home, a Number 23 eased toward the platform. At eleven bloody twenty. The driver, a young guy with pale skin and a ginger goatee in need of a barber's attention, looked like he had never had a care in his life. Lucky him.

Hosam boarded and tapped his transit card, which he had recharged at a nearby machine to be certain it had sufficient funds for the journey. He took a seat on the mostly empty bus and wondered how long they were going to sit there. Not long, thank God. A minute later they were rolling.

He pulled his copy of the *Rubáiyát* from his backpack and thumbed its pages, desperate for a sign from the poet. But Khayyam had no explanation — or justification — for Hosam's theft of the drugs from Jamila's crash cart. He told himself he must have been seized by a compulsion of self-preservation. He had suddenly seen the drugs not as life-saving medications but as lethal weapons he might one day use against the Caliph. He knew the modest danger of midazolam and the extreme danger of rocuronium and succinylcholine. Leila would be terrified if she knew those drugs were in the house, though for some reason she did not have a problem with ketamine. It had taken some convincing to stop her using that powerful, mind-bending drug on her anxious clients.

Although he did feel better knowing he had some kind of weapon in his home, he worried what Omar might do if he came across the lethal cocktail. Kids were endlessly curious and seldom thought about consequences, no matter how potentially catastrophic. Before leaving the house, Hosam moved the three vials from his sock drawer to a nook concealed by the loose ceiling tile above the toilet. The family's vital documents from the United Nations and the Canadian government were hidden in the same place. Leila's earnings — her transactions were always enacted in cash — were stashed in their bedroom, behind another loose tile. They called it Leila's Bank, and Hosam looked after the bookkeeping. He reviewed each week's accounts on Sundays or Mondays when the barbershop was closed. Leila's Bank was growing every week. Inshallah, the steady growth would continue.

The bus groaned in low gear as they ascended the Escarpment via the switchback linking the lower and upper halves of the city. Beyond the downtown office towers and apartment blocks, flames flickered like giant candles from the steel-mill chimneys by the lake. If what many of his haircutting clients said was true, it might not be long before the mills were shuttered, the furnaces unplugged, the flames extinguished.

A few minutes later, McDonald's golden arches were impossible to miss as he approached his destination on Mohawk Road. He was five minutes late when he strode across the Drive-Thru. Headlamps flashed from the parking lot — a dark Ford F-150 pickup with a four-door cab and an extended box. Saramin was at the wheel.

He jumped in without waiting for a further invitation and clicked his seatbelt in place. He sat up straight and offered no apology for his tardy arrival. He may have been coerced into doing the Caliph's bidding, but he was not going to act like a slave.

"Keep your gloves on," she said then levered the gear stick into drive and eased out of the parking lot. Her perfume was the same scent as before but not quite as strong. He did not let on that he noticed.

"Here we are again, I guess," he said to her in Arabic once she had merged with the southbound traffic on Upper Gage Avenue.

She checked her rearview mirror then looked straight ahead. "A busy night ahead of us. I trust you still have not acquired a mobile phone?"

He opened his jacket and everted the linings of its pockets. "No worries there. I cannot afford one."

"Don't even dream about bringing a phone on any of these excursions."

Dreading her reference to future sorties on behalf of the Caliph, he inspected the cab's well-worn interior. It had none of the pristine elegance of Friday night's Lincoln. He hoped that meant Saramin would not be as obsessed about the state of the carpets and upholstery. Extra scuffs and smudges were less likely to be noticed when the rightful owner retook possession at the airport.

"The same drill," he said, "with the valet parking guys at YYZ?"

"Ah, you're learning the local lingo."

"And the modus operandi."

"Don't get smart. The Caliph does not like it."

"You tell him everything? Even our little —"

"Just conduct yourself as if you were in his presence and we'll continue to get along without complications. You must know by now the Caliph hates complications."

"Most certainly."

A kilometre later, she took the eastbound ramp onto the crosstown parkway. In the smooth flow of negligible late-night traffic, the tension around her mouth eased and her shoulders relaxed.

After a few moments, he asked, "Another church, tonight?" At least it would not be as bad as stealing from his own Church People.

She signalled her frustration at his curiosity with a long sigh then pressed the master switch on the door locks. "Baseball diamonds."

"More copper roofs and downspouts?"

She shook her head. "These are country places, mostly for kids. No roofs. No seating. Just simple playing fields." She paused then added, "What they do have are powerful lights for night games."

He checked his Casio and understood the midnight start. "The games will be over by now, I suppose?"

"They rarely play on Mondays. But when they do, they're always gone by ten, ten thirty at the latest."

She exited the parkway at Mud Street. The compass on the dashboard showed they were still heading east. He had a feeling they were travelling to the same district as Friday night but were coming at it from the west instead of from the north.

"What are we going to steal?"

"Copper wire."

"From a baseball field?"

"The lighting system uses a lot of it. Heavy gauge."

"I trust there is a switch we can turn off first."

She laughed. "You are afraid of getting electrocuted?"

"Well . . ."

"No switch. But our guys have that covered. They'll show you."

"Are we working with those two Syrians from Friday night?"

Her glossy crimson lips tightened. "No more questions."

As Mud Street became increasingly rural and deserted, Hosam wondered how a few dozen metres of copper wire could be worth this elaborate cloak-and-dagger effort. How valuable was scrap copper, anyway? He tried to calculate how much wire they might take away with them tonight, but he had no idea. He knew too little about the dimensions of community baseball diamonds and the height and spacing of their light poles. It seemed likely that churches and ballparks were merely the Caliph's testing grounds. He was probably warming up his mob-style operation by amassing a cache of seed money and scrutinizing refugee conscripts in the process. Undoubtedly, he had plans for jobs that were far more lucrative and dangerous.

Less than twenty minutes from their McDonald's rendezvous, it was now pitch dark on either side of Mud Street. No lights anywhere. The truck's headlamps caught a sign that said *Tapley-Town Community Diamond* along with an arrow pointing left. Vesuvius belched in Hosam's belly the moment he recognized the logo beneath the arrow. His father had been a staunch Rotarian. The treachery Hosam was about to commit against a Rotary International project would have his dad cursing from the grave.

Saramin braked and followed the sign onto a smooth dirt road. About 500 metres in, she pulled to a stop a few metres short of a Dodge Ram pickup. There were two men in the cab. She unlocked the doors and told Hosam to join the others.

"They're expecting you."

Hosam's heart leapt into his throat. His tongue felt like a piece of ten-day-old pita. Saramin had not brought him here to steal bits of copper for the Caliph. The boss had ordered his execution. Merde! Merde! Merde!

He swallowed hard and ran his tongue across his lips. He grabbed the dashboard with both hands. "Come on, I know nothing. I bet Saramin is not your real name. I cannot get any of you in trouble. I have no idea who the Caliph is or where he lives. You do not need to kill me. *Please* . . . my wife and son, they need me. Badly. They cannot do without me. *Please* . . ."

She put the truck in park and faced him. "For God's sake, Hosam. No one is going to kill you. Honestly, we're here to snatch a grand's worth of copper wire and get the hell out of here."

He could not take his eyes off the men in the Dodge. The driver was opening the door. He had something in his hand, and it was not just a set of keys.

She reached over and touched his arm. The gesture seemed sincere, but as a gangster's girlfriend, she had to be a good actress. As he looked out the window, he could not believe anywhere could be this black. The big-city lights of Aleppo and Gaziantep had extended well into the countryside. And when the power went out, there had always been the overwhelming brilliance of mortar fire.

"It's okay. Really. Go on. You know these two guys. They'll show you how it's done. Watch what they do and work fast."

He squeezed the door handle hard with his shaking hand. He had no choice but to face the men. If he tried to run in the dark, he would fall and break his neck.

He stepped out of the truck and nearly collided with what had to be the short guy from the other night, the man from Homs City. The man raised his arm. Hosam planted his feet and said nothing. He was not going to beg, and he was not going to let them shoot him lying on the ground like a sick dog.

A shot of light came out of the man's hand. No noise, no pain, no smell. Just a weak glow.

"Here," he said, flicking his extended arm. "Put on this lamp or you'll break your goddamn leg in the dark."

CHAPTER 23

Hosam donned the headlamp and looked around. The baseball diamond seemed to be in the middle of a large, flat field far from any sign of human habitation. They could spend all night here tearing apart the wires linking the diamond's four tall lighting poles, and no one would notice.

Saramin's men opened the cover of their Dodge Ram's cargo box and took out their tools. Theirs was no fine set of surgical instruments, just a shovel, an axe, a crowbar, heavy pliers, and three pairs of heavy-duty leather gloves. The tall, super-muscular guy, who still reeked of chewing tobacco and was no less taciturn tonight than he had been on Friday, removed three empty industrial spools from the back of the truck. He motioned for Hosam to take three more from the fifteen or twenty others like them.

"We are going to wrap the wire around these, uh . . . spools?" Hosam asked, again taking care not to look the tall guy directly in the face.

"That's gonna be your job," said the short guy from Homs City. "It won't take you long to get the hang of it." He threw Hosam a pair of the gloves. "And wear these, or it's gonna be a long time before you get back to your clippers and scissors."

The tall guy led him to the closest lighting pole, and they dropped their spools at its base. Hosam inspected the pole in the light from his headlamp. He gave it a tap with his knuckles. "Aluminium?"

The man shrugged and led Hosam across the dewy grass to where his mate was standing next to a utility pole two hundred metres from home plate. This pole was wooden, well-weathered, and connected to a line of similar posts running alongside the access road. Fifty or more years ago, there had been something here that required a connection to the electrical grid. Perhaps a pump drawing well water.

The short guy pointed to a long pipe attached to the side of the pole. The smooth, grey line of plastic tubing ran from the wires at the top of the pole, down its side, and into the grass-covered ground at its base. "The live feed is inside there," he said. "We cut the power here, and we're safe for the rest of the night."

Before Hosam could ask him how they were going to turn off the power when there was no apparent switch, the man picked up the axe from where he had laid it on the grass. "This is the fun part," he said. "The sparks fly like crazy, so stand back."

"You can do this safely?" Hosam asked.

"Yeah, yeah. Done it lots of times."

Hosam backed five paces away from the pole, then three more for good measure. The tall guy backed up only three casual paces and gave a condescending smirk.

The short guy wiped the axe blade with his thumb. Then, like a golfer, he checked his grip and took a couple of practice swings at the pipe.

"Hey, Mo, you going to wear the gloves?" Tall Guy said, breaking his silence.

Mo examined his hands then shrugged. He wiped his left palm on his jeans, then adjusted his grip and swung at the pipe.

As the axe head severed the wires, Hosam was not sure which was more impressive, the white-hot flash that temporarily blinded him or the roaring boom that set his ears ringing. As he stood there, seeing nothing but a black void peppered with a myriad of coloured spots, his nose filled with the pungent smell of ozone and burnt plastic. And then burnt flesh.

When the ringing had marginally subsided, he heard footsteps and what sounded like the tall guy shouting, "Mo? Mo? You okay?"

A few seconds later, Hosam's vision cleared enough for him to see Tall Guy standing over a human form that was inert and semi-prone on the ground. Tall Guy, his arms extended, was bending forward to rouse his mate.

"Ya Allah!" Hosam screamed. "Do not touch him. You will get electrocuted."

Tall Guy froze, his eyes huge in the beam of Hosam's headlamp. The smirk was long gone from his lips.

Hosam shuffled forward, sweeping the grass with the beam from his headlamp. Above everything else, he had to locate the axe. As long as it was in contact with the live feed, it was a lethal weapon. After several fruitless sweeps, he spotted the axe head glinting in the grass a couple of metres from the utility pole. He left it there where it posed no danger.

The next step was to ascertain whether any part of Mo was touching the pole or its wires. "What do you think?" he asked Tall Guy. "Is he clear of the wires?"

"Clear," said Tall Guy.

Hosam agreed. Mo had fallen well away from the pole. Electrically speaking, his body was not live. But whether the man himself was alive was another question.

"Help me roll him onto his back," Hosam said. "But for the love of Muhammad — *peace be upon him* — do not touch that pole. Any part of the damned thing could be live."

Once they had turned Mo onto his back, they dragged him two paces farther away from the pole and put his arms at his sides. Without the black paint on his face, he looked surprisingly young. Twenty-something.

Hosam told Tall Guy, "Aim your lamp at his chest. I need every bit of light you can give me."

He knelt on Mo's right side and told Tall Guy to kneel on the left. Hosam pressed his fingers into the man's neck, desperate to feel a carotid pulse. Nothing. He tried the other side. Still nothing. He unzipped Mo's windbreaker jacket, popped the buttons on his shirt, and pressed his left ear against Mo's chest below the left nipple. Nothing here either. Electrocution had put the man's heart either into asystole (no action whatsoever), or into ventricular fibrillation (a useless squirming of the heart muscle).

Still on his knees, Hosam straightened up and took a deep breath. If Mo's heart had stopped completely, it was game over for him. Asystole resisted most interventions, even by experts wielding the latest equipment. But if his left ventricle was fibrillating, Mo had a chance. Sometimes a good whack in the chest set the heart pumping again. Hosam made a fist with his right hand and brought it down like a sledgehammer onto Mo's sternum.

Mo showed no reaction to what should have been a painful blow. Still, there was no carotid pulse. Hosam whacked the sternum a second time. Nothing. He threw off his jacket, put one hand over the other, and started cardiac compressions. He had done this so many times — often with the sound of fighter jets and mortar fire booming in his ears — that pumping 110 beats per minute was second nature.

"Shine your light on his face," he told Tall Guy without breaking his rhythm. "What colour are his lips?"

Tall Guy did not answer. His hand was clamped over his nose and mouth and a choking sound was coming from his throat. Clearly he wasn't used to the overpowering smell of freshly burnt flesh. But Hosam had to give the man credit: he had not run away, and his headlamp's beam on Mo's face was unwavering.

"His lips?" said a female voice from somewhere in the darkness. "It's hard to tell under that soot. But they look blue to me. What happened?"

"Glad you are here, Boss," Hosam told her. "You can call 911 and tell them a man has been electrocuted. They need to know he is unconscious, VSA, and we are doing CPR."

"How did it happen?"

"Fool did not wear gloves," Hosam told her between compressions. "Let his axe get wet. Head *and* handle."

"How?"

"Laid it on the grass. Covered in dew. Water conducts 240 volts . . . rather too nicely."

"Is he gonna make it? He's the only one of you the Scarpellinos trust."

"How close to the nearest hospital?"

"Who cares? Nobody's calling 911."

"That is crazy. You have to."

She extended her arm and swept it toward the ball diamond. "How detailed a picture do I have to draw for you?"

"We cannot let him die here. He deserves a fair chance."

"He looks barely even alive to me. If he dies here or in an ambulance, what does it matter?"

Hosam grabbed Mo's jaw with his right hand and pinched the man's nose with his left. He gave him two good mouth-to-mouth breaths. The lungs offered no resistance. It was like blowing into a corpse. Though heartless, Saramin was probably right. Hosam was probably doing CPR on a cadaver. But Mo was under thirty, still warm, and probably healthy until he had swung that damned axe. Hosam resumed the compressions and pondered his next move. How many more minutes of compressions, and how many more blows to Mo's sternum until it was time to give up on the man?

After three more minutes, Hosam was exhausted and could barely catch his breath. It was time for one final manoeuvre. He stopped the compressions, raised his right fist, and whacked the sternum twice as hard as he dared.

A moment later, Mo grimaced and gave a little cough. His eyelids flickered, and drops of red spittle gathered at the corners of his mouth. Hosam's own heart rate shot up twenty points. Tall Guy jerked backwards as if he had just seen Muhammad's ghost.

Hosam dug again into Mo's neck and could barely believe what he found thumping against his fingertips. *Alhamdulillah! Praise be to God!*

He looked at Saramin. "Now, will you call 911?"

She tightened her lips. "We'll take him in the Ford. On the rear seat. And drop him at the hospital."

"An ambulance would be better. The paramedics have the right equipment. His heart has suffered a significant injury. It could stop again at any moment."

She was not going to be swayed. "We can be at Caledonian in ten minutes. We unload him there at Emergency. And as soon as they get him on their stretcher, we take off. We've gotta get these vehicles back to YYZ."

CHAPTER 24

Shortly after nine thirty on Tuesday morning, Natasha stepped from the elevator onto the cardiac ward of Caledonian University Medical Centre. Muriel Simon was expecting her visit.

"Ah, Miss Sharma," Mrs. Simon called from her bed as Natasha stood at the doorway. The woman pointed to the only chair in the cramped four-bedded room and added, "Come in and pull up a seat." Even from this distance, her tiny, sharp-featured face was lined and pinched.

The chair was the sort of simple folding model they sold at IKEA. There was no space in the room for any others. "That one doesn't look particularly comfortable, I'm afraid. But there isn't anywhere more private for us to talk. They say I'm not allowed to leave my bed."

The slight but legendarily commanding school principal appeared dwarfed by her high-tech hospital bed and the flashy machinery surrounding it. The menacing jungle of tubes and wires attached to her arms and chest clashed with the whimsy of her penguin-print pyjama top. The garment's fine piping and classic tailoring suggested Ralph Lauren, but perhaps he didn't do penguins. Natasha couldn't see any logo embroidered on the pocket.

She pulled the chair in close and sat down. "How are you feeling, Mrs. Simon?"

"Well, thanks to you, I'm still in this world. I hate to think what would have become of me had you not been there to call 911." She tapped the hefty-looking intravenous line snaking from the side of her neck into the digital monitor beside the bed. A dazzling array of ever-changing data displayed itself on myriad colourful channels. "This temporary pacemaker has raised my energy level to prodigious heights. But I'm tethered to it, and they won't let me get up in case I dislodge it."

"You are looking rosier. I'm relieved to see it."

"Frankly, I don't know why I haven't been discharged. Those people languishing in the hallways down in Emergency need this bed a great deal more than I do."

Natasha smiled to herself at the woman's understatement of her condition, then took her notebook from her briefcase and studied her surroundings. The space felt confined, airless, and positively claustrophobic. Hamish had once explained that the rooms in this wing were each originally built to house two patients each, not four. But the moment the hospital opened its doors, it was clear it could not satisfy the needs of the city's expanding population. Extra beds were shoehorned into every room, and joyless grey curtains were installed around every bed in an attempt to create the illusion of privacy.

"I gather you feel up to a few questions?" Natasha asked.

The woman ran a hand through the uncombed mousy curls of her salt-and-pepper hair, then made a face as she inspected the greasy film on her fingers. Clearly, she wished someone would come and give her a shampoo. "Be my guest," she said, hiding her hand under the covers. "But first I need to know about my kids. How are Céline and Juan-Carlos?"

"Our nurses were in touch with their families yesterday, and they're doing well. Compared to the other cases, their polio was mild and they've had no setbacks."

"That's a relief. But what about my twelve little ones you have under quarantine?"

Natasha hated the Q-word. *Quarantine* sounded accusatory and hostile. It reminded her of overcrowded sailing ships of the nineteenth century carrying immigrants infected with cholera, tuberculosis, and typhus. "They appear to have the usual assortment of minor illnesses that school kids get. Nothing suspicious of polio. I expect they'll be back to school quite soon."

"What about their blood work?"

"Until Friday, we had no idea what we were looking for. But now, we think we're making progress. We'll be contacting the families today to arrange for some simple blood tests."

Now that they knew to look for evidence of Parvo-W and Zika virus infection among the close contacts of polio victims, active surveillance of potential new cases was becoming possible. It was a relief to be finally infusing hard science into their investigation. Three weeks of empty hypotheses had been exasperating.

"But please," Natasha told her, "let me know if you need a break."

"Seriously, I'm fine."

"I'm wondering about school trips. Has Cathcart Elementary made any in the past few months?"

"That's an easy one. The grade sixes and sevens have been studying the evolution of agriculture, so we took them to the Niagara Peninsula. It's Ontario's fruit basket, of course, and right next door. So an obvious choice for a field trip."

"When was that?"

She paused and gazed at the ceiling for a moment. "A month ago. Early April."

"It would be helpful to know exactly where the students went and what they visited."

"You're not asking difficult questions, Miss Sharma. The region's hydroponic greenhouses were the object study. Tomatoes, cucumbers, ornamental flowers, and . . . well, you get the idea." A guilty look invaded her face and she looked away.

Muriel Simon had more to say. And whatever it was, it could be an important piece in the puzzle. "I understand," Natasha said, "that there have been significant advancements in the way hothouse tomatoes are raised. They're so much tastier than they used to be. Perhaps you and the students were shown other agricultural innovations?"

The principal was uncomfortable about where the conversation was headed. "Well . . . I suppose *innovation* is one way of putting it."

"Yes?"

"It . . . it wasn't part of the original plan." She looked away again. "It just sort of happened."

"Oh, that sounds interesting," Natasha said, hoping she sounded disarmingly chirpy. "What *just sort of happened*?"

Mrs. Simon studied the chips in her nail polish. The colour was unquestionably Cajun Shrimp. "It's a bit embarrassing. Not the sort of thing I'd like anyone to make a fuss about."

Natasha put down her pen and notebook, suggesting that whatever Mrs. Simon had to say would be off the record. "I'm not in the business of making fusses, Mrs. Simon. Just gathering facts. Anything that has no bearing on the polio epidemic, I will keep to myself."

The principal looked anxiously toward the closest privacy curtain, afraid of being heard by whomever was in the next bed. A moment later, her shoulders relaxed and her eyes brightened. "They're deaf as posts in here and barely alive. So I don't know what I'm worried about." She looked at Natasha for a moment, then leaned forward and whispered, "We were given a peek into a cannabis operation."

Natasha admired Muriel Simon's spunk. The woman was far more than the sum of her not-so-mousy parts. "You took the kids to a cannabis grow-op?"

"Now Miss Sharma, it's not a grow-op when it's a sophisticated operation harvesting cannabis for medical use."

"You were allowed inside?"

"Not exactly. The interior is strictly controlled in terms of climate and hygiene. But they do let you look through a glass wall."

"Were the kids spellbound?"

"Um . . ." She paused, then nodded matter-of-factly. "I think that *is* the right word. But I don't want you to think . . ."

"Think what?"

"That, uh . . . that we were corrupting our students. Our teachers made it abundantly clear that this particular cannabis crop was strictly for medical purposes."

"Did you get any blowback from their parents?"

"Do you mean, were they angry that we showed their children the legitimate side of something that has become a key element in many of their lives? Oh, Miss Sharma, our Beasley neighbourhood may be financially compromised, but our families' attitudes are inspiringly . . ." She searched a moment for the right word. "Enlightened."

Her eyes widened with alarm, and she shot a hand to her mouth. "Oh my goodness!" She pushed herself straight up in bed. "You have it in mind that two of my students, and their beloved teacher's aide, came down with polio as a result of their trip to the greenhouses. Exposure to pesticides, perhaps? Oh, dear God, I'll never forgive myself if more of them —"

Natasha rested her hand on the poor woman's arm and glanced at the monitor. Her systolic blood pressure had shot up twenty-five points.

"Take a few deep breaths, Mrs. Simon." Natasha couldn't take her eyes off the numbers in the digital array. "Please try not to upset yourself. We have no reason to think those greenhouses have any direct bearing on the polio outbreak." At this moment, absolute honesty was not nearly as important as the poor woman's blood pressure.

Muriel Simon tightened her lips. She was used to giving instructions — not following them — and ignored Natasha's advice about breathing deeply. "If you don't think the details of our field trip are pertinent to your investigation, why are you asking me these particular questions?"

"We're following every avenue of investigation that presents itself. I know you wouldn't want us to leave any stone unturned."

"You mean like our starfish and dear Pancho and Pedro?"

"We must seem intrusive, and I'm truly sorry about the starfish, but —"

"Your need to discover the source of the polio epidemic has made you desperate for answers. I can see that with crystalline clarity."

The woman was right. Natasha *was* desperate. And so was Zol. Hamish, too, in his own way. And there was no point in trying to deny it to this perceptive woman. "I'm afraid you're right. At this point, I think every one of us at the Health Unit feels desperate to some extent."

Mrs. Simon seemed pleased that she'd scored a point at Natasha's expense. She obviously enjoyed reading people, a skill she must use every day in dealing with her students and their parents. She studied her monitor for several moments then gave Natasha a satisfied grin. "Look," she said, "my blood pressure is settling on its own. We can keep going. What else would you like to know?"

"Are you sure?"

"Of course. I enjoy solving conundrums as much as you do."

Natasha studied the monitor. No alarms were flashing or sounding. "Well then, let me ask you — do you remember where the greenhouses were located?"

She gestured impatiently toward the monitor. "I need this technology to stimulate my heart, Miss Sharma, not my brain. The little grey cells are working just fine."

"Yes, of course. I'm sorry. So . . . the greenhouses . . . they were located in . . . ?"

"That small place not far from Niagara-on-the-Lake. It's on the main road before you enter the town. What's it called? Oh yes, Cicero. A grand name for something that's no more than a hamlet."

Natasha had visited Niagara-on-the-Lake at least a dozen times and had never heard of a village called Cicero. And then it dawned — the woman was confusing her Latin scholars. "Might the place have been called Virgil, Mrs. Simon?"

"Oh, goodness. How silly of me. Of course it was. Named after the Roman poet, not the orator."

Natasha felt her face flush and her own heart rate climb twenty points. Mrs. Simon's students had visited the exact village where Dr. Polgar told Zol a mosquito surveillance team had trapped the

Aedes albopictus. The Cathcart Street students and their teachers could have been bitten by those mosquitoes. And if the mosquitoes were carrying Zika virus, they could have infected Cathcart Elementary's staff and students. What a thrill to be making progress after so many dead ends in the investigation. But it would come apart if the polio victims from Cathcart School had not been on that trip.

Natasha touched Mrs. Simon's arm. "Did Ms. Asante go on the field trip?"

The principal's eyes glistened with tears. "Yes, bless her. She went on all our trips."

"And . . . well . . . it's not fair to expect you to know the answer to this without consulting your records, but —"

"I don't need to consult any records. Both of the children who developed polio were also on that trip. They were helpful translators when it came to interacting with the migrant workers tending the tomatoes and the flowers. The labourers came alive to my students as real people thanks to Juan-Carlos and Céline. Juan-Carlos, as you can well imagine, being from El Salvador, speaks fluent Spanish. And Céline's first language is Haitian Creole."

"We think mosquito bites might be a key element in our polio puzzle. Is it possible —"

"I can stop you right there. The mosquitoes in the tulip greenhouse were nothing short of a scourge. Something to do with our unusually hot April and the humidity in the greenhouse. I got three bites myself. But never in a million years did I think they —"

"Did you notice mosquitoes anywhere else?"

"No, just in the tulip nursery. And, yes, I remember what it was called. Vander Zalm Nurseries, located in the same hamlet with the pretentious name. Virgil."

Natasha couldn't help smiling at the woman's moxie. "Did you happen to notice what those mosquitoes looked like?"

Mrs. Simon was looking pleased with herself. She'd been providing answers her entire working life and seemed to be delighted to keep them coming now, each accompanied by a detailed explanation.

"The older kids thought the mosquitoes looked like the pictures of the children in *The Boy in the Striped Pajamas*. Have you read that book? It's by John Boyne and is set in a World War Two Nazi internment camp. The grade sevens studied the novel this year. To be honest, it packs quite the emotional punch."

Natasha opened her notebook. "You don't mind if I jot down a few points to remind me of this conversation?"

She glanced again the privacy curtain next to her. "I would prefer you didn't mention the . . ."

"It has no bearing, Mrs. Simon. There'll be no mention of it in my notes."

With her pen poised over her notebook, Natasha stopped to think. She'd just confirmed that three of the epidemic's ten polio cases had visited an Aedes albopictus hotspot in Niagara Region during April this year. She needed to find out how many others had done the same. The deceased janitor had lived alone, which might make it difficult to trace his steps. The family of Jamila Khateb — the girl who worked at Petz Haven and was now on a ventilator — didn't strike Natasha as likely to have visited Niagara's greenhouses or to have shopped in Niagara-on-the-Lake's upscale boutiques. They didn't speak English and would have more urgent demands on their limited income. It was, however, possible that Jamila did visit Niagara on a trip sponsored by her high school.

"Do high schools sometimes take their students on field trips, Mrs. Simon?"

"Certainly."

"I'm wondering about Sir John A. Macdonald High School. I need to know if one of their students, a seventeen-year-old girl, visited Niagara Region recently."

"Niagara is a favourite field-trip destination for Sir John A., I do know that. But can't you just ask her?"

"She and her family are recent refugees from the Middle East. Her parents don't speak English, and she's incapacitated at the moment — unable to talk."

"Oh dear, oh dear. That sounds ominously like dear Ms. Asante."

Natasha dipped her gaze to her notebook. "I really can't say."

Mrs. Simon waved a dismissive had. "I understand your situation. You're not at liberty to release confidential information. Especially about a topic as sensitive as this polio epidemic."

"Well, as I say . . ."

"Never mind. I have a friend you can call. She's a guidance counsellor at Sir. John A. If that school took their students to Niagara recently, Marg Bickerton can tell you exactly when, where, and which students were on the trip." She pointed to the locker beside her bed. "My phone's in there. If you hand it to me, I'll give you Marg's number."

The laboratory in Winnipeg had promised to let Natasha know the results of Jamila Khateb's Zika virus testing this afternoon. If Jamila was Zika positive, *and* if she'd gone on a school trip to an Aedes albopictus hotspot in Niagara, that would mean four of the epidemic's ten cases — forty percent — had visited Niagara Region in April this year *and* had been infected with Zika virus.

Natasha wondered if it was too soon to hope she might finally be making headway against the epidemic. The source of the Zika component of the double-virus infection did seem almost in view. The source of the Parvo-W component remained as elusive as ever. Finding it depended on pursuing her word-of-mouth theory. But given the demographic diversity of the cases outside Beasley, that wasn't going to be easy.

Her phone buzzed in her briefcase. She apologized to Mrs. Simon and dug it out. Jesse's too-eager face was beaming at her, announcing his call from the Health Unit. She prayed he had results from Winnipeg, and that the laboratory provided more answers than questions.

Natasha stepped into the hall outside Muriel Simon's room and hit the green button on her cellphone. "Yes, Jesse? You've got results for me?"

"I'm just fine, thank you for asking."

"That's the good thing about you, Jesse. You're always in fine form."

"All the same, it's nice to be asked."

She wondered what earrings he was wearing today. His Day-of-the-Dead pearly skulls, his Long John Silver gold-coloured hoops, or his Steven Tyler feathers?

"Did Dr. Szabo ask you to call me?"

"As a matter of fact, yes. But Dr. Zed is tied up at the moment. He's having a serious conversation with the mayor, who sounded like a bear when he called the office and demanded to be put through to the boss."

The mayor always sounded like a bear when a local outbreak was mentioned more than once in the *Hamilton Spectator* and angry letters to the editor started piling up. Natasha figured it was letters from angry voters, not the plight of innocent citizens, that got him steamed over outbreaks of infection.

"Dr. Zed says you'll be pleased with what I have to report from the good folks in Winnipeg," Jesse continued. "How's *your* day going so far?"

"I'm standing in the corridor of the cardiac ward at CUMC. It's not the easiest place for chit-chat."

"You mean, you'd like me to call back later? At a more convenient time?"

Natasha never liked sarcasm and found the best response was silence. She touched her earlobe. What earrings, she wondered, was *she* wearing today? She'd got dressed so quickly this morning she couldn't remember. Ah yes . . . the sterling silver triangles Zol bought for her last year in Singapore after that disastrous . . .

"You still there, Natasha?" Jesse said, ending the awkward silence.

"I most certainly am."

"Okay, then," he said, his tone conciliatory. "I'll make this quick and snappy."

"Thank you."

"The two most recent polio cases, Jamila Khateb and Bhavjeet Singh Malik, are positive for Parvo-W. In their blood *and* their spinal fluids. That makes each of the ten cases positive for Parvo-W virus. It's invaded the central nervous systems of all our victims, and still we have no idea where it's coming from."

We? What made Jesse think *he* was part of the investigative team? "Did they send us any other results?"

"Yes, indeed." He cleared his throat. "As promised, they ran Zika virus PCRs on the spinal fluids of our polio cases. Eight of the ten are virus positive."

"Hmm . . . Which two are negative?"

"Let me check." She heard paper rattling as he thumbed through Winnipeg's printout. "Oh! That's interesting . . ."

"What?"

"The two without Zika virus in their spinal fluids are the two kids, Juan-Carlos and Céline. They are anti-Zika *antibody* positive but Zika *virus* negative."

That struck Natasha as both interesting and perhaps explainable. The two people in the epidemic with the mildest disease were the two children. Neither had required intensive care, and both had been discharged from hospital after only a few days. Perhaps children neutralized Zika virus more efficiently than adults did, as was the case with other viruses, such as measles, mumps, chicken pox, and West Nile virus.

"Anything else, Jesse?"

"That's it for now. But on my lunch break, I'm going to buy a bucketful of insect repellent."

How much did Jesse know about the epidemiology of Zika virus? she wondered. He'd been hired part-time as an IT guy and receptionist, not as a biologist. "Why's that?"

"Ten fresh Zika infections spread across our fair city means Aedes albopictus, or one of its cousins, can't be far away. I figure a mosquito tiger is in our midst."

"Keep that to yourself, please, Jesse."

"Lips are sealed. Oh . . . Dr. Zed is buzzing me. He must have finished with the mayor. He'll need a large coffee. See ya!"

Natasha returned to Muriel Simon's room to say goodbye. "Before I go, Mrs. Simon, is there anything I can do to make you more comfortable?"

"I'm fine, dear," the principal said. "I need nothing better than you to get to the bottom of this polio epidemic. The board refuses to close my school, but at least I have you people at the Health Unit watching over us."

Out in the hallway again, Natasha phoned the number Mrs. Simon had given her for Marg Bickerton, her friend from the guidance office at Sir John A. Macdonald High School. The call went immediately to voicemail. Natasha dropped Muriel Simon's name in her message and made it clear she would appreciate a return call as soon as possible.

CHAPTER 25

One floor above the cardiac ward, Natasha hurried toward the intensive care unit. At the unit's imposing entrance plastered with curtly worded rules and regulations, she used the wall phone next to the locked doors and explained the reason for her visit.

A receptionist buzzed her in and told her to report directly to the nursing station. There she was directed her to put on a gown, gloves, and shoe covers from a nearby counter. She was told to wait for someone to escort her to Jamila Khateb's room. She was relieved it had been decided that the lack of polio transmission within households meant she wasn't required to wear a mask.

When she walked into Jamila's room a few minutes later, what Natasha noticed first was the noise. The rhythmic *hiss-cluck-hiss* of the mechanical ventilator brought back horrible memories of Cousin Vik's three days in ICU. They didn't call motorcycles *donorcycles* for nothing. Six transplant patients had benefitted from Vik's fatal crash, but that didn't diminish the intensity of the family's nightmare. Vik's mother still worried he'd been removed too soon from life support. Sometimes, she claimed her son was still alive until the doctors killed him by removing his beating heart.

Natasha took a few deep breaths and forced herself to suppress the image of Auntie Saroj wailing at Vik's bedside. Today, it was Jamila in the bed, a beautiful young woman lying peacefully on her back with her eyes closed.

Even with an endotracheal tube in her nose and a disposable bouffant cap askew on her head, she was attractive. Her lashes, long and luxuriant, rested gracefully on her delicate cheeks. There were no lines around her brow or eyelids to suggest she was anxious or uncomfortable. The midazolam dripping into an IV port in her left arm was doing its job.

Standing next to Jamila, their hands resting near her but afraid to touch her, was an exhausted-looking couple: a woman wearing a beige hijab and a man in baggy chinos and a wrinkled shirt. The fear in the couple's eyes, the tension around their lips, and the despair in their shaky hands made them unmistakable as Jamila's parents. How terrifying this must be for them. They'd escaped the horrors of war-torn Syria only to be thrown into another one. This time, in a foreign land where everyone spoke an incomprehensible language.

"As-salaam alaikum," Natasha said as she approached, keeping her hands by her sides and her voice soft yet hopefully audible above the whir of the ventilator.

"Wa-alaikum salaam," the parents responded together, their heads bobbing. Desperate for answers, they peppered her with a rapid string of questions none of which she could remotely understand.

She shook her gently and held up a hand. "I'm so sorry, I don't speak your language."

A tall man, who'd been standing two paces behind the couple and scanning the room as if on the lookout for threats, stepped forward. He had the square, clean-shaven jaw of a Hollywood idol and looked about Zol's age, not yet forty. He had a thick black moustache, and his luminous grey-blue eyes glowed from deep within his tan face. He looked familiar, but she couldn't place him. Did he look like an actor she'd seen on TV?

"May I be of assistance, miss?"

Natasha introduced herself then asked, "These are Jamila's parents?"

"That is correct."

"I believe they have a young son. I spoke to him on the phone on Friday when —"

"Ah yes, you are the kind lady who telephoned the ambulance and perhaps saved Jamila's life. Achraf is her younger brother, and he is at school today. I am hoping that is not a problem?"

Natasha deflected both the compliment and the question. "I'm hoping they have information that might help their daughter."

"My name is Hosam Khousa. And I am their interpreter." He cleared his throat. "And also their friend and fellow countryman."

Natasha swallowed hard at his physically commanding presence. His carefully groomed moustache matched his thick black hair, cut fashionably long at the front and tapered sharply at the back and sides. Like Zol and Hamish, he'd found a skilled barber and visited him recently.

Barber! That's how she recognized him. For the past few months, he'd been Max's barber. They'd exchanged nods and waves from some distance during the few times she'd picked Max up after a haircut at Paradise Barbers. He was also the one who'd been so helpful to Max and Travis after that awful knifing.

She debated mentioning their connection but decided against it. This was anything but a social visit. She needed to stick to her agenda without complicating the situation.

Her first task was to establish whether Jamila had acquired Zika virus locally or somewhere else. "I'd like to know how long the family has been living in Ontario. Would you ask them for me, please?"

"I do not need to ask. I know that they arrived in Canada several weeks before me and my family. That means they are here about eight months."

"Where did they arrive from?"

"The Kingdom of Jordan. They stayed almost three years there. In a camp supported by the United Nations."

Zika's incubation period was no more than a few days. Sometimes it stayed hidden in certain parts of the body for a number of weeks after that but never longer than six months. If Jamila had arrived in Canada eight months ago and had never left, she could only have acquired Zika in this country. "Please ask the parents if Jamila has ever left Ontario since the family first arrived."

Hosam conferred briefly with the patients then told Natasha, "None of us have the papers, the funds, or the wish to leave Canada at the moment."

Natasha gestured to the poor girl motionless on the bed. "Has she ever been on a school trip to Niagara Region?"

His response was immediate. "Her high school took her to Niagara. That was in April."

"Goodness, you seem to know this family well."

"Jamila, she was sitting beside my son on that bus trip. Both the going and the coming home." His eyes turned dark. "To be honest with you, Miss Sharma, I worry that this girl passed her infection to my son and he may be the next victim of your epidemic."

"Let me assure you, we have no evidence that this illness is being transmitted directly from one person to another."

"Then what is the mode of transmission? In the case of classic poliomyelitis, the transmission it is fecal-oral, if I am not mistaken."

Hosam Khousa, she now realized, was no medical layman. He talked like a doctor, and according to Max, he'd acted like one in the barbershop on Friday morning. "You were a physician in Syria, weren't you, sir?"

He smiled. "A general surgeon. Dealing mostly with major trauma."

She couldn't let herself imagine what he'd been confronted with on his operating table. The reports of the carnage caused by the Syrian conflict were horrendous. "You're correct, of course, Dr. Khousa, about classic polio. But what Jamila is suffering appears to be an entirely different entity."

"Different in what respect?"

"I'd like to tell you we understand this disease, but the simple truth is, we don't. We are pursuing a number of avenues of investigation, and one of them has taken us to a specific location in the Niagara Peninsula."

"To the famous Niagara Falls?"

"Not the Falls, but a village not too far from them. Do you know exactly what sites the students visited on that trip?"

Dr. Khousa shook his head. "You are knowing how teenagers are. They are never giving you any details. But when I get home, I can ask my son and see what he can tell us. Omar is at home today. I do not want him at school until this polio business is —"

Frustrated at being left out of such an important conversation, Jamila's father threw up his hands and started talking loudly in Arabic. When Dr. Khousa answered him calmly in their native tongue and pointed to Natasha with a warm smile, the distraught man's face relaxed a little.

"Would you like to borrow my cellphone, Dr. Khousa?" Natasha asked. "To call your son?"

"Thank you," he said, scanning the room. "Are we allowed to make mobile calls from here? They are not interfering with the equipment?"

"There's no problem."

She opened the telephone app on her phone and handed him the device. After a moment's hesitation, he tapped out a number then said, "I press here to complete the call?"

"Yes, this green button."

It seemed to take ages for someone to answer, but once they did, an animated conversation in Arabic ensued. At one point, Hosam mimed a pen and paper. She handed him a ballpoint and her notebook.

After he'd scribbled a few lines in Arabic script, he looked up from the notebook and said, "Omar says they visited one fort. He cannot remember the name."

She mimed a series of upright poles. "Was it made almost entirely of wooden posts?"

Omar's answer, through his father, was a confident nod. Fort George was a standard feature of school trips to Niagara.

"Did they visit any greenhouses?"

Hosam Khousa relayed the question, listened for an answer, then seemed to ask a question or two of his own. He moved the phone away from his ear and nodded. "Yes, a big one. Where they had tomatoes growing. Nothing but rows and rows of tomatoes."

"Did they visit any other greenhouses? One where they grow nothing but flowers, perhaps?"

It took a long time for Hosam to coax an answer out of the teenager. After a lot of back and forth in Arabic between father and son, Hosam finally told Natasha, "They did visit one greenhouse that was only for the growing of flowers. The boys, they stayed outside smoking cigarettes." A flush came to Hosam's cheeks. "He knows I do not like him smoking, but at least he told me the truth. He knows his answers are important for Jamila." He rubbed the back of his neck as his blue eyes seemed to gaze into a troubled past. "Omar has experienced first-hand that in wartime there is no such thing as the truth. Everybody lies and everybody suffers. Inshallah, it will be different in this country."

Except for the ventilator's *hiss-cluck-hiss*, a hushed silence filled the room.

After a long moment, Natasha said, "Did *all* the girls go inside the greenhouse?"

Hosam's face was still sombre. "Yes. And they were given flowers for taking to their homes."

"And Omar is certain that Jamila joined the other girls inside the greenhouse?"

"He remembers yellow flowers. She was holding them while riding the bus back to the school."

"Does he remember the name of that greenhouse?"

Hosam relayed the question to his son then said, "Sorry, he is having no idea."

She took back her notebook and skimmed the notes she'd made earlier this morning. They'd covered nearly everything on her list, but she had to be sure she hadn't missed something important. "During that bus trip, did the students visit anything in addition to what we've talked about?"

Hosam relayed the question then chuckled with her at Omar's answer. "Just the wooden fort, the two greenhouses, and the highlight for the day — a stop at McDonald's. Big Macs for the lunch."

Hosam ended the call, and Natasha slipped the phone and her notebook into her briefcase. Omar's high school group could easily have visited that same Aedes-infested greenhouse as the students from Cathcart Elementary.

Through Hosam, Natasha asked the parents whether Jamila had recently suffered any insect bites. The father shrugged dismissively. The mother nudged her husband out of the way and lifted the bedsheet covering her daughter's legs. Letting loose a torrent of Arabic, she pointed to half a dozen dark lesions around the girl's ankles. Then she lifted her daughter's flaccid right hand from the bed. Encircling Jamila's wrist were five more spots, identical to the others.

Hosam's face went ashen. "Rima says her daughter came home from that trip with those spots. And now, I remember that Omar was having similar lesions on his arms. He scratched at them for days." He steadied himself against the side rails of Jamila's bed. "Those are not innocent insect bites, Miss Sharma. I can tell by your interest in them. My only son, he is in grave danger. And so are the many others who went on that trip."

CHAPTER 26

Hosam fixed his gaze on the beautiful girl lying helpless on the bed half a world away from her home in the shattered city of Hama. He watched her chest rise and fall to the rhythm of the mechanical ventilator that dominated the room like a fierce beast. Was the nightmare ever going to end for any of his people? In Syria, the war had brought rampaging thugs to their homes at midnight and bombs from the air at any time of day. But here, in this gold-plated sanctuary provided by the earnest people of Canada, the threats were less predictable, more difficult to evade, and just as deadly.

"Please, Miss Sharma. You must tell me what terrible thing my son he was exposed to on that school trip."

Her warm smile was long gone. Her lips tightened. "As I said, we are in the early stages of our investigation. All I can say is we are following a new and important lead in the case."

"'Investigation'...'Important lead in the case'...You are using the language of the police. Jamila and my son, are they victims of a crime the details of which you do not choose to share?"

She looked surprised and affronted at his conclusion. "No, we don't expect any criminal activity."

"Then why will you not tell me what you and your colleagues suspect happened on that excursion?" In Aleppo, it was often helpful to point out the connections you had with those in power. Perhaps it worked the same way here. "I know Dr. Zoltan Szabo personally. I am certain he would want me to be in complete awareness of any threats to the life of my son."

Miss Sharma looked down at her obviously expensive shoes and said nothing. The refined design of her footwear reminded him of the days when Leila could afford to similarly adorn her feet so gracefully.

"Can you at least tell me," he pressed, "what you suspect has bitten my son? Was it a tick? A poisonous spider? Some sort of nasty Canadian beetle?"

She looked up from her shoes but avoided his face. "I'm sorry, but I haven't seen your son. And I'm not a doctor. I'm not in a position to say what might have bitten him."

Struggling to suppress his anger, he pointed to the child in the bed. "Jamila, then. What caused those lesions on *her* wrists and ankles? At least tell me that so that I can explain it to her parents. You do not need an interpreter to see how upset her mother is. She is convinced her daughter sustained the bites of some sort of poisonous insect."

Miss Sharma stood for a long time fingering an earring and gazing at Rima, who was sobbing over her helpless daughter. Miss Sharma seemed to be debating with herself. Finally, she looked straight into Hosam's face and said, "Perhaps you've heard of the Aedes mosquito? Specifically Aedes albopictus?"

"Yes, of course," he told her in as confident a tone as possible, colleague to colleague. He had reviewed the chapter about mosquito-borne diseases in his *Toronto Notes*. He could not remember every virus that Aedes mosquitoes transmitted, but he knew they did carry yellow fever. And dengue. And West Nile, or was that the Culex mosquito? On the other hand, he was certain that poliovirus was not transmitted by any type of insect.

"The Aedes," he said, "it transmits certain tropical viruses. But that does not include the poliovirus."

"Exactly."

"So, in Jamila's case, which virus are you suspecting?"

She looked around the room, obviously uncertain how much official information she should release. Finally, she said almost in a whisper, "Zika virus. The people affected by our poliomyelitis outbreak were recently infected with Zika virus. Every one of them."

Into what sort of strange land had he led his family? In January, you could freeze to death in a matter of minutes unless you were wearing multiple layers of the correct clothing. And by April, your child could catch a deadly tropical virus during a brief outing with his school.

He wiped the sweat from his brow with his handkerchief. "An invasion of Aedes mosquitoes has brought the Zika virus to Canada?"

"It appears that way," she admitted.

"And Omar? My son, he must be infected as well. How quickly will he show signs of this horrible disease? Oh, Miss Sharma, there must be something we can do to catch it before . . ."

The blank look on her face confirmed his worst fears. Poliovirus had no antidote. The disease's respiratory paralysis could be managed with a ventilator, nourishment could be administered through various tubings, but nothing could stop the virus from running rampant inside the central nervous system.

"Don't despair, Dr. Khousa," she said. "There is hope."

"I am a realist, Miss Sharma. A surgeon who operated day and night on war-ravaged civilians. For the love of God, I was forced to amputate what was left of my own son's lower leg. Please, do not try to calm my fears with foolish false hope."

"But I'm serious. There *is* hope. And it's because . . ." She paused and again seemed to debate with herself about whether she should explain further.

"Yes?"

"It appears that the expression of this form of poliomyelitis requires simultaneous infection with two distinct viruses."

"*Two* viruses? What is it, the second one?"

"Something the medical community has never reported before."

"Does it have a name?"

"We're . . . we're calling it . . . Parvo-W."

"And there is hope because there is a chance my son is not infected with this second virus?"

"A very good chance."

"How does one contract this Parvo-W?"

"We don't know," she admitted. "No one does. And to be honest, that's a major stumbling block in our investigation."

"So, you have cracked one half of your medical puzzle, but there remains the other half."

"You could say that. But we have a long way to go to prevent more people from acquiring Zika virus locally. We're in the process of pinpointing the exact location of the Aedes mosquitoes that seem to be carrying it."

"Clearly, Jamila visited at least one of them," he told her. "And probably Omar and other children on that outing."

She glanced at her watch. "From what I've learned from you in the last few minutes, that appears to be the case."

"Can you test Omar to see if he has the Zika? A blood test for antibodies, perhaps?"

"We can certainly do that. In fact, I will arrange for Omar's blood sample to be taken this afternoon. At the Health Unit." She tapped the screen on her mobile phone. "Can I reach you at the number you just used to call your son?"

"I will make certain that Omar is at home to answer your call. Can he arrive to your health unit on the city bus?"

"No problem. It's easy to get to." She paused, and her face brightened as if she had been struck by a bright idea. "If we are going to pinpoint the source of the second virus, the Parvo-W, we'll need to establish an hour-by-hour timeline of the polio victims' activities within the past few weeks. Can you help me with that?"

"What would you like me to do?"

"Sit down with Jamila's parents, establish the date when she first developed fever and headache, count back, um . . . say, twenty-one days. Then make a list of everywhere she went and everything she did during those three weeks."

"Everything? Including what she took at every meal? Every

friend she talked to? I am afraid, Miss Sharma, you are asking for the impossible. As a parent myself —"

"I know. You're right. The parents won't remember that degree of detail. And teenagers get up to all sorts of things their parents know nothing about. Just track her movements as best you can. If you can access her cellphone, that might help."

"What are we looking for?"

"I don't know. But if we track the movements of as many of the polio cases as we can, we might see that during the weeks prior to their illness, they visited the same place."

"I will do my best. Shall I take your mobile number?"

She gave him her number, and they shook hands, colleague to colleague. Miss Sharma smiled and thanked him several times for his invaluable assistance without seeming to notice the sweat trickling from his brow.

As he watched her walk away, his mouth felt as foul as the floor of a henhouse. Yesterday, he had reviewed his wife's invoices for the previous month. Jamila's parents were paying off their daughter's account at the rate of five dollars per week. It would take them six months to settle Leila's one-hundred-twenty-dollar fee. Jamila had spent four one-hour sessions with Leila within Miss Sharma's three-week window. If Hosam included them in his report of Jamila's movements, Leila's work would be exposed directly to the health department. And . . .

Leila would be ordered to halt her vital endeavours.

The money they had invested in her equipment would be lost, including the paltry amount the greedy pawnbroker had given them for her ring.

Leila would go to jail.

The Church People would evict them from their townhouse.

He would never save enough money to sit his re-certification exams.

He would be stuck doing low tapers and high fades until he was an old man.

Merde!

CHAPTER 27

Natasha tossed her protective gear into the appropriate bins at Jamila's door and pumped alcohol sanitizer onto her palms. Once the liquid had evaporated, she pumped out a second dollop, and then a third in case she'd missed a spot. Although she knew that no patients from the outbreak had transmitted the disease to any close contacts, she prayed the sanitizer was up to its germ-killing task and it had been okay not to wear a mask.

Still rubbing her hands, she walked over to the nursing station. There, she studied the whiteboard posted not-so-discreetly on the wall above a sink. Among the list of twelve patients currently admitted to the unit, she recognized the names of four: Jamila and the three others whom polio had paralyzed from the neck down — Blessica Velasquez the nanny, Barry Novak the retired labourer, and Lewis Feldman the laid-off menswear salesman. Like Jamila, the others had probably made recent visits to Virgil or Niagara-on-the-Lake. But Natasha knew she had to be certain about their movements. A shudder crossed her shoulders at the idea that any of them had picked up their Zika infection in another locale. A second focus of Zika-infected Aedes mosquitoes spreading the disease within easy visiting distance of Hamilton was too scary to contemplate.

She took note of the room numbers of her polio cases and set off to interview their relatives at the bedsides. She was soon disappointed to find that none of the patients had visitors this early in the day. Most of the staff, however, were crowded into Lewis Feldman's room. By the anxious looks on their faces and the flashing lights on Lewis's monitor, the sixty-three-year-old menswear salesman was in major trouble. Two of the polio victims, Esi and Darryl, had succumbed last week to unexpected cardiac collapse. Hamish called it malignant myocarditis and explained that their heart muscles had turned to mush overnight. Was the same untreatable complication happening to Lewis? And had something similar landed Muriel Simon on the cardiac ward?

Natasha's cellphone chimed in her briefcase. She grabbed it and slipped into an unoccupied utility room.

"How can I help you, Ms. Sharma?" Ms. Bickerton said after they'd introduced themselves and Natasha had explained their mutual connection with Muriel Simon.

"I'm hoping you can give me some details about the trip your school made to the Niagara Peninsula in April."

"What sort of details?"

"Let's start with how many students participated?"

"You've caught me off-guard, I'm afraid. I don't have the exact number at my fingertips. But what I can tell you is, we've sponsored just the one trip to Niagara so far this year."

"Can you give me a ballpark figure, then? Are we talking a couple dozen teenagers or a couple of hundred?"

"Oh heavens! Our teachers and chaperones can handle only one busload of students on a single outing."

"So, we're talking fewer than fifty students?"

"I'd say closer to thirty-five."

"And how many chaperones?"

"Usually two teachers and two volunteer parents or guardians."

"I would be grateful for a list of all the participants. Names, addresses, and phone numbers, to start with. The students and the accompanying adults."

"I must say, this is highly irregular. There are privacy issues involved here. I cannot provide any such information on my own. I'd need the permission of our principal and perhaps our school board's legal department." She paused and cleared her throat. "Who did you say you were with?"

"I work for Hamilton-Lakeshore Public Health Services. My boss is the medical officer of health for our region. He runs the Health Unit."

"Does this person have a name?"

"Dr. Szabo."

"Szabo? Why does that sound familiar?"

"Perhaps because —"

"Ah, you mean Dr. *Zoltan* Szabo, the fellow who's been getting a lot of press these days concerning the epidemic everyone's talking about?"

"That's correct, Ms. Bickerton. And Dr. Szabo would appreciate all the cooperation you are able to give us."

"So this *is* about those cases of . . . oh my God . . . of polio. And you think our kids are at risk because they went on that field trip? For heaven's sake, why didn't you tell me? And seriously . . . we should have been informed long before today."

Natasha struggled to keep the smile in her voice. "We're interested in the exact locations the students visited on that trip. Do you have a list of the stops the bus made and the places the students visited?"

"I'm not sure I have a record of every time the bus came to a stop, but I can tell you what was on the official schedule."

"That sounds like a great start. Thank you."

"I'm going to put you on speakerphone while I find my reading glasses and open up the field-trip file on my computer. I didn't go on that trip this year, so I'll have to read you what's on the official itinerary."

Ms. Bickerton tapped frenetically on her keyboard for at least a couple of minutes, then let out an exasperated sigh. "Stupid thing," she said. "This new database is not being cooperative. The old one was much better." She cursed again under her breath and typed another long sequence. Finally, she said, "Okay, here it is. April Excursion to Niagara-on-the-Lake and Environs. I hope you've got a pen and paper handy."

With her notebook and briefcase balanced on the edge of the utility room's massive stainless steel sink, Natasha fervently hoped she hadn't ducked into the dirty room instead of the clean one. She sniffed the air and was thankful not to catch a whiff of dirty bedpans. "I'm ready."

"Their first stop was Niagara-on-the-Lake. Specifically, Fort George. It's at the far end of the town."

"How long did they spend there?"

"This won't tell me exactly, but the Fort's educational program is always seventy-five minutes long. This year, it ran from, um . . . ten fifteen to eleven thirty."

"Would all of the students have stayed around for that program?"

"The teachers would have insisted on it. Fort George is the major educational component of the day. Our kids always do a unit on the War of 1812."

"I see. And then what did they visit, Ms. Bickerton?"

"Being high school students, they're allowed time on their own until the next scheduled event. Whenever I've gone on this trip, the students have walked into town from the fort and hit the ice cream parlours and the fudge shop on the main street."

"And after that bit of free time?"

"Let's see . . . the schedule has the bus picking them up at the fudge shop at twelve fifteen and taking them down the road to the village of Virgil."

"What did they do there?"

"They'd have started with lunch at McDonald's. It's neither cultural nor educational, but the kids love it, and it's affordable."

"What did they do after they finished their Big Macs?"

"Give me a sec . . . Ah, this year it was Hardeman Hydroponics for a tour of their brand new tomato operation. And after that,

Vander Zalm Nurseries for a look at the tulips. They must have a hundred varieties under one roof."

"Both operations are in Virgil?"

"It's a small village, so they're not far apart."

"I understand there are some medical cannabis growing facilities nearby. Were the students taken to any of those?"

Ms. Bickerton let out a chortle, and Natasha pictured a middle-aged woman with a generous bosom and a floral-print dress. "You must be kidding. The teachers would never have gotten them out of there."

"Are you able to say if they made any other stops? Perhaps something not listed on the schedule?"

"Mrs. Todd, she's the math teacher who accompanied the students and supervised the trip. She goes on this particular excursion every year. She would have typed up the obligatory trip summary and incident report."

Incident report? Natasha didn't like the sound of that. "Did something bad happen to one of the students?"

"No, no. Eleanor Todd is always precise. To her mathematical mind, even an unscheduled toilet stop is an incident."

Natasha's grade twelve math teacher had been like that — delightfully eccentric and reassuringly motherly. "I understand."

"If something was added to the trip at the last minute, Eleanor would have recorded it."

"And did she?"

"Let me read you what she wrote: *The April 6 field trip went well with no hitches, hassles, or hold-ups. We kept close to the prescribed schedule. As usual, the ice cream, fudge, and burgers were the highlights. I suggest that Vander Zalm Nurseries be deleted from the itinerary in future years. The boys refused to be seen looking at flowers of any description, and the mosquitoes were frightful — little striped beasties buzzing everywhere.*"

Natasha tapped her notebook with her ballpoint and said to herself: *Thank you, Mrs. Todd. You've confirmed our Zika outbreak's ground zero.* But why, Natasha wondered, was it Vander Zalm Nurseries of Virgil, Ontario? What was special about that greenhouse? Its location close to New York State? Its microclimate? Its tulips? Its staff?

"I will need that detailed list of trip participants, Ms. Bickerton. How can we make that happen as soon as possible?"

"I think if you get your boss to fax a formal request to our principal, we can get you the information pretty quickly. Is tomorrow morning soon enough?"

Natasha looked at her watch. It was almost noon. Organizing Zika and Parvo-W blood testing for almost forty people was going to take some doing. The sooner she had that list the better. "This afternoon would be more helpful, if you can swing it."

"Our kids *are* in danger, aren't they?"

"At this point, we're not sure whether or not they're at risk of anything serious. But Dr. Szabo would like us to proceed with an abundance of caution. I'm sure you can understand that."

"And you need to understand that many of our parents have limited resources and don't speak English. This is going to throw our entire school into a panic."

"I have no doubt that you and your colleagues are pros at culturally sensitive, multilingual communication. Dr. Szabo will probably call upon your expertise when it comes to contacting the families."

Something clattered at Ms. Bickerton's end of the phone. Natasha pictured the teacher's heavy reading glasses dropping onto her keyboard. "Oh dear Lord. Oh Miss Sharma." The poor woman was groaning as if someone had rushed in and punched her in the gut.

"What's wrong? Ms. Bickerton, are you okay? Do you need me to call someone?"

"The bus driver on that trip, dear Barry Novak. He's an institution at this school. Wonderful with the kids. I just remembered . . . he's been in intensive care at Caledonian Medical Centre for about a week. I understand he's on life support."

Natasha flipped through her notebook. There he was — Barry Novak, polio case number six. But he was listed as a retired labourer, not a school's occasional bus driver. "We had no idea he was a driver. He's listed as a retired labourer."

"He injured his back some years ago working construction and never got properly compensated. Now he drives part-time for the small charter company we use for our field trips. We've been presuming he had a heart attack. But if it's your polio epidemic that's got him . . . My God, we'd better get that list to you fast."

CHAPTER 28

Hosam tucked Jamila's smartphone into his jacket pocket and said goodbye to her parents. Fadi and Rima had been unable to help him fulfill Miss Sharma's request to track their daughter's movements. They knew little of her new life in Hamilton but lent Hosam her phone in the hope it would reveal something to help her desperate condition. Rima, teary-eyed, told Hosam she had watched Jamila type in the phone's password and remembered it because it was Rima's own birth date: 2281.

Hosam had the feeling that neither parent had benefitted from more than a year or two of schooling. As an auto mechanic, Fadi would not have needed to read and write. Rima struck Hosam as a traditional Syrian housewife who may have had street sense but no formal education. He was almost certain their literacy in written Arabic was limited to a few key phrases. Learning English was going to be a huge problem for them; so far, they had made no progress whatsoever. They admitted to being confused, disoriented, and embarrassed every time they ventured from their townhouse. Unable to decipher any of the English script on storefronts and road signs, they told Hosam they felt like imbeciles dropped onto an alien planet. Almost nothing made sense. Even the food in the supermarkets was strange to them, the labels on every package unintelligible. Being government-sponsored refugees, they had no group of private sponsors, like Hosam's Church People, to help them find their way.

Instead of heading directly to the ICU's exit door, Hosam decided to stroll clockwise around the unit and look surreptitiously through the glass walls of each of its fifteen private rooms. If Mo was still alive after last night's debacle, he would probably have been admitted here. Hosam had never worked in an ICU this large, this orderly, or with this much sophisticated equipment. And Canadians were such a courteous bunch that it was a revelation to watch them at work. It amazed him how much they could accomplish without raising either their arms or their voices.

As he glanced into the fourth room along, he saw the occupant in the bed peering back at him through the window. He was a brown-skinned man in his late twenties with a mass of wildly dishevelled dark hair and a sneer of broken teeth. His bare chest and arms were connected to a dozen tubes and leads, and he was sitting with his gown bunched on his lap and his legs dangling over the side of the bed. By the dazed look on his face, he seemed to have no idea where he was. When the man raised his arms and started waving them frantically, Hosam could see that both of his hands were heavily bandaged in layers of white gauze and a great deal of tape.

Hosam stepped to the threshold of the open door and said, in Arabic, "Mo? Is that you, Mo?"

The man's face lit up at being addressed in his mother tongue. "Where . . . ? Where in the blazing flames of hell am I?"

"In the intensive care unit."

"A hospital?"

"Caledonian Medical Centre."

"What . . . ? What happened? Did somebody shoot me?"

"Do you remember who I am?"

"Yeah. You're the doctor . . . the big shot from Aleppo. Who doesn't like getting his precious hands dirty."

Hosam did not know where that came from. He thought he had pulled his weight perfectly well during the church job on Friday night. He looked at his palms and shrugged. "Has anyone explained what happened to you last night?"

Mo shook his head and gestured to the intravenous device in his left forearm. "They poke me with goddamned needles. They take my blood. They ask me dumb questions." He looked down at the cardiac leads attached to his hairy chest. "What are these stupid things?" His eyes followed the wires to the cardiac monitor flashing a host of graphs and numbers beside his bed. "My heart . . . it's got something wrong with it? My chest hurts like hell, and I feel like shit."

"I do not know all the details. But if you like, I can find them out and explain them to you. But you need to tell your nurse I am your official translator. They have rules here. They do not release information without permission."

Mo rubbed his thigh with his heavily bandaged right hand then winced in discomfort. "Sure. Whatever."

Hosam looked around. There was no sign on the door warning visitors away, and the staff seemed occupied elsewhere. He walked in and sat on the bed.

Mo winced as his weight shifted on the mattress. "Careful, I told you my chest was killing me." He gestured toward the left side of his ribcage. "I feel like someone ran over me with their truck. Look at these bruises."

Well, thought Hosam, a few cracked ribs were a small price to pay for a beating heart. "I was there last night," he told Mo. "At the ball diamond."

"What? Oh . . . you mean we pulled another of those wire jobs?"

"Not exactly. We barely got started."

He told Mo the story of the high-voltage wire, the axe that got wet in the dew-covered grass, the thunderous discharge that stopped Mo's heart, the long minutes of CPR, and the desperate final blow to Mo's sternum that brought him around. He didn't mention the nauseating smell of burning flesh.

"You saved my life?" he said, wincing again and examining the bruises.

Hosam nodded. "You could say that."

"How did I get here?"

Hosam described their hair-raising ride in the back seat of the Ford F-150: Mo deeply unconscious and barely breathing, Hosam sick with worry that Mo's heart was going to give out before they reached the hospital, and Saramin driving at a donkey's pace, afraid the cops might nab her for speeding.

"So the bitch dumped me here and took off?"

"She had to return the, um, borrowed vehicle."

"She never came back to see if I made it. My wallet and ID are missing. She must have taken them off me — so if I died, I'd be some nameless corpse that nobody claimed. And she and the Caliph would be in the clear. As always."

Mo was right, of course. But Hosam said nothing. He was not going to get between Mo, Saramin, and the Caliph.

"For shit's sake!" Mo continued. "I know what Saramin is like. If it weren't for you, she'd have left me for dead. She may be gorgeous, but she's one harsh bitch."

"I do not know. She seemed pretty cut up when it looked like we were going to lose you."

After Saramin let it slip last night that Mo had special status with the Scarpellinos, Hosam borrowed Omar's computer to look the family up on Google. He discovered they were Hamilton-based Italian mobsters currently involved in a turf war against their longstanding rivals, the Michelinis. Il Proppo, his moniker derived from the Italian for landlord, was said to be a man called Giuseppe Michelini. Unnamed sources said Il Proppo was the driving force behind the Michelinis' current campaign for dominance that had seen two Scarpellino brothers gunned down in the past month. One brother had been killed outside his home in Hamilton, the other at a suburban restaurant north of Toronto. It was expected that a Michelini or two would soon be meeting a similar fate.

Hosam figured that the operations of the Italian families would have much in common with whatever the Caliph was into. In fact, if the Scarpellinos had put their trust in Mo, it sounded as if the Caliph had entered into a business agreement with them. The Syrian war had turned many young men into sharpshooters, some of whom had made their way to Ontario as refugees. Out of work in a strange land, marginalized by their inadequate English, and craving the surges of battle-fuelled adrenalin that had once flooded their veins, some ex-militiamen would be eager to prove their mettle inside Ontario's mobster fraternity.

"You know, Saramin, she . . ." Hosam paused, unsure how much he should say. "Well, she mentioned something about the Scarpellinos trusting you more than anyone else. I gather the Caliph considers you a valuable asset. That gave me the impression that —"

"Fuck Saramin," Mo said, scowling fiercely into Hosam's face. With his deep-set eyes, long nose, and crooked teeth, he looked like a wolf sizing up his prey. After a tension-filled silence, he lifted his arms and studied the bulky bandages hiding his hands. "Tell me the truth, Doc. Do I have any fingers left?"

"Sorry, Mo. It was too dark last night to see much. And I was so busy restarting your heart that I thought about nothing else. You tell the nurse I am your interpreter, and I will . . ."

Hosam wiped his sweaty palms against his trousers. If he and his family were to have any chance of escaping the Caliph's predatory grip, he had to know exactly what the boss was up to with the Scarpellinos. He had faced a lot of bullies these past few years, but that did not make facing this one any easier. He did, however, have the upper hand. Mo knew he would be downstairs on an ice-cold slab if it were not for Hosam's quick actions last night. Still, with a bruiser like Mo, he had to be careful. The key word was subtlety.

"Yes," Hosam told, aiming his gaze at Mo's wolfish eyes, "I can ask the nurse to tell us the exact condition of your valuable . . . *trigger* fingers?"

Mo's face tightened then relaxed slightly. And though he looked away without a word, his eyes betrayed him. Mo was the Caliph's hitman for the Italian mob. There was not the slightest doubt about it.

CHAPTER 29

"Come in, Love," Zol said as he extended his arms to her that Tuesday afternoon. "You didn't sleep much last night, did you?" He threw her a fake frown and added, "And I bet you haven't taken the time to grab even a quick sandwich for lunch."

He glanced at his office door, to be certain it had closed behind her, then he stood and held her close. As they kissed on the lips, he knew he could never get enough of this smart, beautiful, compassionate woman who was soon to be his bride.

He closed his eyes and let Sarah McLachlan sing a few bars of "Angel" somewhere deep inside his brain. His post-concussion synesthesia never bothered him when Tasha was in his arms smelling of sandalwood. He enjoyed the dreamy sound of Sarah's voice, and he loved everything about Tasha. Well, except for maybe her mother.

"Jesse put Mummyji through to me," he told her. "At eleven thirty on the dot."

"Oh, Zol, I'm so sorry."

"It's okay. I was glad to talk to her."

She gave his arms a playful squeeze. "You don't have to fib. Did she want something specific or was she just calling to be annoying?"

"She wants me to abandon the idea of wearing a business suit at the ceremony."

"Oh, not again! I already told her you'd look ridiculous in a sherwani and turban. What did you say?"

"I told her I'd gone and had my measurements taken at that Punjabi tailor's place in Mississauga. The exact one she recommended."

"No, Zol, you didn't! *Please*, we have to stand up to her. As a couple. Believe me — where my mother is concerned, the wedding turban and sherwani are just the thin edge of a queen-size wedge. You know how manipulative she is. I've spent my entire life —"

"My dearest bride-to-be, it's okay, I've got it all planned."

"But —"

"Just trust me on this, Tasha. There will be no turban, no sherwani, and no business suit."

"What do you mean?"

"I think both you *and* your mother will be pleased with what Mr. Gupta is going to make for me."

"That doesn't sound possible."

He kissed her again. "Well, I know for certain you will love his bit of made-to-measure tailoring. It's going to be perfect, but I'm not saying anything more about it. Like your wedding dress, my attire will be under wraps until our big day." He let go of her arms and pointed to the chair next to his desk. "Now, have a seat and tell me about the rest of your morning. You had impressive success with those teachers."

"Did you catch Dr. Polgar?"

"We had a brief chat," he said and dropped into his chair. "But she's expecting a call from you this afternoon with the details."

"Was she surprised that her Aedes Tigers seem to be transmitting Zika?"

"I'd say disappointed."

Stephanie Polgar had hoped the mosquitoes her staff had trapped in Virgil would test virus-free at the Toronto lab. Tasha's investigation suggested they'd been transmitting the virus to at least a few casual visitors to her region.

"Those school groups stayed how long in Virgil admiring the tulips?" he asked.

"About half an hour."

"Damned efficient little buggers."

"And still, Dr. Polgar doesn't have a single case of polio anywhere in Niagara?" Tasha said.

"None," Zol told her. "Zika is still only half of our polio story."

"Did she have any more ideas about how the virus and the mosquitoes got to that tulip farm?"

"She's concentrating on the migrant workers at this point. Many of them come from Guatemala."

"And from Haiti, according to Muriel Simon."

"Stephanie's going to send her staff to find out exactly when the workers arrived, what routes they took, and test them for Zika." And, of course, she'd be trapping and testing as many mosquitoes in that greenhouse as she could.

Tasha fingered the silver peacock locket she often wore around her neck. Crafted in Punjab, it had belonged to her grandmother and had survived the cataclysm of British India's bloody partition in 1947. Tasha saw her simple locket as symbolic of the enduring strength of the human spirit.

Something — a concern, a bright idea, a distant memory — was niggling at her. He could tell by the faraway look in her eyes. "Do they ever employ women as temporary agricultural workers?" she asked.

"I've never thought about it," he admitted. "Any of the articles I've read on the subject have featured men. We work those guys incredibly hard for half the year so they can put food on our tables. We pay them meagre wages that allow them to accrue minimal savings. We ship them back to their wives and kids for the winter. And then we start the cycle again when spring comes."

"I was thinking of those babies born to Zika-infected mothers in Brazil. They had small heads and tiny brains. You've seen the photos on the internet."

"Sorry," he said, "I was soapboxing there. But, yeah, microcephaly is the nasty side to Zika." And Tasha's discovery this morning of the ease of Zika transmission had magnified the potential scope of the problem. "Oh my God," he said, "you're right. Stephanie will have to offer Zika testing to virtually everyone in her region who's of childbearing age."

"We're only next door and we've got cases already. Are we going to do it too?"

"Another thing to discuss with Hamish tonight." Zol checked his watch. "My task-force meeting on cannabis legalization starts in a few minutes. Hamish and I agreed to meet tonight over supper. At our place. I hope that's okay?"

She looked serious. "Well, it depends."

Shit! What commitment had he forgotten? "Oh no. On what?"

Her scowl dissolved into a teasing grin. "On what you'll be cooking."

He laughed and swept his phone, pen, and keys from the desk. He stashed them in his jacket pockets. "I thought I'd do a . . . well, I'm not sure. *It depends* on what looks fresh at Kelly's on the way home."

He rose to his feet. "I've gotta run. But in words of one syllable, how did you make out with Bhavjeet and his auntie? Has he been tiptoeing through Niagara's tulips?"

She stood and reached for a kiss. "It's a long story. I'll tell you tonight over that delicious meal you're going to whip up."

CHAPTER 30

"Okay, Hamish," Zol told him, pointing to the ingredients he'd assembled on the kitchen counter. "Throw those into the food processor and give them a whirl."

"Everything? You mean . . . all at once?"

Unable to suppress a grin at Hamish's hesitance, Zol gestured to the fresh basil, spinach, pine nuts, peeled garlic, and cubed parmesan awaiting their fate. "Yep. The whole lot."

Hamish jiggled the processor's tight-fitting lid several times then slapped it with his palm. "Stupid thing," he said. "How do I get this part off?"

"What are you talking about? I thought you guys had one."

"I've never used it. That's Al's domain."

"Hasn't he shown you the many things you can do with a food processor?"

"He's afraid if I learn to cook anything more complicated than scrambled eggs, I'll have designs above my station and he'll lose his subservient dishwasher."

Zol laughed and removed the lid with a quick twist. He tipped the basil and other pesto makings into the processor. After he'd secured the lid, he pointed to the pulse bar and told Hamish, "Hold this down for a few seconds at a time. Keep at it until the machine stops rattling and just hums."

"And that's it?"

"Not quite. See this hole in the top? Pour a couple of glugs of olive oil through it, then two generous tablespoons of mayo and a teaspoon of mustard."

"How much is a glug?"

"Doesn't matter, just go for it. Then run the machine for half a minute more."

Hamish returned him a skeptical look then focused on his task.

"Table's set," Tasha said, returning from the sunroom. Nowadays, the place doubled as a dining room because it was her favourite part of the house. "What else can I do?"

"Um . . . Pour the wine." Zol pointed to the fridge. "There's a New Zealand Sauvignon Blanc and a Chilean Pinot Grigio in there. Your choice." He was pretty sure she'd pick the Sauvignon Blanc.

Tasha turned to Hamish, whose gaze was still fixed on the pulse bar of the silent machine. "Do you have a wine preference, Hamish?"

"You know me. Just half a glass of anything white."

While Tasha opened the New Zealand, Zol unrolled his puff pastry onto the counter. These days, he used the factory-made stuff from the supermarket. His instructors at cooking school — it was hard to believe it was nearly twenty years since he'd received his diploma — would have a fit if they saw him using store-bought pastry. A trained professional was supposed to make everything from scratch. But what the heck. This was a helluva lot faster and worked perfectly well for a homestyle Salmon Wellington.

He centred the salmon filet on the sheet of pastry and listened to the food processor labouring under Hamish's awkward but diligent fingers. "Sounds pretty good, sous chef. Is the parmesan totally pulverized?"

"If you mean, is it in tiny crumbs, then yes."

"Great. Now add the wet stuff."

After the machine had whirred exactly thirty seconds by Hamish's Omega, Zol told him, "Okay, turn it off then twist the handle towards you and lift the bowl."

Hamish twisted one way, then the other, then back the other way. Finally, the bowl separated from its base and he handed the whole thing over.

Zol removed the lid and scraped the bright green mixture onto the salmon. Then, recalling the technique he'd learned all those years ago, he folded the pastry over the fish as if wrapping a fine present.

"Looks perfect," Tasha said as he placed the pastry parcel in the oven. "But when will it be ready? I'm starving."

"Then you'd better get out the cashews and put them in a bowl," he said. "This baby has to bake for forty-five minutes."

"What about the boys?" Tasha said. "I'm surprised they're not in here sniffing around. They must be starving too."

"They're okay. They're both masters of the microwave. Filled themselves with the house specialty before I got home. And now they're doing their homework . . . I hope."

Hamish dried his freshly washed hands and grabbed a handful of cashews. "What's the house specialty?"

"Mac and cheese layered with bacon," Zol said. It was a dish that froze well and was always a hit. Even Tasha liked it. She avoided beef and pork, but she'd try a bit of bacon every now and then. As a frequent sleepover house guest at the home of three carnivorous lads, she'd come to accept that bacon was its own food group and occasionally too good to pass up.

She lifted a glass of Perrier and the bowl of cashews from the counter. "Shall we retire to the sunroom, sirs?"

Zol raised his glass in a quick toast then let a citrusy mouthful of New Zealand's south-island finest tickle his throat. As often happened with Sauvignon Blanc, the wine's grassy bouquet conjured Daft Punk from the ether. The opening riff of their "Get Lucky" erupted in his head.

The foot-tapping tune — it was one of his favourites — carried on as he followed the others into the sunroom. He settled next to Tasha on the sofa and took another sip of the wine. Once Daft Punk left the stage, he asked her to bring Hamish up to date on today's events.

Without looking at her notes, Tasha summarized what she'd gleaned from the elementary school principal and her friend the high school guidance teacher.

When Tasha finished, Hamish told her, "Of course, your theory will have to be confirmed by an expert examination of the mosquitoes at that greenhouse. Reports from a couple of school teachers that they *might* have seen mosquitoes, which *might* have been striped, just isn't good enough. We have to know for certain that what those women saw *are* Aedes albopictus, and they *are* carrying Zika virus."

Zol felt his face flush, and it wasn't the wine. Hamish took that arrogant tone with Tasha far too often. He seemed to think he could get away with it because she wasn't a physician. Zol figured it was a status thing with Hamish. She was a woman, and she was smarter than most of the physicians he worked with. The guy couldn't accept those two bare facts.

"Just wait a darn minute there, Hamish," Zol told him. "Tasha did some great detective work today. And the evidence she uncovered is strong. Five people who visited that particular greenhouse in April now have lab-confirmed Zika." Those five also had Parvo-W virus infection along with their clinical poliomyelitis, but for now, he considered that beside the point.

Tasha tapped her notebook. "If there is Zika transmission in that location, it appears to be sustained. The two school groups — Cathcart Elementary and Sir John A. Macdonald — visited the greenhouse several days apart."

Hamish dropped his gaze and studied his wineglass, as yet untouched on the coffee table in front of him. "The vast majority of human Zika infections produce no obvious symptoms. And that means —"

Tasha leaned forward as she beat him to the punch. "If we're going to find every case of Zika acquired on those school trips, we'll have to blood-test everyone who participated."

"Exactly," said Hamish. "Kids, adults, drivers . . ."

"We've got a team at the Health Unit who can arrange that," Zol said.

Tasha then described her afternoon phone conversation with Stephanie Polgar. "She's going to Zika-test the Vander Zalm green-house employees and any mosquitoes her traps catch inside the facility. She's making it a top priority. After that, she'll consider testing the wider Niagara community. Starting with women of childbearing age and their partners, for obvious reasons."

Tasha shifted her notebook on her lap as if uncertain how to phrase what she wanted to say next. She touched Zol's knee and said, "We may even have a sixth case of Zika acquired among those tulips."

"One of the polio cases or someone else?" Hamish asked.

"A polio case," Tasha said.

Hamish made no effort to mask his impatience. "Who is it? Why haven't you told us about this before?"

"Steady there, Hamish," Zol said, glancing at his watch. "Tasha's got an entire day's worth of interviews to tell us about. Let's give her some —"

"Actually," Tasha said, her eyes flashing at Hamish. "*I* shouldn't have to be telling *you*." She paused to let that sink in.

"What?" Hamish said.

Smiling at his momentary befuddlement, she said, "You've had the kid under your nose for the past four days."

CHAPTER 31

When the adults were somewhere in the middle of their noisy discussion in the sunroom, Travis rapped on Max's bedroom door. It was open as usual, but Travis knocked anyway and waited to be invited in. His mom, an army colonel, had a strict code of politeness she expected him to live by. And as far as Max could see, he mostly did.

"I need a break from algebra," Travis said.

Max tossed his pencil onto his desk and covered a yawn with his hand. "Me too. Do you wanna go downstairs for some OJ?"

Travis closed the door and spoke in a low voice. "I don't know, KB. Your dad sounds kind of upset down there."

There was a network of ducts in the house that circulated the cool air back to the furnace. The ducts carried every bit of sound from the sunroom downstairs to the landing outside the boys' bedrooms. Upstairs, they could hear what was going on downstairs, and vice versa. When Travis first came to stay, he showed Max how to cover the vent in the downstairs computer room with a piece of cardboard. After that, they could game and razz each other as much as they liked and no one could hear what they were saying.

"Your dad and Hamish have been arguing," Travis continued, "and I don't want to snag any spillover. We'd better stay up here out of the way."

"Nah, it's okay," Max told him. "Dad was reminding Uncle Hamish to be more respectful towards Tasha. That's all."

"Does Hamish have a problem with women? My mom says the army's full of guys that hate taking orders from women."

"Dad says Uncle Hamish's mom is an extreme narcissist — a female version of Donald Trump who's always treated her son like shit."

"And he takes it out on Natasha?"

"I dunno. Dad never said it in so many words."

Travis pointed to the sunroom below them. "This polio thing is getting pretty heavy, eh?"

"Yeah, it's on Dad's mind every minute. And Tasha's. And you know what Uncle Hamish is like. It's getting to him big time. Everything does."

"It's got Omar freaked too. He was on one of those bus trips they're talking about down there."

"I know. And he sat beside that girl who got sick. I'd be scared too."

"Do you think *we* need to worry?"

"About getting polio?" Max shook his head. "It won't help. Worrying doesn't make anything better. That's what the Dalai Lama says."

"What?"

"My dad quotes him a lot. Dad says a wise person knows that worrying steals the strength you need to deal with the present."

"Then we better check in with Omar. He's one worried dude."

Max glanced at his math text. He was only about halfway done the day's assignment. "Now?"

"Yeah. We weren't exactly helpful to him yesterday after school."

"I know."

But what, Max wondered, were they supposed to tell Omar?

Travis was looking serious. "We need to tell him something he can hold on to. Like his dad has, um, a perfectly good reason for keeping those meds on hand."

"And what would that be, Trav?"

"Maybe he needs them to put a sick animal out of its misery?"

"We gotta get real, here," Max said. "Omar's dad, our barber, is mixed up with some bad characters. So we gotta stay out of Omar's life as much as we can."

"We *are* out of it. Omar doesn't know anything about us except we're a couple of kids he plays *Fortnite* with. He doesn't even know our real names, just our IGNs."

"You're forgetting something."

"What?"

"He knows my dad's the doctor leading the polio investigation. Don't you remember? I told Omar that yesterday."

"Oh yeah." Travis rubbed at his neck with both hands. "And your dad's picture is all over the news. Ten times a day. Omar must know exactly who he is. "

Max rammed his pencil against the metal lid of his math set. "And sooner or later, Omar and his dad are going to put their facts together and figure out exactly who we are and how much we know."

"We gotta message Omar," Travis said. "Tell him to shut up about those notes from the warlord. And to shut up about the meds. His father needs to think no one knows he grabbed those drugs and stashed them in with his socks."

"Yeah. Least of all, the two of us."

"But what if Hosam uses them?" Travis said.

"You mean, what if he kills someone with them?"

Trav's birthmark was on fire. "Would we keep quiet about it forever?"

Max rammed his pencil against the desk until it broke in two. "I dunno. Maybe it would depend on who he kills."

Trav's eyes were bugging out of his skull. "Like, it's okay if he executes a warlord?"

"Shit, Trav, I dunno."

"Holy crap. Racking up a few bombs on *Fortnite* was just supposed to be something to do for kicks after school."

CHAPTER 32

"It took some prodding," Natasha told them, "but I think I got the truth out of Bhavjeet Singh Malik and his auntie this afternoon."

She took a tissue from her briefcase and wiped the sweat from her palms. Twice, her tall glass of Perrier had nearly slipped through her fingers and crashed onto the new coffee table she'd chosen when rejuvenating the sunroom.

Hamish's eyes narrowed. "What do you mean you *think* you got to the truth," he said, his cheeks still scarlet. "Either you did or you didn't. Which is it?"

She'd never seen Hamish in such a lather. For some reason, this polio thing had him spooked. Did he know one of the cases? If so, he hadn't said anything. She couldn't see how. The guy was status-conscious. She couldn't see him having ties to the collection of low-paid workers that this epidemic was preying upon.

"They were cagey with me, Hamish. That's what I mean."

"Hell's bells. The boy's a step away from the ICU and a ventilator, and they're being evasive?"

"Not everyone is comfortable with authority, Hamish," Zol said then gave her a smile. "No matter how benign a form it takes."

Sitting beside her on the couch, he pressed his arm gently into hers. As always, the warmth of him boosted her confidence.

Hamish gulped back the last of his wine. He opened his mouth as if to speak, but when he glanced at the two of them, a united front, he held his tongue.

"Anyway," Zol said, "what did you get out of the Singhs?"

She described visiting Bhavjeet on the medical ward at Caledonian Medical Centre after she'd interviewed Jamila's parents in the ICU with the help of the barber-surgeon from Syria. Bhavjeet's cousin and uncle were at work at their gas bar, so only the auntie was with the lad in his isolation room. She was a small woman with a sharp face, a missing front tooth, and suspicious eyes. Her pea-green shalwar kameez, though threadbare in places, had been expertly ironed. Her loose polyester scarf — its shade of maroon was particularly muddy — kept slipping off her head onto the back of her neck. It was irritating to watch her fidgeting with the silly thing. As Natasha's mother told anyone who would listen, there was nothing elegant about a garment that had to be constantly adjusted.

Natasha had started by asking if Bhavjeet had ever visited the Niagara Region. Before the teenager could get a word in, the auntie said that yes, she and her son had taken him to see the Falls about a month ago.

When she then asked if they'd visited anywhere else nearby — Niagara-on-the-Lake for shopping or a tour of a winery — Bhavjeet seemed either too shy or too intimidated by his auntie to respond. The answer from the auntie was a grim-faced *no*. The woman then looked Natasha up and down and made it obvious she didn't like what she saw: a South Asian woman, most probably Hindu, with a pixie haircut, bare legs, and a bare head. Auntie told Natasha that they had no time for shopping and, being a Muslim family, they did not drink alcohol in any form.

"But I kept digging," Natasha told Zol and Hamish.

"I should hope so," Hamish said. "That kid's Zika did not appear out of thin air. We have to know where he got it."

"Exactly," Natasha said. "And he's been in Canada too long to have acquired it anywhere else but in this country."

"What about that tulip greenhouse?" Zol said. "I don't suppose he ever set foot in there?"

"That's where they got cagey on me."

"How so?" said Zol.

"I asked them specifically about Vander Zalm Nurseries and the acres of tulips they have under plastic. I could tell Bhavjeet knew exactly what I was talking about, but before he said anything, his auntie cut in and said they hadn't visited any indoor gardens."

"Did you believe her?" Zol asked.

"The two of them carried on an animated discussion in Punjabi."

Zol chuckled. "Which they figured you couldn't understand?"

"Bhavjeet told his auntie they should be truthful with me because I was trying to make him better. Auntie said it wasn't anyone's business why they were buying second-quality tulips for resale, and the greenhouse had nothing to do with Bhavjeet's illness."

Zol put his head back and laughed. "And then you broke it to them?"

"I told them, in Punjabi, of course, that Bhavjeet's life depended on them answering my questions with the absolute truth. A bit of an exaggeration on my part, but . . ."

"How did they react?" Zol said.

"Bhavjeet didn't look surprised. He's a smart kid. He knew Sharma was a common Punjabi name and there was a good chance I would understand their language. The auntie looked at me as though I were some come kind of heathen Hindu ghost."

Zol was beaming. Even Hamish looked a little impressed.

"Well done," Zol said. "Did they have anything else to say?"

"Nothing other than verifying that it was Vander Zalm Nurseries, not some other tulip farm, that they'd visited."

"So," Hamish said, "that makes how many polio cases visiting that greenhouse?"

"Let's count the ones we know about," Natasha said. "Two

pupils and one teacher's aide from Cathcart School. Jamila and the bus driver from the high school. And Bhavjeet."

"Hmm," Zol said. "Six."

"Out of ten," Hamish said. "That's more than half of them."

"So," said Zol, throwing Hamish a no-nonsense look. "Vander Zalm's is definitely our Zika hotspot. But what about the Parvo-W?"

"I asked your Syrian barber friend to track Jamila's movements with her parents," Natasha told him. "We'll have to do that with the others and see if they intersect somewhere."

"That's going to be a huge task," Zol said.

"And," said Hamish, lifting his professorial index finger, "between poor memories and cagey personalities, how reliable is the tracking data going to be?"

"There's more work to be done than the three of us can handle," Zol said. "We'll need to expand our team."

Hamish looked puzzled. "How are you going to do that?"

"Hamish is right," Natasha said. "We all remember what happened that time they forced so-called *help* on us from Toronto."

Zol laughed. "Poor Wyatt Burr. He barely survived us."

"Or we him." She couldn't suppress a *tsk*. "But he brought it on himself." The guy was an arrogant so-and-so who rode in on his high horse from Toronto's ivory towers. In the middle of what looked like Canada's first human outbreak of mad cow disease, Dr. Wyatt Burr discounted Zol and Natasha's groundwork and local knowledge, then jumped to erroneous conclusions. He quickly made a complete mess of their investigation and exposed them to the wrong sort of international attention. In the end, they sorted the situation themselves.

"Don't worry," Zol said. "I wouldn't dream of asking Toronto for assistance." He paused and scrubbed at his five-o'clock stubble. "I think we should ask Jesse to join us."

"Jesse?" Natasha said, making no attempt to hide the surprise in her voice. "Zol, you must be kidding."

"Who's Jesse?" Hamish asked.

"Our receptionist," Natasha told him.

"That's not fair, Tasha," Zol said. "He's a lot more than a receptionist."

"Okay, so he fetches your coffee and helps us with our IT problems."

"Hey," Zol said. "Jesse completely revitalized our communication system with his nifty out-of-the-box approach to computer networking. Remember?"

"Okay, but that's a far cry from the footwork involved in field epidemiology."

"He's got the gift of the gab and a charming manner," Zol said. "You have to admit he's disarming. It would be impossible for him to come across as an intimidating government official."

"Which of our polio cases are you going to assign him to?" Natasha said.

Zol thought for a moment. "Let's give him one of the deceased. The young janitor who worked at Limeridge Mall. What was his name?"

"Darryl Oxman," she told him. "I guess Jesse can't do too much damage if we give him Darryl. The poor guy lived alone, and there were no next of kin listed in his hospital record."

"Okay, then," Zol said. "We'll send him to Limeridge tomorrow where he can speak to Darryl's employer. It's a long shot, but maybe Jesse can dig up something on the guy's movements over the past few weeks."

An ear-piercing siren filled the house, and footsteps thundered down the stairs. In a flash of plaid shirts and sneakers, Max and Travis raced into the sunroom

"Dad," shouted Max. "The fire alarm. What's going on?"

And then they saw it: a cloud of black smoke billowing from the kitchen.

"Oh my God," Zol said, looking at his watch in disbelief. "I forgot about the Wellington. The puff pastry must be in flames. Shit."

They raced into the kitchen, coughing and fanning the dense haze in front of them with their arms. Travis grabbed the fire extinguisher beside the stove. Zol opened the oven door. Flames leapt toward him.

Zol jumped back. "Go ahead, Son," he told Travis, shouting to make himself heard above the wail of the alarm. "The salmon is ruined at this point. But stand well back."

Beaming as if this was the best fun ever, Travis pulled the extinguisher's trigger and sprayed the oven with gusto. In seconds, the flames disappeared, but the boy was enjoying himself too much to stop. By the time he'd emptied the canister, he'd covered the entire oven with three layers of foam.

Max and Natasha opened the doors and were working on the windows when Zol climbed on a chair, reached toward the ceiling, and pressed the silence button on the shrieking smoke detector.

"Damn," Zol said, "I can't get this thing to shut up."

"There's too much smoke," Hamish said bluntly. "It's the same model we installed in our new kitchen. When there's this much smoke, you can't turn the thing off. No matter what you do, the fire department gets called." Looking much too proud of his insider knowledge, he added, "And there's no calling them off. They'll be here any minute . . . sirens, trucks, hoses. The whole shebang."

CHAPTER 33

Natasha couldn't believe the hullabaloo caused by Zol's flaming Salmon Wellington. The poor thing was not only flambéed but reduced to a solid brick of charcoal. Never before had she experienced the frenzied and cacophonous yet thoroughly professional onslaught of a fire brigade responding to a call. Before Zol could stop them, the firefighters had unspooled their hoses and were storming the front door with axes in hand. Despite Zol's protestations that the kitchen fire was now out and had been limited to the interior of his oven, the firefighters insisted that everyone vacate the premises immediately.

While Natasha shivered with the others on the front lawn, five men and one woman in helmets and heavy gear spent several minutes searching the house from top to bottom. Presumably, they were looking for an ongoing source of smoke and flames. Much to Zol's obvious relief, they left their hoses outside. Hamish, flapping his arms and shifting his feet in a vain effort to keep warm, gave a wary eye to the coils looped across the grass. He pronounced, most unhelpfully, that if the firefighters turned those hoses on, Zol's kitchen would be destroyed as quickly as Hamish's own had been on Friday night when his brand new pipes burst.

After a while, four of the firefighters exited the house through the front door. They told Zol they were satisfied that the danger had passed and nothing further needed to be done. The female firefighter repaired directly to one of the firetrucks. She told her colleagues she was getting started on the paperwork, an essential component of the proceedings the men seemed pleased to leave to her.

The tallest member of the brigade, the unit commander, gathered Natasha and the others on the front steps. His name, d'Onofrio, was emblazoned in large, luminous letters on his helmet and on the front and back of his heavy jacket. Natasha shivered when she realized the reason for such clear identification. She pictured a well-toned body collapsed on a heap of flaming debris.

Officer d'Onofrio cleared his throat and asked, "Which of you is the homeowner?"

Zol put up his hand and said meekly, "I am. And, sorry to say, the inattentive chef."

D'Onofrio chuckled. "Except for some charring inside the oven, there appears to be no harm done."

"Not even smoke damage?" Hamish asked. He seemed disappointed by the clean bill of health delivered so swiftly.

"The place will smell smoky for a few hours, but I don't think it'll be permanent," said the officer. "But I gotta warn you, that fire extinguisher made one right mess of your kitchen, and your drapes will need a good dry cleaning." He turned to Zol. "Is that your pipe I saw in the room that looks onto the Escarpment, sir?"

"Yes," Zol said. "Afraid so."

"So you'll be used to the smell of smoke in your house." D'Onofrio paused, coughed into his fist, then added, "You don't ever smoke in bed, do you, sir?"

"Never," Zol said. "Only in the sunroom. Where you found my pipe."

The officer turned to Max and Travis. "Video games and smoking don't mix, boys. We see a number of fires started when cigarettes are left unattended by distracted gamers." He chuckled again and his eyes twinkled. "Especially gamers who play *Fortnite*. It's particularly absorbing."

The boys' eyes grew huge. Travis shook his head vigorously, and Max said, "We don't smoke, sir." The earnest tone in his voice seemed a little forced.

"Well, that's good then." The look in the officer's eye made Natasha wonder if he'd found smoking materials in one of the boys' rooms. Cigarettes? Weed? Or had Max *borrowed* one of his father's pipes? It wasn't her business, and she certainly wouldn't push the issue. She was, however, going to keep her eyes open.

The last two firefighters came out through the front door, each with a small device in his hand. Officer d'Onofrio stepped to the side, conferred with them briefly, and turned to Zol. "It's safe to go back in now. My men have verified that carbon monoxide has not accumulated in any of the rooms." He looked at Hamish hugging his chest against the cooling night air. "They closed the doors and windows, so you'll warm up fairly quickly."

As Hamish and the boys dashed into the house, Officer d'Onofrio said to Zol, "Do I recognize you from the . . . from the news, sir?"

"Perhaps," Zol said, reluctant to elaborate.

"Regarding the, um . . . the polio epidemic?"

"Guilty as charged," Zol said, looking around us as if worried this incident at his home might also make the news and perhaps further complicate his relationship with the public and the media.

"My sister's nanny was diagnosed with the polio and is fighting for her life in intensive care at Caledonian Medical Centre," said d'Onofrio.

"Goodness," Zol said, "I'm sorry to hear that." He gestured toward Natasha and continued, "We at the Health Unit are doing everything we can to bring this outbreak to an end."

"I don't mind telling you," the officer replied, "our entire family is terrified. Blessica attends all our family functions. Any of us could come down with it next. My sister has two little kids and I've got three."

Zol looked at Natasha and lifted his eyebrows. He turned to the officer. "The good news is, we haven't seen any polio transmission between family members. As far as we can tell, the micro-organisms causing this infection are not capable of being passed from one person to another."

"That sounds a bit weird," said d'Onofrio, frowning. "So how did Blessica come down with it?"

"That's the big question we're working on," Zol said. "Day and night."

"Which explains the salmon dish catching on fire," Natasha said. "We were so busy reviewing some exciting new information we collected today that we forgot about our dinner baking in the oven."

"Well," d'Onofrio said. "Tiffany has been going crazy cleaning her house with bleach and Lysol ever since the ambulance took Blessica to the hospital."

"Tiffany?" Natasha said. "That's your sister?"

"Yeah, Tiffany Fonseca. She married a guy from the Azores. My Italian parents weren't too happy at first, but he's turned out to be a good guy."

Natasha was suddenly struck with how cold she'd become. They'd been standing outside for going on half an hour wearing only indoor clothing. "Let's go inside, officer. I'm freezing, and I'd like to ask you a few questions. If I may."

"Good idea," Zol said. He took Natasha by the arm and added, "I'm sorry, Officer d'Onofrio, I should have introduced you earlier. This is Ms. Natasha Sharma. She's our chief investigator on the polio file."

Inside, Zol led the officer into the sunroom. Natasha grabbed her coat from the front-hall closet where she heard Hamish running the water in the adjacent bathroom. She pulled on her coat and joined the two men. She found her pen and notebook lying where she'd dropped them on the coffee table.

"We've been unable to get hold of Blessica's friends, family, or employer," Natasha told the firefighter, who'd undone the top buttons of his jacket and was holding his helmet in his lap. "One of my colleagues visited the address associated with her health card a couple of times but was unable to find anyone at home."

"That's no surprise," d'Onofrio said. "Tiffany's husband commutes every day to Toronto and never gets home till late. He's a lawyer on Bay Street. The Royal Bank. And Tiffany is busy at her shop. Ten hours a day, six days a week."

"She has her own business?" Natasha asked.

"Yes, and as the wedding season approaches, things heat up for her." He paused, looked down at his boots, then added, "She's been feeling incredibly guilty that she hasn't been able to visit Blessica in the hospital. It's not that she doesn't care."

Natasha nodded empathetically then asked, "What sort of business is your sister in?"

"Sorry, I should have said. My sister is a florist. She owns Blossoms by Tiffany. It's on Sydenham Street. In downtown Dundas."

Really? A flower shop? She could tell Zol was also thinking about a connection to Vander Zalm Nurseries.

She grabbed a tissue and coughed into it several times before the harsh tickle in her throat settled. She couldn't see any smoke in the air, but she could certainly smell it, and her breathing passages were rebelling.

"Where does she get her flowers from?" she asked him.

D'Onofrio shrugged. "From all over the world, I guess. Why? Is it important? Does this polio thing have something to do with flowers?"

"Not directly," Zol said, "but it's important we talk to the families swept up in this outbreak. We have to piece a lot of information together if we're going achieve the results everyone expects of us."

D'Onofrio nodded and fished a cellphone from deep inside a trouser pocket. He tapped the device a few times and held the screen for Natasha to see. "Here's Tiffany's number and the address of her shop. I know she'll want to help you as much as she can. And it can't hurt to tell her you were talking to her big brother Vince."

He looked over at Zol and winked. "You don't have to mention the incinerated salmon."

After they'd said their goodbyes at the front door, d'Onofrio paused at the threshold and looked serious. "So, it's okay to tell my wife to lay off the Lysol? She's been —"

"Yes," Natasha told him. "No need to go crazy with the disinfecting. I'll tell your sister the same when I visit her tomorrow."

They waved the officer off, and as Zol was closing the door, Hamish came out of the bathroom. His face looked freshly scrubbed and his hands glowed bright pink. They'd been subjected to fifteen minutes of hot water and soap. A ritual cleansing usually put him a good mood.

"What are we going to eat?" he asked. "I'm starving."

"It'll have to be takeout, I'm afraid," Zol said.

"Fine with me," Hamish said. "Do you want me to call that Thai place on Upper James? My treat?"

"Thanks, Hamish," Zol said. "We love Thai. And please order enough for five."

"Five?" Hamish said. "You're *that* hungry?"

"The boys love pad Thai," Zol said. "And I think they earned it tonight, don't you?"

"Yeah, yeah," Hamish answered absently. "Sure thing."

Feeling almost warm again, Natasha hung up her coat and removed the scarf from a pocket. She draped it over her shoulders and secured it around her neck with a quick knot. She turned toward the stairs. "If you excuse me for a few minutes, I have a phone call to make before the food comes. And don't worry about choosing for me. I like everything that place has on the menu."

As she climbed the stairs and headed toward the privacy of their bedroom, Natasha's mind was full of questions raised by the revelation that Blessica Velasquez's employer owned a busy flower shop smack in the middle of downtown Dundas.

Had Blessica acquired Zika virus infection because, like the school kids, she'd visited Vander Zalm Nurseries? And if so, had she gone on a tulip-buying trip with her employer, who may also have acquired the infection? And had Tiffany's children gone with them?

Or, had Tiffany Fonseca unwittingly introduced a few Zika-infected Aedes albopictus mosquitoes to Dundas in a shipment of tulips from Vander Zalm Nurseries? If so, had Blessica been bitten at the flower shop? Or had Tiffany brought an arrangement of mosquito-infested tulips to her house, and that's where Blessica — and potentially other family members — had acquired the Zika virus?

How close were Blessica and the other Filipina nanny also hospitalized with the polio, Emmalita Pina? Had Emmalita acquired her Zika infection the same way Blessica had?

Of course, tulip-mediated Zika might not be limited to Tiffany Fonseca and her household. If her Dundas flower shop was infested with Aedes albopictus, who amongst her many customers had been bitten? And what about Vander Zalm Nurseries's other wholesale customers? How far afield from Virgil, Ontario, did the nursery ship its tulips? Natasha felt nauseated at the thought of Zika-infected mosquitoes breaking out of tulip buds everywhere from Sarnia to Shawinigan, Windsor to Waskesiu.

The more questions she asked herself the faster her heart thumped against her chest. At the top of the stairs, her stomach queasy and her lungs gasping for air, she whipped off her scarf to fend off escalating claustrophobia. She had a phone call to make.

And tomorrow, she would be standing on the doorstep of Blossoms by Tiffany the moment it opened. But before that, a stop at a drugstore for a bottle of insect repellent containing plenty of DEET. There was no way she was going to let herself get bitten by any hungry Aedes Tigers lurking inside Tiffany's tulips.

Not in her condition.

CHAPTER 34

After that exhausting and emotional Tuesday morning at the hospital, Hosam retreated to his desk in·the afternoon and tried working on his studies. His mind was in such a whirl that he was unable to concentrate. Nothing stuck. He read one full chapter of his *Toronto Notes* and could remember none of it. In the late afternoon, while Leila was still working on her clients, and Omar was social-networking on his laptop, Hosam gave up trying to study. He closed the text, descended the stairs, and put together a light supper for the three of them. None of them had appetites, and much of the modest dinner went to waste. Omar quickly retreated to his room, and while Hosam cleared the table, Leila set to Facebooking on the tablet that had consumed six months of their savings.

He had once hoped Leila's nightly Facebook ritual might defend her from the loneliness Hosam could see was draining the life from her soul. He saw little evidence of it working. Before the war, she'd been a lively, confident professional with a vast network of friends and admirers. In the aftermath of Farah's death and their flight to Gaziantep, she'd gradually regained her smile and her confidence. In the refugee camp, her skills as a professional, a networker, and an organizer found many outlets. But here in Canada, the long hours she worked in their windowless garage were robbing her of the opportunity to make the friends and connections that were the foundation of her vitality. The vicious attack in the barbershop and the Caliph's ensuing threats and demands had her terrified that their lives in Canada would never be happy or fulfilling.

"Habibi," she said as she dried the dishes he had stacked on the rack, "I never expected to feel this way, but I wish we were back in Gaziantep. Life was not easy there, but I had plenty of friends, and I was able to continue my profession without hiding like a criminal." A string of sobs racked her shoulders. "And . . . Omar was not . . . living under a sentence of death . . . after an innocent school trip."

"Omar is going to be okay, Habibti. The woman from the health department assured me that all the polio cases had the misfortune of catching two rare viruses simultaneously. The chance that our son —"

"But what is to say he has not already caught that second virus? He sat beside poor Jamila Khateb during that entire bus trip."

Having no rational answer, Hosam said nothing. Omar had visited the health department this afternoon, and now it was the stressful matter of awaiting the result of the Zika test. Hosam opened his arms and embraced his wife with as much encouragement as he could muster. With nothing left for either of them to say, she returned to her laptop and he went upstairs to his desk.

He opened his *Toronto Notes* to the chapter he had tried and failed to absorb this afternoon. It covered a subject to which he had paid little academic attention during those years he was qualifying as a surgeon: "Assessing the Patient with Anxiety and Depression." He tried reading the opening paragraph, but again the words danced meaninglessly in front of him. The incriminating appointments in Jamila's calendar, which he'd found so easily on her phone during the bus ride home from the hospital, pawed relentlessly at his conscience. But as he and Leila had discussed while they were setting the table for supper, the procedures she'd performed on Jamila could have nothing to do with the girl's polio.

The mosquitoes transmitting Zika virus were an hour's drive away in Niagara, and Leila's equipment was brand new, including the sterilizer she used without fail. There was no denying that his decision to cover up Jamila's four recent appointments at Leila's office was dishonest. But it was a white lie that would keep Leila out of jail and allow the family to prosper in this expensive and complicated land.

He heard the kitchen telephone ring four times before Leila answered it and called up to him, "Hosam, it is for you. Ms. Sharma from the health department."

His hands were slick with sweat by the time he descended the stairs and took the receiver from his wife.

"Hello . . . Hosam Khousa here."

The competent young woman he had met earlier today introduced herself and wasted no time in getting to the matters at hand.

"Yes," he told her in response to her first query, "Omar, he did have the blood test today. The people at your health department were quite helpful. When will the result be available?"

"I will put a rush on it, which means we should get the result by Friday. How does that sound?"

He glanced at Leila, who was leaning against the counter wringing her hands. "Thank you, Ms. Sharma. My wife wishes it could be processed instantly, but we are not expecting the impossible."

"Did you have any luck with Mr. and Mrs. Khateb?"

His tongue turned to parchment. "L-luck?"

"I mean, were they able to give you a detailed account of Jamila's movements over the past three or four weeks?"

"She . . . she does not lead a complicated life. The parents are rarely leaving the house without her. She must navigate every situation for them."

"Yes, a lack of English must make this new life of theirs quite difficult."

Hoping to find encouragement, Hosam looked into Leila's eyes. He saw only distress. "Jamila's movements were only involving her school, her job at the pet store, and grocery shopping trips with her parents, Ms. Sharma."

"What about her doctor's appointment?" she asked.

Hosam knees threatened to fail him, and he sank onto the nearest chair. "Sorry?"

"You see, Dr. Khousa, Jamila's supervisor at the pet store said the girl called from her mobile to say she'd been held up at a doctor's appointment and would be fifteen minutes late for work. That was only a few days before she became ill."

"I did not find any such appointment listed in her phone."

"And her parents mentioned nothing about visiting a doctor?"

"They did not. As I said —"

"I need you to check again because this is important. We do need the name of that doctor. Jamila's appointment could have an important bearing on her case." She paused, then said, "How familiar are you with smartphones, Dr. Khousa? Perhaps you need someone to help you with Jamila's calendar."

Hosam's heart threatened to leap out of his chest. He pictured himself in the operating theatre, forcing himself to maintain a steady hand while the patient on the table threatened to bleed to death. Now, as then, he took long, slow breaths in through his nose. "It is similar to the model I used every day in Aleppo. I am thoroughly familiar with the calendar application."

He forced himself to take three more slow breaths. Even if Dr. Szabo or Miss Sharma insisted on having a look at Jamila's phone, they wouldn't understand a word of what was on it. Everything was in Arabic. Well, everything except for one entry on Facebook where she told her friends what a difficult time she was having with her teeth.

"Well, please speak with her parents once more and specifically ask about the afternoon of the Friday before she became ill. See if they can tell you where she was at that time. Perhaps you might try interviewing the parents separately. Perhaps the mother knows something that Jamila didn't want her father to know about."

"Yes, Ms. Sharma, the Friday afternoon before last. I have taken note of it."

"I'm worried she might have been up to something else. Not a doctor's appointment but something she was ashamed of that exposed her to the Parvo-W and is playing a vital role in our outbreak."

When the persistent young woman urged him once again to speak with the parents and said she'd be in touch again tomorrow, Hosam's hand shook so badly he could barely return the telephone to its cradle.

CHAPTER 35

On Wednesday morning, Zol awoke to the vague smell of old smoke and the sound of retching. The latter was coming from the bathroom. He reached across the bed for Tasha. She wasn't there, but her pillow was still warm.

He debated with himself about checking on her versus leaving her be. On the rare occasions he found himself vomiting, what he wanted most was to be left alone. The only thing worse than heaving your dry stomach into the toilet was someone watching you do it.

After three more paroxysms echoed from the bathroom, he opened the door a crack and peeked in. Poor Tasha. Her favourite bathrobe was bunched across her back, and she was kneeling in front of the toilet as if in prayer.

He pushed the door open and squatted beside her. Pressing his arm firmly around her waist, he said, "My poor darling. Not that damned gastro again." He'd been sure the cryptosporidiosis thing they'd both had several weeks ago was well behind them. They'd succumbed to the allure of fresh fruit out of season — parasite-infested raspberries from Guatemala — and had paid the price.

He ran a facecloth under the tap, wrung out the excess warm water, and handed it to her as he helped her to her feet.

"I'm so sorry," she said, "I didn't mean to wake you. But this time, I knew I wouldn't make the other bathroom in time."

After she'd wiped her face, he took the facecloth from her and rinsed it with more warm water before returning it. "Don't worry about me. I'm just sorry you're having a relapse."

She gave him a wry smile and wiped her face again. He left her to brush her teeth and clean herself up behind the closed door. What had she meant by *this time*? Had she been ill for a few days without telling him?

He returned to bed and checked his phone for an email from the province's public health directorate in Toronto. They often sent alerts and updates overnight, but this morning's message held only housekeeping issues. A good start to the day.

When Tasha returned to the bedroom, she looked exhausted. Huge, dark circles had formed around her eyes. "I think you better take the day off," he told her. "It will speed your recovery. Last time we both went back to work too soon. Remember? This polio thing has been hard on us both. Perhaps you're not getting enough sleep."

"I'm not sick, Zol. I'm fine."

"You don't look fine. Well . . . I mean, you will always look lovely to me, but right now —"

"I don't need a day off. I'll feel better in a few minutes."

"How can you be so sure?"

"I've been feeling like this for the past week or so. You haven't noticed because I've been making it to the other bathroom in time."

"Do you think you need another round of antimicrobials? There's a repeat left on the script Hamish gave us."

"I don't think antimicrobials are indicated."

"Just rest, then?"

"Zol, darling, have you noticed what I've been drinking lately?"

"You opened that bottle of Sauvignon Blanc last night. We all had some, even Hamish. It was pretty good."

She shook her head. "I had sparkling water. I've been drinking quite a bit of it lately."

He thought for a moment and remembered the dozen green bottles in the recycling bin. Perrier. Women drank sparkling mostly when they were dieting or they were . . .

He remembered her almost jumping off the bed last night when his thumb had grazed her nipple.

Was she?

Her lips were forming an impish grin.

"Oh my God," he said. "You're pregnant." He jumped out of bed and took her in his arms. "This is wonderful. Absolutely fantastic."

"You're pleased?"

"Of course I am. Oh Tasha darling, I'm so happy."

She kissed the base of his neck then pulled away. "The timing is terrible."

"Who cares about the timing, love."

"My mother."

"For heaven's sake, you always say we shouldn't let her judge us. Or interfere in our affairs."

"But this is different."

"How so?"

She had no answer, just dark eyes brimming with tears and a quivering lower lip. He took her into his arms again and held her close. As always, he loved the warmth of her — emotional and physical.

After a long, quiet moment, he whispered into her ear. "How far along are you?"

"Seven weeks, today."

"Oh my! Not that it matters, but I thought we had this birth control thing covered. We *are* in the business of helping families plan ahead for healthy parenthood."

"I've been thinking about that. I must not have absorbed my birth control pills when I had that ten days of diarrhea. I guess they slid right through me without doing their job."

He felt the coolness of her tears on his neck. "I hope those are tears of joy because I'm so happy I could burst."

"Really?"

"Of course. Along with Max, you're the best thing that has ever happened to me. And now, with another little Max or Maxine on the way? What could be better?"

"Maybe if you weren't so horny, I would have recovered completely from my gastro before —"

"I'm much more than horny, Tasha. I'm absolutely besotted."

"But still, the timing is terrible. What if —"

"Let's look at this rationally. You're seven weeks now. The wedding is in another . . . How many days is it?"

"Seven weeks plus three days."

"That means you'll be fourteen weeks on our wedding day. Not even showing."

"But what about this morning sickness?"

"It will be over by then, don't worry."

"My mother says she vomited for six months straight when she was carrying me."

"And you believe her? You know we have to divide everything she says by ten to get even close to the truth."

"So you're not upset?"

"Upset? For heaven's sake, I'm ecstatic. But look, if you're worried about the timing, we can get married this week. A private civil ceremony here at home or at City Hall. Or anywhere else you'd like. We could invite a couple of witnesses and swear them to secrecy." He loosened his embrace so that he could gaze fully into her face. "Would that make you feel better?"

"Absolutely not. If my mother ever found out, she'd see it as a shotgun wedding and would never let me forget it."

"Fine, then. We'll keep the wedding plans as they are. How tight-fitting is your dress?"

"That's why I've been avoiding Dinesh Ramsay, Mummyji's dressmaker. I was afraid he'd notice me filling in as the weeks went by, and he'd tell Mummyji what was going on. He's a terrible gossip."

"Will you be able to find something that suits the occasion and will accommodate" — he winked and made air quotes with his hands — "this *filling in* of ours?"

"I think I found the perfect dress on the internet."

"Well, go for it, my darling. In the knowledge that your groom is absolutely thrilled you'll be blossoming inside it." He squeezed her again. "Now, I want you to take this morning off. I'll make that trip to Tiffany's flower shop."

"No, no. I'm perfectly capable of —"

"Ms. Sharma, the boss insists. You're having the morning off. With the option of the entire day if you need it."

"Zol, it's not necessary."

"Maybe not, but I'd like the chance to test my skills in the field. I've been spending too much time in my office lately."

"Well . . ." she said with a cheeky look in her eyes. "I suppose I can work from home this morning if the boss insists. But I've got to visit that refugee women's cooperative at lunchtime. You know, the place where Rima Khateb, Jamila's mother, has been helping out."

"That's today?"

"I need to be there by noon or so."

"Even though we've pretty well ruled out foodborne transmission?"

"For the optics, if nothing else. The other women will be antsy about Rima's presence among them. And who knows? I might find an important tidbit among the hummus and tabouleh." She grabbed his arms and pressed her thumbs into his biceps. "But before you set foot in Tiffany's flower shop, you have to promise me something."

"What?"

"That you'll pick up some DEET and do a proper job of applying it before you enter that shop. If Tiffany's got Zika-infected Aedes albopictus buzzing around her flowers, I don't want you getting bitten and infecting me and Junior here," she told him, releasing her grip and patting her tummy.

"Yes, ma'am."

CHAPTER 36

At the Health Unit, Zol took the back stairs two at a time, tossed his Stetson onto the rack, and dropped his briefcase on his desk. On the drive over, he could think about nothing but the baby in Tasha's womb. They'd talked about having a child at a time that was best for Tasha's career. But now that it looked like an infant would be arriving before the end of the year, the practical issues whirled inside his head. The only way he was going to accomplish anything at work today was to knuckle down and concentrate.

He picked up the phone and buzzed the reception desk. "Good morning, Jesse, it's —"

"Hey, Dr. Zed. What can I do you for?"

"I need to talk to you. I mean . . . in person . . . here, in my office."

"Uh-oh. Sounds serious."

"Nothing to worry about, Jesse. It's good serious."

"Be right there, Dr. Zed. Do you need a coffee?"

"Maybe later."

Thirty seconds later, Jesse was rapping on the door and sliding into the room. As usual, his shirt was loud. A Hawaiian number, today. And his earrings were long. Blue feathers that matched the birds on the shirt. At least he'd shaved today. When he tried the stubble thing, it was always too patchy for a good look.

Zol invited him to take a seat but Jesse eyed the chair with suspicion and said, "How much trouble am I in, Dr. Zed? Maybe I should just stand and . . . and take it like a man."

"Relax, Jesse. I'm offering you a promotion."

The young man's eyes widened in amazement, and he settled his lanky form onto the chair without a word.

"The polio file is getting more complicated by the day," Zol told him, "and I'd like you to join our investigative team."

"Are you serious? That would be wicked. Majorly wicked."

"Tasha tells me you've been following the outbreak closely and you understand a good deal of the science involved."

"I've always been fascinated by bugs, Dr. Zed. I had a butterfly and beetle collection when I was a kid. The other boys thought I was . . ." The innocent smile vanished from his face. "Well, you can probably guess." He stared at his hands in his lap and picked at his well-bitten fingernails.

Watching Jesse's earrings twirl with every movement of his head, Zol imagined there were many things the other boys had taunted him about. Jesse was a talented guy who'd been born . . . well . . . different. There was no nicer way to put it. And it was clear he'd experienced more than his share of shaming and name-calling.

"I'm looking for someone with plenty of smarts who has the insight to look beyond the meagre amount of info we've assembled so far."

"I've never been known for conformity," he said, his eyes brightening a little as he fidgeted with an earring.

"If we're going to piece this polio thing together and bring the outbreak to a halt, we have to find the source of the Parvo-W."

"You're looking for the one obscure thing that links all the cases, right?"

Zol nodded. "That's the guiding principle of epidemiological investigation, but —"

"I'll bet it's something kind of weird. Outside the mainstream. Which is why it hasn't turned up yet. I'm guessing it's something embarrassing or shameful. Something a person would want to keep underground."

"We've found it impossible to interview any of the cases properly," Zol told him. "Two lived alone and died quickly, three are still in medically induced comas, and all of the next of kin have been cagey or difficult to contact."

Zol reviewed with Jesse how the outbreak clustered around the Beasley, Limeridge, and Dundas sections of the city. When he described Tasha's theory that word-of-mouth was likely how the three neighbourhoods became linked, Jesse agreed that her theory fit the underground angle. "My guess is we're looking for something illegal, Dr. Zed. Or something on the black market. Whatever it is, it seems to involve people living on the margins."

Zol and Tasha had already noticed that the ten people afflicted by the outbreak were financially vulnerable. Until now, that had not struck him as particularly unusual. In public health, almost every issue came down to living standards. Poor people lived shorter and less healthy lives than rich people.

"When I looked at their profiles," Jesse continued, "I noticed they were all earning minimum wage or less. And working for the kind of employers who don't provide benefits."

"I'm not going to say anything more, Jesse. I want you to use your own instincts, your unique point of view, and maybe your computer skills."

"Where do you want me to start?"

Zol handed him a photocopied page from Tasha's notebook. It outlined the precious little they knew about Darryl Oxman, the young janitor from Limeridge Mall. "This fellow was case number seven and the second death. He lived alone and was alienated from his family, which makes tracing his story a particular challenge."

Jesse took the page and studied it eagerly, pumped by the challenge.

Zol said, "I want you to interview his employer at the mall. See what you can discover about him. Maybe the boss can point you toward Darryl's friends, hobbies, habits — good and bad."

"If this Darryl guy had a secret life, his boss probably doesn't have a clue," Jesse said, then quickly looked down.

Zol paused then cleared his throat, knowing he was about to tread on shaky ground. "Before you go, Jesse, I'd like to give you one last word of advice."

Jesse looked up and smiled warmly. "It's okay, Dr. Zed. I'm going to change the shirt and ditch the earrings."

Five minutes later, the phone buzzed. Zol picked it up.

"Hey, Dr. Zed."

"You're still here?"

"I asked Amanda to cover the phones for me, but she can't start until eight thirty. Dr. Wakefield is on the line. He sounds super anxious. Can I put him through?"

"Of course."

"We've got another one," Hamish said.

"Where?"

"In ICU. I'm with her now. She had a respiratory arrest in the ambulance on the way to Emerg. They've got her stabilized on a ventilator, but she's one sick lady."

"Give me the thumbnail, will you?"

"Asian female, thirty-five. First name Thuy, last name Nguyen." Hamish spelled the names out then continued. "It's impossible to get much out of the sister who came with her in the ambulance. The woman's hysterical. But from what I can make out, the patient first showed signs of illness three or four days ago. She immigrated from Vietnam fifteen years back and now runs a nail salon with her husband and the sister. You'll never guess where it is."

"Okay, I'm not guessing."

"Dundas. I checked the place out on Google Maps. It's a hole-in-the-wall on Sydenham Street."

"You're kidding."

"Of course not. Why would I be kidding?"

"Sorry. Figure of speech. How close is it to Tiffany's flower shop?"

"Three doors down."

"Holy shit. Maybe we're getting somewhere. Any connection to Vander Zalm's Nurseries?"

"Hard to say. The hysterical sister has never heard of Virgil or Niagara-on-the-Lake. And she told me the patient visited the Falls only once, and that was a long time ago."

"The Zika link must be with Tiffany. I'll check it out when I visit her shop this morning."

"I thought Natasha was —"

"Something's come up."

"Another polio case?"

"Something else. Listen, I need you to trace every move your patient made over the past three weeks."

"We're expecting the husband to arrive shortly. I'm hoping he speaks English and won't be blubbering like the sister."

"See if your woman's been into something dodgy or frankly illegal. There's a good chance our Parvo-W is eluding us because its source is underground. It may involve a conspiracy of some sort."

"Exactly how am I going to do that, Zol? If they're using their nail salon as a front for laundering money, dealing drugs, or importing endangered species, they're certainly not going to enlighten me with the details."

"They might if you play your super-specialist doctor card and put the fear of God into them. Tell them if they're not completely truthful with you, that woman is going to stay on a breathing machine for the rest of her life. And the blubbering sister is going to be next. And their kids, if they have any."

"Are you serious, Szabo?"

"Not quite. But it *is* time we played a bit of hardball, Hamish. The polite, light-touch approach hasn't got us anywhere. One way or another, we have to find where that goddamned Parvo-W is coming from."

CHAPTER 37

Shortly after nine o'clock on Wednesday morning, the receptionist buzzed Hosam into the intensive care unit at CUMC. He'd slept poorly last night, but that no longer mattered. Now his heart swelled with the familiar thrill of being part of a medical community. He was not a surgeon here, of course, but yesterday they had awarded him official status as the Arabic interpreter for both Jamila and Mo. He was cautioned to share medical information only with bona fide family members and warned that the patients' charts were strictly off limits. The charge nurse suggested that if his efforts proved satisfactory, the hospital would call on him in future to interpret for other families. As a volunteer, he knew there would be no money in the work, but that did not matter. He would be part of the hospital team and treated to a fly-on-the-wall view of how medicine was practised in Canada among the sickest of the sick.

He peeked first into Jamila's room. She was still connected to the ventilator and sedated to the point of unconsciousness. As no one was visiting her, there was no reason for him to linger. He headed toward Mo's room where a few paces short of the open door he heard a man and a woman arguing in Arabic. He could not catch everything they were saying, but it sounded like the woman was offering an ultimatum rather than sympathy and encouragement.

The last words Hosam heard the woman say were "end up like that stupid barber, you *will* keep your mouth shut."

"Hey, it's my doc from Aleppo," Mo said when he spotted Hosam standing at the door. Mo's gaze darted nervously around the room. "Come in. Saramin was just leaving."

Saramin threw Mo a dirty look then eyed Hosam up and down as if expecting to find something she could criticize.

"The nurse wants to change my dressings," Mo said. "I told her she had to wait till you got here."

Hosam gave Saramin a brief nod then stepped into the room. He gestured to Mo's bandages. "Have you ... um, seen your fingers yet?"

"Shit, no." Mo's face was drawn, and whoever had shaved him this morning had done a poor job of it. They had probably used an electric razor with a dull cutter head and missed half his whiskers as a result.

Saramin drew close and leaned into Hosam's ear. "The Caliph has another job for you. Be prepared for tomorrow night."

He looked around Mo's room. Its walls were mostly windows and glass panels on three sides. Doctors and nurses were striding by in a never-ending stream. This was a strikingly public place that felt secure.

"Sorry," he said, surprising himself with his boldness, "the barbershop will be reopening tomorrow. After ten hours on my feet, I will be exhausted. Too tired for a night job. I would not perform well for you."

"Listen to you," Saramin said, her voice full of contempt. "You seem to think you have a choice."

"As I said, not tomorrow night." He had no idea how long he would be able to fend off the Caliph's demands. But this was a start, and it felt good.

Saramin scowled and threw back her hair. She was on the point of jabbing his chest with her index finger when they both sensed movement at the doorway.

She lowered her hand and pretended to look for something in her handbag.

"Hello, nurse," Mo said. "This my doctor."

Hosam touched his palm to his chest and told the nurse, "I am not his doctor. I am his interpreter."

The nurse — blond, freckled, and trim — consulted a folded piece of paper from her pocket. "Mr. Khousa?"

"That is correct."

"Mo was insistent that you be here when I unwrapped his dressings for the first time."

"He worries about his fingers," Hosam told her. He lowered his voice and added, "He is terrified he might not be having any left."

The nurse smiled awkwardly and turned to a side table on wheels where a dressing tray was waiting for her.

"Time for me to split," Saramin said in English. "I'm no good with blood." She gave Hosam a piercing, cold-hearted look the nurse could not see, then said in Arabic, "The Caliph will be in touch. Like I said . . . be prepared."

After readying everything on her tray and donning a pair of sterile gloves, the nurse wheeled her table next to Mo's bed and motioned for him to put both of his hands on a sterile drape. She forced a nervous smile and asked Mo which hand he would like her to start with. Hosam translated the question and Mo's reluctant answer: the left.

Sitting on the edge of the bed, Mo winced several times and swore loudly in Arabic as the nurse gradually removed layer upon layer of gauze from his left hand. When she stripped the final piece of Vaseline-impregnated netting away and revealed the flesh beneath it, Mo's face turned white and his eyelids fluttered. Hosam gripped the poor fellow's shoulders to steady him. If the guy had been standing, he would have fainted.

Despite himself, Hosam swallowed hard. What remained of Mo's left hand was a blistered thumb and the sutured stumps of the four other digits. His fingers had vanished beyond their second knuckles.

Embarrassed by the tears brimming in his eyes, Mo bit his lower lip and looked away.

The nurse remained silent as she continued her task. Hosam said nothing. The hand was speaking for itself. With practice, Hosam figured, the hand could be reasonably useful. But there was no way that Mo could see that now. All he could see was the devastation left by the high-voltage spark that had run up that axe handle.

The nurse soaked Mo's hand in a basin of sterile saline and wiped away as many crusts of dried blood and debris as Mo could tolerate. Even the lightest touch against his wounds caused him to wince and swear. The nurse offered him a dose of intravenous morphine, but he refused it. She patted the wounds dry, spread on a thick layer of white ointment, and applied a new set of bandages.

Before the nurse started on the right hand, Hosam convinced Mo to accept a shot of morphine. The nurse's generous dose slowed his heart rate on the cardiac monitor but did nothing for the terror in his eyes. Hosam eased into position beside Mo on the bed and put his arm around his shoulders. He gripped Mo with the same intensity he had held Farah and Omar during those horrifying bombing raids on Aleppo. It was strange to think that in his arms was the same hard-hearted thug who had seemed on the point of shooting him through the head two nights ago.

By the time the nurse removed the last of the gauze from Mo's right hand, it was clear that the thing — and that is was it was, *a thing* — would never be much use. The thumb and fingers were missing right down to the palms. The hand was nothing more than a club.

Mo's body tightened beneath Hosam's grip. His heart rate shot up on the monitor. His face glowed blood red as a torrent of curses stormed from his mouth.

The nurse jumped back in fear and surprise, nearly knocking her bowl of saline to the floor.

Mo's torrent ended as abruptly as it had started, and the three of them froze in position as if hoping that what lay before them was no more than a bad dream.

Hosam broke the silence. "It is okay, nurse. Please to not worry. He is not being angry at you."

When the nurse's posture made it clear she was reluctant to finish her task without a security guard by her side, Hosam added, "One must admit his hand does look rather bleak."

She lifted her eyebrows and took several deep breaths. Examining her own gloved hands, she cautiously approached her work table once again. "You're right," she said softly. "Poor guy. This *is* nasty."

The nurse injected a second dose of morphine into Mo's IV then resumed her task.

Perhaps it was the morphine, but as the nurse redid the bandage, layer by layer, Mo became surprisingly chatty.

"If you're smart, Doc," he said, speaking in Arabic, "you'll keep clear of the Caliph."

Hosam wondered how that would be possible. He may have put Saramin off for a few days, but like Satan, the Caliph would come calling sooner or later.

"Have you ever met him?" Hosam asked, his arm still tight around Mo's shoulders and sensing every time the fellow winced.

"The Caliph?" Mo said. "Nobody meets him. Not even his enforcers. We only meet Saramin."

Hosam pictured a troop of rough guys like Leo and Ghazwan. And, of course, Mo himself.

"Some guys don't last too long," Mo continued. "Like Ghazwan. He went too far at the barbershop. And ... well ... now the idiot's at the bottom of the friggin' lake."

Hosam's stomach tightened as Mo confirmed his fears. "Saramin told you that?"

"A warning. To remember to keep my friggin' mouth shut."

Hosam looked at Mo's newly bandaged hands. "Is the Caliph going to look after you now that ... ?"

"Guess again, Doc."

Ya Rab, thought Hosam, what was going to become of Mo? The guy's English was rudimentary at best. He had been living in the shadows and at the mercy of the Caliph. Probably barely eking out a living. And now, all he had was half of one hand. What had he been doing for a living in Syria before the war turned him into a mercenary? Had he ever learned to read and write Arabic? Yes, he was a thug. But every thug had once been his mother's little boy.

"What is her story?" Hosam asked.

"Saramin's? Shit, who knows? The word is she ran off with a Canadian guy who was visiting her island down south."

"Saint Lucia?"

"Could be. Anyway, the husband brought her here then turned jihadist and went to Syria to fight for al-Nusra. He didn't last long. Got himself killed after a few weeks. When it was clear he wasn't coming home, she wanted revenge and fell in with the Caliph."

"Because he was ex-al-Nusra? I heard he fought with them for a few years then landed here as a refugee."

"He's no friggin' refugee. He snuck in by some back door."

"And now the two of them have joined forces with the Italians ... the Scarpellinos?"

Mo made a face but did not argue. "You can't make a friggin' living stealing copper from churches and baseball diamonds. The big money is in racketeering and the odd mob hit."

Hosam looked around to make sure no one was in earshot.

Mo raised his arms, stared at his bandaged hands for a long moment, then turned and heaved huge sobs into Hosam's shoulder, soaking his shirt.

Half an hour later, after another dose of morphine, and long periods of awkward silence, Mo fell asleep. Hosam took his leave.

As he was passing the nursing station on the way out of the ICU, he noticed a whiteboard listing the names of the patients admitted to the unit. *Vent* was written in brackets after Blessica's name, presumably because she was on a mechanical ventilator. He examined the list for the names of potential Arabic-speaking patients for whom he might act as interpreter. By the time he reached the bottom of the list, he felt physically ill. He grabbed for the counter bordering the station, certain he was going to pass out.

The receptionist saw him wobbling and rushed to his side. She took hold of his arm and handed him a face cloth. "Yes," she said, "some of these cases are heartbreaking. Especially these younger people with polio." She gestured toward the other side of the counter and said, "Come with me and sit down for a few minutes."

"No, no, miss. I am fine."

"But it's my job to keep an eye on you, sir."

Oh my God. What does she know? "Let me assure you, miss, there is nothing wrong with me."

"Don't feel embarrassed. This often happens when our interpreters come here for the first time. They get quickly involved with the patients' lives and take everything to heart." Her grip on his arm was surprisingly strong for a young woman. "And a lot of what happens in this unit can be hard to stomach."

Alhamdulillah! She has no idea. "Whatever you think is being best," Hosam told her meekly and allowed her to lead him to the chair. He was glad of the face cloth and wiped the ocean of sweat from his forehead.

From the chair, he had a clear view of the whiteboard. In addition to Jamila's name — and Mo's — there were four names on the list that he recognized. And each had the word vent written after it.

They were not common names. There was no reason for him to recognize them except . . .

While no one was looking, he eased Jamila's phone from his pocket and snapped a quick shot of the board. He would show it to Leila, but like Mo's devastated hands, the names spoke for themselves. And what they were saying filled him with horror.

CHAPTER 38

Zol pulled the minivan into a vacant parking spot on Sydenham Street and killed the ignition. He grabbed the packet from the drugstore and struggled to cut through the tough plastic packaging with his nail-clipper keychain. Finally, he removed the bottle and gave the lotion a sniff. As soon as the smell of DEET hit his nose, "Hakuna Matata" from the *Lion King* soundtrack boomed in his head. The band and singers kept their lively number going until he'd rubbed a generous amount of lotion over on his exposed skin and put the bottle in his briefcase.

It felt strange applying insect repellent this early in the spring. The mornings and evenings were still cool, and he hadn't seen a mosquito for months. The bug season didn't usually start until later in May. As he stepped out of his vehicle, he checked his watch: it was coming up to nine fifty.

He was soon standing in front of Blossoms by Tiffany. The lights were on, but when he tried the door handle, he found it was locked. The opening hours posted on the window said the place opened at ten. He rapped firmly and peered inside. He gave a friendly wave when the woman behind the front counter looked up from her paperwork. Instead of waving back, she shook her head, pointed to her watch, and went back to her papers. He pulled his Ontario Public Health photo ID card from his wallet, held it up, and rapped once more. She looked up again, made a face to let him know she would indulge him but was moderately annoyed, and came to the door. She didn't open it. He pointed to the ID card and raised his eyebrows. He smiled and lifted his palms to let her know he was looking for a favour, not a confrontation.

The woman pulled the door partway open and stood in the entrance. She had long, dark, wavy hair tied back in a ponytail, an arching nose, and a slim physique. Zol thought she was probably about Tasha's age. Early thirties at most. She took his ID and studied it. "Is this some sort of inspection? If it is, I've never heard of such a thing. My business license —"

Zol held out his hand, quickly introduced himself, and said, "This isn't an inspection, ma'am. I'm hoping Ms. Fonseca can help us with an investigation we're carrying out at the Health Unit."

"I'm Tiffany Fonseca," she said sharply and handed him back his card. "What kind of investigation? I've done nothing wrong."

Feeling ridiculous standing on the sidewalk like a rebuffed Jehovah's Witness, Zol said, "May I come in and explain it to you?"

"Look, I'm extremely busy. I've had a heck of a time arranging childcare and there's a ton of things I need to get done before I open the shop."

Why, he wondered, was everyone reluctant to help with this investigation? The woman had given him no choice but to drop the bombshell in her lap. "We're afraid something in your flowers may be playing a role in the polio outbreak."

"Oh my God. You can't be serious. I know my nanny's in ICU, but she couldn't have gotten sick because of my —"

"Ms. Fonseca, if you let me come in, I can describe the situation to you before your customers start arriving. I don't think you want them hearing what we're saying and coming to conclusions of their own."

Her face had turned from annoyed to anxious. "Well . . . okay, I guess," she said and stepped aside to let him in.

She locked the door and returned to her stool behind the counter. "I suppose you're here with news about Blessica? My life is hell without her. How soon will she be up and about?"

"I'm sorry, I have nothing to tell you about Ms. Velasquez's condition. That needs to come from her doctors at Caledonian Medical Centre. I'm sure they would be happy —"

"So . . . why are you here? What can my flowers possibly have to do with Blessica's illness? I mean —"

"Why don't I start with a few simple questions, Ms. Fonseca? And then together we might draw a clearer picture of how this outbreak came about."

"I don't know a thing about polio."

"But you do know a lot about flowers."

Suddenly, he was hit by an intense floral scent. Lily, perhaps, or something more exotic. To fend off what he knew would come next, he pinched his nose and held his breath. It didn't work. Seconds later, Drake was in his head singing "Passionfruit" at full volume. It was a terrific number, another one of his favourites and at the top of the charts, but the timing was terrible. This woman, already irritated by his unexpected presence, was going to think he was having some sort of fit unworthy of the region's medical officer of health.

He fumbled in his pocket for a Kleenex and made a show of blowing his nose.

"Allergic to flowers, are you, Doctor?"

Still covering his sniffer with the Kleenex, he nodded vigorously and told her, "Sort of. Give me a minute, please. That's all I need."

Drake cut out after a few more bars, and Zol put the Kleenex in his suit jacket pocket. The shop was full of scents, a veritable jukebox of aromas that could force-feed his synesthesia for an entire day. He should have stayed outside and interviewed the woman on the odourless sidewalk.

"Sorry about that," he said. "I should be okay for a while."

She looked at her watch. "Can we get on with the questions?"

"Sure, sorry. First off, we're interested in the tulips you buy from Vander Zalm Nurseries in Virgil." He'd phoned Vander Zalm's this morning and confirmed she was a regular customer and had taken delivery of their tulips for the past two or three years.

"So, I get my tulips from Vander Zalm's. How's that a problem?"

"Do you ever visit the nursery or do the shipments get delivered directly here to the shop?"

"I haven't been there for at least a couple of years. I checked the place out initially, liked what I saw, and negotiated a fair price for their flowers."

"What about Blessica? Has she visited Vander Zalm's anytime in the past few weeks?"

"Certainly not. It's a wholesale nursery. Why would she go there?"

"You're sure?"

"Of course."

"Do you know if she's made a trip to Niagara Region in the past couple of months? Perhaps the Falls? Niagara-on-the-Lake? The wine country?"

"She and her friends don't drive, she doesn't drink, and she's pretty much a homebody. On her days off, she hangs with her chums in Hamilton and Mississauga. There would be no reason for her to go to Niagara."

"You're certain about that?"

Tiffany Fonseca looked him straight in the eye and showed no hint of deception. "Absolutely. She and her Filipino friends hang out at Square One. It's easy for them to get there by bus, so that's where they congregate."

The mall was in Mississauga, an hour's drive northeast of Hamilton. Niagara lay in the opposite direction. If Blessica Velasquez hadn't acquired her Zika infection from a mosquito anywhere in Niagara, she had to have been bitten in this shop.

"How often does she come into this store?"

Tiffany's face tightened. "Twice a day. With Marigold. I'm still breastfeeding." She paused, overcome by her own dark thoughts. Her eyes flooded with tears. "Oh my God, are you saying my daughter is going to get polio too?"

"What can you tell me about a woman called Thuy Nguyen? Do you know her?"

"From the nail salon? Of course. Why?"

"She comes here often?"

"Three times a week, at least. Her salon may be tiny but she keeps it beautifully decorated. Thuy has an uncanny eye for arranging flowers. Don't tell me she's sick too?"

Zol looked toward the back of the shop without answering her question. "May I have a look around? And please keep the door locked until I'm finished."

"Please, Doctor. How could anyone catch polio from my flowers? Did something contaminate them?"

Zol spent about fifteen minutes looking around the shop, which included a large cold room at the back. He saw a few ants and aphids crawling on various leaves and petals, and there were house-flies buzzing at the windows. He saw no mosquitoes, even among the tulips.

When he returned to the front counter, Tiffany was on the phone. He caught the tail end of her conversation: "And you're a hundred percent sure she doesn't have a fever? I'm telling you, Mother, be sure to call me if that sniffle gets even the tiniest bit worse."

She hung up and turned to Zol. "Marigold's got a runny nose. Just started this morning. Do you think it could be the start of . . ." She was soon sobbing so forcefully she couldn't get another word out.

"No, ma'am," Zol said. "Polio doesn't start with a sniffle." He opened his briefcase and handed her a Kleenex. "I don't think you have anything to worry about."

When she'd stopped sobbing, she wiped her nose and gestured to the rear of the store. "What were you looking for back there?"

"Mosquitoes. Have you seen any in here lately?"

"At this time of year?"

"Well, with global warming, anything's possible. Have you noticed any insect bites on your skin?"

She started to shake her head then stopped. Her eyes widened as she stashed the Kleenex into her apron pocket and thrust her left elbow toward his face. "This thing here, it's itchy. Do you think it's a bite?"

Above her elbow was a small, raised red papule. "How long has it been there?"

"A few days, I guess." Her face darkened again. "Oh my God. Does it mean I'm gonna get polio? *Please*, Doctor, tell me I'm gonna be okay."

He explained that every person affected by the current outbreak of polio had been infected with two viruses simultaneously. Even if she had been bitten by a virus-infected mosquito, the chance she would acquire the all-important second virus and come down with polio was minuscule.

"But Blessica got both viruses," she said, "so why not me? She goes pretty much everywhere I go."

The poor woman had a good point, and he had no answer that would make her feel better. "Let's look at the places Blessica went to that you didn't. Perhaps we should start with her days off."

"I told you. She usually goes to Square One."

"How often does she get a day off?"

"Once a week. Sundays."

"And the evenings? Where does she go after the dishes are done and your daughter goes to bed?"

"To her room. She lives with us."

"She never goes go out?"

"As I said, she's a homebody."

"What about hobbies, night courses, sports?"

"None of that."

"Has she needed any time off during the day, lately? For an appointment of some sort?"

Tiffany started to dismiss his question with a wave of her hand but stopped and picked up her phone. She tapped the screen a few times and said, "I'm looking at my calendar. I had to get my mother to take Marigold a couple of times in April because Blessica did have two appointments."

"What sort of appointments?"

"She was fussing about her teeth. Said she had a toothache. Her teeth looked perfectly fine to me but she insisted on seeing a dentist. It was extremely inconvenient because the dentist doesn't work on Sundays. Mother had to give up her bridge game to take care of Marigold. Two weeks running."

"When was that?"

She studied the calendar. "April 12th and 19th."

Parvo-W was a brand new virus, so no one knew its incubation period. Those April dates, however, did seem to be in the right ballpark. "Blessica goes to your dentist?"

"Oh no. The Filipinos have their own. They wouldn't trust anyone else. They call her Doctor Elle, and she charges them less than the going rate, which is a big plus."

A dentist who charged less than the going rate and serviced an immigrant community of modest means — maybe he was getting somewhere. "She? What's her full name and address?"

"I have no idea. She's in Hamilton somewhere, I know that much."

"The dentist must have given Blessica a receipt. Do you think you could find it?"

Tiffany shook her head. "Cash only. And never a receipt. My husband gave her an advance on next month's earnings to cover it."

Zol dipped into his briefcase and pulled out the page he kept with the names and demographic data of the outbreak's now eleven cases. Tasha retained everything in her head. He needed the cheat sheet. "Does the name Emmalita Pina mean anything to you?"

"Sure. She's a friend of Blessica's."

"A nanny, I understand? From the Philippines?"

"Last I heard she was out of work. And couch-surfing."

"Oh?"

"I don't know what the real story is." Tiffany paused as if uncertain how much she wanted to divulge. She ran a hand along her ponytail then said, "Blessica says Emmalita quit when the husband came on to her. I wouldn't be surprised if she was fired for incompetence and made up the whole story, though. She's not the sharpest knife in the drawer."

"Has she visited this shop lately?"

"Until Blessica got sick, she hung around quite a bit. I didn't need two nannies, but if she was a help to Blessica, I didn't mind. She asked for money to pay her dental bill, but I said no. If you give these people an inch they —"

Without thinking, Zol rubbed at a sting on his temple. A moment later, when he looked at his fingers they were wet with fresh blood. It couldn't be a shaving cut — the spot was near his eye where whiskers didn't grow.

Tiffany stepped back and made a face. "That looks like blood. What's it from?"

He brought his hand closer to his face. There was more than blood on his fingers. He could make out the squashed remains of a delicate insect — legs, body, wings.

The damned thing had black and white stripes. Like a tiger.

Shit!

There was no way you could miss them.

CHAPTER 39

Jesse pulled his Mazda into a parking spot near Limeridge Mall's south entrance. He'd been raised within cycling distance of this place in the part of Hamilton that everyone called the West Mountain — local code for the neighbourhood built in the 1960s above the rim of the Niagara Escarpment in the city's southwest. As a teenager, he'd hung here with his friends. The place was so big that kids skipping school or chilling on weekends blended in with the serious shoppers, and no one in authority gave them grief. The shops were constantly undergoing renovation, and the rotunda had been redesigned a few times, but he knew the place well. From the entrance, he walked past the Hudson's Bay Company's fragrance and cosmetic counters on the ground floor and took the escalator to the mall's administrative offices on the second. It was down the hall from the washroom in which he'd had his first kiss. (A bit disappointing; their second kiss was better.)

He showed the receptionist his Ontario Public Health ID card and asked to speak with Darryl Oxman's boss. The woman's eyes glistened as she said how sorry everyone was about Darryl. She introduced herself as Rose and asked Jesse to wait for a moment; she would see if Mr. Melville was available.

A minute later, Rose led Jesse from the counter to one of four offices in a pod behind it. She introduced him to Mr. Richard Melville, physical operations manager.

Jesse showed his card to the heavyset middle-aged man seated at a desk. Holding the card in his beefy fingers, he scrutinized it then said, "Health department? Again? What've we done wrong now? You guys never —"

"Nothing, sir. I'm not here to . . . um . . . point any fingers."

"So, what do you want, son?"

"I'd like to learn as much about Darryl Oxman as you can tell me."

"Darryl? What a tragedy. And it happened so fast. We certainly didn't see it coming." Mr. Melville picked up the ballpoint on his desk and clicked it several times. "Best janitor I ever had." He stared at his desk for a while then wiped his nose with a tissue from his pocket. "Always on time. Never missed a speck of dirt. Of course, he could only work half days, four days a week. But still . . ."

Jesse did the math then asked, "Was there a reason he worked only sixteen hours a week?"

Mr. Melville looked up. "That was all he could take. Any more and his outbursts would start. Just harmless mutterings to no one in particular. But he had a loud voice at times, and it would upset the shoppers. There'd been complaints."

"Why did he have them, these, uh, outbursts?"

"What's wrong with you guys? Don't you have his medical file?"

"We do know he collapsed at work . . . on . . ." Jesse tried to flip through his notes to find the date, but his hands were so sweaty that the pages stuck together.

"April 26th," said Melville. "Right here in this office. I was the one who called the ambulance. Three days later, he was dead. April 29th."

"It must have been a shock."

"To us, you bet it was. But to his family . . ." Melville shook his head in disgust. "Well, I haven't heard a peep out of any of them. They haven't even called about the stuff in his locker."

"He was estranged from his parents and siblings?"

"I guess that can happen when you're on the spectrum."

"Darryl was autistic?"

"Big time. But it never worried me. My son's the same. Works for a computer gaming outfit. Half the guys on their payroll are on the spectrum."

Jesse pictured a locker stuffed with Darryl Oxman's belongings. It could be teeming with the sort of clues Dr. Zed had sent him hunting for. "I've been sent to trace Darryl's movements during the three weeks prior to his collapse. We know he must have come in contact with whatever is causing the polio outbreak, but —"

"Needle in a haystack."

"I'm sorry?"

"Good luck tracing Darryl's movements. He was here like clockwork, eight a.m. to twelve, Mondays to Thursdays. Outside of that, it was anyone's guess what he was up to."

"He was secretive?"

"A loner. And liked it that way. Loved puzzles and codes. You know, *DaVinci Code* stuff. I never saw him write anything down in plain numbers and letters. Always in code. What do you call that? Ciphering?"

"Do you know if he kept a diary?"

"You kids these days are obsessed with your phones," Melville said and eyed Jesse's iPhone peeking from the front pocket of his pants. "But Darryl, he didn't have one. He was scared of it being hacked. He probably had a diary of some sort. He was always well organized."

"May I look in his locker?"

The man thought for a moment. "I don't see why not." He looked at his watch, and his eyes hardened. "Darryl collapsed two weeks ago tomorrow. If his family cared two hoots about his things, they'd have let us know by now." His jowly face brightened slightly.

"Tell you what. You seem like a nice kid. You sign for them, and I'll let you take the entire contents away with you."

Jesse's phone buzzed in his pocket. The ring tone told him it was a voice call, so it couldn't be a friend or his roommate, and it certainly wasn't his sister.

He could feel himself blushing as he reached for his pocket. "Sorry, Mr. Melville. This might be my boss."

"So, go ahead. Answer it. That's what it's for."

Jesse whipped out the phone and saw the caller's face on the screen. "Hey, Dr. Zed. How's it going?"

"I don't have much time, so listen carefully. I came across a promising lead a few minutes ago."

If the lead was so promising, why did Dr. Zed sound upset? Was he angry? No, it sounded like nerves straining his voice, not anger. "You found something in the flower shop?"

"Have you talked to the young janitor's boss?"

"I'm with him now." Jesse looked up and caught Melville's eye. "Mr. Melville is being incredibly helpful."

"Ask him about your guy's teeth. We need to know if he'd seen his dentist recently. If he had, I want the dates of his appointments."

"Sure thing."

"We think she's running a clandestine operation. You know, without a license."

"That sounds kinda weird, Dr. Zed."

"Yeah, long story. Her office won't be easy to find."

"Her?"

"She goes by Dr. Elle."

"Like the magazine, E–L–L–E? Or is it L as in Lima?"

"I suppose it could be either." Dr. Zed coughed and cleared his throat. "You know? I never asked. But listen, Jesse, the name and address of that dentist are absolutely essential to our investigation. Without them, we're cooked."

Thanks for the pressure, Dr. Zed. It makes the job so much easier. "On it, Dr. Zed."

"Call me as soon as you get anything. Even the smallest tidbit. See you later."

"Sorry, son," Mr. Melville said when Jesse asked about Darryl's dentist. "Darryl never missed work for any reason. He arranged his appointments for the afternoons. And for Fridays, I guess. I never had to know about them."

"Did he talk about having tooth problems?"

Melville thought for a moment then picked up the phone. "Rose, did Darryl ever talk to you about his teeth? Really, eh? That much pain? And then what? A root canal?" He caught Jesse's eye. "Poor guy, I hate those. When did he have it, Rose?" Mr. Melville jotted her response on a pad by the phone. "And the name of the dentist? Oh . . . that's too bad. You're sure? And no address? I know, Rose, that *was* just like Darryl."

"You followed that?" Melville said. "Rose says Darryl had a root canal that involved two or three appointments around the beginning of April."

"Does she have any idea who the dentist was?"

"None."

CHAPTER 40

By mid-morning, Natasha's nausea had disappeared and she'd devoured a container of blueberry yogurt, a bowl of granola, and a piece of toast with peanut butter. She'd felt antsy sitting at home when there were so many unanswered questions surrounding the polio patients and their next of kin. But now, in the car on her way to Caledonian Medical Centre, she was struggling to blink away the tears and feeling like a fool for having them in the first place. She pulled into the McDonald's parking lot on Mohawk East, put the car into park, and had a good cry.

When he'd called from his car, Zol had broken it to her as gently as he could. But damn it to hell! Why had he let himself get bitten by one of those freaking Aedes Tigers? She'd warned him to be generous with the DEET so that neither an Aedes albopictus nor the Zika virus would get him. He hadn't been generous enough with the repellant. She pictured him in ICU with a big tube in his nose and that awful machine going *hiss-cluck-hiss* beside him.

She studied her face in the mirror and dabbed her mascara-smeared cheeks with a tissue. Sure, he had saved the tiny messy carcass in a clean sandwich bag. And he had asked Hamish to get the thing tested for Zika virus ASAP. But why did life always have to get complicated? Why couldn't the concerns of her early pregnancy simply be nausea and vomiting?

At least, she told herself, Zol's visit with Tiffany hadn't been a bust. Now they knew that her Dundas flower shop was infested with Aedes albopictus, which had hitchhiked there on Vander Zalm's tulips. Zol was preparing the cease and desist order to close Blossoms by Tiffany until the mosquitoes were eradicated. Stephanie Polgar would be dealing with the Vander Zalms' Virgil operation in the same way.

The lead Tiffany had given Zol about a cut-price, cash-only, no-receipts dentist named Dr. Elle was promising and gave the investigation something specific to hone in on. How many dentists in the city could be named Elle? Finding her through the Hamilton Academy of Dentists should be a piece of cake. Unless . . . Natasha didn't like the sound of the dentist's cash-only business model. The fact that her patients, like the polio cases, might be predominantly vulnerable immigrants was unsettling as well. If the woman was operating underground like the Botox "doctors" who gathered clients in people's homes and injected them at kitchen tables, finding her would be close to impossible unless someone talked.

A few minutes later, Natasha was at CUMC taking the stairs to the third floor. According to the various online sites she'd visited these past few days, gentle exercise was good for morning sickness. It seemed to be working.

On Ward 3-South, a general medical ward, she showed her ID card to the ward clerk and explained she was here to speak with Emmalita Pina and Bhavjeet Singh Malik. The clerk gave her their room numbers, pointed out that both were in isolation in private accommodation, and asked Natasha to follow the instructions posted outside their rooms.

When she stopped at Emmalita's room and was confronted by the reality of the isolation measures, a shudder of apprehension shot down her spine. Was she exposing her fetus to unnecessary risk? She knew she shouldn't be too worried about getting polio. Its mode of transmission seemed too tangled to be a threat. But should she be concerned about acquiring Zika, a virus that could damage her unborn child's brain? It was foolish to worry, she told herself. There were no mosquitoes in hospital isolation rooms, and transmission from patients required intimate contact. She put on the gear and entered the room.

Emmalita Pina was a sad-looking sight, more waif than thirty-year-old woman. She didn't move when Natasha approached the bed but did open her eyes and mutter something that sounded like *Hello miss.*

Natasha explained why she was there and that she had only a few simple questions. Emmalita's answers were brief and so barely audible that Natasha had to lean in close to hear her.

The story of Emmalita's single visit to Blessica's dentist came out in monosyllables. Natasha had to ask more leading questions than she usually liked but did ascertain that Emmalita's tooth had bothered her for weeks. Blessica arranged for the two of them to have appointments on the same afternoon, and they went together on the bus. Emmalita's toothache had been so severe that day that she could barely remember the bus ride and recalled nothing of the visit except that a female doctor froze her mouth and put a filling in the problem tooth. Blessica paid the dentist's thirty-dollar fee — which sounded like a remarkable bargain — and Emmalita promised to pay it back as soon as she found a new job.

Before entering Bhavjeet's room a few minutes later, Natasha went through the same performance with the protective gear. The boy was alone and looked more lively today than yesterday afternoon. His eyes were brighter and he was more inclined to talk. He was more comfortable conversing in Punjabi, though she had to strain to catch his rural dialect. It was a relief — to both of them — that his overbearing auntie was nowhere in sight.

"I'd like to know about your sore tooth, Bhavjeet," she said. "How did it start?"

He wasn't sure. The pain in his jaw began a few weeks back, well before he came to the hospital. As the pain got worse, his face swelled and he started to shiver. His aunt and uncle drove him to a dentist who his uncle said would charge a reasonable fee for her work, not like the others.

"Where was the dentist's office?"

The boy looked back at her with a doleful face and shrugged. "I was thinking about the pain in my face, nothing else."

"Well, was it near your uncle's home?"

He shook his head and screwed up his face as if recalling the misery. "Long way. Very much long."

"So, the dentist was in a different part of the city from where you've been living?"

"Auntie gave me cold cloth. I hold it over my face to help the pain."

"So you didn't see where your uncle was taking you?"

"I see but not pay attention." His gaze drifted to the floor. "Sorry."

"What about after you arrived at the dentist and your uncle parked the car. What did the building look like?"

He shrugged again and offered nothing.

"I really need your help, Bhavjeet," she told him. "Was the dentist in a tall building, the kind with an elevator? Or was it —"

"No elevator. Look like my uncle's townhouse."

Good, they were getting somewhere. "Do you remember anything else about it? Something special like a high fence, fancy cars parked outside, a vicious dog, a big store next door?"

Bhavjeet thought for a moment then said, "She work in garage."

"Who? Who worked in a garage?"

"Lady dentist. No cars inside. Her surgery only."

A cut-rate dentist working out of a garage in a townhouse — this fit their assumption that the mysterious Dr. Elle was running an unlicensed operation. There were thousands of townhouses in every district of the city, many of similar design. The woman and her Parvo-W-contaminated instruments could be anywhere.

"Can you tell me what she looked like? Young? Older? Dark skin? Light skin? Long hair? Grey hair?"

The boy scrutinized the little of Natasha's head and body that were not covered in protective gear then said, "Longer hair than yours, miss. Same colour. Skin lighter."

"Would you recognize her if you saw her again?"

He shook his head and mimed a surgical mask covering his nose and mouth. "She was having one of those things."

"The whole time?"

"Yes, miss."

"Now, what did she do for your toothache? Did she pull your tooth?"

Bhavjeet nodded and held up two fingers. "First, spray for the pain. Freezing second." He mimed a series of injections with a long needle followed by two brisk twists of the wrist.

"And then she pulled two teeth?"

He nodded, opened his mouth, and pointed to a large fleshy hole in his lower jaw. It was crisscrossed by black sutures.

After Natasha figured she'd milked all the information out of Bhavjeet she was going to get, she said goodbye then removed the gear, washed her hands in the sink provided — twice — and smothered her palms and fingers in alcohol-based hand sanitizer. She looked down at her still-flat stomach and whispered, "Okay, Junior. I'm doing everything I can to keep you safe." It would be a lifelong task. She was beginning to realize that.

Upstairs in the ICU, she stopped at the nursing station and looked at the whiteboard. Jamila, Barry, Blessica, and Thuy were still on the list. Lewis Feldman was not.

One of the nurses recognized Natasha and approached her with slow, measured steps. She had that universal *I've-got-bad-news* look on her face. "I'm afraid Mr. Feldman passed away about an hour ago."

"I'm so sorry. I noticed a lot of activity in his room yesterday. The crash cart and everything."

"He had a bad night. We did everything we could but . . ."

"Of course."

"It's heartbreaking when a patient dies alone. I wish he'd had some visitors. We had him heavily sedated, of course, but he would have known they were there."

"No one came to see him?"

"A woman who used to work with him was here once, a few days ago. She seemed nice enough but stayed no more than a minute or two." The nurse offered Natasha a knowing look. "She was terrified she'd catch his polio and barely stepped past the door."

"Have you been able to notify Mr. Feldman's family?"

"That's the awful thing. There's no next of kin listed in his chart, and when the doctor dialled the one number we had for him, a landline, all he got was one of those recordings that tell you the number is out of service."

After being cast aside by the crumbling department-store empire for which he'd worked, Lewis Feldman had been so cash-strapped he couldn't pay his telephone bill. At sixty-three, he'd been out of a job, cut off by the phone company, and likely struggling with his teeth. Like the nurse, Natasha was saddened by the loneliness of the man. And frustrated that she was still no closer to finding the elusive Dr. Elle. There were still the families of Thuy Nguyen, Barry Novak, and the two kids from Cathcart Elementary that might help pinpoint the dentist. Hamish was working with Thuy's husband and sister. Muriel Simon was getting the secretary at her school to phone the families of Céline and Juan-Carlos to see what she could dig up. That left Barry Novak, the labourer-cum-bus-driver, to Natasha. He was sedated and ventilated, but his chart said he was married.

When Irene Novak answered the phone on the second ring, Natasha's heart skipped a beat. She explained why she was calling and held her breath for a helpful answer.

"Heavens, dearie. I don't do dentists. Never have. Why, even the mention of the word can send me into a dead faint. You see, I had every tooth in my head pulled when I was twenty-one. And now, with a full set of dentures in perfect condition, no one ever comes at me with needles and drills."

"I see. But what about Mr. Novak? I do need to know if he's been to a dentist lately."

"Then you'll have to ask my husband when he comes around. I have no idea."

"Did he mention having a toothache lately? Or has he shown any signs of a frozen mouth, a new filling, maybe a pulled tooth?"

"Now, miss, you've got to stop using those words. You'll send me crashing to the floor."

"Are you sure you can't help me, Mrs. Novak? If you whisper the name of his dentist, I'll let you go immediately. After that, I promise I'll never bother you again. Please, that's all I'm asking. Just a name and address."

"She's a woman, and he pays cash to keep the cost down because we don't have insurance. He's never told me her name. And now I'm hanging up, dearie."

Sitting like a ninny with a dead phone in her hand, Natasha didn't know which bothered her most: her anger, her frustration, or how ridiculous it was to be listening to the dial tone.

CHAPTER 41

Jesse emptied the garbage bag containing the contents of Darryl Oxman's locker onto the kitchen table. His roommate, Morgan, wouldn't be home from work until five at the earliest, so he had the entire afternoon to examine the stuff uninterrupted. As a law student, Morgan knew about discretion and confidentiality. But she'd gone into law because she was fascinated by what she called the messy narratives of other people's lives. She'd have a heyday pestering Jesse over Darryl's stuff and dreaming up hypotheses about the poor guy's *narrative*. Until he'd proven himself to Dr. Zed, Jesse didn't need that kind of interference. And besides, he had signed a confidentiality agreement as a condition of his employment at the Health Unit, and there was no way he was going to breach it.

Darryl had replaced the mall-issued padlock on his locker with one of his own. Of course, no one had a clue what the combination might be. Mr. Melville, red-faced at Darryl's flaunting of the regulations, got one of his maintenance men to crunch the lock with bolt cutters. Why a shopping mall needed to keep such a tool handy, Jesse had no idea.

The locker contained a complete change of clothes that were more or less wrinkle-free and neatly hung up — white cotton t-shirt, plaid sport shirt, chinos, Toronto Blue Jays ball cap, sneakers, and a windbreaker. Presumably, Darryl had worn these civvies on his way to work and changed into a uniform when he got there. Going through a dead man's trouser pockets was creepy, and Jesse had to force himself to do it. He found an open pack of chewing gum (none of it already chewed, thank God!), half a roll of cough drops, a wad of used Kleenex (ugh!), a small penknife (a nice little piece with a deer-antler handle), and a set of earbuds (smudged with Darryl's earwax!). In the windbreaker's pocket was a Sony CD Walkman with a patent date of 1990 on the back. (The guy certainly was a Luddite.) Apart from a comb and half a bottle of Tylenol Extra Strength, Darryl had kept no grooming aids or toiletries at work. Alongside the locker's original padlock with its key in the lock, there were two keys on a Toronto Maple Leafs ring, neither of which was for a car.

At the bottom of the garbage bag were three ballpoint pens, an HB pencil with an eraser at the end, a pad of blue Post-it Notes, and three paperbacks: *Prime Numbers and the Riemann Hypothesis*, *The Fibonacci Sequence: Nature's Code*, and *Ultimate Sudoku: 300 Challenging Puzzles*.

Fascinated since high school by the role of prime numbers in keeping encrypted messages safe on the internet, Jesse picked up the prime-number book and flipped through it. It was written for a general audience, and the chapter titles referred to many of the fun facts he already knew. Next, he picked up the Sudoku book. Knowing whether Darryl used an indelible pen or an erasable pencil when working on a puzzle could help sketch the guy's character (and help fill in his *narrative*). Was he one of those who wrote tiny numbers in the corners of the squares to help with the solutions? Or was he a purist who kept everything in his head and wrote in ink even when solving the most infuriating puzzles?

For a paperback, the Sudoku book felt heavy. When Jesse opened it and flipped past the title page, he found that most of its centre had been cut away to create a recess. Inside was a pocket-sized daily planner. He remembered his dad using such a thing, a leatherbound Moleskine. Nowadays, most people kept track of their agendas on their smartphones. But, of course, Darryl didn't have a phone. Melville had said the guy didn't trust them.

His heart racing at what Darryl's hidden planner might reveal — and, if Jesse was honest, would cement his promotion to Dr. Zed's investigative team — he lifted the little volume from its hiding place. He turned immediately to Darryl's entries for April this year, his mouth dry with excitement. A numbers guy who hung his clothes neatly in his locker and aligned his sneakers perfectly on a piece of newspaper was bound to have his dental appointments noted with the doctor's contact details written out for easy reference.

The planner showed that Darryl visited a doctor three times in April: at nine o'clock on the morning of Friday the 6th and at three o'clock on two Monday afternoons, the 9th and the 16th. Wow! This had to be the Dr. Elle that Dr. Zed was so desperate to locate. But when he tried to read what should have been the doctor's name and address, Jesse's heart sank into his gut. Darryl had written the appointment details in code. The doctor was listed as *Dr. 8-4.* What followed, which might be her address, was part code and part riddle: *Marble Taker 11 + 59.*

Jesse opened Google Maps on his phone and searched for Marble Street, Hamilton. Google drew a blank immediately. Similarly, it found nothing under Marble Avenue (or Lane, Crescent, Boulevard, or Court). He switched to regular Google and typed in *marble, Hamilton, Ontario.* The first hit to come up was Marble Slab Creamery on Upper James Street. It was followed by ten local places that sold marble, granite, and quartz countertops. Google Maps showed that the creamery was located in a strip mall devoted exclusively to eateries. There was nothing nearby that looked remotely like a dentist's office. The countertop places were in the rural outskirts of the city, well away from dental-office territory.

He wondered who else dealt with marble and might take it from one place to another. Cemeteries, he figured. They made marble headstones. But a dentist wouldn't work there. What about a marble quarry? Was there one nearby? No. Google said there weren't any quarries mining marble anywhere in Ontario.

He pulled a pencil and a scrap of paper from a kitchen drawer and started doodling. Sometimes it helped him to think. And sometimes it just made a mess of a blank sheet. If marble wasn't the name of a street or a business, what was it? Darryl had liked number puzzles. What about crosswords? Had he been keen on those as well? If so, why didn't he have a book of crosswords in his locker? Maybe he'd stuffed it into a pocket of the uniform he'd been wearing when they'd carted him off to the hospital.

Jesse typed *Marble Taker* into Google. The first dozen hits were faraway businesses selling commemorative marble plaques and tablets. No help there. He pressed his pencil firmly into the paper as he doodled, desperate for creative thoughts to pop out of nowhere. He examined Darryl's entries again.

The words *Marble* and *Taker* were capitalized. Was that significant? Perhaps the clue was asking for the name of the person who took the marbles. Did the dentist share a name with a childhood acquaintance who had duped Darryl out of his marbles? A clue *that* personal would be impossible for an outsider to solve.

But what if the clue wasn't personal? What if someone famous took the marbles in question? Google was great at finding famous people.

He asked Google: *Who took the marbles?*

The answer came in a millisecond: Thomas Bruce, the 7th Earl of Elgin, took the marble sculptures from the Parthenon in Athens to the British Museum in London in the 1800s. Something rang a faint bell far back in Jesse's memory. He let it keep ringing until . . . grade eleven history class . . . yes, the Elgin Marbles. Had Darryl known enough about the Elgin Marbles to create a clever clue? If he'd done crosswords often enough, he could have stuffed his brain with all kinds of fascinating trivia. On the other hand, perhaps he was parroting a puzzle clue that had stuck in his mind. Either way, it didn't matter, Jesse knew he was onto something. *Thomas Bruce*, the *Earl* of *Elgin*. That gave him four Hamilton street names to consider, and a street number: 70, the sum of 11 plus 59.

He typed *Thomas* and *Hamilton, Ontario*, into Google Maps. Surprisingly, there was no street by that name in the entire city.

When he searched for a street or avenue called Bruce, he found one. A single block in the centre of the city. From the images on Google Maps, it was in a neighbourhood of small, detached redbrick houses, probably built in Victorian times. Given that the addresses of several of the polio cases were clustered in the city's central core, a dentist operating out of a house on Bruce Street fit the bill nicely. Jesse checked the street numbers on Bruce Street with Google and verified them on Canada Post's website. The houses ranged from number 3 to number 31. No number 70. (Damn!)

He searched for Earl Street and found it in the city's central core. It was four kilometres from Jamila's high school and only three from Cathcart Elementary, the school attended by the first three polio cases. Canada Post said the house numbers ran from 55 to 308. The pictures on Google Maps showed a neighbourhood of modest, mostly detached houses, a few barren lots, and a couple of small warehouses. Number 70 was obscured by trees; Jesse couldn't tell whether there was a house there or an empty lot.

A search for Elgin Street yielded another residential street in the central core, dab in the middle of the Beasley neighbourhood that Miss Sharma had circled as an area of interest. It was 500 metres from Cathcart school. (Perfect!) On the east side, the street numbers ran from 245 to 2499. On the west, they started at 246 and ended at 2500. Google's photos showed Elgin Street to be more of a hodgepodge than the other streets suggested by Darryl's riddle. It included detached Victorian homes, newly constructed town-houses, and several empty lots. The Good Shepherd Food Bank took up a full block on the east side. The northern end terminated at the Hamilton-Wentworth Detention Centre, the notorious Barton Jail. This was not the sort of street in which a dentist would set up shop, and there was no number 70. (Damn!)

He looked again at Darryl's cryptic numbers and nearly kicked himself for being simple-minded. Darryl had been too much into numerology to use the addition and subtraction of plain numbers in his clues. Jesse eyed the prime-number book and remembered reading a novel told from the viewpoint of a deeply intelligent boy with autism. The book had a long title that mentioned something about the night and a dog. The title was beside the point; the boy was fascinated by prime numbers and headed his chapters with them in sequence: 2, 3, 5, 7, 11, 13, etc.

What if Darryl had used prime numbers in his code?

Jesse opened Darryl's prime-number book and turned to the chart that listed the first five hundred primes in order. The page was covered in smudges and greasy finger marks, indicating it had been referred to a lot. Darryl had called the dentist *Dr. 8-4.* The eighth prime number in the chart was 19; the fourth was 7. Nineteen minus seven was twelve.

Dr. Twelve. What could that mean? Was twelve a number in the Fibonacci Sequence? No, the introductory chapter of the Fibonacci book showed the first few numbers were 0, 1, 1, 2, 3, 5, 8, 13, 21, 34 (each being the sum of the two before it).

The doctor's name would start with a letter, of course. The twelfth prime was 37, which wouldn't denote a letter of the alphabet. What was the twelfth letter? Jesse counted on his fingers. Dr. Zed had said to find Dr. Elle. And here she was in Darryl's book! She was Dr. L as in Lima, Lighthouse, Limburger, Lichtenstein, Loretta. Not Elle, but a name that started with L. Did the dentist's patients call her Dr. Elle because her last name was long and difficult to pronounce? Or was it out of the same friendly respect with which Jesse called his boss Dr. Zed? Or, could it be that her name actually was Elle and Darryl had simply turned it into code?

He looked again at the numbers Darryl had written after *Marble Taker*. If his code was consistent (autistic people craved consistency, didn't they?), then 11 + 59 meant the eleventh prime plus the fifty-ninth prime. Jesse looked at the chart and counted out the primes. The fifty-ninth was 277, the eleventh was 31. Their sum was 308.

But . . . was he looking for house number 308, or for the 308th prime, which was 2029? Either way, Elgin Street and Earl Street warranted a detailed look. In person, of course. The photos on Google Street View didn't tell the whole story and were years out of date.

He pocketed Darryl's daily planner and stuffed everything else into the garbage bag, which he stashed under his bed behind his camera case, well away from the clutches of Morgan's curiosity. His Nikon D3500 was great for weddings and wildlife, but the thing was too showy for surveillance work. His smartphone would be fine for snapshots and his tiny IP camera perfect for continuous surveillance. He grabbed the gear and his car keys.

CHAPTER 42

"Hush, Hosam," Leila told him over her lunchtime pita and hummus in their kitchen. "You do not need to shout. You will frighten Omar."

"I was not shouting. Besides, we have never hidden our problems from him. Now is not the time to be deceptive."

The ICU's overmotherly receptionist had brought him a sickly sweet coffee and watched him drink it down before deeming him recovered from his near faint. With her blessing, he had left the hospital immediately and caught the first bus home.

And though it was good to be home, he could not shake the feeling that as a family they were under attack from every side. The horrifying murder at the barbershop, the virus-infected mosquitoes on Omar's school trip, the escalating threats from the Caliph, and now, the names on the ICU's whiteboard that made it almost certain that a lethal microbe had contaminated Leila's equipment.

"Again, we must dig ourselves out of the mess others have thrust upon us," he told her. "If we do not step carefully, we will both be thrown in jail and Omar will be orphaned."

"Hosam, please. Do not say such things." Leila mimed covering her ears. "I cannot bear to hear you talk like that."

"I am only speaking the truth."

"Your vision of the truth." She paused and they both looked around the modest kitchen. Their house in Aleppo had a kitchen four times this size, and it opened into a garden resplendent with oranges, olives, and apricots. "What are we going to do?"

"Suspend your practice as of this minute."

She glanced at her watch, conscious that time was running out on her luncheon break. "I cannot do that. My afternoon clients will already be on their way. And people are counting on me." She opened her appointment planner and stabbed at the weeks of crowded entries. "Look — I have bookings more than a month in advance. I cannot cancel all these people at a moment's notice. And you know as well as I, as long as you're off work, we won't be able to pay the bills without the money I earn."

"We have no choice. You must call this afternoon's clients on their mobiles and put your practice on hiatus until this polio business goes away."

Tears flooded her cheeks. She tried to dry them with her palms, but the more she rubbed at her cheeks the more the tears flowed. "How can you be so certain I am . . ." she could barely bring herself to utter the word, ". . . *responsible* for this nightmare?"

As soon as he had returned from the hospital, he had compared his photo of the ICU's whiteboard with Leila's appointment log. Of the fifteen patients listed on the board, five were Leila's clients. He had expected as much, but seeing it confirmed in black and white was a punch in the gut. As soon as Leila finished with her last patient of the morning, he led her to the kitchen and showed her the startling evidence. Together, they had confronted the unthinkable: five of Leila's patients, all with appointments in April, were now attached to ventilators in Caledonian's high-tech ICU.

He grabbed Jamila Khateb's phone from the table and held up the damning photo again. "How many times do I need to show you? The evidence is undeniable."

She pointed to the screen. "Then you must send that picture to the health department and tell them what you discovered. The man in charge — you cut his hair, do you not?"

"Well, yes."

"Then you can make him understand. Tell him we did not mean any harm."

"He would not see it that way."

"How can you be so sure?"

"I helped you commit a criminal act that led to unthinkable consequences. The authorities will be anything but forgiving."

"Criminal? You're exaggerating. It is a matter of incomplete paperwork, nothing more. We agreed about that."

He said nothing. Months ago, they had told themselves that Leila would be committing a minor bureaucratic violation when she started her practice. Her qualifications back home were exemplary and it would be worth the risk. It was their best shot at a good life in this new land. He would have done the same except a surgeon needed a hospital and an operating theatre. Neither was available to him without the proper credentials vetted by the Canadian authorities.

"What about the other polio cases?" she said after her tears had begun to abate. "Surely, I am not responsible for those as well?"

All he could tell her was what he had seen half an hour ago on the television news. The outbreak total now stood at eleven and included three deaths. For the sake of the privacy of the families, no names were being released.

"If the six others are not my patients, then something else is responsible for the polio. I have always operated a spotless clinic, you know that. The equipment you purchased for me may be basic, but it works perfectly well. I refuse to believe I am responsible for this."

Hosam pulled this morning's *Hamilton Spectator* from the recycling bin under the kitchen sink. He opened it to a story on page four that talked about the city's small but tightly knit Ghanaian community. At breakfast, he had skimmed through the article and taken little note of the details. Now, as he read it again, he saw that the Ghanaians were organizing a candlelight vigil for a woman named Esi Asante who had been the first to die in the polio outbreak. A teacher's aide, she had been working to establish her credentials as a teacher. The community was raising money to send Esi's body home for burial in Africa.

"Look at this," he told Leila as he pointed to the woman's smiling face in the newspaper. "Do you remember her?"

Leila's face turned to ashes. "An extraction and two restorations. The woman had not seen a dentist in years." Leila put her head in her hands and sobbed so forcefully she could barely get any words out. "Oh my God. That makes six!"

Hosam knew there were bound to be more of Leila's patients among the epidemic's unnamed victims. But he refused to go to jail. Another incarceration would break him. It would kill Leila. And it would scar Omar forever.

The only answer was to go through Leila's supplies and equipment drawer by drawer and cupboard by cupboard. They had to find where the Parvo-W was hiding and destroy it. He looked toward the garage door. The virus was in there somewhere. And they were going to find it.

Bang!

It was only a sharp fist on the front door, but it hit both of them with the force of an explosion. Hosam's heart leaped into his throat as Leila screamed and covered her mouth. Seconds later, they heard the squeak of Omar's footsteps retreating up the stairs. *Merde*, the boy had heard everything.

The hinge on the mail slot creaked and something hit the floor with a soft thud. It could not be the mailman. He never came before two o'clock.

CHAPTER 43

Once he hit Barton Street, Jesse drove eastward toward Sherman Avenue. Ahead on the right, the striped brick steeple of St. Stanislaus Polish Roman Catholic Church rose above the fast-food joints and the We-Fix-Anything shops. He knew the Ukrainians' church was in the block beyond the Poles', but he couldn't make out its distinctive metal dome.

One block before St. Stan's, he turned left onto Earl Street (as in the 7th Earl of Elgin, the *Marble Taker* who swiped the Parthenon's statues and gave them to the British Museum). Jesse drove slowly, studying the house numbers as he went. There weren't many to check, the street being a mere two blocks long. Between the tired Victorian houses and empty lots resplendent with windblown litter, flat-roofed industrial blocks sat abandoned, their windows opaque with grime. One property stood out because of the lushness of its well-tended lawn, the gleam of its black iron fence, and the harmony between its high-pitched roof and arched front windows: the All Slavic Full Gospel Church. If it weren't for churchgoing Eastern Europeans, Jesse decided, this world-weary part of the city would be a heck of lot bleaker.

He'd memorized Darryl Oxman's cryptic daily-planner entries for the critical dates in April. If Jesse was on the right track as a code breaker, the possible numbers for Dr. L's (or Elle's) street address were 70, 308, and 2029. Here on Earl Street, number 70 was a vacant lot. The highest number was 310 where the road dead-ended at the railway tracks transecting the city's north end. Unit 308 was home to Happy Hydroponics. It was housed in a Frankenstein cross between a single-bay garage, a warehouse, and a budget self-storage facility. It looked like a respectable business, but any dentist who had set foot in the place had been set on gardening, not drilling teeth.

Jesse put the Mazda through a three-point turn at the tracks, headed back to Barton, and turned right toward downtown and Elgin Street.

At Barton Jail (that place was always in the news because of some scandal or other), he turned right at Elgin into a short block that once again terminated at the train tracks. No buildings fronted this block. The entire east side was taken up by the sizeable grounds of the jail. Along the west side stretched the parking lot that served the cut-price grocery store in the next street.

After another three-point turn, this time under the watchful eyes of the jail guards, Jesse drove south on Elgin. He crossed Barton at the Beer Store and started checking the street numbers. The first house on the left was 2129, the end of a row of nice-looking townhouses. The block had six front doors, 2119 to 2129, and two double-car garages, one at each end. After a slight gap, there was an identical six-unit row. Jesse hit the brakes when he spotted the number on the end unit's door: 2029. The 308th prime number, exactly as predicted by Darryl's code! (Could it be true?) The unit had an attached garage and nothing to indicate it was anything but a private residence. No sign on the lawn, nothing written on the front door, no notice in a window.

It was a decent-looking place that could easily accommodate a dentist's clandestine office, and Jesse's palms were slick with sweat at the possibility he'd cracked Darryl's code. Still, there were two other numbers on Elgin he had to investigate.

He drove into the next block. One hundred metres in, Elgin ended at a playground. There was no number 70. Number 308 was a small business, Beasley Glass and Window. A pickup outside it showed the same name and logo as the shop. There was no way this place was fronting for an underground dentist.

His heart thumping, he drove back to the townhouses. On the west side of the street, opposite number 2029, sat a derelict Honda Civic with rusted wheel wells, large patches of denuded paint, and four flat tires. It looked like Moses had been the last one to drive it and had faced it the wrong way for that side of the street. Jesse checked his left blind spot and drew in behind it. He took out his phone and snapped a few pics of house number 2029 to show Dr. Zed what he'd found (the boss couldn't help but be impressed).

A moment later, a tall woman cloaked in black from head to foot, and walking alone, rounded the corner from Barton Street. As she approached along the opposite sidewalk, Jesse could see that most of her face was covered with one of those black Muslim veils. A niqab, was it? Her gait slowed as she passed the first row of townhouses and got closer to the Honda in front of him. Jesse pulled his ball cap over his forehead and pretended to be asleep.

She stopped opposite number 2029 and looked up and down the street. She seemed satisfied that no one was watching and strode to the front door. She pulled something (an envelope?) out of a pocket with a gloved hand. She rapped on the door, slipped the envelope through the mail slot, then turned sharply and jogged back toward Barton Street. Her gait was no longer a woman's. The figure under the clothing had beefy shoulders, Jesse realized, and a long, athletic stride. He was wearing construction boots.

Jesse hunched down in his seat and snapped the retreating figure through the front passenger window. Then he opened his backpack and pulled out the gear he'd assembled at home.

He took the tiny, high-resolution IP camera, connected it to the battery pack, and switched it on. The battery-strength indicator was at ninety-seven percent, which would run the camera for forty-eight hours. The data-only cellular service via the camera's

SIM card showed four bars — full strength. In *Settings*, he chose the time-lapse mode at five frames per second and the day/night option that made the camera switch automatically to infrared after sunset. Finally, he made sure the images would be sent continuously to his Dropbox account in the Cloud. Now, from any computer or smartphone, he would be able to observe the comings and goings at number 2029. (Well, as long as no one spotted the camera and snatched it.)

Before getting out of the car, he studied the little Victorian house beside him. Every curtain was drawn. Across the street at numbers 2029, 2027, and 2025, the blinds were in various degrees of closure, and he could see no one in the windows. If he was quick, no one would see him. He stuffed the gear in his windbreaker pocket, stepped out of the Mazda, and eased the door closed.

The Honda looked so derelict that Jesse figured it wouldn't be locked. He was wrong. He'd have to stash the camera and battery somewhere on the outside of the car. He bent down and examined the two wheel wells that faced the street. The back half of the car was rusted so badly there were numerous peepholes that would do nicely for the camera. He massaged a wad of adhesive putty and pressed it onto the inner surface of the right rear wheel well. Bits of metal crumbled under the pressure, and the hole got larger than he would have liked. But he figured he could make it work. He pressed the camera into the putty, secured the battery pack in a similar fashion, and stood back to examine his handiwork. Unless you knew the camera was there, you wouldn't see it. The battery was completely out of sight.

He turned the Mazda around and drove back to the playground at the south end of Elgin Street. It was a good bet the Honda was a permanent fixture the neighbours had stopped noticing, but they'd be quick to spot an unfamiliar vehicle parked behind it. He killed the engine, opened his Dropbox account from his phone, and called up the live image from the camera. The lens angle needed adjustment. It was aimed too much at the sidewalk and not enough at number 2029's front door. He also needed to make the angle oblique enough that he would be able to read the license plates of passing vehicles. If Darryl had a reason for writing Dr. L's address in secret code, other than his penchant for cryptography, Jesse might not be the only one keeping Dr. L's place under surveillance.

He locked the Mazda and walked back to the Honda while appearing to be texting on his phone like any other twenty-something with nothing better to do. Again, he checked the windows, roadway, and sidewalk for prying eyes. Satisfied that the street was still deserted, he put his hand inside the wheel well and adjusted the camera's aim until he liked the image he saw on his phone. Anyone observing him would think he was assessing the condition of the bodywork and posting photos of the rusted parts on Facebook or Instagram (well, he hoped so).

He could see on the screen that behind him 2029's front door was opening. He turned and leaned against the car as casually as he could and made a show of thumbing furiously on his phone. He hoped he looked as if his attention was focused a million klicks from everything and everyone on this street.

A thirty-something man with dark hair stepped out through the door and called to someone inside as he left. His voice was sharp and tinged with anger, and the words didn't sound like English. When the guy turned to walk down the front steps, Jesse stepped in front of the IP camera, not yet satisfied he'd hidden it perfectly. He stole a look at the man's face. Above a luxurious black moustache, a pair of grey-blue eyes gaped in terror.

CHAPTER 44

At one thirty, Hosam locked the front door behind him and walked to Barton Street. As directed, he turned right at the Beer Store and kept walking. His shoes felt as if they were filled with the sands of a thousand deserts.

The note through the mail slot said the Caliph had one more job for him. It told him when and where to meet then said: *You will be released from your obligations if your performance on a final job is satisfactory. But if you choose not to show up as directed, your family will pay the price. None of you will be spared.*

At first, Leila had warned him not to go. But when she read the note for herself, the consequences of defiance were too much for either of them. Buying their freedom with one more act of petty thievery seemed like a reasonable offer. But was it foolish to think that after this final demand the Caliph would leave them alone?

Across Barton Street, the Detention Centre did not look as intimidating in the pale sunshine as it did at night, but he knew the Caliph was still playing with his head by forcing him to walk past it. Up the street, on the far side of Ferguson Avenue, was a Tim Hortons. A car would be waiting.

When he reached the Tim's, Hosam scanned the parking lot. He had no idea what sort of vehicle to look for. A small grey Ford, a Focus, flashed its headlamps. Behind both the wheel and an oversized pair of sunglasses was his chauffeur. He breathed a sigh of relief. He had been down this road before and knew more or less what to expect.

Saramin lowered the Ford's passenger window and told him to get in.

"We do not usually meet in the daytime," he said as he buckled his seatbelt. "Or in such a modest vehicle."

"It's fully paid for. That's what matters."

"Is it not a little small for a job?"

"We're not going on a job," she said.

"No?"

"Not yet."

"Let me guess. I am about to receive an offer I cannot refuse?"

"Keep quiet and let me drive."

She turned to the right out of the Tim's onto Barton Street and then left at the second street, Victoria. Ahead of them, two complete city blocks on either side were taken up by the Hamilton Centre for TLC. Once a trauma centre, it was now a chronic-care institution run by a Christian church he had never heard of before, the Mennonites.

Behind the institution's main building, a multi-storey parking garage rose from the industrial lands around it. She steered left into its entrance and took the ticket offered by the machine. When the gate went up, she drove sedately to the fifth floor. She parked in a lonely spot and turned off the ignition. Only three other vehicles were in sight, and they were a long way off.

"Okay," she said, flipping her iron-straight locks behind her shoulders. "Here's the deal. The Caliph needs you to take Mo's place."

"You cannot be serious."

"The Caliph is always serious. Anyway, I haven't told you what the job is."

Should he tell her he had already guessed that Mo was the Caliph's man with a pistol? No. The less he said the better.

"Okay, I am listening."

"It requires only a steady hand." She looked at his hands. "You're a surgeon, so your two will do nicely. I have seen them at work, remember."

"What . . . what does the Caliph have in mind?"

"A quick job. At close range. With a special instrument."

"What instrument?"

"I think you can guess."

The terrible scene in the barbershop overtook him. He could see the doctor's son crumpled on the floor. And Marwan's carotid artery saturating the towels faster than Hosam could change them.

"I am not hacking anyone to death with a knife. No matter what, I will not do that for anyone, not even the Caliph."

"Not a knife, for God's sake."

"Then, what?"

"A Glock."

He felt the sweat streaming down his temples. "I have never used one."

"It's easy. You get close to the target, and you pull the trigger. We'll take you somewhere to practise. And we'll arrange for you to get close to him." She threw him a steely look. "Extremely close."

Putain! They had their plan laid out and ready to go. And had placed him at the centre of it. "Who is the target?"

"You don't need to know that yet." She touched the side of her nose. "Safer for you that way until we are given the final go-ahead from our colleagues. They're verifying credentials."

Credentials? They must be watching him. He took a deep breath and plunged in. "Why do the Scarpellinos not hire their own hitman? Are they testing your partnership?"

She looked affronted. "We don't need testing. We're their equals in every way." She paused for a long moment as if wondering how much she was prepared to tell him. Her face relaxed. "It's a business decision on their part."

It seemed the Caliph was offering hitmen at a discount. How much would the Scarpellinos pay the Caliph for a Syrian refugee to knock off a Michelini and begin to even the score? A lot less than they would pay an Italian, Hosam was certain of that. And it was a safer tactic. Refugee Syrians were as low on the social scale as you could get, and those who spoke English could hide in plain sight. And, as Mo's accident had proved, they were expendable.

But how, *Allah have mercy on us*, was he going to get out of this and keep his family safe? He pictured the lethal cocktail of anesthetic agents he had stashed above the bathroom ceiling tiles and bemoaned the limits of its effectiveness. The drugs might neutralize Saramin on a dark night, but the two of them were never completely alone. He would be discovered immediately, and killing her was unthinkable anyway. The real threats to his family were the Caliph, his henchmen, and the Scarpellinos. To neutralize all of them, he needed a militia, not a bag of medical tricks.

CHAPTER 45

Hosam's "appointment" with Saramin, though it left him with a leaden heart, did not last long. He returned directly home, and by four o'clock that afternoon, he and Leila had gone through all the supplies in her clinic searching for possible breaks in her chain of sterility. Transmission of microbes between dental patients was a well-known problem, especially in low-income countries during desperate times. Doctors and dentists had transmitted HIV, Hepatitis C, and other infections via contaminated needles and medications. But Leila used disposable, single-use needles and syringes for every injection. The local anesthetic she favoured, generic lidocaine, came in small plastic vials from a respected Canadian pharmaceutical firm. She opened a fresh vial for each patient.

"I never double dip," she told him. "To save money, some dentists use what is left from previous patients. But I always open a new vial." Her eyes filled with tears at the accusations hanging over her like the yellow flag on a plague ship.

The metal amalgam she used for her fillings was manufactured in Israel and arrived by Canada Post. Again, she used single-use packets to avoid cross-contamination. The packs always arrived intact and came from a distributor well respected in dental circles.

The mouth rinse and dental floss she purchased in Hamilton at Walmart. The company offered the best prices, and if their products were carrying Parvo-W, Hosam figured the polio problem would not be limited to the City of Hamilton. There would be dozens, maybe even hundreds, of polio cases worldwide. The long arms of Walmart reached into the far corners of several continents.

"Now, we must look at your instruments," he told her. "Maybe your autoclave is not achieving the proper temperature."

"It always gets extremely hot when I run it," she said.

"Is there a temperature readout?"

She pointed to an analogue gauge on the side of the autoclave. "That is it, right there." It looked surprisingly crude for something made in the digital age. "The arrow moves to the green side every time we run it," she said. "My girls know to check for that."

"And they write it down with the date and time?" In Syria, before the war, his hospital had kept a detailed log of the temperature and pressure achieved each time the autoclaves were put through their sterilization cycles. Every tray of instruments sent for sterilization included an indicator strip that turned colour if the proper microbe-killing conditions were achieved. Of course, once the war hit, the strips became unavailable and many other safety measures were tossed aside. Sometimes, something as simple as bringing a pan of water to the boil had been impossible.

A guilty look overtook Leila's face. "They wrote everything in a notebook when we first started. But then we got busier than I ever expected." Her cheeks flushed as she added, "Sometimes, we have to cut a few corners to cope with the pace in here." She stared into his face and her anger flared. "Do not look at me like that. You of all people know that everything cannot be perfect all the time. But I promise you, we never do anything that puts our patients at risk."

"What about the indicator strips? Do they always turn the proper colour in the autoclave?"

She bit her lower lip and looked away.

"What?" he said.

When she still didn't answer, he said, "Ya Rab, Leila. Tell me."

She sighed heavily as if he had no business putting her on the spot. "They are on order."

"Since when?"

"I do not remember. Six weeks?"

In his head, he counted back six weeks. The timing hit him like a mortar shell. "You have not been using indicator strips since March?"

"I told you, the temperature gauge always goes into the green."

"But it could be faulty."

"The machine is still new. You said it was a good one when you ordered it."

"Yes, but equipment can always go wrong."

"Do not raise your voice at me."

She was right. He was almost shouting. He did the same in the operating theatre when he was losing a patient on the table. "I have been reading about parvoviruses," he said, taking care to lower his voice. "They can survive higher temperatures than other viruses. If your autoclave is not working properly, we may have found the problem."

"But where did the parvovirus come from in the first place?"

He threw up his hands. "Your patients come from the four corners of the Earth. Any of them could have cursed us with that virus."

There was a firm knock on the outside door.

Leila looked at her watch. "That must be Mr. Zadran. He is booked for four o'clock. He didn't answer when I called to cancel his appointment. Perhaps he was running his saw and didn't hear the phone."

"You cannot let him in here."

"I know that, Hosam. You do not have to tell me."

"What will he bring us from his shop today, do you suppose?" Last time it was a leg of lamb with the bone removed. Before that, three roasting chickens. He had the best halal meat in this part of the city.

"Whatever it is, I must give him some cash. If I cannot work on his teeth, I cannot accept his offerings without paying for them."

Hosam told her not to reward the butcher too generously and walked toward the inside door that led to kitchen. "I am going to Omar's room. There cannot be a worldwide shortage of autoclave test strips. Surely Amazon can deliver us a box of them by the weekend. I will not sleep until we get this issue settled."

"I may never sleep again," she said softly then she threw cold water onto her face from the hand basin and dabbed at her blood-shot eyes.

CHAPTER 46

Zol left the house on Thursday morning feeling guilty about leaving Tasha to her morning sickness. She'd shooed him out the door and told him not to fuss, reminding him that she'd perked up yesterday by ten o'clock and put in more than a full day's work. She had indeed. She'd calmed the women's fears at their lunch cooperative and confirmed that, in addition to Blessica Velasquez, three polio cases had been treated recently by a female dentist. According to Bhavjeet, she worked out of a garage attached to a townhouse. In what part of the city she plied her trade was still anyone's guess.

Anxious to know what Jesse had discovered from Darryl Oxman's employer — and frustrated that he'd received nothing more from the kid than a brief text saying he was working on a lead — Zol was doubly disappointed that Jesse was nowhere to be seen when he arrived at the office at eight o'clock. Young people never answered their phones. And getting a young man to respond to your text message with more than five cryptic words was like . . . well, it was like pulling teeth.

Shortly after nine, Jesse rapped on Zol's office door, a large messenger bag hanging from his shoulder. The earrings were back. Well, just one — a Long John Silver hoop through his left earlobe.

"Hi, Dr. Zed. Is this a good time?"

"Where have you been? We're supposed to be working as a team, you know."

He looked hurt for an instant, then recovered quickly. "Sorry I haven't been at my desk. But when I show you what I've got, I think you'll be —"

Zol pointed to Jesse's bag. "Is that your laptop? What've you been up to?"

Jesse flushed. "It's best if you don't ask too many questions, Dr. Zed."

"Show me what you've got. And then I'll decide about the questions." Zol pointed to the chair beside his desk. "Have a seat."

Jesse made himself comfortable and pulled a notebook and a small daily planner from his bag. He showed them to Zol and told a complicated story about Darryl Oxman's root canal, the first five hundred prime numbers, the Fibonacci Sequence, a doctor called either L or Elle, a crossword puzzle clue about stolen marbles, two streets in the city's central core, and a surveillance camera he'd hidden in a rusted-out Honda Civic.

How sure was the kid that overnight someone hadn't stolen his camera and the video footage? Parts of the North End could be rough. "When will you have something on video to show me? Or is that where you've been, retrieving the tape?"

Jesse laughed. "There's no such thing as tape anymore, Dr. Zed. Everything is digital."

"All the same, are you sure your camera hasn't been stolen or tampered with?"

"It's got a built-in SIM card." Jesse paused to see if Zol was following, which he wasn't completely. "Like a cellphone. It connects directly to the internet and sends video images in real time to an account I have in the Cloud."

"You mean you've got something to show me? Right now?"

Jesse pulled the laptop from his bag and beamed from earlobe to earlobe as he set it on Zol's desk. "You bet."

With a few strokes on the keyboard, Jesse brought up an image of a row of townhouses. It was difficult to tell whether it was a still or a video image because nothing was happening.

"What you are seeing here are two townhouses in a six-unit row: 2027 and 2029 Elgin Street," Jesse said. "If I have it right, number 2029 fits Darryl Oxman's code. And as you can see, it has an attached garage."

Bhavjeet hadn't been able to remember much about the dentist who had extracted his teeth, but he'd told Tasha that her office was in a garage attached to a townhouse. Maybe Jesse was on to something.

"Looks pretty quiet," Zol said. "Is that what's happening now, or was that recorded sometime yesterday?"

"Yesterday afternoon."

"Where is this street?"

"Partway between Cathcart Elementary and Sir John A. High. In Beasley."

Before Zol had time to react to what could be fine work on Jesse's part or just a coincidence, he saw the front door of unit 2029 begin to open and what looked like a man's foot step through it. Then the screen went black. Jesse hit Fast Forward and said, "Sorry about that, I was just getting the camera set up at the time."

"A problem with it?"

"No, I was afraid the guy was going to spot me fiddling with the Honda. So I stepped between him and the camera and made it look like I was texting."

"Like everyone else your age. I get it. Did you get a look at the guy?"

"Yeah. Thirty-something. Big black moustache. Greek or maybe Italian. A movie-star look about him. Like Javier Bardem. He was in —"

"I know who you mean. He won an Oscar a few years back. *No Country for Old Men.* One of my favourites. You think your guy lives in that townhouse?"

"He has a front-door key."

"My barber kind of looks like Bardem. I hope you weren't spying on him."

Jesse patted the top edge of the laptop as if it were a friend. "It's okay, Dr. Zed. He comes back."

"Did you see a woman who might be living or working there?"

"Sorry. No glimpses of Darryl's dentist . . . if that's where she works."

"How many hours of footage do you have there?"

"About eighteen."

Zol looked at his watch. "Holy smokes, Jesse. We can't sit here for eighteen hours."

"It's okay, Dr. Zed. The software automatically makes an abbreviated version containing only segments that show something moving."

"You've had a look at that?"

Jesse's face filled with pride. "I've been up since five listing a summary of yesterday's activity for you."

"I'm ready to be impressed, Dr. Jay."

The kid's eyes sparkled as he fanned himself with his notebook. "It's a quiet street. Not many cars go down it. Lots of people walk by without showing an interest in any of the houses. I don't think you want to hear about every one of them."

"Good thinking."

Jesse nodded and continued. "A few cars go by now and then, most of them without stopping or slowing down. None of them park." Jesse consulted his notes. His printing was surprisingly neat — like calligraphy. "Moustache guy comes back at 13:58, opens the door with a key, and goes inside."

"Sounds like he lives there."

Jesse tapped the keyboard and brought up a video of a man in his fifties approaching the townhouse from the left of the screen. He was carrying a small duffle bag and wearing an unusual wool hat the shape of an English pork pie. It was beige, soft-sided, and flat on top. The lower edge was rolled.

"That's him?" Zol asked "I thought you said your guy was in his thirties. That man is closer to sixty."

Jesse hit pause and the man stopped in mid-stride. "Sorry, sometimes this program jumps ahead faster than I'd like. This is a different fellow. He arrived at 15:58. If you don't mind, I'll run the clip and see what you think of him."

Jesse tapped the keyboard and the man continued walking toward the townhouse. He went straight to the left side of the garage and began knocking. The camera angle didn't show what he was knocking on. It could have been a door, a window, or the exterior wall. When no one answered him, he put down his duffle bag, looked at his watch, and shook his head as if puzzled by the lack of response. He knocked again. A person must have finally come to the door, because the video showed the man lifting his duffle bag and talking with someone unseen. In the course of the conversation, he shrugged as if in resignation, then pulled a plastic grocery bag from the duffle and coaxed the person at the door to take it. A moment later, he received something in return — an envelope or perhaps a few bills — then gave a friendly wave and walked in the direction from which he'd come.

"What was that about?" Zol asked. "It certainly wasn't a dental appointment. What was he selling?"

"I Googled the hat," Jesse said. "It's called a pakol. Worn by Afghani tribesmen, especially in the cooler months."

"So what's an Afghani tribesman selling door-to-door at an address that Darryl Oxman wrote in secret code? You seemed to have cracked the cipher, but I'm not sure you're on the right track here, Jesse."

"Please, Dr. Zed. Can I show you a couple more highlights?"

"Only if you think they're significant to our investigation."

With a few keystrokes, Jesse brought up a clip showing a black Lexus SUV. The driver was wearing a ball cap and aviator sunglasses. He slowed to walking speed as he passed unit 2029. It looked like he might stop, but he didn't.

"I have four clips just like that," Jesse said.

"Same vehicle?"

"And driver."

"When was that?"

Jesse pointed to the date and time stamp on the screen. "That was at 17:01. The other three are within half an hour of it."

"Impressive," Zol said. "Your camera's so good it picks up the plate number."

Jesse smiled. "Wouldn't you love to know who owns that vehicle?"

"We'd have to get permission, and I have no idea how to do that. A warrant from a judge, I suppose." Zol shook his head. "Forget it. If there was a dentist operating out of that garage, you'd have captured people coming and going at regular intervals. There was only that one man, right? In the hat?"

Jesse wasn't listening. He was clicking away at the keyboard. A second later, a mugshot filled the screen.

"Who's that?" Zol said.

"The vehicle owner. Charged with extortion last year but quickly released because of lack of evidence."

"How do you . . . ?" Zol held up his hands. "Wait. Don't tell me. I don't want to know. And as an employee of the Health Unit, you shouldn't . . ."

"His name is Andrea Scarpellino."

The family had been all over the papers lately. "Two Scarpellino brothers were recently gunned down at close range," Zol said. "Am I right?"

Jesse smiled. "In a turf war with the Michelinis."

"You'd better retrieve your camera. If they find out you've been spying . . . Shit, Jesse. I should never have —"

The kid was clicking again. "Before we pull the plug, let me show you the guy who looks like Javier Bardem."

The time stamp was dated yesterday at 13:58. A tallish man with a bushy moustache was walking along the sidewalk toward the townhouses. When he got to unit 2029, he inserted a key in the front-door lock. Before opening the door, he turned around as if checking to see if he'd been followed. He looked straight into the lens of Jesse's camera.

The room began to spin.

Zol felt Jesse's hand grip his shoulder. "Dr. Zed, are you okay? I think you need a glass of water."

"My God, Jesse, that *is* my barber."

CHAPTER 47

On Thursday afternoon Max and Travis were in the kitchen guzzling their after-school dose of OJ when Max's dad called from work.

"Hi Dad," Max said. "What's up?

"I . . . I just want to be sure you're not planning to go back to the barbershop for a while."

"If you mean the one where Hosam works, it doesn't matter if they haven't cleaned the place up perfectly. We don't mind a little blood."

"I don't care in the least how clean it is, Max. You're not going."

Max rubbed a hand across the back of his scalp. His fade needed a trim, and badly. "But I need a haircut. Hosam only did Trav's hair before those guys . . . Well, when can I go back?"

"Maybe never."

Max's heart rate jumped from zero to sixty. Had Dad found out that Marwan's killing wasn't a one-off personal vendetta? Had he found out about the Caliph and his gang? Was he going to force Travis and him to go to the police and tell them what they suspected? "Why, Dad?"

"Where are you?"

"In the kitchen."

"What kitchen?"

"Da-ad — you called me on our landline. You know what kitchen I'm in. Are you okay? You don't sound right."

"Is Travis there with you?"

"Yeah."

"Anyone else?"

"No. What's this —"

"Put the phone on speaker. I want you both to hear this because I'm only going to say it once. Got it?"

Max pressed the speakerphone button and handed the phone to Travis, who made a show of setting the device carefully between them in the middle of the table.

"Okay, Dad. We're listening. Both of us."

"I . . . I have reason to believe that the barber's murder had something to . . . well, something to do with a turf war between two families, the Scarpellinos and the Michelinis. Do you know what a turf war is?"

The boys looked at each other and rolled their eyes.

"You mean," said Max, "it was an *Italian* mob hit?"

"Well . . . I guess . . . yes. That *is* what I mean."

Max leaned back in his chair. Clearly, his dad didn't have access to the same insider facts that he and Travis did via Omar. If Dad thought the Italians were involved, then he had no idea about Hosam's threatening notes from the Caliph. Dad was fingering the wrong mob. Max knew a lot more about the local mobster scene than his dad imagined. He and Travis had a student in their class, Joey Scarpellino, who'd recently missed school after two of his uncles got shot through the head. Joey bragged that a thousand people filled the cathedral for each funeral Mass and that his family was preparing to get revenge on the Michelinis.

"I want you boys to give Paradise Barbers a miss for the time being."

"Okay, Dad," said Max. It wasn't the Italians he and Travis were afraid of, but Dad was right. They did need to give Paradise Barbers a wide berth. "But I'm not going back to that barber on Garth Street. His breath stinks."

"So we're good, Max?"

There was a ping on Max's laptop. Omar. Hosam still wasn't letting him go to school, so the kid was bored. These days, he was messaging them as soon as he figured they'd be home from school and ready for a game of *Fortnite*. He was bursting to hit another dub, but lately his game had been off and his kill counts were down.

"Max?" Zol said. "We're good?"

"Yeah, Dad. Gotta go. See you at supper."

KB. you home from school?

> *We're here. Me and Travman. How's it going, Omar?*

terrible.
lady from the health place
call today. she speak to me
first
then my dad. he home early
from werk because no one
coming
to barbershop after murder.

> *What did the lady say?*

my blood test is bad. my
dad say i get polio if i go in
my mother garage.

> *What blood test?*

i think she say zeeka. from
my mosquito bites.

> *Who called you? Someone from the health department?*

name Miss Charmin. like
toilet paper on tv. she sound
nice.

Travis nudged Max's arm. "He means Tasha."

"What?"

"As in Sharma. You know, Charmin? Sharma?"

"Good one, Trav."

"But don't tell him we know her."

I'm glad she was nice.

my dad talk to her then
hang up.
my parents get angry. my
mother cry.
tell me not go in garage. if i
do. i die.

*Don't worry, Omar. They're
exaggerating to make you listen
because they think it's
important. They don't really mean
you are going to die.*

exaggerating??? wait. let me
check google translate.
no, i not exaggerating. my
parents very serious.
yesterday they stay hours
in garage. cleaning and
shouting.
he say she doing bad werk
and making people sick.
she say she making money to
buy food plus my laptop and
other special things.
now my father force her to
stop working because he say
polio
hiding in garage.

> *Did Miss Charmin tell you not to go
> into the garage?*

!!! no. garage is big secret.
nobody know. only clients
know.
my dad say goverment not
like it. put my mother in jail.

"What's his mother doing in their garage, KB?" Travis said. "She can't be a mechanic because cars and trucks don't give you polio. She must be a hooker. That's why she's afraid of going to jail for transmitting germs."

"You can't get polio from sex, Trav."

"Who knows for sure? Your dad and Tasha both said this kind of polio is different from the kind they had in our grandparents' day."

That got Max thinking. "Holy crap, you could be right. Omar's mother could be a hooker. She obviously has clients who don't want anyone to know what they're up to."

"Ask him what she does in the garage. But . . ." Trav's eyes were huge. "But for shit's sake, don't let him know we think his mom's a hooker."

Max rolled his eyes. "What kind of idiot do you —?"

"I'm just saying . . ."

"Sometimes I like it better when you don't say."

Travis smacked his good arm. "Yeah, yeah, whatever. Just go ahead and ask him."

> *What sort of work does your
> mother do in the garage, Omar?*

big secret. i cannot tell.

> *But if your life is in danger, maybe
> we can help you.*

you help? how?

"He's right," Travis said. "How *can* we help him? If his parents

302

are frightened about the government, reminding him about your dad being in charge of the Health Unit will scare him off."

> *I'm not sure Omar, but we are your friends. And friends always help friends.*
> *We'll think of something. It always helps to talk. That way you know you aren't alone and things don't seem so scary.*

you are my real friends? not
just fortnite squad friends?

> *Yes.*

for sure?

> *100 percent.*

promise on grandmother
grave to keep garage
secret?

> *Yes, definitely.*

KB and TRAVMAN? both?

> *Both of us.*

promise?

> *We promise.*

okay.
my mother she fix teeth.
back home she is dentist.

> *Her dental office is in your garage?*

my dad make it for
her. extra water pipes.
equipment.
special chair.
sorry KB. my father coming
now. must close laptop.

> *Your secret is safe with us, Omar. On our grandmothers' graves.*

We will think of some way to help you.

remember friends never
break promise.

Omar logged off.

"What do we do now?" Travis said.

"About what?"

Max knew perfectly well what Travis was talking about, but he was stalling while his mind spun.

"Do we tell your dad that Hosam's wife is doing dental surgery illegally in their garage?"

"We promised Omar we wouldn't. On our grandmother's graves. Between us, that's four of them in total. And soon I'll be getting a new grandmother who's going to die sooner or later and that will be a fifth grandmother's grave."

"Don't be a smartass, KB. People's lives are at stake."

"We don't know that for sure. And neither does Hosam. He's probably overreacting. The polio epidemic has him spooked because he found out his son's Zika virus test is positive, and he feels guilty that his wife is operating an illegal dental clinic that could get both of them in trouble. Do you actually think we should rat on them?"

"Doing the right thing is not ratting," Travis said. "It's being a good citizen."

"As always, you have the theory perfect. But this is personal, Trav. Omar is a lonely kid who has no one but us to talk to. He trusts us to keep his secret — we promised. And Hosam's a good guy. He took great care of us after that attack, remember. Don't you think we owe him some major slack?"

Travis drummed his fingers on the table while he did some serious thinking. Finally, he said, "Can we compromise?"

"How?"

"We search Google for anything that connects dentists, polio, and parvoviruses. Your dad told us a parvovirus is playing a cru- cial role in the polio epidemic, right? If we find no connection between parvo and dentists, we don't report Hosam and his wife to your dad."

"If you insist."

Max logged onto Google. Travis gave him the search terms he wanted, and Max typed them in.

They didn't get any hits that connected parvoviruses with dentists. There were lots of sites that described parvovirus infections in animals: dogs, parrots, starfish, crickets, and weird-looking cats in Asia called civets. If Omar's mom was operating an illegal vet clinic, they would have to worry. It seemed it was a good thing she was a dentist.

"Okay, you win," Travis said. "We keep quiet." He returned the OJ carton to the fridge and said in his no-nonsense voice, "For now."

CHAPTER 48

On Friday morning at six fifteen, Hosam stepped off the Route 34 Upper Paradise bus at his usual spot, made the short walk to the barbershop, and unlocked the door. He locked it behind him immediately and checked that the closed sign was still lit. He made sure the blinds were tightly shut. Unless he had been frightened off like so many of their other regular clients, Joe Smith would be arriving anytime between now and six forty-five. Sometimes he arrived from one direction, sometimes from the other. He never parked in exactly the same spot — sometimes up the street, sometimes in the parking lot at the front. Though he varied his route and arrival time, he came to his appointment every Friday without fail. Today, that loyalty to Paradise Barbers was going to be tested. And so was his vanity.

Every week, "Mr. Smith" came for the same service: a hot-lather shave, a businessman's trim, and a twenty-minute colour rinse in Midnight Brown. He paid the going rate plus a seventy-five-dollar tip in cash, which Ibrahim and Hosam were only too glad to accept. As the shop's senior barber, Ibrahim usually looked after Mr. Smith. But on days like today when he couldn't get to the shop early enough, he asked Hosam to take his place. Understandably, Mr. Smith did not want anyone to know he had his hair dyed, which explained the clandestine nature of his weekly visits. His name may have been Smith, but he had the complexion of a Hussein, an Onassis, or even a Khayyam. And like many Mediterranean men, he had a heavy beard and appreciated the straight-razor shave that left his neck, chin, and cheeks feeling like an infant's bottom.

Mr. Smith was extremely fit, and rather vain, admiring himself in the shop's large mirror a couple of times every visit. The muscles of his neck, arms, and shoulders were impressive. He admitted to lifting weights regularly. And he probably took androgens. If he was not careful, the hair on his scalp would thin more than it had already. No amount of Midnight Brown would fix that. He had told Hosam he was in commercial real estate: buying, selling, and renting. From the size of the diamond attached to the cross around his neck, it was clear that Mr. Smith was a wealthy man.

Today, he arrived at six forty. And, for the first time since Hosam had met him, he was not alone. Someone else had driven his black S-Class. The driver parked close to the barbershop's door and remained with the vehicle. Mr. Smith studied the shop with a suspicious eye as Hosam locked the door behind him. Was he looking for threatening figures or for signs of the bloodbath he would have heard about on the news? The few clients who turned up yesterday morning had done the same.

Hosam took the man's suit jacket, and by the time he had hung it up, his client had already undone the top buttons of his shirt and was making himself comfortable in Hosam's chair.

"Looks like they cleaned the place up pretty good," Mr. Smith said.

"They are thorough, these special cleaning companies."

"Do you have any idea who those two guys were working for? I doubt it was a random attack."

Hosam shook his head and busied himself with his preparations. He removed Mr. Smith's badger shaving brush and Jermyn Street (London) shaving soap from their place in the cupboard. He had already prepared the towels, loaded the razor with a new blade, and run the water until it was hot.

Mr. Smith never talked while Hosam was shaving him. Sometimes, he relaxed so much during the experience that he fell asleep. Today, he seemed preoccupied. Did he have a major business deal on his mind? He did not seem the type of man to be bothered by the fact that a week ago the chair beside him had been dripping in blood.

Ninety minutes later, well before the shop was due to open at nine o'clock, Hosam sprayed a little of Mr. Smith's favourite cologne on his neck, removed the cape, and showed off his artistry in the hand mirror.

"As usual, a great job. You'd never know I'd had it done. Thanks, Hosam."

"Always a pleasure, Mr. Smith."

They walked together to the front desk and the man pulled out his wallet. "Shit. I'm sorry, Hosam. I gave all my cash to my kid last night. He's twenty-two, and I'm still paying for his beer and pizza. Go figure."

Hosam smiled. He genuinely liked this man. He admired his appealing mix of physical strength, wealth, and folksy demeanour. And if it were not for the man's vanity, Hosam would have fewer dollars in his pocket at the end of each month.

"No problem," Hosam told him. "You can pay next week."

"No, I'm gonna pay now. Business may be slow in here for a while. You take Visa?"

"Certainly."

"Great," he said and handed Hosam a small green envelope the size of a credit card. It took Hosam a second to realize it was an RFID protection sleeve with the Visa card inside it.

Hosam slid two fingers into the open end of the envelope. Two cards slipped out. The Visa credit card, in the name of Joe Smith, stayed between his fingers. The second card dropped onto the desk. When Hosam picked it up to return it to the envelope, he saw it was a driver's license.

The face in the photo was the one he had just shaved.

The name on the license said Giuseppe Michelini.

Hosam swallowed hard, and with shaky hands returned the license to the envelope as rapidly as he could, hoping Il Proppo had not noticed. He processed the payment on the cash register and inserted the Visa card into the reader. The man took the reader, studied the screen, and pressed the required sequence of buttons that included his PIN. Before handing the device back, he said, "It's better for you if I don't put the tip on the card. I'm gonna send someone tomorrow with the cash."

Hosam waved one hand dismissively. The other was holding onto the desk while every drop of blood drained from his cheeks. He was trying to look natural, but he had never been able to keep his surprise, or his darkest thoughts, from showing on his face. He knew his eyes would be black and his skin a sickly shade of green. "Um . . . You do not need to do that, um . . . sir. Next time, um . . . next you come in —"

The man lunged across the desk, grabbed Hosam by the neck of his polo shirt, and twisted hard.

It felt like his eyes were about to pop out of his cranium.

He could not breathe.

"You saw, didn't you?"

Hosam lifted his arms and shoulders in a flaccid half-shrug. He tried to cough, but the man had his neck in a steely, two-handed grip.

"So what're you going to do about it?"

Hosam had learned at the hands of the Mukhabarat that battling torturers made everything worse. If the man wanted answers to his questions, he would have to let go of his throat.

Il Proppo glanced at the door as if expecting reinforcements to storm through it any second. "Speak up, or I'll make the bloodbath you had in here last week look like a Sunday-school picnic."

Hosam pointed at the thumbs on his trachea. "Cannot . . . talk."

The man gave the windows a quick study. Satisfied the blinds were closed, he let go of Hosam's neck and pointed to Hosam's apron. "Empty your pockets. All of them."

Hosam removed the scissors and comb from his apron and his wallet from his trousers. He held them out for Il Proppo to see.

"Drop them on the desk."

He did as he was told.

"Now take off that apron. And your shirt."

He draped them over the chair beside him.

"Drop your pants."

Wondering what was coming next, Hosam simply stood and stared.

"Don't give me that look. You know I'm not a goddamn pervert. I need to see for myself you're not wearing a wire."

Hosam undid his belt and let his trousers fall to his ankles.

"Turn around."

He steadied himself with the chair as he turned three-sixty degrees. He prayed that Il Proppo would not comment on the web of scars left by the Mukhabarat's daily lashings. He did not want this man's pity. His anger was bad enough.

"Looks like you're clean. Put your clothes on. And then tell me what you know about my family."

Hosam did not know what to say. If he told this guy the unvarnished truth, he would call his bodyguard out of the car and the two of them would turn him into hamburger meat.

"Stop stalling."

"Your . . . your rivals," he said, buttoning up his shirt, "they have been hassling me."

"The Scarpellinos? You owe them money?"

"I owe them nothing. I have not even seen them."

Il Proppo scanned the shop like a jackal. "What? They want you to pay protection? Don't worry, I can take care of that."

Hosam shook his head. "It is not about protection."

"Then what do those fuckers want?"

"I must perform a job for them. If I do not, they will do terrible things to my wife and my son."

Il Proppo thought for a moment. "I get it. They know you're a surgeon. They want you to cut a stiff into pieces for easy disposal?"

"They are not interested in my surgical skills."

Il Proppo flexed the fingers of his massive hands. The implication was obvious.

Hosam looked Il Proppo in the eye and told him straight. "They want me to kill you. Or a powerful person in your family business. They have not revealed the exact target."

"What? You're supposed to slit my throat while you're shaving me?"

"He wants me to use his Glock."

"Whose Glock?"

Hosam swallowed hard but could not get any words out.

"Come on, cough it up. Who's your contact?"

"They call him the . . . the Caliph. In Syria, he was a warlord. Now, he is working with the —"

"Yeah, yeah. I heard the Scarpos were in with some slimy Arab." Il Proppo spat on the floor. "He can only be a two-bit punk. No one else would be foolish enough to go into business with the goddamned Scarpos."

"The Caliph makes good on his threats. Look at what his guys did to our barber." Hosam blinked back the tears. "He was just a kid."

Il Proppo crossed his arms. The rage had left his eyes. He seemed pleased with the way the conversation was going. "So . . . What are you going to do?"

"I know one thing only. I will not kill anyone."

"You don't have to. My guys will take out the Caliph when we're doing the same with the Scarpos." He looked into the unseen distance as if imagining the deathly scenario. "Our problems will be solved. Yours *and* mine."

"No one ever sees him. You will not find him."

"What, he's a ghost? How does he contact you?"

"Through his girlfriend. She is Syrian as well. Tall. Long blond hair down to her waist. Bright red lips. Tough as nails."

"Where does she hang out?"

"Every time we meet, it is in a different place. And a different vehicle."

"So, she's a ghost too?"

Hosam eyed his wallet on the desk next to the scissors and comb. Inside it was a scrap of paper that could be the Caliph's death warrant. And possibly Saramin's. Was he prepared to go that far to secure his family's safety? Now that the Caliph had upgraded his demands from petty thievery to murder, the answer was not so difficult.

He pointed to the wallet. "I wrote down her license plate. The last time we met, she was driving a small Ford. A Focus. That one, I do not think was stolen. Perhaps its plate number will be of use."

Il Proppo smiled as he rubbed his jaw with his fingers, enjoying the baby-fresh smoothness of the professional, triple-lather shave. "No problem. That's all I need."

When Hosam could not conceal his surprise, the mobster chuckled. "We've got plenty of friends among the boys and girls in blue. They'll be only too happy to help us get one more scumbag off the streets."

CHAPTER 49

The next day, Saturday, proved to be a long, drawn-out day at the barbershop. As he had predicted, many of Hosam's regulars, spooked by last week's events, did not come in for their monthly and biweekly cuts. By four o'clock, the flow of patrons had trickled to a halt, and Ibrahim left Hosam to man the place on his own until closing time at six.

Hosam's only hope was that the shop's reputation for excellent service would bring the customers back after a bad cut or two somewhere else. But that could take weeks, and would Ibrahim be forced to lay Hosam off in the meantime? He pictured the Church People's patronizing faces as they arrived at 2029 Elgin Street with hampers of macaroni, tinned tuna, peanut butter, and inedible casserole concoctions. The thought of Leila tiptoeing into the Good Shepherd Food Bank around the corner from their townhouse brought on a sweaty chill.

Sitting alone in the empty shop and watching the clock, his gut churned and his mind reeled. He could not stop thinking about Il Proppo and what he had asked the man to do. Had he, Hosam Khousa, facilitated a gangland killing? Is that what it had come to in this quiet country, this supposed haven of politeness and civility? Had he stooped so low as to order a hit on a mobster? And what if the Michelinis bungled it and the Caliph found out who had betrayed him? The Caliph's treatment of Marwan showed that second chances were nowhere in his lexicon.

By the time Hosam arrived home, he was desperate for a Canadian cold one. Instead of a beer, he was greeted in the kitchen by a wife who was simultaneously annoyed and triumphant. Yesterday's red, puffy eyes had disappeared. She had put on a little makeup and spruced up her lashes. Her face was glowing.

"Do you see what this is?" she said, holding up a small strip of paper.

"They arrived?"

"This morning." She held the strip close to his face. "Look at it and tell me what colour you see."

The crucial line running the length of the sterilization indicator strip was a bright, purplish red. "I do not know what you call it," he told her. "Some sort of purple?"

"Exactly. It started out grey, but now it's vivid magenta."

"Is that good news?"

"Your Dr. Szabo will have to find his Parvo-W somewhere else. My autoclave is working perfectly well."

"You tested it?"

"With a full tray of instruments."

He gestured toward the garage. "Then there is something else in there that is harbouring the parvovirus."

She waved the strip at him. "That's impossible, Hosam, and you know it. We turned that place upside down."

"I still say we missed something."

She made a face then tossed the strip onto the table and gripped his arm. "There's another thing I need to show you. Come with me." She led him into the living room at the rear of the townhouse.

There was not much in the small room other than a couple of chairs and the television. The Church People had beamed with pride when they unveiled the generous, high-def flatscreen. Omar, who loved watching international soccer matches almost as much as playing *Fortnite*, had been thrilled. And Hosam had to admit it helped the three of them with their English proficiency.

"You will be responsible for paying your cable bills every month," the committee chairman had said after explaining the complicated system of television channels and associated billing options. But now, if Leila could not work and Hosam's fearful clients stayed away, there would be no money for cable bills. The TV's screen would remain a huge black eye on the wall.

Leila pressed the remote, and the local news channel flashed in front of them. "They've been playing the same story all day."

The television at the barbershop was permanently tuned to the golf channel, and Hosam had never thought to change it after Ibrahim had left for the day. Golf had been an agreeable distraction. "What?"

"A triple murder. Last night on Barton Street. At the far east end. A scrapyard."

"A shooting?"

"Gangland style, they say. Shot through the forehead."

"Who?"

"Two men and a woman. No names yet, officially. But anonymous sources say it's two Scarpellino cousins and a female associate. You can watch the details for yourself, later." Before he had a chance to think, she had pressed the remote again. "What sort of car was that awful woman driving when she picked you up on Wednesday?"

"A small Ford," he told her. "A Focus. What is this about?"

Now on the screen was a list of programs the machine had recorded. Leila selected one from earlier today, and soon a freeze-frame of a grey, compact sedan was filling the TV.

"Is that it?" she asked.

He could see the familiar brand name on the oval disk above the front grill. "Well, it *is* a Ford, and it does look like a Focus."

"Did you ever take note of her license plate number?"

Of course he had. And had seen it again yesterday in the barbershop when he was sealing her fate by handing her over to Il

Proppo. The combination of letters and numbers on Saramin's vanity plate had seared itself into his memory: STLU 414.

In the fuzzy image, the front license was visible, but only half the digits were in focus. He strained to make them out. The initial *STL* was clear enough, and so was the final *4*.

His brow grew cold with sweat. His heart raced. "It looks like he . . . Oh my God, I cannot believe it happened so fast."

Leila's made-up eyes grew huge. "Don't tell me you arranged it, Habibi. Have we sunk as low as this?"

He said nothing. He could not take his eyes off the television.

"Will the Caliph suspect you're involved? Allah have mercy on us, how much danger are we in?"

"We must keep our doors and windows locked. We cannot open them to anyone. Least of all a patient. You never know who the Caliph will send disguised as a man with a toothache and armed with a knife."

Leila dropped onto a chair, the brightness in her eyes and the confident glow on her face long gone. "But —"

"No *buts*, Habibti."

They would have to tread extremely carefully until he had a private talk with his high-tipping client.

CHAPTER 50

Zol poured three glugs of grapeseed oil into the frying pan and turned up the heat. It had been more than two weeks since his Salmon Wellington fiasco, and it was time he prepared his favourite fish again. He thought about baking it, but that would be tempting fate. He would have better control of the fillets in the cast-iron pan because he'd be watching them every second.

He had the romaine lettuce and cherry tomatoes on five plates ready to receive the cooked salmon. The shaved Parmesan and his own version of Caesar dressing made without raw egg were waiting in the fridge. The wedges of Yukon Gold, Max and Trav's favourite, were crisping in the oven. In a minute or two, attracted by the smell of oven-caramelized garlic and potatoes, the boys would be down here with their mouths open. If they didn't appear without being called, it meant they were playing *Fortnite*, not doing their homework.

In deference to Tasha's as yet unannounced pregnancy, and the fact that it was a weeknight, everyone would have ice water instead of wine. Hamish wasn't much for alcohol anyway. When he'd called half an hour ago to say he had some important news to share, Zol eyed the salmon and romaine and decided he could easily stretch the servings from four to five.

"You know how I hate the phone," Hamish said when he asked if he could come over. Who was he kidding? Hamish loved Zol's cooking more than he hated the telephone, especially on the nights Al was working the late shift at the paper. And Zol suspected that Hamish might be happier for the company than he was willing to admit.

As Zol was moving the salmon from the pan to a warm plate, Hamish rang the front doorbell and walked in. He hung his jacket in the closet and strode into the kitchen. The guy's timing was perfect, but his hair was looking shaggy. Zol had never seen him go this long without a haircut. His flattop needed weekly attention to stay the way Hamish liked it. The murder of the Scarpellino cousins after Zol's warning of Hosam's potential involvement with the criminal underworld had Hamish giving Paradise Barbers a wide berth. And it looked like until he found another barber who was an expert at flattops, he was eschewing haircuts altogether.

It was now a full two weeks since they'd seen a new case of polio. Before that, the longest hiatus in the outbreak had been four days. Had Dr. Elle felt the heat and suspended her practice? If so, how long would it be before she started it up again? He knew she was bound to. You didn't go to the expense and effort of setting up a dental office and then abandon it forever.

Thuy Nguyen, the outbreak's most recent case, was still in the ICU on the ventilator, as were Jamila, Blessica, and Barry. Emmalita had improved enough to be discharged to the care of Filipino friends in Toronto. Bhavjeet had vanished from the hospital and apparently from the city. When Tasha tried to reach the family, there was no response from any of the phone numbers in his chart, and his uncle's address turned out to be fictitious.

"The table's set," Tasha told him as she gave Zol a peck on the cheek. "Anything else I can do?"

"Is the ice water poured?"

"Done."

"If you get the Parmesan and the dressing out of the fridge, I'll plate the salmon. Hamish, will you go and call the boys?"

Hamish ran a hand through his hair. His face tightened. "We got two more cases this afternoon."

"Of polio? Shit," Zol said.

"They're twin sisters. Mid-teens. Refugees from Syria. They've been here a few months, so they didn't bring it with them."

"How sick are they?" Tasha asked.

"One was in the process of being intubated when I left, the other is close behind."

"Any connection with a dentist?" Zol asked.

"Same story — parents don't speak English, and the girls were too out of it to answer questions. But . . ." He paused and wagged his professorial finger. "They both had extractions within the past few days. I saw the sutures in their mouths."

"Any idea who their dentist is?" Tasha said.

"None. An Egyptian woman came up from the pharmacy to translate for me after I found the stitches. But, same story. Parents were short on details, and the girls weren't capable of even nodding yes or no."

"So Dr. Elle's back in business," Zol said.

"And hasn't cleaned up her act," Hamish said and went upstairs to call the boys for supper.

The bad news was a conversation killer around the table, though Tasha tried her best to keep the mood upbeat for the sake of Max and Travis. The salmon Caesar vanished from every plate far too quickly. He'd mismatched the portions with the appetites. He'd have to fill them up with potatoes and ice cream.

"More potatoes, anyone?" he said. "There are a few left in the oven."

"I'll get them, Dad," Max said, jumping up from the table. Zol wondered how many wedges the boy was going to sneak before he reappeared with the remnants on the baking sheet.

Hamish looked at his watch and said, "Are you ready for my other update? It may be more positive." He looked at the boys dividing up the potatoes as if unsure they should hear what he had to say.

"Sure," Zol said. "And don't worry about the boys. They know almost as much about the outbreak as we do."

Max and Travis exchanged smirks pregnant with hidden meaning then stabbed at the few wedges on their plates with exaggerated gusto. With teenaged boys, everything had a subtext that was impossible to figure out. Zol imagined that life with teenaged girls would be infinitely more complicated. He glanced at Tasha and wondered what sort of little person she was carrying in her belly.

Several days ago, a dark cloud began to hover over the happy thoughts of Tasha's pregnancy. Hamish's colleagues in entomology had confirmed it was an Aedes albopictus mosquito that had bitten Zol at Tiffany's flower shop. And the virology lab had confirmed the presence of Zika virus in its bloody remains. It would be a month before he'd know for certain whether or not he'd been infected with the virus. For now, his intimate moments with Tasha were under drastic curtailment. Neither of them was willing to entrust the integrity of their baby's brain to the flimsy walls of a latex condom.

CHAPTER 51

Ignoring the boys now passing bowls of chocolate ice cream around the table, Hamish fixed his gaze on Zol. "Did you ever meet Ahmed Khan? He was a trainee of ours. Sponsored by the Government of Pakistan."

Zol looked at Tasha. "Can't say I remember him. Did he do a stint with us?"

"Don't think so," she said. "I don't recall any Pakistani nationals spending electives at the unit."

"He was born with a natural talent for medical practice," Hamish said. "And we turned him into an excellent infectious disease consultant. He called me yesterday."

"From Pakistan?" Zol asked.

"From Lahore. He took a posting at a university hospital there. Two or three years ago."

"The King Edward or the University of Health Sciences?" Tasha asked. Before the partition of British India in 1947, her family had been prominent members of Lahore's medical community. Being Hindu, they had fled across the newly created border separating Muslim Pakistan and Hindu India.

Hamish waved his hand dismissively. "King Something. Doesn't matter."

"So," Zol said, flatly, "did Dr. Khan have something interesting to say?"

"He read about our polio outbreak on a newsfeed and wanted to compare notes."

"Don't tell me they've been experiencing something similar over there?" Tasha said.

"Surprisingly so," Hamish said. "An outbreak of polio among adults and older children."

Zol had been reading a lot about polio lately. According to the WHO, there were only three countries with ongoing poliovirus transmission: Nigeria, Afghanistan, and Pakistan. Almost all of the cases were non-immunized children less than five years old. What Hamish was talking about sounded quite different.

Zol turned to Tasha. "How far is Lahore from Pakistan's polio hotspots?"

"Far enough," Tasha told him, "but they do get an occasional childhood case in Lahore every year."

"So, until the outbreak, your friend Dr. Khan didn't have a lot more experience with acute poliomyelitis than we did?"

"As a physician who looked after adults, not children," Hamish said, "he had no experience whatsoever."

"Did he and his colleagues assume the affected adults had received defective vaccine, which left them susceptible?" Tasha said.

"Exactly," Hamish said, "but when the number of cases grew to more than thirty, and many of the victims were people of significant means with a history of good quality health care, they realized they had something new on their hands."

"An emerging pathogen," Zol said. "Same as us."

"What did they find?" Tasha asked.

"Zika," Hamish said. "In every case."

"Fascinating," Zol said. "What about Parvo-W?"

Hamish raised his hand. "Not yet, but I'm getting to that. Zika infection is widespread around Lahore, but the polio cases were confined to one section of the city. Ahmed began to suspect that a second pathogen might be involved, so he looked further into the particulars of the affected individuals."

Hamish raised his eyebrows to be sure he still had Zol's attention, then paused for a couple of mouthfuls of ice cream.

When Hamish dipped into his bowl for a third time, Zol said, "Come on, Hamish. Enough with the chocolate. Spill the goods before I burst my gut."

"Okay, okay. You're never going to believe this, but in just about every case, the patient had visited a dentist within three weeks of the onset of illness."

From across the table came a series of clatters and crashes. Max had been lifting his bowl for another scoop of Chocolate Heaven from Travis when both boys dropped everything on the floor.

"Steady, boys," Zol said.

Travis collected the ice cream and broken dishes and carried them to the kitchen. A moment later, he reappeared, caught Max's eye, and pointed to the ceiling. Both boys raced upstairs.

"What was that about?" Hamish said as Max's bedroom door closed with a deliberate thud.

"I have no idea," Zol said. "But I'm getting them back to help with the dishes."

Tasha folded her serviette, placed it on the table beside her empty bowl, and smoothed it with her palm. She turned to Hamish. "To finish your story, what did Dr. Khan and his colleagues find in the dentists' offices?"

"So far, nothing. Their public health resources are zero to none, and the dental lobby is making inspections of their equipment close to impossible."

"That's why he called you, eh?" Zol said. "He was hoping you could point him toward something specific to search for."

"All I could do was tell him about our Parvo-W," Hamish said, "and wish him good luck."

Moments later, the boys were back. Max's face was as long as the Trans-Canada Highway — St. John's to Victoria. Travis had the upright posture and solemn brow of a young man who has just won an argument but isn't certain that's a good thing.

Max stood behind Tasha's chair and gripped the back of it with his right hand. Travis angled himself behind Max and, being that much taller, looked over Max's head.

"We've got something to tell you," Max said, his voice cracking. "Travis wanted us to say something before, but we promised a friend on our grandmothers' graves not to say a word."

"Sounds serious, boys," Zol said. "What's this about?" The salmon and garlic were churning in his stomach.

"It has to do with what Uncle Hamish said is happening in Pakistan."

"Pakistan?" Zol said.

"You know we have a *Fortnite* friend named Omar, right?"

"Didn't you tell me he was a refugee from Syria, not Pakistan?"

"He *is* from Syria and lives here now. We message each other on Facebook."

"Okay."

"And his dad . . . well, his dad is Hosam from the barbershop."

Images of mobsters, drive-by shootings, and gory vendettas flashed in Zol's mind. "Oh my God, boys, has your so-called friend got you in trouble with the mob?"

"No, Dad. Nothing like that. He only knows me by my *Fortnite* name, KB. And he has no idea where we live."

Travis frowned and whispered in Max's ear. Max shook his head in response and continued. "Omar's dad is a doctor, right?"

"Well, he was," Zol said. "Back when the family lived in Syria."

"So he knows about medical things?"

"Sure."

"Well, he, um . . . he told Omar not to go into the garage or he'd come down with polio and maybe die."

"What garage?" Zol said.

"The one where . . . um . . ." Travis gave Max a nudge in the ribs. "Where his mother has her dentist's office. It's attached to their house."

Tasha looked aghast. Red blotches flared across the base of her neck. "What's Omar's mother's name?"

Max turned to Travis, and they both shook their heads. "We don't know." Max's face was a beet-red lantern. His body was shaking, and he was holding onto Tasha's chair as if his life depended on it. "But Omar says if the government finds out she's working as a dentist, they'll put her in jail. Then send her back to Syria."

For the first time in years, Max's eyes brimmed with tears. "Please, Dad, don't let them send Omar's mom back to the war."

CHAPTER 52

It took Zol the entire morning to secure the warrant to search "The Domestic Premises and Attached Garage at 2029, Elgin Street, City of Hamilton, Province of Ontario."

First, he had to find someone at the police station who was willing to talk to him. Then, he spent an hour helping them complete the warrant application with enough specific details to impress a magistrate. It took another hour with the magistrate and her assistant to successfully plead his case. Both the police and the magistrate were troubled by the fact that Zol didn't know the dentist's first or last name. The hearsay nature of his evidence against this unnamed person almost had the magistrate laughing him out of her office. She warned him that if the warrant was later successfully challenged in court, any evidence he collected would be inadmissible. Zol told them he was not bothered by the outcome of any court case, all he cared about was preventing further polio cases in his city. In the end, the three beautiful teenaged girls among the seven people currently on ventilators in Caledonian's ICU struck a chord with the magistrate, who had photographs of her grandchildren on three walls of her office.

He found it frustrating that no one could imagine that a dental office would be the scene of a crime other than sexual assault. If he had claimed that the dentist in question was engaging in sex with her patients, the police would have been in there in a flash. It was difficult to interest them in the transmission of microbes, no matter how deadly.

The warrant in hand, he located Detective Sergeant Kathleen Bergman at the Hamilton Police Service and asked her to help him execute it. The two of them had crossed paths during the arrest of a murder suspect on the Grand Basin Indian Reserve a couple of years earlier when she worked for the Ontario Provincial Police. She had trusted his judgement then, and, thank God, she was willing to trust it today. It seemed her promotion to detective sergeant in the city's force gave her new authority and flexibility.

She agreed to pick him up with Tasha at the Health Unit at one thirty. Her police partner, Constable Rodrigues, would be coming with them. They'd be driving an unmarked car.

In the car, he and Tasha summarized the evidence implicating the phantom dentist they were calling Dr. Elle. He explained that her husband, the barber/surgeon, would be at work this time of day. Their teenaged son, Omar, hadn't been attending school lately and would likely be at home with his mother.

"You've got photos?" Sergeant Bergman asked. "So we'll know them when we see them?"

"Sorry," Zol said. "Not even a description. We do know the son is fifteen and lived through the Syrian civil war."

"So, let me get this straight," said Officer Bergman. "We're looking for a woman who may be a dentist and probably looks Middle Eastern plus a person who could've been misrepresenting himself to your son online. This so-called kid could turn out to be a two-hundred-and-fifty-pound MMA master with anger management issues." She nudged her partner who was riding shotgun beside her in the front seat of the Chevy. "Good thing they brought us along, eh?"

Constable Rodrigues turned to her and patted his holstered

handgun. Although he said nothing, the broad smirk on his face revealed a set of unnaturally white teeth that said everything.

The sergeant had no trouble finding Elgin Street and the two, six-unit townhouse blocks that Jesse had described. Number 2029 looked exactly as it had in Jesse's surveillance video, including its attached garage.

"Remember," Sergeant Bergman said, stopping in front of the driveway's entrance and catching Zol's eye in the rearview mirror. "Rodrigues and I are executing the warrant. You two are here as consultants to the police. We take the lead. That means we knock on the door, we do the introductions and, to start with, we ask the questions." She turned around. "Understood?"

Zol tapped Tasha's arm and nodded for both of them. "Yes, ma'am."

"But we can touch things, right?" Tasha said. "And have a good snoop?"

"Once I give you the go-ahead. And as long as you're wearing gloves. You brought some, right?"

Tasha held up her duffel bag. "And Tyvek suits."

"Good," Bergman said. "We may or may not need them. Depends on what we find."

Bergman led the way to the front door, buttoning her suit jacket as she went. Immediately behind her, Rodrigues did the same and fluffed his shiny hair with his fingers. Bergman's dull, nondescript bob looked strictly wash-and-wear. Zol and Tasha followed five steps behind them.

The sergeant rang the doorbell and waited. She was about to ring it a second time when a brown-haired woman appeared at the window beside the doorframe. She shook her head dismissively, dropped the curtain, and turned away. The officers held their badges to the window, and Rodrigues pounded on the door with his fist. The woman returned and this time looked startled. She squinted at the badges, appeared paralyzed with fear, and opened the door only when Rodrigues pounded so hard it threatened to come off its hinges.

"Is this the Khousa residence?" Bergman asked.

"Y . . . yes," said the woman tentatively. She was slim, medium height, in her thirties, and had gorgeous dark eyes much like Tasha's. She was wearing a white blouse with black slacks and no hijab.

After identifying herself and her colleague, Sergeant Bergman said, "Are you Mrs. Khousa?"

"Y . . . Yes."

"Your husband is Hosam?"

The woman grabbed the door frame. "Something has happened to him? I told him —"

"No, ma'am. I just wish to establish your identity. What is your name?"

"I am Hosam's wife. Leila. Leila Khousa."

"Is Omar home?"

The woman was taken aback that the officer knew her son's name. "He . . . he is upstairs."

"Please ask him to come down. We need to see him."

Leila's face turned ashen. "Why? He is just boy. Please, I beg of you. Do not take him away."

"We need to account for everyone in the house. Other than that, we have no interest in your son. Please, ma'am, there is no reason to be concerned. We just want to have a look inside your house."

"But why you need to look?"

"Please, ma'am, just call your son."

The woman turned and shouted something in what sounded like Arabic.

A moment later, a skinny teenaged boy appeared beside her. He had short dark hair, olive skin, and acne on his cheeks. He was about Trav's height but not as muscular.

"Is there anyone else at home at this time, ma'am?" Bergman asked.

"My husband, he is at work. We have no visitors."

Bergman explained the search warrant to Leila and told Rodrigues to secure the premises while everyone else waited outside on the steps. Zol watched two angry crows squabbling over a piece of roadkill near the cop car. Were they a mated pair with chicks on the way? Neither was giving ground to the other, so he hoped not.

Moments later, Rodrigues returned — out of breath and his face flushed. "All the rooms are clear, Sarge. But holy Hannah, you won't believe what's in that garage."

CHAPTER 53

The young officer led Natasha and the others into the kitchen and stopped at a door on the left. On it was a green and white sign displaying the Islamic star-and-crescent and two words written in Arabic script. Below them was their English translation: *Prayer Room.*

Sergeant Bergman locked the front door behind them as Constable Rodrigues put his hand on the knob of the prayer room door. He flashed his toothy smile at Natasha then said to Zol, "This is what you've come to see, Doc. No doubt about it."

Leila planted her feet and put up her hands. Looking beseechingly at Natasha as if she was a potential ally, she pointed to the sign and said, "Stop. Entry is forbidden. Muslims only. It is our holy place. Non-Muslims must not foul it with their presence."

Natasha said nothing but watched as Bergman stepped back and threw her colleague a piercing look. "Which is it, Rodrigues? A potential crime scene or a holy place?"

Rodrigues pointed to the sign. "That's a scam, Sarge. A hoax to keep us out. There's nothing holy about what's inside here."

The sergeant paused, considered what her colleague had said for a moment, then stepped forward. "Okay." She turned to Leila. "Sorry, ma'am, but this is where we start our search."

Leila put a hand to her mouth and looked at her son, her face stricken. The young lad stared at the floor and said nothing.

Rodrigues opened the door and stepped aside so the rest of them could go through. Before leading the way, Bergman said, "Remember, nobody touches anything unless I give the okay. And only with gloves on."

Rodrigues was the last one in and closed the door behind him. It was clear it was going to be Bergman's job to supervise the searching and Rodrigues's to prevent Leila and Omar from tampering with anything or fleeing the scene.

It was a single-car garage without a car or a garden tool in sight. The walls were made of bare cinderblock, and patches of oil stained the concrete floor, but the place was otherwise spotless. As Natasha looked around the room, its function was immediately apparent. It was a dentist's waiting room with chairs for three, a reception area, and a procedure room — all in one. Two mobile room dividers on casters had been pushed to the side. They were probably wheeled in place around the dentist's chair to give her and the patient a degree of privacy. Along two of the walls ran white, IKEA-style kitchen counters and cupboards. On each end, they were anchored by a deep double sink. It was impossible to tell for sure, but Natasha hoped that one sink was for the dentist to scrub up, the other for handling contaminated equipment. The taps had wing-shaped handles that could be operated by the flick of an elbow, just like in a hospital OR.

Rodrigues led Leila and Omar to the waiting-room chairs and told them to sit put. Bergman pulled a pair of vinyl gloves from her suit jacket pocket and began opening cupboard doors. She looked inside but touched nothing as if wanting a general overview before the search got into full gear.

Before stepping away from the door, Natasha handed Zol a Tyvek suit and a pair of gloves from her duffel bag.

"Good idea," he said. "I'll put on a suit before I touch anything biological."

Tasha's face darkened. "No, you'll put it on now, before you take another step. This place could be crawling with parvovirus. If that mosquito gave you Zika, you're a target for full polio if the parvo gets you. I'm not even sure you should be in here."

He hung his suit jacket on the door handle then slid one foot into the Tyvek. He paused and lifted his gaze to her belly. "What about you? You're sure you're okay with this?"

She swept the room with her hand. "Look at this place. It's immaculate. Nothing is going to jump out and bite us. If we're careful, we'll be fine with gloves and these suits."

He'd be careful. Damned careful.

They zipped up their suits, and once Tasha had donned her gloves, she asked Sergeant Bergman, "May I look in a few cupboards?"

The sergeant pulled out her smartphone and said, "We'll do this together. You open the drawers and cupboards one by one while I watch. Let me take photos of each before you touch anything. You know what you're looking for. I haven't a clue. If you find something, great. If not, we'll get the forensics teams in."

As Natasha opened the first cupboard, she heard Zol asking Leila about her autoclave and how she tested whether it was working properly. She heard them discussing temperatures, test strips, instruments, needles, and drill heads. She left them to it.

It took a good forty-five minutes for Natasha to go through every drawer and cupboard with Dr. Bergman taking photos. Leila may have been practising dentistry illegally, but her operation seemed exemplary. She was a well-organized person who kept everything in its place. It was difficult to imagine that this could be a hotbed of Parvo-W transmission and the epicentre of the city's polio outbreak. Each time Natasha glanced at Leila and her son riveted to their chairs — Leila crying silently and Omar scowling — a growing horror fermented inside her. Did she and Zol have it completely wrong? Were they tormenting a highly competent woman who was running a much-needed service for the city's disadvantaged?

After they'd looked at every vial, package, and box in every drawer and cupboard, Sergeant Bergman held up her iPhone for Natasha to see and pointed to a photo. "You didn't pull all these out and look behind them."

"Aren't they just women's sanitary supplies?" Natasha said. "I guess some of her patients can't afford to buy —"

"A favoured hiding place," she said, shaking her head. "Admittedly, it's usually drugs, guns, or money. But you never know . . ."

"Which cupboard was it?"

They backtracked several cupboards until they found the one in question. "Pull everything out," Bergman told her.

Once Natasha had placed all the packages on the counter and checked that nothing was hidden behind them, Bergman said, "We'll do this together."

"Do what?" Natasha said.

"We examine each package, feel its weight, and check for signs of tampering."

As Natasha glanced at Leila, the escalating fear in the woman's eyes suggested that either Zol had found a flaw in her sterilizing procedures or Officer Bergman was onto something.

When Natasha lifted the third box of two-dozen tampons with a Costco label, she could tell it was heavier than the others. "There's something funny about this one," she told Bergman. "It's too heavy."

"For God's sake don't shake it. Just put it down. Slowly."

Natasha eased the box to the counter and stepped back. The look on Bergman's face told her she should be scared to death.

"Get out your wand, Rodrigues," Bergman said. "I need you to check out this pack of so-called tampons." She turned to Natasha then looked at Zol. "It may be boobytrapped."

Rodrigues put on a fresh pair of gloves and lifted a slender box from his jacket pocket. Working on the white IKEA countertop on the other side of the room, he opened the box and removed a device that looked like a TV remote. He took a small cellophane packet from the box, ripped it open, removed whatever was inside, and attached it to the end of the device.

With the loaded wand in his hand, and every eye in the room fixed on his movements, Rodrigues approached the jumbo-pack of Costco tampons. With a light and practised touch, he dragged the device back and forth across the top and sides of the suspicious box.

When he'd finished, he pressed a couple of buttons on the device and looked at it closely. "Negative for residues. It's not going to blow up."

Telling everyone else to gather on the other side of the door while she opened the box, Bergman stepped toward the counter.

Seconds later, she called, "All clear, you can come back in now."

When Natasha looked into the wide-open box, she saw it had been opened and resealed with Scotch Tape. The top two rows of tampons had been disturbed, and they were doing a poor job of concealing a row of what appeared to be medicine vials beneath them.

"Told you," the sergeant said, making no attempt to hide her triumph. She pointed to the shiny blue containers. "What are those?"

Natasha adjusted her gloves, pulled the white sleeves of her Tyvek suit down over her wrists, and lifted out one of six identical 30-ml plastic bottles.

"Zol," Natasha said. "Take a look at this."

She glanced at his hands to be sure he still had his gloves on and handed him what was less a vial and more a small plastic bottle with a pull-off top.

He read the label aloud. "Ketamine nasal spray. Extra strength." He turned to Leila. "Dr. L . . . that's what they call you, isn't it? Tell me, what's this for?"

Positioned on her chair again, stone-faced and red-eyed like one of her patients with a toothache, Leila said nothing.

"Please, Dr. L," Zol continued, "you've been running an incredibly clean operation. And I'm impressed, I truly am. But you hid these away for some reason. We need to know why."

"My husband, he is not approving."

Zol held up the bottle. "Why? Is there something wrong with this preparation?"

"It is perfectly good."

"Then why doesn't he approve of it?" Natasha said.

Leila waved a dismissive hand. "Hosam is out of date. He is thinking ketamine is powerful anesthetic belonging only in operating theatres. That was true in former times."

"But not now?" Natasha pressed.

"I am using much smaller doses than the anesthetists. Very safe."

"Hosam doesn't know you are using this?" Zol said.

Leila's face was long and sheepish.

The thing looked like a bottle of over-the-counter, pump-action nasal spray. Natasha used a steroid from a similar bottle every September when her hay fever peaked. "Tell me how you administer it," Zol said.

Leila tightened her lips and stared at the floor.

Sergeant Bergman held up her car keys and rattled them. "You can tell us here or tell us at the police station," she said, her tone offering no flexibility. "Your choice."

Leila's eyes widened at the sight of the keys. She swept a wayward strand of hair off her cheek and took a long, deep breath as if suppressing a sob. Her eyes filled with tears. "When . . . when patient arrive in a great discomfort, I spray once or twice. Each nostril."

"What does that do?" Zol asked.

"It remove their pain. Help them relax."

Natasha thought of what Bhavjeet Singh had told her. He'd mentioned receiving some sort of spray. Perhaps he was vague about the details of the visit not because of his pain but because of the ketamine Leila had administered. As an anesthetic agent, it would dampen the brain as well as a toothache. "So," she said, "say I arrived in terrible pain from a tooth abscess. Before you froze my mouth and pulled my tooth, you'd spray a couple of shots of this into my nose?"

Leila nodded. "To make your experience less unpleasant."

"And less memorable?"

"That is possible."

Omar, who'd been growing increasingly agitated on his chair, had a pained look on his face. He said something to his mother in Arabic.

Leila turned to Sergeant Bergman. "My son, he would like to use the toilet."

Bergman frowned. "Can't he hold it?"

Leila shot a questioning glance at her son, and when he shook his head she said, "I do not think so."

"Okay," said Bergman. "But he can't leave the house. And he has to back as soon as he's done."

Omar shot out of his chair and was out the door before his mother had finished repeating the sergeant's instructions in Arabic.

Zol took a closer look at the little spray bottle, then said, "These are designed for multi-use, right? One vial can make several patients comfortable."

Leila examined her fingernails and pulled at her cuticles.

"What do you do with the nozzle between patients?" Zol asked her. "Plastic doesn't stand up well to autoclaving."

Leila gave a heavy sigh. "I wash. According to directions. Hot soapy water."

Zol was looking paler by the minute. "Where do you get this stuff from? I doubt that it's licensed for sale in Canada in this form."

"Alibaba," Leila said.

"What?" Zol's mouth was wide open. He never shopped online. Natasha knew he must be imagining the original Ali Baba and the Forty Thieves.

She touched his arm. "It's an Asian online shopping site."

Officer Bergman pointed to the bottle. "What Dr. Szabo has in his hand is a prescription drug that comes to you directly from overseas?"

Leila nodded.

"And Canada Customs never intercepts it?"

Leila didn't answer.

Natasha knew how it worked. "They come marked as a gift, don't they, Leila? Canada Post. One or two bottles at a time?"

Leila's silence spoke volumes.

"Importing prescription drugs without a license is a serious offence," Bergman told her. "Ma'am, you could be in major trouble. I suggest you do your best to cooperate with us."

"Oh, my God," said Zol, holding up the bottle again and squinting at the tiny letters on the label. His hands shook as he returned it to Natasha. "Look where it's made."

She turned the thing around a couple of times before she found what he was talking about. Her heart raced at the sight of it. Her skin burned and tingled beneath the Tyvek suit. In all probability, this not-so-innocuous little bottle was the key to two deadly revivals of epidemic poliomyelitis on opposite sides of the globe: Dr. Khan's in Lahore and their own here in Hamilton. Dr. L's ketamine nasal spray, sent to her through the mail by Alibaba, was made by Tru-Meds Pharma in Lahore, Pakistan.

"What?" said Officer Bergman. "Where's it made and why does it matter?"

Without waiting for an answer, Bergman tensed, turned, and grabbed her holstered handgun with her right hand. With her left, she pointed across the room at the doorway. "Rodrigues, for shit's sake, what's that kid got in his hand?"

CHAPTER 54

Omar *did* have something in his fist. A syringe. And attached to it was a long, uncapped needle.

The boy stared at Zol, his face filled with revulsion. "I know you. From TV. You father to KB."

Zol couldn't take his eyes off Omar's weapon. A needle that size would blind you if it pierced your eyeball. And what was the boy talking about? "KB? I don't know what . . . oh . . . you mean from *Fortnite?*"

"But KB full of bullshit. Big fat liar."

Sergeant Bergman threw Zol a *what-the-hell?* frown as Leila pointed at the syringe and shouted something to her son in Arabic. Zol hoped she was telling him to put the damned thing down before someone got hurt.

Omar shouted back, his tone defiant. He took several steps into the room and waved the weapon in an arc in front of him like a knight with a lance. He narrowed his eyes and pointed the needle at Zol, his right arm fully extended. "KB say we are real friends, not fake *Fortnite* friends. He make promise on grandmother grave. But he break it."

"I'm sorry, Omar," Zol said, acutely aware that the kid and the needle were three short steps away from his eye. "What promise did my son break?"

The boy spat on the floor. When he looked up, his cheeks were wet with tears. "You know. He tell you the secret. He tell you about our garage, and now you come . . . you come for put my mother in jail."

Leila said something brief and sharp to her son in Arabic. He mumbled a brief response, then swept the room with his teary gaze and raised the syringe above his head. "In here, three drugs. My father bring them. From the hospital. He hide them. But I find them and look on Google. They used for execution purpose." He looked directly at Zol. "Capital punishment."

His mother, utterly aghast, tried to speak, but no words came out. She threw up her arms in defeat then dropped them and sobbed into her palms.

Tasha eased toward Leila and sat on the chair next to her, the Tyvek rustling with every step. Tasha's hands shook as she reached out to comfort the woman, but her eyes stayed clear. And resolute.

The officers, knees flexed, hands gripping their pistols, looked poised to pounce at the first sign of weakness from their prey.

Omar waved the syringe again and filled the room with his hate-filled gaze. "KB, he know about this. I tell him on Facebook." He studied the syringe as if verifying its integrity, then added, "Anybody want, they can ask him."

Half a second later, the boy lunged, jabbing the needle through Zol's Tyvek suit and into his biceps. The large-bore point hit bone and hurt like hell as the kid jammed the barrel against Zol's arm with the entire weight of his upper body.

Omar locked eyes with the sergeant, raised his left hand, and slowly aimed his thumb at the plunger. "You police, you leave now. If you take my mother . . . I execute KB father. Only fair. Like *Fortnite* — one v. one."

No one moved.

Every eye was riveted on the teenager's thumb.

Zol scanned the room and forced himself to think. If the worst happened, could any of these people do a proper job of mouth-to-mouth? Did police detectives take CPR training? Tasha had taken a basic life-support course a long time ago. Would she remember enough of it to keep him alive until the paramedics arrived? And would they know enough about Omar's lethal cocktail to ventilate Zol until the paralyzing drugs wore off? And what about Leila? She'd likely be better at mouth-to-mouth than any of the others, but would she do it?

Zol's arm burned, the sweat poured off his chin, his legs felt like rubber. If Omar had somehow found some potassium chloride and added it to the mix, Zol knew he could be dead before he hit the floor.

Why the hell had Max not told him about Omar's lethal cocktail?

Movement flashed at the doorway. A figure shot into the room. Omar's left knee buckled beneath him. The boy went down, and . . . holy shit! . . . a prosthetic foot scuttled across the floor.

Standing astride the moaning teen and struggling to catch his breath was Zol's barber, Hosam, the syringe now in *his* fist. Zol massaged his sore arm and wondered how much of its contents had shot into his biceps. In a few seconds, he could be down beside the boy. Out cold.

Hosam glowered at his wife, and in what sounded like Arabic, let fly a string of invective that echoed across the bare walls of the garage.

Leila gasped then mumbled something into her hand as her fearful gaze twitched between her furious husband and wide-eyed son.

Hosam looked around the room, tears threatening to flood his crumpled face. "Jamila is dead. That sweet girl from Hama City, she is dead. Just like our dear, dear Farah."

Zol caught Tasha's eye. Jamila's death was news to them. "I'm so sorry," Tasha said. "Did she pass away this morning?"

"Her father, he called me from the hospital. Sobbing an ocean of heartbreak. Minutes before, he watched his daughter's cardiac monitor flatline for the fourth and final time. The parvovirus, it had invaded her heart, and she battled at the brink of life all night long."

Hosam glared at his wife. "That makes it four of your patients, Leila — four of them dead."

Tasha straightened her back and settled her palm against her lower abdomen. Zol felt a string of heartbeats catch in his throat. "And did Fadi tell you about Iman and Yara?" Tasha said.

A flash of surprise lit Hosam's face. "They are from Damascus. Like us, newcomers. And living close by. But . . ." He thought for a moment then said, "Of course, Miss Sharma, you have their names on your list."

"Fadi told you he'd seen them admitted last night to intensive care, didn't he?" Tasha said. She touched Leila's forearm. "And, of course, you know them as well, Leila. When was their last appointment with you?"

Before Leila could respond, Hosam shouted, "I told her, weeks ago, she must suspend her practice."

Leila got to her feet, her stance suddenly defiant. "Those twins, they were in terrible pain. No other dentist would touch them without guarantee of payment. I had to help them."

Hosam shook the syringe. Zol tensed at the thought of the needle flying off the damned thing like a rogue dart. "That's why I came home early. I had to —"

"You had to what?" said Sergeant Bergman. "Bury your tracks deeper this time?"

"Ya Rab, no! Upon the name of the Profit, you must believe me," Hosam said, looking beseechingly at Zol. "I knew we must . . ." His voice trailed off as the words choked in his throat.

"Spit it out, Hosam," Zol said.

"I . . . I knew we must put aside our selfish goals." His face dissolved as he looked at Leila. "Even if my wife might . . . might be sent to jail."

Bergman holstered her gun but motioned to her colleague to

keep his drawn. She threw her shoulders back. "You expect us to believe you were going to come clean?" Even without her weapon drawn, the detective sergeant was a commanding presence. "You two have been running a cozy little operation in this garage for some time. Why would you give it up?"

Leila crossed her arms against her chest. "*Our* selfish goals, they are not." She thrust an accusing finger at her husband. "They are his. *He* is the one wanting thousands of dollars for licensing exams." She fixed Hosam with a laser-sharp gaze. "It is *you* that is hungry for status as surgical hot-shot."

Hosam, still standing astride his terrified but immobile son, swept the sweat off his brow with the back of his left hand. "It is not about status. I was born to be a surgeon. My place, it is in the operating theatre. You said so yourself. Many times."

"And you said no problem with me working quietly without license." She held up her left hand and spread its bare fingers. "You traded my ring for" — she swept the room with her outstretched arms — "all this gear. And said not to worry about foolish paperwork because no one will find out."

Hosam's face went white. He turned to Bergman. "But that was before. As soon as Fadi told me about Jamila and the twins, I raced home to tell Leila we had to go to Dr. Szabo. You can ask Ibrahim. He gave me money from the till. Two twenties. So I could jump into a taxi instead of waiting for the bus." He pulled a loose twenty-dollar bill from his pocket and held it out. "Here is the change."

Leila sank onto her chair. "Ibrahim? He knows? Since when?"

"Since minutes ago only," Hosam said. "I told him I was coming to collect you, and we were going to Dr. Szabo's office as fast as we could get there."

Zol felt the room swim and the lights darken. The feeling went out of his legs as they collapsed beneath him. He heard a crack as his shoulder hit the concrete floor.

CHAPTER 55

"Seriously, Doctor?" asked Hosam. "A pair of old rubber boots?"

"Three pairs, as it turned out," said Dr. Szabo, dipping his chin while Hosam ran the clippers up the nape of the good doctor's neck.

The man was getting married tomorrow, so this had to be the best low fade he had ever had. It was the least Hosam could do after Dr. Szabo had smoothed things over for Omar by not insisting that assault charges be laid. Still, the boy was slated to appear before a juvenile court judge who might think otherwise. He had retreated to his room and was still refusing to attend school.

The province's Royal College of Dental Surgeons had sealed Leila's dental clinic until it reviewed her credentials. Depending on the outcome of the legal proceedings, they might allow her to serve in a disadvantaged community under close supervision. Or they might come down hard and prevent her from practising anywhere. Hosam continued to be flabbergasted that she had imported the ketamine spray behind his back. And devastated that she had treated the two sisters from Damascus after promising to suspend her operation. Yes, those girls had been in terrible pain, needed immediate extractions, and did not know where else to turn. But that did not negate the fact that the consequences had been horrendous.

Everyone who mattered agreed that there was no criminal intent in Leila's actions. The Crown Prosecutor was of the opinion that Dr. Szabo's hastily obtained search warrant would probably not stand up in court. Consequently, the Crown decided not to charge her with the illegal importation of a Schedule I drug but was considering a lesser charge: the administration of a noxious substance. Her court-appointed lawyer was pushing for a charge of mischief, to which she was ready to plead guilty. She was no longer facing jail time or deportation, which was a huge relief. But the episode and its aftermath still clung to them like a rotten smell. How long that smell would affect their marriage, he did not know. He had consulted Omar Khayyam, but the poet had little to say about the complicated topic of forgiveness.

The polio story was not without good news: the bus driver from Omar's school, the Filipina nanny, the lady from the nail salon, and the twin sisters from Damascus were now breathing on their own and expected to recover. Why some of the polio victims died and the rest recovered remained a mystery.

"Yes," said Dr. Szabo, "three pairs of dirty boots from a single Guatemalan village caused a lot of heartaches. And damn near gave me a Zika virus infection. But I struck it lucky on that score."

"The Customs people, they did not check the luggage when those men arrived for the growing season?"

Beneath the cape, Dr. Szabo's shoulders shrugged. His right one did not seem to be paining him anymore. The hairline crack in the proximal humerus had warranted a few weeks in a sling but had healed. The heat inside Dr. Szabo's Tyvek suit, not Omar's lethal cocktail, had caused him to faint onto Leila's floor.

"What would Customs be on the lookout for?" Dr. Szabo asked. "Mosquito eggs are pretty well microscopic. And Zika virus even more so."

"But how could the eggs be alive after such a long trip?"

"The rubber protects them. And when the right conditions of warmth and moisture come along, the eggs hatch into larvae."

"Which are maturing into adults and spreading Zika to my son and the other innocent people who are visiting that flower nursery?"

Dr. Szabo lifted his head and cleared his throat. Hosam understood the message. Omar was not exactly innocent. The boy had a lot to learn about good citizenship.

There was one more thing to which Hosam needed a definite answer. It had been keeping him awake at night for the past month. The guilt and the uncertainty gnawed like a cancer. "Are you having any results from Leila's spray? Is it containing the parvovirus?"

"I'm afraid so, Hosam. Winnipeg got the results back to us this week. They isolated the same Parvo-W from that nasal preparation as from the polio patients."

Hosam switched off the clippers and laid them on the worktable. "Leila and I have been expecting that result." He grabbed a towel and wiped the sweat from his palms. "We are extremely sorry —"

"I know, Hosam, I know. You've apologized many times. But if there is a silver lining, we were able to alert our colleague Dr. Khan that the same ketamine spray, manufactured in his home town of Lahore, was likely responsible for their outbreak as well."

The polio outbreak in Pakistan involved so many people that it had made the international news. "I understand they are having a great many cases."

"Over a hundred," said Dr. Szabo. "Ten times the number we had to deal with."

"Still . . . it should not have happened here."

"Have you heard of a rather strange, cat-like animal called a civet? We don't have them in North America, but they're found in many parts of Asia."

He shook his head and picked up the cordless trimmer. "Perhaps the Middle East is too dry for them."

"They're nocturnal and like to live in people's homes between the ceiling and the roof."

"They are probably leaving their urine and feces everywhere."

Dr. Szabo smiled then gestured toward his friend, Dr. Hamish Wakefield, who was in Ibrahim's chair having his flattop trimmed to perfection. "At the suggestion of my best man over there, Dr. Khan visited the factory which made the ketamine spray. He found animal droppings on the floor. After some persuasion, the plant manager allowed Dr. Khan to set up an infrared surveillance camera. It turned out that the civets were leaving their nests above the ceiling and exploring the factory's equipment during the night."

"Looking for food?"

"I guess."

"They carry parvovirus, these civets?"

"You bet," said Dr. Szabo, "and they touched, licked, and urinated on virtually everything in the plant."

In her own way, Hosam realized, Leila had helped bring a stop to an extensive polio epidemic in Pakistan. There was irony hidden in there somewhere. And perhaps a little comfort.

Dr. Szabo took in the redecorated barbershop. "Looks like the new decor has been good for business, Hosam."

The shop's posters of the Colosseum, Piazza San Marco, and the Dolomite Mountains left no doubt about the heritage of the new owner.

"We are looking for a fourth barber. The boss is wanting him to be Italian, like Luigi who started last week."

"Looks like Luigi brought a lot of his customers with him."

Hosam smiled but said nothing. He switched on the trimmer and worked carefully around Dr. Szabo's ears.

A few clients loyal to a mediocre barber had not revived the shop. The new owner, Hosam's *influential* client, Giuseppe Michelini (Mr. Joe), alias Mr. Smith, was its saviour. The new boss — never to be addressed as Il Proppo — let it be known among his colleghi that they should support his new venture. In a show of triumph after eliminating the Scarpellinos' key players, Mr. Joe purchased the strip mall housing the beleaguered Paradise Barbers. When the Michelinis' lawyers processed the paperwork for the new investment, they discovered that the barbershop's leaseholder was a recently murdered woman named Saramin Wassef. As she had no descendants and was in no position to pay the rent, Mr. Joe took over the shop as a pet project.

Hosam shuddered as he pictured Saramin's crimson lips and Madonna locks but could not help smiling as he watched Ibrahim massage shampoo into Dr. Wakefield's scalp in preparation for the final sculpting of his flattop. Ibrahim had been a new man — smiling and full of amusing stories — ever since they had discovered that the Caliph was nothing more than an odious fiction. Saramin had invented the one-eyed monster to control her ragtag mob. Runaway militiamen would never have accepted orders from a woman. Not even in their wildest nightmares.

I'm investing in you, Mr. Joe had told Hosam. *You helped us get another jump on the Scarpos and saved my life. And now I'm investing in yours. First as my barber, and later as my surgeon.*

When Hosam expressed his wariness of gifts that came with hefty strings attached — the Trojans and their famous horse came to mind — Mr. Joe laughed and said, *You have nothing to worry about, mio amico. The only favours you will return to me and my family will take place in the operating room.*

Hosam smiled to himself, picked up a comb, and exchanged clippers once more. "You are ready for tomorrow, Dr. Szabo?"

"I picked up my tuxedo from Mr. Gupta yesterday."

"Custom made, I am trusting?"

"My new mother-in-law would never forgive me for presenting myself in anything less. I hope she likes the colour."

"Yes?"

"Midnight blue. Not quite as dark as navy, and with a subtle pattern in the weave that you can see only in certain lights."

That is what he liked about this man. He believed in the power of nuance. "And the boys? They will be serving in the wedding party?"

"Natasha got them fixed up at Hudson's Bay. Nothing custom made, but they do look sharp in navy. They'll be here for their haircuts any minute."

"Is it your tradition not to see the bride's gown until the wedding day?"

Dr. Szabo chuckled. "You've got that right." With a broad smile, he caught the eye of the slim young man coming through the front door. "Good, here's Jesse now. One of my employees. He proved to be a creative detective on . . . on a challenging case we had recently. Unfortunately, his talents went unsung."

"Oh?" Hosam was not surprised about the unsung talents. The boy did not look like a detective. He was wearing long earrings made from feathers and carrying a scuffed backpack and a camera case. His stringy hair needed a proper cut.

"It was mostly my fault," said Dr. Szabo. "Anyway, he's got his teeth into something challenging at the moment."

"It involves photography?"

"The camera's for a photo-story of the wedding process. Start to finish. Including shots of you and Ibrahim getting us fixed up today." Dr. Szabo raised his hands. "If that's okay?"

They heard a shriek at the door, and a woman dressed in yoga gear charged into the shop. "Does anyone in here know first aid?" She pushed Jesse to the side. "An elderly woman just got hit. By a big truck. I think she's unconscious." The woman leaned against the desk to catch her breath. "One of her legs is broken — there's a bone sticking out. Oh my God, it's awful."

"We'd better go," Dr. Szabo said, pulling at his cape. "Whip this thing off me, will you?"

They raced together toward the door, but Dr. Szabo stopped short. "You know what, Hosam? What she needs is a trauma surgeon. You go ahead. This is *your* show, my friend." He grabbed the phone. "I'll call 911 and bring you a stack of towels."

ACKNOWLEDGEMENTS

It takes a village to publish a book, and Zol Szabo is fortunate to have found a happy and productive home at ECW Press where Jack David and David Caron have been pillars of support from the start. My barbers Marwan Haydar and Rewar Kamil, along with Dersim Kamil, sparked the idea that became this tale. My tireless editor, Cat London, revived the plot and the characters wherever they stumbled. Yousery and Margaret Koubaesh, and Jen Knoch, got things back in tune when they strayed off-key. Video gamers Kevin and Eric Peng introduced me to the basics of *Fortnight*'s jargon and culture. Rick McIsaac's knowledge of electricity and skulduggery added plenty of Hamilton colour. And, as always, Lorna inspired the better angels of my characters' natures.

ROSS PENNIE has been a jungle surgeon, pediatrician, infectious-diseases specialist, professor, and novelist. He lives with his family in Southern Ontario.

ALSO BY LAURA ESQUIVEL

Like Water for Chocolate

THE
LAW OF LOVE

LAURA ESQUIVEL

Translated by Margaret Sayers Peden

CROWN PUBLISHERS, INC.
NEW YORK

Grateful acknowledgment is made to the following for permission to reprint previously published material:

EMI Music Publishing: Lyrics to "Burundanga" by Rafael Oscar M. Bouffartique. Copyright © 1953 renewed 1981 Morro Music Corp. All rights controlled and administered by EMI Catalogue Partnership, Inc. All rights reserved. International copyright secured. Used by permission.

Liliana Felipe: Lyrics from "Mala," "A Nadie," "San Miguel Arcángel," and "A Su Merced" by Liliana Felipe are reprinted by permission of Liliana Felipe/Ediciones El Hábito.

Universidad Nacional Autónoma de México: Poems from *Trece Poetas del Mundo Azteca* by Miguel León-Portilla are reprinted by permission of the publisher. Copyright © Secretaría de Educación Pública. All rights reserved.

Published by Crown Publishers, Inc., 201 East 50th Street, New York, New York 10022. Member of the Crown Publishing Group.

Random House, Inc. New York, Toronto, London, Sydney, Auckland
http://www.randomhouse.com/

CROWN is a trademark of Crown Publishers, Inc.

Originally published in Spanish by Editorial Grijalbo, S.A. de C.V., in 1995
Copyright © 1995 by Laura Esquivel

Printed in the United States of America

Design by Lauren Dong

Library of Congress Cataloging-in-Publication Data
Esquivel, Laura, 1950–
    [Ley del amor. English]
    The law of love / by Laura Esquivel ; translated by Margaret Sayers Peden.
    I. Peden, Margaret Sayers. II. Title.
    PQ7298.15.S638L4913 1996
    863—dc20   96-22952

ISBN: 0-517-70681-4

10 9 8 7 6 5 4 3 2 1

First American Edition

For Sandra

For Javier

THE
LAW OF LOVE

1

I am drunk, crying, filled with grief,
Thinking, speaking,
And this I find inside:
May I never die,
May I never disappear.
There, where there is no death,
There, where death is conquered,
Let it be there that I go.
May I never die,
May I never disappear.

Ms. "Cantares mexicanos," fol. 17 v.
Nezahualcóyotl
Trece Poetas del Mundo Azteca
Miguel León-Portilla

When do the dead die? When they are forgotten. When does a city disappear? When it no longer exists in the memory of those who lived there. And when does love cease? When one begins to love anew. Of this there is no doubt.

That is why Hernán Cortés decided to construct a new city upon the ruins of the ancient Tenochtitlán. The time it took him to size up the situation was the same that it takes a firmly gripped sword to pierce the skin of the chest and reach the center of the heart: one second. But in time of battle, a split second can mean escaping the sword or being run through by it.

During the conquest of Mexico, only those who could react in an instant survived, those who so feared death that they placed all their instincts, all their reflexes, all their senses, at the service of that fear. Terror became the command center for all their actions. Located just behind the navel, it received before the brain all the sensations perceived by smell, sight, touch, hearing, and taste. These were processed in milliseconds and forwarded to the brain, along with a precise course of action. All this lasted no more than the one second essential for survival.

As rapidly as the Conquistadors' bodies were acquiring the ability to react, new senses were also evolving. They learned to anticipate an attack from the rear, smell blood before it was spilled, sense a betrayal before the first word was uttered, and, above all, to see into the future as well as the keenest oracle. This was why, on the very day Cortés saw an Indian sounding a conch in front of the remains of an ancient pyramid, he knew he could not leave the city in ruins. It would have been like leaving a monument to the grandeur of the Aztecs. Sooner or later, nostalgia would have prompted the Indians to regroup in an attempt to regain their city. There was no time to lose. He had to obliterate all trace of the great Tenochtitlán from Aztec memory. He had to construct a new city before it was too late.

What Cortés did not take into account was that stones contain a truth beyond what the eye manages to see. They possess a force of their own that is not seen but felt, a force that cannot be constrained by a house or church. None of Cortés's newly acquired senses was fine-tuned enough to perceive this force. It was too subtle. Invisibility granted it absolute mobility, allowing it to swirl silently about the heights of the pyramids without being noticed. Some were aware of its effects, but didn't know what to attribute them to. The most severe case was that of Rodrigo Díaz, one of Cortés's valiant captains. As he and his companions proceeded to demolish the pyramids, he could never have imagined the consequences of his fateful contact with the stones. Even if someone had warned Rodrigo that those stones were powerful enough to change his life, he would not have believed it, for his beliefs never went beyond what he could grasp with his hands. When he was told there was one pyramid where the Indians used to conduct pagan ceremonies honoring some sort of goddess of love, he laughed. Not for a moment did he allow that any such goddess could exist, let alone that the pyramid could have a sacred function. Everyone agreed with him; they decided it was not even worth bothering to erect a church there. Without further thought, Cortés offered Rodrigo the site where the pyramid stood, so that he could build his house upon it.

Rodrigo was a happy man. He had earned the right to this parcel of land by his achievements on the battlefield and by his fierceness in hacking off arms, noses, ears, and heads. By his own hand he had dispatched approximately two hundred Indians, so he did not have to wait long for his reward: a generous tract of land bordering one of the four canals running through the city, the one that in time would become the road to Tacuba. Rodrigo's ambition made him dream of erecting his house in a grander spot— even on the ruins of the Great Temple—but he was forced to content himself with this more modest site since there were already plans to build a cathedral where that temple once stood. However, as compensation for his plot not being located within the select circle of houses the captains were building in the center of the city as witness to the birth of New Spain, he was granted an *encomienda;* that is, along with the land, ownership of fifty Indians, among whom was Citlali.

Citlali was descended from a noble family of Tenochtitlán. From childhood she had received a privileged upbringing, so her bearing reflected no trace of submission but, rather, great pride verging on defiance. The graceful swaying of her broad hips charged the atmosphere with sensuality, spreading ripples of air in widening circles. This energy displacement was much like the waves generated when a stone is dropped suddenly into a calm lake.

Rodrigo sensed Citlali's approach at a hundred yards. He had survived the Conquest for good reason: he possessed an acute ability to detect movements outside the ordinary. Interrupting his activity, he tried to pinpoint the danger. From the heights of the pyramid he commanded a view of everything in its vicinity. Immediately he focused on the line of Indians approaching his property. In the lead came Citlali. Rodrigo instantly realized that the movement that had so disturbed him emanated from Citlali's hips. He was completely disarmed. This was a challenge he did not know how to confront, and so he fell captive to the spell of her hips. All this happened as his hands were engaged in the effort of moving the stone that had formed the apex of the Pyramid of Love. But before he could do so there was a moment for the powerful energy generated by the pyramid to circulate through his veins. It was a lightning current, a blinding flash that made him see Citlali not as the simple Indian servant that she appeared to be, but rather, as the Goddess of Love herself.

Never had Rodrigo desired anyone so greatly, much less an Indian woman. He could not have explained what came over him. He hurriedly finished dislodging the stone and awaited her arrival. As soon as she drew near him, he could no longer restrain himself; he ordered all the other Indians off to install themselves at the rear of the property and right there, in the heart of what had once been the temple, he raped her.

Citlali, her face motionless and her eyes wide open, regarded her image reflected in Rodrigo's green eyes. Green, green, the color of the sea that she had seen once as a child. The sea which still brought fear to her. Long ago she had sensed the enormous destructive power latent in each wave. From the moment she had learned that the white-skinned men would come from beyond the boundless waters, she had lived in terror. If they possessed the power to dominate the sea, surely it meant that they carried inside them an equal capacity for destruction. And she had not been mistaken. The sea had arrived to destroy all of her world. She felt its furious pounding inside her. Not even the weight of the heavens above Rodrigo's shoulders could halt the frenzied movement of that sea. Deep within her its salty waves burned like fire, and its battering made her dizzy and nauseous. Rodrigo entered her body the same way he made his way through life: with the luxury of violence.

He had arrived some time earlier, during one of the battles that preceded the fall of the great Tenochtitlán, on the very day that Citlali had given birth to her son. As a result of her noble lineage, Citlali had been closely attended despite the fierce battle her people were waging against the Spanish. Her son had arrived in this world to the sounds of defeat, to the groans of a dying Tenochtitlán. The midwife who attended her, trying somehow to compensate for the child's untimely arrival, begged the Gods to provide him with good fortune. The Gods must have foreseen that the child's best fate lay not on this earth, for when the midwife handed the baby to Citlali to embrace, the mother held him in her arms for the first and last time. Just then Rodrigo, having killed the guards of the royal palace, burst in on her, wrested the newborn from her hands, and dashed him to the ground. Seizing Citlali by the hair, he dragged her a short distance away and stabbed her. He cut off the arm the midwife raised against him, and as a final gesture, set fire to the palace.

O that we might decide at what moment to die. Citlali would have chosen to die that very day, the day her husband, her son, her home, her city, all died. O that her eyes had never witnessed the great Tenochtitlán robed in desolation. O that her ears had never rung with the silence of the conches. O that the earth she walked upon had not responded with the dull echoes of sand. O that the air had not been heavy with the odor of olives. O that her body had never felt another so loathsome inside itself, and O that Rodrigo in leaving had taken with him the smell of the sea.

And now, as Rodrigo rose and was adjusting his clothing, Citlali begged the Gods for the strength to live until the day that this man should repent for having profaned not only her, but the Goddess of Love. For he could not have committed a greater outrage than to violate her on such a sacred site. Citlali was sure that the Goddess must be greatly offended. The force she had felt circulating inside her, urged on by Rodrigo's savage appetite, in no way resembled the energy of love. It was a brutal force she had never known before. Once, when the pyramid was still standing, Citlali had participated in a ceremony on its heights that had produced an entirely different effect. Perhaps this difference stemmed from the fact that the pyramid was now truncated and lacked its highest point, so that amorous energy swirled about madly without any order. Poor Goddess of Love! Surely she felt as humiliated and profaned as her devoted follower Citlali, and surely she not only authorized, but eagerly awaited, the hour of their revenge.

Citlali decided that the best means of accomplishing this was to vent her rage upon someone Rodrigo loved. That was why she was delighted to learn one day that a Spanish lady would soon be arriving to wed Rodrigo. Citlali surmised that if Rodrigo was planning to marry, it must be because he was in love. She did not know that he was doing so only to fulfill one of the requirements of the *encomienda*. This specified that to combat idolatry the *encomendero* was obliged to begin constructing a church on his lands within six months from the date of receiving the royal grant; he was also to erect and inhabit a residence within eighteen months, and to transport his wife there or marry within the same period. Therefore, as soon as construction was sufficiently advanced for the house to be occupied, Rodrigo sent to Spain for Doña Isabel de Góngora, to make her his wife. The marriage took place immediately, and Citlali was placed in the lady's service as a maid in waiting. Their first encounter was neither agreeable nor disagreeable. It simply never occurred.

For a meeting to take place, two people must come together in the same space, but neither of these women inhabited the same house. Isabel continued to live in Spain, Citlali in Tenochtitlán. They had no way of ever meeting, much less communicating, for they did not speak the same language. Neither of them could recognize herself in the eyes of the other. Neither of the two shared a common landscape. Neither of the two could understand what the other said. And this was not a matter of comprehension, it was a matter of the heart, for that is where words acquire their true meaning. And the hearts of both were closed.

To Isabel, Tlatelolco was a filthy place swarming with Indians, where she was forced to go for supplies and where it was nearly impossible to find saffron or olive oil. For Citlali, Tlatelolco was the place she had most loved to visit as a child, not only because there she could savor a wealth of smells, colors, and sounds, but because there she could witness a marvelous spectacle: a man all the children called Teo, but whose real name was Teocuicani or "Divine Singer," would dance small gods on the palm of his hand. These clay gods he had shaped would speak, wage war, and sing in the voices of conches, rattles, birds, rain, thunder, all of which poured forth from the prodigious vocal cords of this man. Citlali could not hear the word "Tlatelolco" without those images springing to mind, just as the sound of the word "Spain" threw a shroud of indifference over her soul.

For Isabel it was just the opposite: Spain was the most beautiful place she knew; Spain, the richest in meaning. It was the grass of the plains, where countless times she had lain observing the sky; it was the winds off the sea that chased the clouds till they scattered across the mountain peaks. It was laughter, music, wine, wild horses, bread hot from the oven, sheets spread out in the sun to dry, the solitude of the plain, its silence. And within this solitude and this silence, made even deeper by the sound of the waves and of cicadas, Isabel had a thousand times imagined her ideal love. Spain meant the sun, heat, and love. For Citlali, Spain was the place where Rodrigo had learned how to kill.

This great difference in associations stemmed from their great difference in experience. Isabel would have to have lived a long time in Tenochtitlán to know what it meant to say *ahuehuetl*, to know how, after participating in a ceremony in its honor, one felt to rest beneath its shade. Citlali would have to have been born in Spain to know how it felt to sit among olive trees gazing at flocks of sheep. Isabel would have to have grown up with a tortilla in her hand not to be offended by its dank smell. Citlali would have to have been suckled in a place filled with the aroma of fresh-baked bread in order to delight in its taste. And both women would have to have been born with less arrogance to be able to set aside all that separated them and to discover the many things they had in common.

They walked on the same paths, were warmed by the same sun, were awakened by the same birds, were caressed by the same hands and kissed by the same lips; yet they found not a single point of contact, not even in Rodrigo. While Isabel saw in Rodrigo the man she had dreamed of long ago in Spain, Citlali saw only her son's murderer. Neither of the two saw him as he really was, for Rodrigo was not easy to fathom. Two people lived inside him. He had but one tongue, yet it slipped into the mouths of Citlali and Isabel in very different ways. He had but one voice, yet its tones were like a caress to one and an assault to the other. He had but one pair of green eyes, yet for one they resembled a warm, tranquil sea; for the other, a sea that was restless and violent. This sea nonetheless generated life in the wombs of Isabel and Citlali indiscriminately. However, while Isabel awaited the arrival of her son with great joy, Citlali did so with horror. She aborted the fetus as she had done each time she became pregnant by Rodrigo. She could not stand the idea of bringing a being into the world that was half Indian, half Spanish. She did not believe it could harbor two such distinct natures and live in peace. It would be like condemning her child to live constantly at war with himself, fixing him forever at a crossroads, and that could never be called living.

Rodrigo himself knew this better than anyone. He had to divide his body into two separate Rodrigos. Each fought for control of his heart, which would completely change according to which of the sides was winning. To Isabel he behaved like a gentle breeze; but with Citlali, his unrestrained passion, stubborn desire, scorching lust, all caused him to act like a male in rut. He pursued her constantly; he besieged her, he lay in ambush for her, he cornered her; yet every day she seemed farther away.

During the Conquest, his sensory acuity had enabled him to survive; now it was killing him. He couldn't sleep, couldn't eat, couldn't think of anything except losing himself in Citlali's body. Now he lived only to detect the sensuous swaying of her hips in the air. No movement she made, however slight, went unnoticed by Rodrigo: he would sense it immediately, and a searing urgency would impel him to become one with its source, to unburden himself between those legs, to fall down with Citlali no matter where, to mount her day and night, trying to find relief. No day went by that he did not accost her repeatedly. His body needed a rest. He could not take any more. Not even at night could he find respite, for the moment she turned over on her straw mat, the movement of her hips created waves that swept over him with the force of a powerful groundswell. He would rise from his bed and rush like an arrow straight for Citlali.

Rodrigo thought there was no better way to show his love for Citlali; yet, Citlali never took it that way. She suffered his assaults with great stoicism, but never responded to his passion. Her soul remained unknown to him. Only once did she attempt to communicate something to him, to ask him a favor; unfortunately, on that one occasion Rodrigo could do nothing to satisfy her wish.

That evening Citlali had been watering the flowers along the balconies when she spotted a group of people dragging along a madman whose hands had been cut off. Her heart froze when she saw it was Teo, who had made the clay gods dance on his hands in the market of Tlatelolco when she was a girl. Driven mad during the Conquest, he had been discovered wandering about, singing and dancing his clay gods before crowds of children. Now he was being brought before the Viceroy, who was dining at Rodrigo's home, so that his fate could be determined. They had already cut off his hands to make sure he would never again disobey the royal edict forbidding clay idols. As soon as the Viceroy heard the case, he determined they must also cut out this madman's tongue, for he was known to incite rebellion with his stirring words in Nahuatl.

With her eyes Citlali begged Rodrigo to be merciful with Teo, but Rodrigo was caught between the sword and the wall. The Viceroy had come to visit him because there had been alarming reports that Rodrigo was becoming too lenient with the Indians of his *encomienda*; his neighbors had also witnessed him treating Citlali with uncommon indulgence. The Viceroy had subtly threatened to strip Rodrigo of his Indians, along with the other honors and privileges he had won during the Conquest. So now Rodrigo could not speak in favor of the Indian, because by doing so he would risk being accused of encouraging idolatry among the natives, an offense severe enough to retract the *encomienda*, and the last thing Rodrigo wanted to risk was losing Citlali. So he lowered his gaze and pretended not to have seen the entreaty in her eyes.

Citlali never forgave him for this. She spoke not another word to him for the rest of her life, and shut herself off forever inside her own world.

And so the house was left inhabited by beings who never communicated with one another. They were beings incapable of seeing each other, hearing each other, loving each other; they were beings who rejected each other in the belief that they belonged to very different cultures. They never discovered the true reason for this rejection. It remained unseen, issuing from the subterranean forces of the stones that had formed the Temple of Love and those of the house later built upon it: from the vexation of the pyramid, which was only awaiting the proper moment to shake off those alien stones and thereby regain its equilibrium.

Citlali's plight was similar to that of the pyramids, with the exception that, for her, regaining her former equilibrium meant not shaking off stones but seeking a means of revenge. Fortunately for her, she did not have long to wait. Isabel gave birth to a beautiful golden-haired boy. Citlali never left her side during the delivery, and as soon as the baby was delivered into the midwife's hands, Citlali took it in her arms to present to Rodrigo; then, pretending to trip, she let the child fall. He died instantly, and as he fell to the ground Citlali's lifelines fell from her hands with him.

Her time on earth was now marked in the air, among Isabel's wails and laments; it no longer belonged to her. In the confusion of the moment, Rodrigo dragged Citlali from the room by her hair, thus removing her from the scene before anyone else had time to react. He could not allow someone else's hand to harm her. Only he himself could give her a worthy death. There was no escape for Citlali, that much he knew; but he also realized that this body he had so often held, this body that he knew so well, that he had longed for and kissed so many times, merited a loving death. With great sorrow Rodrigo drew his dagger and, just as he had seen the Aztec priests do during human sacrifices, he split open Citlali's chest and took her heart in his hand, kissing it repeatedly before finally ripping it out and hurling it far away. It happened so quickly that Citlali did not experience the least suffering. Her face reflected great tranquillity and her soul at last could rest in peace, for she had wrought her revenge. But what she never realized was that her revenge lay not in having murdered the infant but in having committed an act warranting death. For it was by her own death that she finally achieved what she had so longed for after that first encounter with Rodrigo: that he be made to howl in pain.

Isabel died at almost the same time as Citlali, convinced that Rodrigo had gone mad at the sight of his dead son and so had brutally murdered Citlali. That is what was whispered in her ear; that was all they told her. For there was no need to tell a dying woman that immediately after her husband had killed Citlali, he had killed himself.

Can it be that this earth is our only abode?
I know nothing but suffering, for only in anguish
    do we live.
Will my flesh be sown anew
In my father and my mother?
Will I yet take shape as an ear of corn?
Will I throb once again in fruit?
I weep: no one is here; they have been left orphans.
Is it true we still live
In that region where all are united?
Do our hearts, perhaps, believe it so?

Ms. "Cantares mexicanos," fol. 13 v.
Nezahualcóyotl
Trece Poetas del Mundo Azteca
Miguel León-Portilla

2

The pyramids of Parangaricutirimícuaro
are parangaricutirimicized.
He who can unparangaricutirimicute them
will be a great unparangaricutirimizator.

There is nothing easy about being a Guardian Angel. But being Anacreonte, Azucena's Guardian Angel, is really tough, because Azucena never listens to reason. She is used to having her own blessed way, and let me tell you, in her case, "blessed" has nothing to do with divine. She simply won't recognize the existence of any will superior to her own, and so has never followed a single order except that dictated by her own desires. Using poetic license, shall we say that, for all she cares, you can take divine will and hurl it to kingdom come. To top it off, she has the royal nerve to decide that it's only fitting and just that she finally encounter her twin soul, since she has already suffered enough and isn't in the mood to wait another lifetime. With serene stubbornness she has worked her way through all the red

15

tape necessary to convince the bureaucrats to let her make contact with Rodrigo.

I'm not criticizing her; it seemed like a good idea to me. She knows how to listen to her inner voice and, through sheer force of will, to vanquish every obstacle in her path. So she is convinced that she has triumphed because of her nerve, but that's where she's wrong. If everything works out, it will be only because her inner voice happens to be in complete accord with Divine Will, with the cosmic order in which we all have a place, a place that is ours alone. When we find it, all is in harmony; we glide smoothly along the river of life, at least until we meet an obstacle. For when even one stone is out of place, it hinders the flow of the current and the water becomes stagnant and putrid.

It's easy enough to detect disorder in the "real" world; what's difficult is to discover the hidden order in things that cannot be seen. Few have this power, and among them are artists, who are supreme Reconcilers. With their special perception they decide where on the canvas to place the yellow, blue, and red; where the notes and silences fall; what the first word of the poem should be. They go along fitting these pieces together, guided only by that inner voice telling them, "This goes here," or "That doesn't go there," until the last piece falls into place.

This predetermined ordering of colors, sounds, or words means that a work of art achieves a purpose beyond the simple satisfaction of its creator. It means that even before it is made, it has already been assigned a unique place in the human soul. So when a poet arranges the words of a poem in accordance with Divine Will, he reconciles something within each of us, for his work is in harmony with a cosmic order. As a result, his creation will flow unimpeded through our veins, creating a powerful unifying bond.

If artists are the supreme Reconcilers, there exist along with them some consummate Wreckoncilers—those who believe that

16

theirs is the only will that matters and have power enough to *make* it matter; those who believe they have the authority to decide others' fates. Substituting lies for truth, death for life, and hatred for love inside our hearts, they repeatedly dam the flow of the river of life.

Surely the heart is not a fitting place to house hatred. But where is its place? I don't know. That is one of the universe's Unknowns. It would seem that the Gods truly delight in messing things up, for in not having created a particular spot to house hatred, they have provoked eternal chaos. Hatred is forever hunting down a refuge, poking its nose where it shouldn't, taking over sites reserved for others, invariably forcing out love.

And Nature, which, unlike the Gods, insists upon order—to the point of neurosis, you might say—feels the need to get into the act and put things back in place, thereby preserving the balance. She simply will not permit hatred to take up permanent residence in the heart, for its energy would block the circulation of love, with the grave danger that, just like stagnant water, the soul would putrefy. So instead she attempts to root out hatred whenever it settles in the heart.

This is relatively easy to do when it has made its way there by mistake or carelessness. In most of these cases all one needs to do is to be exposed to art created by a Reconciler, for in the process the soul can separate itself from the body: through the subtle alchemy of colors, sounds, forms, the soul is enabled to rise to great heights. The energy of hatred, on the other hand, is so heavy that it cannot detect subtleties, and so is unable to ascend with the soul. It remains with the body, but since its host has vacated the premises, it decides to search elsewhere for a promising spot. When the soul then returns to the body, there is room once again for love to resume its place in the heart.

The real problem arises when hatred is planted in our hearts through the conscious designs of a Wreckonciler, as when we find ourselves harmed through robbery, torture, lies, betrayal, murder. In such cases, the only way hatred can be removed is by the aggressor himself. As stipulated by the Law of Love: the person who causes an imbalance in the cosmic order is the only one who can restore balance. In nearly all cases, one lifetime is insufficient to achieve that, so Nature provides reincarnation in order to give Wreckoncilers the chance to straighten out their screwups. When hatred exists between two people, life will bring them together as many times as necessary for that hatred to disappear. Again and again they will be born near each other, until finally they learn how to love. And one day, after perhaps fourteen thousand lives, they will have learned enough about the Law of Love to be allowed to meet their twin soul. This is the highest reward a human being can ever hope for in life, and it will happen to all, you may be sure, but only at the appointed hour.

And that is precisely what my dear Azucena fails to understand. The moment finally has come for her to meet Rodrigo, but it is not yet time for them to live together side by side. First of all, she had better get some control over her emotions, and he too has some outstanding debts to pay. He has to put a few things in order before he'll be able to unite with her for all time, and Azucena is going to have to help him. Let's hope it all works out to the benefit of both mortals and spirits alike.

But I know how hard it will be. To succeed in her mission, Azucena will need a lot of help. As her Guardian Angel, I am obliged to come to her aid. And, as my protégée, she is supposed to yield and follow instructions. And that's where the tough part comes in. She doesn't heed me in the slightest. I spend five minutes explaining to her that she has to deactivate the protective auric field around her apartment so that Rodrigo can get in, and it's as if I were talking to the wall. She's so excited about the idea of meeting him that she has no ears for any suggestions from me. Well, we'll see if the poor guy doesn't get zapped as soon as he tries to get through that door.

But at least it won't be my fault. I've told her a thousand times what she has to do, but No Way! What worries me most is that if she isn't even capable of following such a simple order, what's going to happen when her life depends on it? In any case, may God's will be done!

3

It wasn't until her apartment alarm began to sound that Azucena realized what Anacreonte had been trying to tell her. She had completely forgotten to turn it off! This was serious, since Rodrigo's aura was not registered in the electromagnetic system protecting her apartment. If she did not deactivate the alarm immediately, the apparatus would process him as an unknown body and his cells would be prevented from correctly reintegrating inside the aerophone booth. After waiting all this time, how could she end up doing something so stupid! At best, Rodrigo would run the risk of disintegrating for twenty-four hours. She had only ten seconds to act. Fortunately, the power of love is invincible, and what the human body can accomplish in emergencies, truly amazing. In a flash, Azucena crossed the living room, deactivated the alarm, and returned to the aerophone door with time remaining to adjust her hair and put on her best smile to welcome Rodrigo.

A smile Rodrigo never saw; for as soon as his eyes fixed upon hers, the most marvelous of all encounters began: the meeting of twin souls, where physical features play a minor role. The heat from the lovers' gaze melts the barrier imposed by the flesh and allows a mutual contemplation of souls—souls that, in being identical, recognize each other's energy as their own. This recognition begins in energy receptors in the human body called chakras. There are seven chakras, each corresponding to a note on the musical scale and to a color in the rainbow. When a chakra is activated by the energy originating from the twin soul, it vibrates at its highest potential, producing a sound. In the case of twin souls, as each chakra resonates, so does that of its twin, and these two identical tones generate a subtle energy that courses through the spinal column, rising to the brain center and bursting outward to fall like a shower of color saturating the aura from top to bottom.

During their soul coupling, Azucena and Rodrigo repeated this process with each of their chakras until their auric field formed a complete rainbow and their chakras sounded a wondrous melody.

There is a vast difference between the coupling of bodies with unlike souls and the bodies of twin souls. In the former case, there is an urgency for physical possession, and, however intense the relationship becomes, it will always be conditioned by the physical. Thus a perfect communion of souls can never be achieved, however great the affinity between the two bodies. The most they can experience is great physical pleasure, but nothing more.

The case of twin souls is so intriguing because the fusion of souls is complete, occurring on all levels. Just as there is a place within a woman's body meant to be filled by the male member, so there is space between the atoms of each body free to be filled by energy from the twin soul. In this reciprocal penetration, each space becomes at the same time both contained by and containing the other: fountain and water, sword and wound, sun and moon, sea and sand, penis and vagina. The sensation of penetrating space is comparable only to that of feeling oneself penetrated; moistening, only to that of being moistened; sucking, to that of being sucked; flooded with warm sperm, only to that of ejaculating it. And when all the spaces between all the atoms in the body have filled or been filled—for the effect is the same—what follows is profound, intense, prolonged orgasm. There is nothing separating the two souls, for they form a single being. Thus restored to their original state, they are made aware of the truth: each sees, in the face of the partner, all of the faces the other has had during the fourteen thousand lives prior to their encounter.

At this moment Azucena no longer knew who was who, or what part of her body belonged to her and what to Rodrigo. She could feel a hand, but she did not know whether it was his or hers. Nor did she know who was inner and who was outer, who above and who below, who in front and who behind. All she knew was that with Rodrigo she formed a single body that, lulled by orgasms, danced through space to the rhythm of the music of the spheres.

Azucena came back to earth in her bed to find a strange leg on top of her own. She knew instantly that this leg did not belong to her: it was neither hers nor Rodrigo's. Rodrigo must have seen it too, because they screamed in unison as they discovered the body of a dead man lying between them.

The return to reality could not have been more brutal. Their honeymoon chamber was suddenly filled with policemen, reporters, and curious onlookers. Abel Zabludowsky, microphone in hand and perched on Azucena's side of the bed, was at that very moment interviewing the campaign manager of the American candidate for Planetary President, who had just been assassinated.

"Do you have any idea who might have shot Mr. Bush?"

"I haven't a clue."

"Do you believe that this assassination is part of a plot to destabilize the United States of America?"

"It's hard to tell. This cowardly assassination has definitely jolted our consciousness, and I, as well as all the inhabitants of the Planet, can only lament the fact that violence has returned to cast its dark shadow over us all. I want to take this opportunity to publicly express my total condemnation of any act of this nature, and to demand that the Planetary Prosecutor General conduct an immediate investigation into the cause of this crime, as well as the identity of those who masterminded it. Today is certainly a day of mourning for us all."

The manager of the presidential campaign, like everyone else around the world, was aghast. For more than a century, crime had been nonexistent on Planet Earth. This inexplicable act, however, presaged a return to an age of violence that everyone believed had been left behind.

It took Azucena and Rodrigo a moment to recover from their shock. Rodrigo had no idea what was going on, but Azucena did: she had forgotten to turn off the alarm clock on her Televirtual set. She groped for the remote control on her night table and shut it off. Immediately, the images of everyone at the murder scene vanished, though the bitter taste lingering in their mouths did not. Azucena felt nauseous. She was not used to confronting violence, much less in such a brutal, immediate way.

Televirtuality in effect transports the viewer to the site of news events, placing one right in the middle of the action. Strangely enough, that was why Azucena had bought her set, because it was so pleasant to wake up during the weather report. She might find herself anywhere in the world, or the galaxy, for that matter. She could revel in exotic landscapes or delight in the ordinary; open her eyes to the dawn on Saturn, or hear the sound of the Neptunian sea; luxuriate in the luminous dusk on Jupiter or in the freshness of a forest just after a downpour. There was no better way to wake up before going off to work.

She certainly had not expected such a violent jolt, especially after such a marvelous night. What a nightmare! She could not get the picture out of her mind: a man with a bullet in his head lying right in the middle of her bed. Her bed! The bed that was Rodrigo's and hers, now tainted with death. But as she gazed once again into Rodrigo's eyes, she regained her soul and her horror evaporated. And at the touch of his arms, she was again in Paradise. She would have remained there forever had Rodrigo not gotten up. He wanted to go to his apartment to collect his belongings and return to her, never to be separated again. Before he left, Azucena promised that he would find no disagreeable surprises upon his return, for she would disconnect all electronic devices in her home and leave the aerophone alarm deactivated. Rodrigo responded with a broad smile . . . and that was the last image Azucena had of him.

The first thing Azucena missed when she reawakened was a sense of well-being upon seeing the sunlight. Anguish unfolded its black wings above her, engulfing her in darkness, stifling her voice, extinguishing pleasure, freezing the sheets on her bed, silencing the music of the stars. The party was over before they had danced their tango, before she had wept with pleasure at dawn, before she could tell Rodrigo that he drove her mad with delight. She felt the words knot in her throat; she could not bear to speak them or to hear them. A large part of her being had flowed out to fill the spaces between the cells of Rodrigo's body. She had literally been emptied. And of her night of love, all that remained was a sweet pain in her intimate parts, and here and there a bruise of passion. That was all.

But these bruises faded in time, and what were once violets in the fields of ecstasy became pale witnesses to her abandonment and her loneliness. As her physical pain diminished, her internal muscles, which with such pleasure had received, squeezed, clung to, moistened, and savored Rodrigo, resumed their former state, and her body was left with no palpable memory of her brief honeymoon.

What doubt can there be that distance is one of the greatest torments for lovers? Azucena felt a profound, consuming emptiness. Losing her twin soul meant losing her very being.

Azucena knew this, and sought desperately to find Rodrigo's soul. She began by retracing his footsteps, by penetrating the spaces where he had been. This popular home remedy worked for a while, since at first Rodrigo's soul was still very much there; but as time passed, Azucena could scarcely perceive his aura, could barely remember him, his smell, his taste, his warmth. Her memory clouded over with suffering. The spaces between the cells of her body shrank back in sadness as, inevitably, Rodrigo's soul began to escape her.

Rodrigo's disappearance had left her completely disheartened, without recourse to reason. What explanation could she give to her body, which was begging to be caressed? And, above all, what was she going to tell that busybody Cuquita, her super? Azucena had rushed to her that first day to ask her to register Rodrigo's aura in the building's master control as soon as he returned, and now she felt like a fool. Every time she ran into Cuquita, the super would ask, sarcasm dripping from each word, when her twin soul would be returning. Cuquita hated her. They had never gotten along, because Cuquita was a social malcontent who belonged to the Party for the Retribution of Inequities—the PRI.

Cuquita had always spied on her, trying to catch her at something, just once, in order not to feel so inferior to Azucena. She had never succeeded, but now she had Azucena at a disadvantage, and it irritated Azucena to be the object of her ridicule. What could she tell Cuquita? She didn't know. The only one who had answers, who definitely knew Rodrigo's whereabouts, was her Guardian Angel, Anacreonte, but Azucena had broken off communication with him. She had not been interested in any information he had to offer. Now she was furious. He had known perfectly well that the only thing in life that interested her was finding Rodrigo, so why hadn't he warned her that Rodrigo might disappear? What the hell good was it to have a Guardian Angel if he couldn't prevent that kind of disaster? She would never listen to him again. That good-for-nothing would see she didn't need him to manage her life.

Her worst problem was that she didn't know where to begin. Besides, even going out of the house depressed her. In the wake of the assassination, the atmosphere was tense and everyone was afraid. If someone had dared commit murder, what next? That was it—the assassination! Why hadn't she thought of it before? What happened to Rodrigo probably had something to do with the murder. Perhaps new disturbances were preventing him from returning, and there she was, behaving like a catatonic jerk, waiting for her lover to fall out of the sky. Quickly, she switched on her Tele-virtual. It had been a week since she'd paid any attention to the outside world.

Azucena's bedroom was instantly converted into a cocoa plantation that was being destroyed by army troops. The voice of Abel Zabludowsky reported: "Today the American Army struck a ferocious blow against cocoa trafficking. Several acres of the drug were destroyed, and one of the most powerful chocolate lords was captured after being sought for some time by police. No further information is available at this time. The names of the leader and his group are being withheld so as not to jeopardize the investigation, which has targeted the entire Venus cartel."

Azucena's bedroom was then transformed into a laboratory filled with computers for the ensuing documentary on how crime had been abolished from Planet Earth. This had resulted from the development of an apparatus that, from a single drop of blood or saliva, a broken fingernail or a hair, could reconstruct the entire body of a person and indicate his whereabouts. Criminals, therefore, could be arrested and punished minutes after committing an offense, no matter where they had transflashed themselves.

Predictably, however, the candidate's assassin had been very careful not to leave any traces behind. All the spit on the sidewalk had been analyzed, to no avail. There had been no sign of the criminal. Suddenly, the laboratory images vanished, to be replaced by Abel Zabludowsky and Dr. Díez. Both were sitting on Azucena's bed, one on either side of her. Azucena was shocked to see her colleague at the clinic being interviewed by Abel Zabludowsky.

"Welcome, Dr. Díez. Thank you for joining us here on our program . . ."

"My pleasure."

"Tell us, Doctor, just what is this new device you've invented?"

"Well, it's really very simple. It photographs a person's aura, and detects traces of others who have been in contact with that person.

This device makes it easy to determine who was the last person to approach Mr. Bush."

"Just a moment, I don't think I completely understand. You mean that with this apparatus you've invented, you can capture, in a single photograph of someone's aura, *all* the people who have been in contact with that person?"

"That's correct. The aura consists of energy, which we have been able to photograph for quite some time now. We all know that when a person penetrates our magnetic field, he contaminates it. We have countless aurographs recording the moment at which an aura is affected but, until now, no one has been able to analyze and determine to whom the aura of the contaminating body belonged. That is what my device can do. And if we have the aurograph of the contaminating party, we can reproduce the body of the person to whom it belongs."

"Let me get this straight. Mr. Bush was assassinated as he was making his way through a large crowd. Many people must have been close enough to have contaminated his aura. So how can we be sure which is the assassin's?"

"By its color. You recall that all negative emotions have a specific color. . . ."

Azucena did not need to hear any more. Besides being her colleague, Dr. Díez was a close friend, so all she had to do was to go see him, have her own aurograph taken, and thus be able to find Rodrigo. Thank God! She grabbed her purse and rushed out, without even putting on shoes, without combing her hair, and without turning off her Televirtual set. Had she waited just another minute, she would have seen Rodrigo leaping about her bedroom like a madman. Abel Zabludowsky had moved on to the interplanetary newscast. Korma, a penal planet, had just suffered a volcanic eruption. All Televirtualites were being asked to send aid to the victims, since the inhabitants of that planet, members of the Third World, were living in the Stone Age. Among them was Rodrigo, who was desperately trying to escape a sea of lava.

⁎

Rodrigo was the last to enter a small cave toward the top of a mountain. Even the smallest of the primitive creatures inhabiting the planet Korma could run more rapidly than he. He lacked calloused feet to protect him against sharp rocks and heat, and his muscles were not used to such physical exertion. The most he had been called on to do in his lifetime was walk to the nearest aerophone booth to be transported elsewhere on the planet. He did not remember at what moment he had entered the booth that had flashed him here. In fact, he did not remember anything at all; he only felt a sense of anguish, as if he had failed to do something vital. His body longed for something he did not know; his feet wanted to tango, his lips felt the urgent need for a kiss; his voice strained to speak a name that was erased from his memory. He was at the point of uttering it, but his mind drew a blank. The only thing he was sure of was that he missed the moon . . . and that this cave stank to high heaven.

The concentrated humors of some thirty primitive creatures—men, women, and children—were unbearable. The combined sweat, urine, excrement, semen, rotting food, blood, earwax, mucus, and other secretions accumulating for years on the bodies of these savages was powerful enough to make anyone reel. But even more powerful than the stench was Rodrigo's need to catch his breath after the marathon he had just run, so he gulped in great mouthfuls of air and then collapsed on a large rock, as far as possible from the others. His legs were cramping from the exertion, but he didn't have the strength to rub them. He was completely drained and too exhausted even to cry, let alone scream in anguish like the woman nearby who had just lost her son. She was walking in circles, carrying the burnt remains of the small body in her own scorched hands. Rodrigo could imagine how she must have plunged those hands into the boiling lava to rescue the boy. The odor of burnt flesh spiraled around her as she paced before the entrance to the cave. Outside, in the unbearable heat, everything was tinged with glowing lava.

Rodrigo closed his eyes at the sight, regretting his own escape. What was the point of fighting to survive in this place where he did not belong? Although he no longer remembered who he was or where he came from, he had a profound sense that he had once lived in a privileged moment. And now—bereft, racked with sorrow—he existed in an endless void. It seemed as though half his body had been ripped away. He didn't know what to do: there was no means of escape, and besides, where could he go? He had no family, no one even to weep for him. How long could he survive on this planet? On his own, not even a day, yet even as a member of this tribe he had scarcely any hope. He was constantly aware of the suspicious glances the savages directed at him. He could not blame them. He was male, but hairless and unaggressive; he lacked their brute strength; he possessed no scars; and furthermore, he had all his teeth—something unknown to an adult male on Korma. Instead of defecating in the cave, he would go outside and hide behind a tree; instead of attacking dinosaurs, he would use the tip of a spear to clean the dirt from his fingernails; instead of eating his nasal mucus, he would blow his nose with his fingers, covering his face with his other hand so that no one would see; and to top it off, he had never fornicated with any of the women of the tribe. All these things made him highly suspect and universally scorned.

Only one woman was attracted to him, and no one knew why. The fact was, she had been the only Kormian to witness the landing of the spacecraft that had brought Rodrigo to Korma. She had watched it descend from the heavens amid fire and thunder, and she had later seen Rodrigo, naked and confused, emerge from the strange device as from a floating womb. Thus for her, Rodrigo was some strange god born of the stars. More than once she had saved his life, defending him like a tigress against the other males of the clan, but she could not find a way to show him her feelings. Sometimes she would lie down before him and spread her hairy legs, in a clear invitation for him to mount her as other primitives did at the least provocation, but Rodrigo would pretend not to see her, and things would progress no further.

Still, this primitive woman had not lost faith and felt that, now that her god was wounded, she had her chance. Crouching at his feet, she tenderly began licking the wounds he had sustained escaping the flood of lava. He opened his eyes at her touch and attempted to draw back his feet, but his muscles would not obey. After a few seconds, he realized how soothing it was to feel her moist tongue stroking the burned soles of his feet. He felt so comforted that he set aside his resistance, closed his eyes, and allowed himself to enjoy it. The licking intensified as it proceeded upward. Occasionally the woman would pause to remove a thorn stuck in Rodrigo's leg, then she continued upward, past his knees, lingering over his thighs—where clearly there was no wound—until she finally arrived at her main objective: his groin. Lecherously, she licked her lips before continuing her labors. Rodrigo grew apprehensive. He knew very well what she wanted, this repulsive, hairy-chested woman who stank like a beast, had pestilent breath, and was lasciviously wiggling her ass. What she wanted was precisely what he had been avoiding from the start.

Fortunately, one of the primitive males had not missed a single bit of what was going on between them. Not for a second had he taken his eyes off the female's raised hindquarters: that she was on all fours made her even more desirable. Without a thought he grabbed her by the hips, and began fornicating with her. She grunted in protest and received in return a thump on the head that subdued her. Rodrigo, while grateful that the male had taken over, was disturbed by his methods. Since the woman had saved his life on several occasions, he felt obliged to return her favor. Not knowing from where, he found the strength to get to his feet and pull the male off her. The latter, enraged, lashed out with a wallop that left Rodrigo feeling as though he had been mauled by a dinosaur. Rodrigo could not take any more and burst into tears of impotence. What had he ever done to deserve such punishment? What crime was he paying for?

Everyone stared at him in amazement. His tears disillusioned even the female who had so greatly admired him. And from that moment on, he was unanimously shunned for being queer.

4

Dr. Díez's aerophone did not admit Azucena, an indication that he was occupied with a patient and had put a block on it. So Azucena had no choice but to go to her own office next door and from there make an appointment with her colleague, as she should have done in the first place. Azucena realized she had been wrong in keying in the doctor's aerophone number without calling first, but she had been so desperate that she had ignored the basic rules of courtesy. And what was technology for, if not to prevent people from forgetting their manners? So Azucena was forced to behave in a civilized fashion. As she waited for her office door to open, she realized she hadn't been there in a week and would be sure to have countless messages from all the patients she had abandoned.

The first thing Azucena heard as she entered her office was a collective "It's about time!" She was stunned, but then felt a pang of guilt. Her plants had just spent seven days without water, and so had every right to greet her this way. She always left them connected to the Plantspeaker, a device that translated their electrical emissions into words, because she liked hearing them welcome her each day when she arrived at work.

Ordinarily Azucena's plants were well behaved and extremely affectionate. They had never before spoken a harsh word to her. But Azucena could not bring herself to scold them, since she herself knew what it felt like to be left stranded. So before she did anything else, she watered them, pleading with them to forgive her, singing songs to them, caressing them as though she were the one being consoled. The plants soon calmed down and began purring with pleasure.

Azucena then played back her aerophone messages. The most pressing one came from a young man who was the reincarnation of a famous twentieth-century soccer player named Hugo Sánchez. Since 2200 the youth, once an athlete, had played for the Earth All-Stars, and with the Interplanetary Soccer Championship coming up soon, everyone was hoping he would be in top form. The problem was that his experiences as Hugo Sánchez had traumatized him; his teammates had been so jealous of him that they had made his life hell. As much as Azucena had worked with him during several astroanalytical sessions, she still could not completely erase the bitter experience of having been barred from playing in the 1994 World Cup.

The next message came from his wife, who in a previous life had been Dr. Mejía Barón, the trainer who had not permitted Hugo to play that year. The two had been brought together once again so that they could learn how to love, but Hugo still could not forgive her and would give her a thrashing at every opportunity. The woman couldn't take any more and begged Azucena to help her; if not, she was determined to kill herself.

There were also several calls from the youth's current trainer. He wanted his star player spiritually aligned in time for the Earth–Venus match, which was just around the corner. Azucena thought it best to give the trainer the name of one of her other patients, who was the reincarnation of Pelé, since at present she was in no condition to treat anyone. She was terribly sorry, but what could she do? That's how it was. In order to function as an astroanalyst, you had to be cleansed of all negative emotions, and Azucena clearly was not.

Before she could listen to the rest of her messages, she was interrupted by her plants, which were shrieking hysterically. Through the thin office wall, they had been listening to an argument coming from Dr. Díez's office, and they were jarred by its harsh vibrations. Azucena immediately went into the hall and knocked on Dr. Díez's door. The doctor was the most peaceful person she knew, so something awful must have been going on for him to explode like this.

Her knocking silenced the quarrel. No one came to the door, however, and she was about to knock again when suddenly the door flew open and a burly man shoved Azucena back against her own door, shattering the glass reading *Azucena Martínez, Astro-analyst*. After that man came a second, even more enraged, and after him Dr. Díez. At the sight of Azucena lying on the floor, he stopped in his tracks and rushed over to help her.

"Azucena! So it was you! Are you hurt?"

"I don't think so."

The doctor helped Azucena to her feet and quickly checked her over.

"You seem all right."

"But what about you? Did they hurt you?"

"No, we were just having a discussion. But it was lucky you came."

"Who were those men?"

"No one, no one important. But God, what's happened to you?"

"It's nothing, they just knocked me against the door."

"I don't mean that. What's the matter with *you*? Are you sick? You look awful."

Azucena could no longer hold back the tears. The doctor gave her a paternal hug, and Azucena, her voice choked with sobs, unburdened herself, telling him how she had found her twin soul, and how briefly that joy had lasted. How in one day she had gone from the tender bliss of her lover's embrace to a desolate, tormenting void. She told him how she had already searched everywhere, but still could find no trace of Rodrigo. Her only remaining hope was to locate him by means of Dr. Díez's new invention. As soon as Azucena mentioned the word "invention," the doctor became anxious, looking around him to be sure no one was listening. Then he took Azucena by the arm and led her into his office.

"Come along with me. We can talk better in here."

Azucena took one of the comfortable leather chairs facing the doctor's desk. Dr. Díez spoke in a low voice, as if someone might be listening.

"Look, Azucena, you're a good friend and I'd love to help you, but I can't."

Disappointment made Azucena mute. Her eyes misted with sadness.

"I put together only two machines. The police have one, and they would never lend it to me, because they're using it around the clock to find Mr. Bush's assassin. As for the second one, I can't let you have it either. I don't even have authorization to enter the Center for the Oversight of Previous Existences, where it is, although . . . Let me think. You know, there *is* an opening at COPE. Maybe if you got the job, you could use the machine on site."

"Are you kidding? They don't accept anybody but born and bred bureaucrats. There's no way they'd hire me."

"What if I have a way to help you become a bureaucrat?"

"You do? How?"

The doctor removed a tiny instrument from his desk drawer and showed it to Azucena.

"With this."

The female bureaucrat quickly put her tasty tamale back in the drawer and carefully wiped her fingers on her skirt before addressing Azucena Martínez, the final candidate she had to interview for the position of Official Investigator.

"Please have a seat."

"Thank you."

"I see you're an astroanalyst."

"Yes, I am."

"That's such a high-paying job . . . Why would you want to apply for a clerical position like this?"

Azucena felt extremely nervous. She knew a photomental camera was recording her every thought and she only hoped that the microcomputer Dr. Díez had installed in her brain was sending out thoughts of love and peace. If not, she was lost, for what she was really thinking right then was that interviews like this were a joke and that government offices were mired in crap.

"Well, you see, I'm emotionally exhausted, so my doctor recommended taking a break. My aura has been charged with negative energy and needs to recuperate. You know how it is . . . I work really long hours listening to all kinds of problems."

"Yes, I understand. Just as I'm sure you'll appreciate how important it is for us to have knowledge about a person's prior lives in order to know how they will conduct themselves in their work here."

"Of course."

"So I assume you'll have no objection to our directly examining your subconscious; this will enable us to reach our final conclusion as to whether or not you are suitably qualified to fill the position of Official Investigator."

Azucena felt cold sweat trickling down her back. She was frightened to the core, for now the test of fire awaited her. Although no one could delve into another person's subconscious without prior authorization, she would have to allow them to do so if she really wanted a job at COPE. Of course, she would never allow them access to her true subconscious, since the information the analysts were looking for concerned her moral and social integrity. They wanted to learn whether in any of her lives she had tortured or murdered someone, how honest she was at present, what kind of tolerance she had for frustration, or if she was likely to involve herself in some revolutionary movement. Azucena was very honest, and had already spent several lifetimes improving her karma, paying for sins she had committed in previous lives. However, her tolerance level for frustration was close to zero. She was a born agitator and rebel—all the more reason to hope that Dr. Díez's apparatus continued to work properly. If not, she would not only find herself without a job as Official Investigator, but would be dealt a more fatal blow: they would erase all trace of past lives from her memory, and that would really mean Good-bye, Rodrigo!

"What is your password?"

"Buried Potatoes."

The bureaucrat typed the words into the computer and handed Azucena a helmet containing a photomental camera that would record her subconscious thoughts, translating them into images of virtual reality. These in turn would be transmitted to the Data

Control Office, where they would be minutely analyzed by a team of scientists as well as a computer.

Azucena put on the helmet and closed her eyes; in a moment she was listening to some very pleasing music.

In the adjoining office, the Mexico City of 1985 was being reproduced in virtual reality. The scientific bureaucrats were thus able to walk along Avenida Samuel Ruiz just as it had been two hundred and fifteen years earlier, when it had been known as Eje Lázaro Cárdenas. They reached the Metropolitan Cathedral, which looked just as it had before it was damaged, and continued along Eje Central, arriving at Plaza de Garibaldi, where they stopped beside a group of mariachis playing for some passing tourists.

A heated discussion ensued among the scientists over the clarity of the images they were viewing. Ordinarily, the mind recalls events in a confused and disorganized way. Azucena was the first person they had seen who recalled every detail of her past with such precision. The images she projected followed a perfect sequence. They were not at all fragmented, which suggested that either this girl was a genius, or she had illegally slipped in a micro-computer. One scientist suggested notifying the police. Several others favored an internal investigation. The remaining ones, however, moved by the sound of the mariachi trumpets, were reduced to tears.

Fortunately in these cases, there is only one whose opinion holds any weight, only one who can render the final verdict: the computer. And the computer accepted without hesitation the information provided by Azucena. The opinion of the scientists was taken into account only when the computer failed to function, and this had happened only once in the past hundred and fifty years, during the time of the Great Earthquake, when the Earth gave birth to the New Moon. And at that time no one was interested in scientific opinion because all that mattered was saving one's skin.

Azucena meanwhile, completely isolated from everyone, was listening to the music coming from the audiophones in her helmet. She felt as though she were literally floating in time as the melody gently transported her to one of her past lives. Her true subconscious had begun to work spontaneously, bringing forth an image she had seen once during an astroanalysis session. She had never been able to get beyond it, because something was blocking that past life from her; but evidently the melody she now heard had the power to break through that barrier.

CD
Track 1

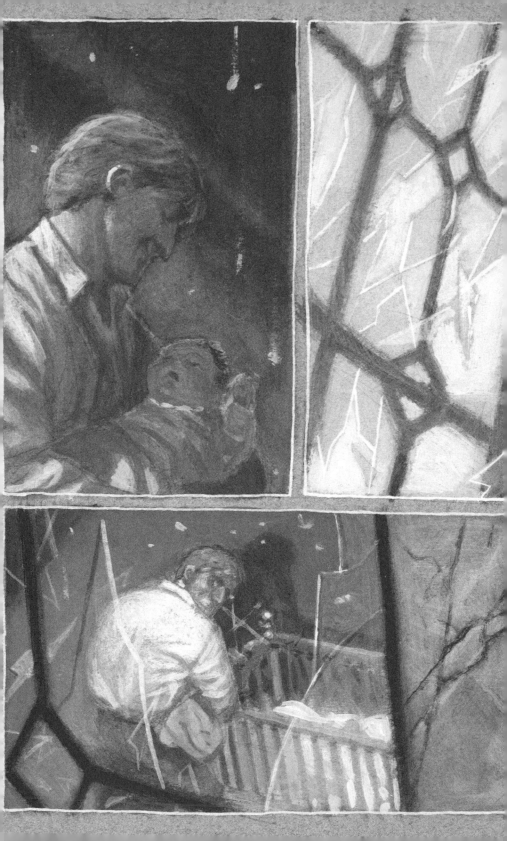

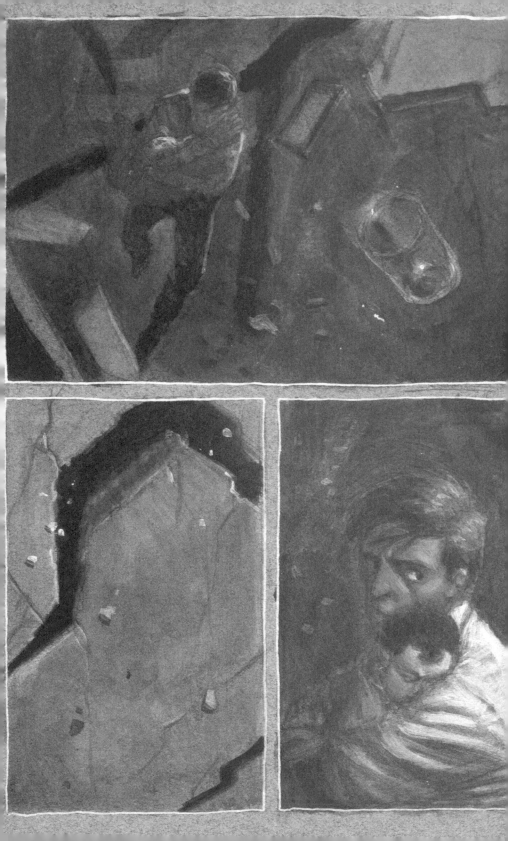

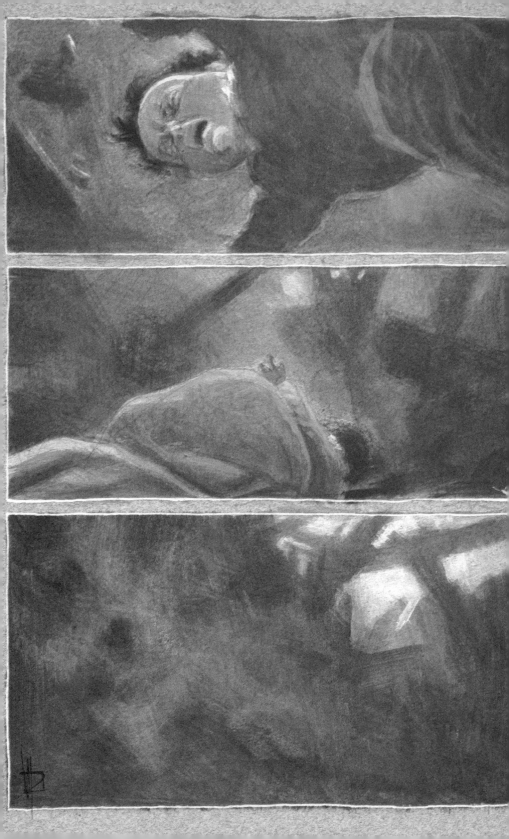

Suddenly the music stopped, leaving Azucena's mind blank. Her helmet had been disconnected. How could the bureaucrat be waking her just when she saw Rodrigo? Azucena was absolutely certain Rodrigo was that man who had scooped her into his arms from the cradle and saved her life. She recognized his face as one of the fourteen thousand from his previous lives, which she had seen on the day they met. She hadn't the slightest doubt. It was Rodrigo! She must know what that music was that had led her to him.

"That will be all, thank you. Now we'll have to wait for the final decision."

"That music I was listening to, what was it?"

"Classical music."

"Yes, I know, but who wrote it?"

"I don't know, seems to me it's from an opera, but I'm not sure."

"Do you think you could find out?"

"Why are you so interested in it?"

"Oh, it's not that I'm interested personally. But in my work as an astroanalyst it's very useful to be familiar with music that can induce altered states of consciousness."

"I can imagine. But since you won't be working as an astroanalyst for some time, it hardly matters."

Through a slit in the desk, the computer spit out a sheet of paper. The bureaucrat read it and then handed it to Azucena.

"Hmmm. Congratulations, you passed the exam. Just take this paper to the second floor. They'll take an aurograph there for your ID. As soon as you have it, you can report for work."

Azucena was beside herself with joy. She couldn't believe how lucky she had been. Although she tried to hide her emotions, she could not suppress a smile of triumph. Everything was working out perfectly. She'd show that Anacreonte how to solve problems!

On the second floor, there were about five hundred people waiting to have their aurographs taken. This was nothing compared to the endless lines Azucena had stood in before, so she took her place at the end of this one with the usual resignation. Meanwhile a photomental camera was constantly scanning all of them as a final test, registering the frustration tolerance of these future bureaucrats. It turned out that her fellow applicants in line had what it takes to be bureaucrats and easily withstood the test. Azucena did not. Each passing minute sapped her patience. The nervous tapping of her heel on the floor was the first thing to raise the eyebrows of the qualifying judges. It completely contradicted the thoughts she was emitting. The photomental camera focused on her face, capturing her impatient frown. The total disparity between Azucena's thoughts and her appearance was highly suspicious. This may have been why the moment she reached the window to be helped, the "Closed" sign went up. Azucena's blood was boiling. This couldn't be! She *couldn't* have such bad luck. She had to bite her lip so she wouldn't scream obscenities; shut her eyes so they wouldn't release the daggers she wanted to bury in the woman's throat; clamp her feet together so she wouldn't kick the window to smithereens; knot her fingers to keep them from shredding to bits all these papers they were handing her as they told her to return next Monday.

Monday! And it was only Thursday morning now. She couldn't just sit around waiting for Monday to come. But what *could* she do? She would have loved to continue that regression to the past life where she had seen Rodrigo, but she didn't know the name of the opera they had been playing and, even if she did, it wouldn't be easy to obtain. The latest discoveries in music therapy had complicated the sale and purchase of CDs. It had been known for some time that musical sounds have a powerful influence on the human organism and can alter psychological states, inducing at times neurotic, schizophrenic, psychopathic, and—in extreme cases—even murderous behavior.

Recently, however, it had been discovered that a single melody had the power to activate our memory of past lives. Music was currently being used in the area of astroanalysis to induce regressions to former incarnations. As might be expected, it was not appropriate that just anyone use music for these purposes, since not everyone had achieved the same stage of evolution. Sometimes it was thought best not to lift the lid on the past, for if an awareness was blocked, it was usually because the person in question was not ready to deal with it. There had been too many times when, for example, a former king had sought to recover jewels from a crown belonging to him in a past incarnation—things of that sort. So the government had decreed that all records, stereos, cassettes, CDs, and other audio equipment should fall under the jurisdiction of the Director of Public Health. If you wanted to buy a CD, you had to demonstrate your moral integrity and your level of spiritual development by presenting a certified letter from an astroanalyst stating that the holder would not be running any risk by listening to the music in question.

As an astroanalyst, Azucena could cut through that red tape without difficulty, but it would take nearly a month to do so. And that would be an eternity! She had to think of another way, because if she went back to her apartment without making some progress in locating Rodrigo, she would go mad. She wanted to see him face to face, and as soon as possible, to find out why he had abandoned her. Had she done something wrong? Wasn't she attractive enough? Or did he have another lover whom he could not abandon? Azucena was prepared to accept any explanation, but she wanted to hear it coming from his lips.

What she couldn't bear was all this uncertainty. It reawakened in her all the insecurities she had worked so hard to overcome through astroanalysis. Her lack of self-confidence had prevented her from forming a stable relationship in the past. Whenever she had found someone worthwhile who treated her well, she had invariably ended up breaking it off. Deep down, she had always felt she didn't deserve happiness; yet she still had had a profound need to feel loved. It was in an effort to resolve these problems that she had decided to find her twin soul, thinking that with him she couldn't go wrong. It had taken so long to find him! And then to have lost him so soon! It was the greatest injustice she had suffered in all her fourteen thousand lives.

Azucena knew she had better do something fast to assuage all this anguish and considered that her best bet would be to go stand in line at the Consumer Protection Agency. There at least she could pick a fight with somebody, or simply complain, scream, demand her rights. The bureaucrats on duty in such places were among the most forbearing of government employees, having been assigned there expressly so that people could take out their frustrations on them. Yes, that was what she would do.

✦

The Consumer Protection Agency looked like the anteroom to Hell. Complaints, laments, and tears filled the stifling room, where thousands of people stood crammed together. By the time Azucena made her way to the line for Twin Souls, she was drenched in sweat. So was Cuquita, who was standing a few feet away. Cuquita! There was the super from Azucena's building, in the Astral Ascension line right next to her. They both pretended they had not seen each other, for the last thing they wanted was to have to speak. But fate seemed determined to bring them together, because the moment Cuquita reached the window,

Azucena moved up in line and found herself nearly elbow to elbow with her.

From where she stood she could not avoid hearing all of Cuquita's conversation with the bureaucrat. Communication between the two was complicated by Cuquita's repeated efforts to impress the woman by using language she considered elegant and cultivated. However, since she didn't know what half the terms meant, she only ended up annoying the clerk.

"Listen, Señorita. You have any idea how meretricious I've been?"

"I beg your pardon?"

"I've levitated my soul high enough to merit scatological treatment."

"I'm sure you have, Señora, but the problem is you have to pay for everything in life, either in installments or cash on the barrel-head—but you still have to pay."

"I know, but look, I've paid off my karmic dues, verbatim. And now I want my divorce."

"I'm very sorry, Señora, but our records indicate that you still owe outstanding debts to your husband from prior lives."

"What debts?"

"Do I need to remind you of your life as a film critic?"

"Well, okay, I admit I was pretty nasty, but not enough to deserve this! I've spent enough time paying off karmas from posterior lives not to be stuck with a man guilty of default and battery. Just look at this eye! If you don't grant me a divorce soon, I swear I'll kill him."

"Do what you like, but you'll still have to pay. Next, please."

"Look, isn't there some way we can work this out between us, so that I can meet my twin soul?"

"No, Señora, it won't work. Let me tell you, lots of people are in the same boat. They all want beauty, money, health, or fame—

without ever doing anything to deserve them. But still, if you really want to go ahead and meet your twin soul without earning the privilege, we can always work out a credit. That is, assuming you're willing to pay interest."

"How much interest are we talking about?"

"If you sign this form, we can put you in touch with your twin soul in less than a month, but you'll have to commit to spending ten more lives with your current husband, taking beatings, humiliation, whatever he chooses to dish out. If you agree to this, we can arrange it immediately."

"No way!"

"Well, here we go again . . . People are willing to ask for anything, but they're never interested in paying up. I suggest you think about what you really want to do."

Azucena was embarrassed to have overheard Cuquita's complaints. Although she didn't like Cuquita, still she didn't enjoy seeing her suffer, and the worst of it was that Azucena knew poor Cuquita didn't stand a chance of meeting her twin soul at present. Who could tell how many more lives she would have to wait? By this time Azucena had come to believe that love and waiting were one and the same. Love always meant waiting, yet love, paradoxically, spurred her to action because waiting kept her going. Azucena's love for Rodrigo had caused her to stand in countless lines, to lose weight, to purify her body and soul. But his disappearance had prevented her from thinking about anything that wasn't connected with learning his whereabouts. She had let herself go. She didn't care whether her hair was combed or her teeth brushed. She didn't even care whether or not her aura was luminous. Nothing that happened was of any importance unless it could be related to Rodrigo.

All this while, the person behind her in the line had been telling her about his past lives, but Azucena had not really heard a word of it, although it had nearly put her to sleep. The man hadn't noticed, because Azucena's face kept the same neutral expression through-out his monologue, and to look at her, you could never tell she was about to drift off to sleep. This man was the perfect cure for the galloping insomnia that had plagued her ever since Rodrigo disap-peared. She had tried everything, from linden-flower tea to warm milk and honey, to her foolproof method of remembering all the lines she had stood on in her lifetime. The trick was to count back-ward, one by one, every person who had been at a window before her. This method had never failed until she lost Rodrigo. Now each time she thought of a line, she would remember how hopeful she had been as she stood there, dreaming about being kissed and caressed . . . and then sleep was frightened away once and for all. But now—maybe it was the combination of the heat and her com-panion's chatter, for this man could numb an entire battalion—the truth was, she was about to fall asleep on her feet.

"And did I tell you about my life as a ballerina?"

"No, I don't think so."

"Well, in that life . . . It's funny how things turn out. I didn't want to be a ballerina, I wanted to be a musician, but since I'd been a rock star in a previous life and had made quite a few people deaf with my racket, they wouldn't hear of giving me a good ear again, so I had no choice but to be a ballerina. But I don't regret it—it turned out to be great! That is, except for the bunions I got from those toe shoes. But all in all, I still loved dancing on pointe. It felt like floating, like floating on air . . . like . . . like— Oh, I don't know how to explain it. But the worst thing was, they killed me off when I was only twenty years old. Can you believe it? Oh, it was awful! I was just leaving the theater one night when some men tried to rape me; I fought back, and one of them killed me."

Azucena softened a little at the sight of this big ugly man crying like a little kid. She gave him her handkerchief to dry his tears, and tried to imagine him dancing on pointe, but failed.

"It was really unfair, because I was pregnant . . . and I never got to see my baby. . . ."

He had pronounced the crucial phrase to capture Azucena's attention: "I never got to see my baby." If there was one thing Azucena knew, it was the pain of losing someone. She immediately identified with the sorrow of this poor man, who never got to see the little creature he had so loved and waited for. She could find no way of consoling him; she could only gaze at him with sympathetic eyes.

"That's why I came here, to file a complaint. I was due a woman's body in this life to finish my apprenticeship in the other life, but by mistake I was born in this nightmare of a body. Pretty ugly, isn't it?"

Azucena wanted to cheer him up, but she couldn't think of a single pleasantry. This man's ugliness seemed like a slap in the face to God.

"Oh, you don't know what I'd give to look like you. I hate having a man's body. And since I don't really like women, I have to have homosexual relationships. But most men are brutes! They don't know how to be tender with me, and that's what I crave. Oh, if I were only slender and delicate, then they'd treat me gently."

"Haven't you ever asked for a soul transplant?"

"Are you kidding! I've been standing in lines like this for ten years, but each time there's a body available, they give it to somebody else, never me. I'm desperate."

"Well, I hope they give you one soon."

"So do I."

The man returned the handkerchief Azucena had lent him. She took it gingerly by one corner, because he had liberally blown his nose in it, but then decided to give it back to him rather than put it in her purse. He thanked her warmly and then hurriedly said good-bye, because it was almost Azucena's turn at the window.

"You're next, so thanks, and good luck!"

"You, too."

"Next?"

Azucena approached the window.

"Uh, look, Señorita . . . You see, they processed my documents in Astral Ascension a long time ago."

"All Ascension affairs are in that line over there. Next."

"Listen, let me finish. They told me there that I was ready to meet my twin soul; they put me in touch with him, and we actually met."

"If you've already met him, what are you doing here? Your problem's been solved. Next . . ."

"No, wait! I'm not through! The problem is that he just disappeared, overnight, and I can't find him. Can you provide me with his address?"

"What? You met him, but you don't know his address?"

"No, because all they gave me was his aerophone number. I already left a message for him, and he came to my house."

"Well, call him again. Next . . ."

"Come on, you must think I'm some kind of idiot, right? I've called him day and night, but no answer. And I can't go to his house because I'm not registered in his aerophone. Will you please give me his address—or would you rather have me create a scene? Because, believe me, I'm not leaving here without that address! You tell me whether it's going to be the easy way or the hard way."

Azucena's shouting was accompanied by a threatening glare that succeeded in terrorizing the bureaucrat. With great meekness, she took the paper Azucena handed her, read Rodrigo's particulars, and diligently searched for information on him in the computer.

"No such person exists."

"What do you mean, he doesn't exist?"

"I mean he doesn't exist. I've searched all the files under Embodied and Disembodied, and he doesn't show up on any list."

"That's not possible, he *has* to be there."

"I tell you, *he doesn't exist.*"

"Look, Señorita, please don't give me that crap! I'm living proof he exists, because I'm his twin soul. Rodrigo Sánchez exists because I exist. Period!"

Not a single person in the entire Consumer Protection Agency was spared from Azucena's shrieking, but no one was more shocked by it than her companion in the line. Even after Azucena in her fury had swept up her papers from the counter and turned to leave, he still stood there, not knowing whether to step up to the window for his turn, or to follow Azucena out the door.

As she left the building, Azucena felt a tap on her shoulder that made her jump. She turned to see a shady-looking character whispering something to her.

"Need a body?"

"A what?"

"A body—I can get you one in excellent condition and at a good price."

This was just what she needed to top off her memorable morning in the realm of bureaucracy. She had made the mistake of answering this *coyote*, and that was enough to make him stick to her like a leech for several blocks at least. These kinds of characters were always seen hanging around outside government office buildings. You had to ignore them completely if you wanted to walk down the street in peace, because as soon as they noticed you observing them, even for a second out of the corner of your eye, they insisted on pushing their services on you.

"No thank you."

"Come on, you won't get a better price anywhere."

"I said no! I don't need a body."

"Well, I don't want to say so, but yours looks a little beat up."

"What's that to you!"

"Okay, I'll shut up, but . . . Come on, we just got some new ones in, really beautiful—blue eyes and all. . . ."

"I don't want any!"

"What can you lose, just taking a look?"

"I said no! Do you understand?"

"If you're worried about the cops, let me tell you, we only deal in bodies with no registered auras."

"I'm not worried about the police, I'm going to *call* them, if you don't stop being such a damn pest!"

"Oooh, what a temper!"

It hadn't gone too badly; it had only taken a block and a half at top speed to shake him off. At the corner, Azucena looked back to be sure he still wasn't following her, and spotted him bearing down on the "ballerina" instead. She hoped that in his desperation to have a woman's body he wouldn't fall into the clutches of the *coyote*. But for the time being, she had too many problems of her own to worry about. From now on, the world could fall apart before her eyes and she wouldn't care. She walked along, so involved in her thoughts that she did not even notice the spacecraft circling the city to announce the nomination of a new candidate for Planetary President: Isabel González.

CD
Track 2

Bad because you don't love me
Bad because you never touch me
Bad because you have a mouth
Bad whenever you please

Bad as lies
Bad breath, constipation
Bad as censorship
As a bald rat in garbage
Bad as poverty
As a driver's license photo
Bad as a rubber check
As smacking your granny

Bad as trichinosis
Bad as a hit man
Bad as spiders
Bad and full of cunning

Bad as order, decency, or a good conscience
Bad wherever you look
Bad as a throbbing root canal
Bad as a rusty nail
Bad as a Czech film
Bad as cold soup
Bad as the end of the century

Bad by nature
Bad from head to foot
Bad, bad, bad
Bad, but so damn beautiful

LILIANA FELIPE

5

Being a Demon is an enormous responsibility, but being Mammon, Isabel's Demon, is truly a blessing; for Isabel González is the best student I've had in millions of years. She is the most beautiful flower of meekness ever to blossom in the fields of power and ambition. Her soul has yielded to my counsel with profound innocence, and without any doubts: she takes my suggestions as orders, and carries them out instantly. No one—nothing—stands in her way. She eliminates whatever must be eliminated without a trace of remorse. So persistent is she in attaining her goals that she will soon be made part of our collegiate league, and on that day I shall be the proudest devil in all Hell.

I consider myself fortunate to have been chosen as her teacher. After all, they could have selected any one of the other fallen angels that inhabit these shadowy domains, many of whom have better teaching credentials than I have. But, thank God, I was the lucky one. And thanks to Isabel's diligence, I'm going to earn the promotion I've been waiting for all these centuries. Finally I shall be given the recognition I deserve, because up until now I've received nothing but ingratitude. All that hard work for such little pay! The ones who have always carried off all the applause, all the medals and glory, are the Guardian Angels. I ask myself, where would they be without us Demons?

An evolving spirit must pass through every imaginable horror before reaching enlightenment, for there is no way of arriving at light except through darkness. A soul is tempered only by suffering and pain. There is no way for human beings to avoid this predicament, nor is it useful to give them lessons in advance. The human soul is basically very stupid and cannot comprehend an experience until it lives it out in the flesh. Likewise, no knowledge ever reaches the brain without first passing through the organs of the senses.

Before realizing it was wrong to eat the forbidden fruit, man first had to experience its enticing scent; to anticipate the delight of biting into its flesh, of hearing its skin give way, of savoring each morsel, sensing its contours, its succulence, its gentle caresses as it makes its way through the esophagus, the stomach, the intestines. Not until Adam ate the apple did his mind open to new knowledge. Only when his intestines digested it, did his brain comprehend that he was walking around naked in Paradise. Not until he suffered the consequences of partaking in the wisdom of the God who created him did he realize his transgression. Simply telling him not to eat of the Tree of Good and Evil would never have been enough. There is no way for human beings to accept a priori a line of reasoning; they have to live it out in all its fullness.

And who is it who provides these opportunities? The Guardian Angels? Hell, no! It is we, the Demons, who do it. Thanks to our labors, man suffers. Thanks to all the trials we subject him to, he is able to evolve. And what do we get in return? Rejection, ingratitude, bad press. What else is new? Our role in life has always been to play the part of the bad guys. After all, someone has to do it. Someone has to be the teacher, the discipliner, man's guide through the murky darkness. And I can tell you, it is not easy. To educate is to fight a constant battle, administering pain, suffering, punishment, without relief. It is sheer torment to watch man continually suffer—all because of us.

And it doesn't help knowing it's for their own good, because that knowledge does not alleviate their agony. How I would love to be one of those who give relief, who console, who dry the tears, who offer the protective embrace. But then, who would push man to evolve? Someone has to wield the whip. What would become of a piano if nobody ever struck its keys? We would never hear the unique tones it is capable of sounding.

Sometimes you have to do violence to matter in order to reveal its beauty. The blows of a chisel convert a block of marble into a masterpiece. We must know how to strike without pity, without remorse, without fear of discarding the bits of stone that stand in the way of its splendor. To know how to produce a work of art is to know how to discard the extraneous. All creation follows the same process. In the maternal womb, the cells themselves know what to discard; some sacrifice themselves so that others may exist. In order for the upper lip to separate from the lower, thousands of cells that once joined them must die. Were that not so, how could man speak, sing, eat, kiss, or sigh with love?

The soul, unfortunately, is not as wise as those cells. It is merely a diamond in the rough, which must abide the blows inflicted by suffering in order to shine in all its brilliance. You would think it might learn to stop resisting punishment. But it will not consent to be the cell that commits suicide so the mouth can open and speak for us all; human beings never want to be the piece that is chiseled away to reveal the work of art. So, there is no recourse but to slough some of them off for the benefit of all humanity.

The ones chosen to perform these necessary acts are those who inflict violence: those who respect neither the place nor the order of things. Those who have no awe of life, who never stop to marvel at the beauty of the evening sky; those who know that the world can always be changed to their advantage; that there are no boundaries that cannot be encroached upon, no order that cannot be undone, no law that cannot be rewritten, no virtue that cannot be bought, no body that cannot be possessed, no sacred text that cannot be burned, no pyramid that cannot be destroyed, no opponent that cannot be assassinated.

Such persons are our strongest allies, and, among them all, Isabel reigns queen: the most merciless, ambitious, cruel, and sublimely obedient of all the violators. Her brutal blows, struck with such virtuosity, have produced the most extraordinary music. Thanks to the tortures she inflicted, there were many who received Lucifer's benedictions; thanks to the wars she provoked, great advances were made in science and technology. Because she practiced corruption, men found themselves able to exercise generosity; due to her abuses of the privileges of power, her lack of respect, her obstinacy, her need to control every act of her subordinates, many were finally able to achieve enlightenment and knowledge.

A person can learn the value of his legs only when they've been cut off. To appreciate solidarity, one must first be an outcast. To learn to value order, one must first feel the effects of chaos. Thus if a man is to value life in the universe, he must first learn to destroy it: to regain Paradise, he must first regain Hell, *and above all, he must love it.* For it is only by loving what we despise that we evolve. The only way to arrive at God is by means of the Devil. So Azucena should be very grateful to be included in the destiny of my precious Isabel, for soon, very soon, it will bring her into contact with God.

6

Let us rejoice, Oh friends,
And embrace each other here.
Now we walk on the flowering earth.
No one here need put an end
To flowers or songs.
They will live on in the house of the
    Giver of Life.

This earth is the realm of the fleeting
    moment.
Is it the same, as well, in that region
Where somehow one still exists?
Is one happy there?
Is there friendship there?
Or is it only here on earth
That we come to know our faces?

AYOCUAN CUETZPALTZIN
Trece Poetas del Mundo Azteca
MIGUEL LEÓN-PORTILLA

As Isabel's house filled up with flowers and congratulatory faxes, her heart was seized with fear. Life could not have granted her a greater prize than being chosen as the Americas' candidate for Planetary President. She had finally attained her dream of reaching the heights of power and gaining the respect and admiration of all. But now she was terrified. A mounting fear prevented her from enjoying her triumph. The more that people showed their support, the more threatened she felt, for she knew that any number of them would love to be in her shoes. Realizing how she was envied and closely watched only made her feel more vulnerable. She considered everyone around her a potential enemy and began taking extreme precautions. Knowing that human beings are by nature corruptible, she trusted no one. Anybody might betray her. She slept with her door locked, was constantly detecting strange odors that only she seemed to notice, and had become hypersensitive to tastes as well. In short, she sensed an imminent physical danger and was convinced the entire world was plotting against her.

As long as she had had nothing to lose, she had lived a tranquil existence, but now that she was on the verge of having it all, she was shaky as a poppy in the wind. She felt the way she had as a child, when she refused to walk in the dark for fear that the bogeyman would jump out at her. She had the same sensation even when watching love scenes in movies, for she knew that they usually preceded disasters. So instead of enjoying the lovers' kisses, she was anxiously scanning the screen, anticipating the moment when the dagger would come into view and be thrust into the man's back. It was the same with film music: she knew frightening music always accompanied horror; so instead of enjoying the love theme she was always listening for the slightest variation in its melody, so she could shut her eyes and avoid the jolt to her soul.

Anyone knew that this kind of constant strain was bad for one's health. The Department of Public Health and Welfare had gone so far as to prohibit suspense music in films, which had been linked to liver damage in spectators. Isabel herself had enthusiastically endorsed the measure. Her only regret was that there wasn't a similar organization to regulate the intrusion of tragedies into everyday life, some means of preventing the fact that from one moment to the next you could pass from wedding bells to an ambulance's wail; some way of warning people when something terrible was approaching, so that she would be able to shut her eyes in time. The situation Isabel found herself in was stretching her nerves to the limit. Everyone wanted to see her, interview her, be close to her—close, that is, to power. She had to meet every situation head-on, with her eyes wide open, be extremely vigilant, trust no one, not leave the tiniest loose end dangling so that one of her enemies could use it to destroy her. She had to be on the alert and to steel her heart whenever necessary. Although she had no problem there: she had already shown herself capable of eliminating her own daughter, so she certainly could do the same to anybody else who got in her way.

That daughter had been born in Mexico City on January 12, 2180, at 21 hours, 20 minutes, under the sign of Capricorn, with Virgo in the ascendant. Her astrological chart indicated she would have many problems with authority due to the opposition of Saturn and Uranus, Saturn representing authority and Uranus, liberty and rebellion. In addition, the position of Uranus in the sign of Aries indicated extreme assertiveness, so that when this girl decided to be stubborn, she would be singleminded about it, if not impulsive and irresponsible. The position of Uranus in the eighth house suggested that she might become involved in shady dealings in her desire to challenge authority.

With all the subversive traits predicted by this chart, it was almost a given that the girl would grow up to be a perennial thorn in the side, especially for Isabel, who had always planned on becoming Planetary President. And this was not just some pipe dream of hers, for Isabel's astrological chart indicated it as well, predicting further that when this occurred, an era of peace would finally be established for all humanity. With this knowledge, Isabel did not want to have her own daughter impeding her. So before she could begin to feel any affection for the child, she ordered her to be disintegrated for one hundred years, so as not to thwart the destiny of the human race.

From time to time Isabel thought about that daughter. What would she have been like? Would she have been pretty? Would she have looked like her mother? Would she have been slender? Or fat like Carmela, her other daughter? Now that she thought of it, perhaps it would have been a good idea to have had Carmela disintegrated as well. All she ever did was embarrass Isabel. Just like this morning. The first thing Isabel had done upon awakening was to turn on the Televirtual for the broadcast of the interview she'd given following her nomination. She found it very pleasing to watch herself in virtual reality in her own bedroom. How thrilling to think that she had been in houses all over the world. She was told she had been seen by millions of viewers. The only problem was that Abel Zabludowsky had come up with the bright idea of interviewing Carmela. How embarrassing! Her pig of a daughter had also been in all those homes. She just hoped they had found some way of squeezing Carmela in without crowding her own image out. Talk about hogging the camera! She wondered what people thought of her. That she was a terrible mother not to put her daughter on a diet? What a nightmare! She didn't know what she should do about Carmela. And today Isabel was expecting crowds of people to stop by and fawn over her. Preparations were already under way for a press luncheon on the patio. She certainly didn't want her daughter to be anywhere in sight. But how could she hide her? Now that Carmela had been on the news, they'd all be asking about her. She had to come up with something. Her thoughts were interrupted by her daughter's voice.

"Mommy, may I come in?"

"Yes."

The door opened and there was Carmela, all dressed up for the luncheon. She had chosen a beautiful white lace dress because she wanted to look her best on such a special day for her mother.

"Get that dress off!"

"But . . . it's the nicest one I have."

"It's atrocious. You look like an overstuffed tamale. How in the world could you ever choose white, being as fat as you are?"

"But it's a luncheon, and you've always told me black is only for evening."

"You remember what I tell you well enough when it suits *you*, don't you? Try suiting *me* for a change. Get on another dress! And when you come back, show me the purse you'll be using, too, so I can see if it goes with your dress."

"I don't have a black bag."

"Then go find one somewhere! I don't want you coming down without a purse. Only whores parade around like that. Is that what you want, to look like a slut? Is that what you had in mind? To make a complete fool out of me?"

"No."

Carmela could not hold back her tears any longer. Extracting a tissue from her pocket, she dabbed at the stream running down her cheeks.

"What is *that*? Don't you have a handkerchief? How could you think of going anywhere without one? When have you ever seen a princess blowing her nose in a tissue? From now on, I want you to learn to behave appropriately for the daughter of someone in my position. Now get out of here, you make me furious!"

Carmela turned to leave, but before she reached the door, Isabel stopped her.

"And remember to keep out of range of the cameras."

Isabel was outraged. She was sick of dealing with young people. They always wanted to have their own way, disobey, impose their own wishes, challenge authority—that is, challenge *her*. She didn't understand why she always had the same effect on everyone. They couldn't see her as their superior without immediately wanting to rebel. Well, right now she needed to see if her employees had set up the patio exactly as she had told them.

The patio resembled a frenetic beehive, with countless workers scurrying all over the place under the direction of Agapito, Isabel's right-hand man. Agapito had had to work more frantically than ever to please his boss, because, considering the importance of the function, she'd given him almost no time to organize it. Isabel hadn't any reason for holding a press luncheon so soon. Her nomination had only been announced the day before, so nobody could have expected her to be prepared to have so many people; but she wanted to impress everyone with her organization. Agapito had taken charge with great efficiency, to assure that everything was perfect. The tables, tablecloths, floral arrangements, wines, food, service, invitations, press, music—all had been coordinated personally by him. No detail escaped him. He had at his fingertips the press clippings concerning the nomination, as well as a list of everyone who had called to congratulate Isabel. He knew only too well that the first thing she would want to know was who was on her side—and, by default, who was not, so that she could have them placed on her list of enemies.

As soon as he saw Isabel approach, Agapito felt a surge of apprehension. Having exerted himself to the fullest so that everything would be just right, he was in sore need of his boss's approval. Isabel glanced around the patio. Everything seemed to be in order, but then suddenly her eye was drawn to the center of the patio, where the remains of an ancient pyramid had poked up through the tiles. It was not the first time this problem had occurred. Now again Isabel had to remind them to cover it up, since it would not be at all convenient for the government to find out her house was sitting atop a pre-Hispanic pyramid. In such cases the State invariably ended up nationalizing the property. Then archeologists would arrive on the scene to begin their excavations, and, in the process, they would be likely to unearth a part of Isabel's past she preferred to keep buried deep beneath the earth.

"Agapito! Why haven't they covered the pyramid?"

"Well . . . we thought it'd be good for your image if people saw your concern for our pre-Hispanic past . . ."

"*We* thought? Who's 'we'?"

"Well, the boys and I . . ."

"The boys! The boys are idiots who can't think for themselves—they're supposed to follow *your* orders. If you can't control them, then what good are you? I'll just have to hire somebody who can make them obey."

"They obey me. It was my decision . . ."

"Then you're fired."

"But . . . why?"

"*Why?* Because I'm sick and tired of playing schoolteacher to a bunch of morons. I've told you a million times, anyone who doesn't do as I say can get the hell out!"

"But I did everything you told me to . . ."

"I never told you to leave that pyramid exposed."

"But you didn't say to cover it, either. It's not fair to fire me for one slipup. Everything else is perfect, you can see for yourself . . ."

"The only thing I see is that you're not a professional, so I want you out of here right now. Tell Rosalío to take over."

"Rosalío isn't here."

"Not here? Where did he go?"

"Downtown."

Isabel brightened at this news, and whispered to Agapito, "To get my chocolate?"

"No, you gave him permission to take his papers to the Consumer Protection Agency."

"Well, fire him, too. I'm fed up with both of you!"

Isabel cut short her screaming and put on her most charming smile the second she saw Abel Zabludowsky arriving with his cameras and crew. She was terrified. Had he heard her screaming? God, she hoped not. That would kill her image for sure. Just in case, she patted Agapito on the back to give the impression she'd been joking with him. Then her heart nearly froze as she saw Carmela steaming in, all six hundred sixty pounds of her. Isabel had to prevent Abel Zabludowsky from interviewing her again, let alone spotting the protruding pyramid.

Agapito was sharp enough to divine Isabel's thoughts, and came up with a brilliant solution that won him back his job and completely restored Isabel's former confidence in him.

"What if we sit Carmela right there on top of the pyramid, and tell her to stay put?"

And thus it was that the voluminous Carmela, black bag in hand, came to the rescue, preventing anyone from discovering that in the midst of her mother's patio a pyramid was about to be born.

7

Azucena walked home. Walking always restored her tranquillity. When she arrived at her corner, she saw Cuquita entering their building. Azucena was surprised to see her coming back so late, since she had left the Consumer Protection Agency long before Azucena. When she spotted the large bag Cuquita was carrying, Azucena realized that she must have gone shopping before returning home.

Cuquita, in turn, had caught sight of Azucena on the other side of the street, and seemed not at all pleased. She obviously wanted to get inside as quickly as possible to avoid meeting Azucena, but she found this difficult because her fat, drunken husband was sprawled across the doorway. Nothing unusual about that. Cuquita's husband was practically an architectural fixture in the neighborhood, and no one was surprised anymore when they saw him stretched out on the stairs, covered with vomit and flies. The neighbors had already filed a complaint with Health and Welfare, and Cuquita had been notified that she could not go on letting her spouse use the street as a bedroom.

Poor Cuquita! thought Azucena. No wonder she wanted to change husbands! On the other hand, she must have done something in her other lives to end up with karma like this. Azucena watched as Cuquita tried to drag her husband inside the building; he woke up, enraged, and began giving her an awful beating. This type of injustice always infuriated Azucena. It made her blood boil, and turned her into a force unleashed by nature. In an instant she was beside the mismatched pair. Grabbing Cuquita's husband by his hair, she slammed him against the wall and gave him a kick in the crotch. Then for good measure she added a right hook to the kidneys and, once he was on the ground, finished off with a flurry of kicks to vent all her remaining rage. Azucena ended up exhausting herself, but felt a great sense of relief.

Cuquita didn't know whether to kiss Azucena in gratitude or to gather up the contents of her shopping bag, which had spilled down the stairs. She decided to make her thanks brief and then rushed to collect the scattered articles before anyone noticed them. As Azucena leaned down to help, she was surprised to discover that the bag had been filled not with groceries but with an impressive assortment of Virtual Reality Books.

Some months before, Cuquita had asked Azucena for help in obtaining some of these VRBs for her blind grandmother, who was depressed about not being able to read or watch Televirtual. The VRB was a sensational device that had just come on the market. It consisted of a pair of spectacles that bypassed the eyes altogether, allowing the blind to "see" films in virtual reality with the same clarity as people who had vision. Cuquita's grandmother had been the first to put in a request for the apparatus, and the first to be rejected. She was not eligible for such indulgences because her blindness was karmic: as a former member of the Chilean military she had blinded several prisoners during torture.

Cuquita, however, seeing her grandmother weeping day and night, had worked up the nerve to ask Azucena for a letter of recommendation stating that she was the grandmother's astroanalyst, and could certify that the old woman had already paid off her bad karma—none of which was the case. Azucena, as might be expected, had refused. It was contrary to the ethics of her profession to do that sort of thing. But now Azucena saw to her surprise that Cuquita had gotten her way and somehow managed to obtain the books. Azucena was intrigued as to how she had done it. Whom had she bribed? Cuquita left her no time to speculate. Running over to Azucena, she snatched the VRB out of her hands, and quickly stuffed it back in the bag. As she did so, she asked Azucena, in a tone of direct challenge:

"Well, are you going to perpetrate me?"

"What?"

"To the police! Don't even think of it, I'm warning you! Because when it comes to defending my family, I'm capable of anything."

"Oh, don't worry, I won't go to the police. . . . But listen, could you tell me if they also have compact discs where you bought those VRBs?"

Cuquita was amazed by Azucena's sudden interest.

Azucena seemed more bent on taking advantage of Cuquita's connections than on denouncing them. The urgency in her eyes made that clear, so Cuquita decided on impulse to trust her.

"Well . . . yes. But the thing is, it's dangerous to buy them because, I'm warning you, they're totally explicit."

". . . I don't care if they're illicit, just tell me where to get them, please! There's one I have to find!"

"At the black market in Tepito."

"How do I get there?"

"You've never been?"

"No."

"Well, if you've never gone, it's a bitch to find. I'd take you, but my grandmother is waiting for her supper. We can go tomorrow if you want."

"Thanks, but I'd rather go today."

"Okay, go ahead. When you get to Tepito, just ask around."

"Thanks, Cuquita."

Azucena sprang to her feet and, without even a good-bye to Cuquita, ran to the aerophone booth on the corner to transflash herself to Tepito. In a matter of seconds, Azucena was in the heart of the Lagunilla marketplace. The door of the aerophone booth opened, and she was facing a crush of people pushing and elbowing their way into the booth Azucena was vacating. She struggled against the tide and began wandering through the market. Making her way through throngs of people, she headed straight for the stalls where antiques were sold.

Each of the objects there cast its spell on her, making her wonder who had owned it, and in what place and time. She passed several stalls brimming with tires, cars, vacuum cleaners, computers, and other discarded objects, but could find no compact discs. Finally, in one of the booths she saw a portable sound system. Surely they sold CDs there. She walked over to the stall, but the dealer was busy and couldn't wait on her. He was arguing with a customer who wanted to buy a dentist's chair with all sorts of clamps, syringes, and molds for taking dental impressions. Azucena couldn't understand how anyone would be interested in buying such instruments of torture but, after all, in this world there are all sorts of tastes. She waited a while for the haggling to stop, but the two men were equally obstinate and neither of them wanted to budge. There was a pause when the dealer, bored with the discussion, turned and asked Azucena what he could do for her, but she could not summon the words to respond. She didn't have the nerve to ask out loud where to find black-market compact discs. To avoid looking foolish, she asked instead the price of a beautiful silver serving spoon.

Behind her, she heard a woman's voice saying, "That's my spoon. I had set it aside there to buy." Turning around, Azucena found herself face to face with an attractive, dark-haired woman who was reaching for the spoon Azucena was holding up. Azucena gave it to her immediately and apologized, saying she hadn't realized it was already spoken for. She turned and retreated, feeling deeply frustrated. There was a big difference between knowing there was a black market and dealing with the people who ran it. She hadn't the least idea how to begin, where to go, what to ask. Her status as a Super-Evo without any experience in shady dealings certainly had its drawbacks. Her best bet would be to come back another day and bring Cuquita with her.

As she searched for a way out of the labyrinth of booths Azucena suddenly heard a melody emanating from a stall filled with stereos, radios, and television sets. The first thing she noticed when she got there was a sign reading "Music To Cry To," and, below that, in small print, *"Authorized by the Department of Public Health and Welfare."* Although everything appeared to be strictly legal, Azucena had a feeling she would find what she was looking for here. The music was in fact making her cry. It stirred up a deep nostalgia and with it came a wealth of memories. As she listened, Azucena remembered how it had felt to become a single being with Rodrigo, what it had been like to surpass the barrier of skin and to have four arms and legs and eyes; and twenty fingers and nails with which to tear open the gates to Paradise. As Azucena stood there weeping inconsolably, the antique dealer regarded her with great tenderness. After she dried her tears, the dealer quietly removed the CD and handed it to her.

"How much is it?" she asked.

"Nothing."

"Nothing? But I want to buy it . . ."

The dealer smiled amiably. Azucena felt a current of empathy flow between them.

"No one can sell what isn't his," he replied, "nor receive what she hasn't deserved. Take it, it belongs to you."

"Thank you."

Azucena put the CD safely away in her purse. She could hardly tell the dealer that she also needed a player, because she was sure this strange man, who seemed so oddly familiar, would have offered her one as well, and that would be pushing his generosity too far. Just before Azucena left, the dark-haired woman with the silver spoon walked up to the dealer, greeting him warmly, "How are you, Teo!" The dealer hugged her in return. "My dear Citlali," he exclaimed, "what a pleasure to see you!" Azucena walked away quietly, leaving the pair in animated conversation.

At a stall farther down, she bought a Discman so she could listen to her CD, and then she went directly to the nearest aerophone booth. Impatient as a child with a new toy, she was anxious to get home and listen to the music. But when she arrived at the row of aerophone booths, she nearly lost hope. So many people were crowded there that she thought she'd never get in. Eventually, however, she managed to elbow her way through and reached her goal in record time: a half hour. Her feeling of good fortune vanished, however, when she was shoved aside by a man with a large mustache, who forced his way into the booth before her. Infuriated by this latest injustice, her face transformed by rage, Azucena grabbed the man's arm and yanked him back out. He was sweating profusely, and seemed desperate as he pleaded with her.

"Lady! Please let me use the booth!"

"No, you listen to me! It's my turn. I waited just the same as you to get here."

"How long can it hold you up to let me go first? It'll only take me thirty seconds to free up the booth."

People behind them began whistling and shouting, and some of them tried squeezing past the two into the booth. Just then the mustached man saw the adjoining booth had been vacated, and like any sharp transcommuter, dashed inside. Before anyone else could push ahead of her, Azucena claimed her own booth and the matter was resolved.

What a nightmare! It was hard to believe that in the twenty-third century a human being could act like such a beast, especially when one considered the great strides that had been made in the field of science. As she keyed in her aerophone number, Azucena thought of all the benefits she enjoyed as a result of technological advances. To disintegrate, to travel through space and be reintegrated in the blink of an eye. What marvels!

The aerophone door opened and Azucena was about to step into her apartment, but couldn't, because the electromagnetic barrier was preventing her. As the alarm began to sound, she suddenly realized that this was not her own place but, rather, somebody else's, and a couple was passionately making love there. Well, come to think of it, technological advances in Mexico were not so reliable after all. These kinds of mishaps frequently occurred when aerophone lines were crossed or damaged. Although fortunately in such cases there was no danger of being killed, that did not make the incidents any less uncomfortable or annoying.

When the lovers heard the alarm, they abruptly suspended their amorous activities. The woman cried, "It's my husband!" while frantically pulling down her skirt. Azucena did not know what to do or where to look. Her eyes roamed around the room, finally fixing on a photograph on the far wall. Her voice caught in her throat. The mustached man in the photo was none other than the one she had fought with a few moments earlier. No wonder the poor man had been in such a hurry to get home!

Azucena surmised that he must have keyed in his aerophone number before she had jerked him from the booth, and that was why she ended up at his apartment. Desperately, she keyed in her own aerophone number. She had never been in such an embarrassing situation. Before she left, she attempted an apology.

"Sorry, wrong number!"

"Let's see if you can get it right, stupid!"

The aerophone door then closed and reopened a few seconds later. Azucena breathed a sigh of relief to find herself in her own apartment. Or rather, what was left of it. The living room had been ransacked. Furniture and clothing had been tossed in all directions, and right in the middle of the whole mess was the man with the mustache, dead! Blood streamed from his ears. This was what happened to anyone who ignored the sound of the alarm and broke through the protective magnetic field of a house that wasn't his own: the cells of the body would not reintegrate properly, and an excess of pressure would burst the arteries. The poor guy. So the aerophone lines really had been crossed, and in the man's frenzy to catch his wife in the act, he must have dashed out of the booth, without even hearing the alarm. But . . . wait! Azucena hadn't turned the alarm on, for she still had hoped Rodrigo would return and didn't want him to have any problem getting in. So then what *had* happened? And why had her apartment been ransacked?

The first thing she did was to go check the registry box of her building's protection system. There she discovered that someone clearly had tampered with it. The wires had been crossed, and badly reconnected. That meant that someone had intended to kill her. It was only through the ineptitude of the Aerophone Company that her life had been saved. The accidental crossing of the two lines from the aerophone booths had caused this man to die in her place. That was fate for you: she owed her life to incompetence. But now she had new questions. Why had someone wanted to kill her? And who? She had no idea. The only thing she was sure of was that anyone wishing to adjust the master control of the building needed a work permit, and that Cuquita was the only person who could grant them access.

⊶⧉⊷

Azucena knocked at Cuquita's door. She had to wait a minute before Cuquita opened up, her eyes filled with tears. Azucena regretted having intruded at the wrong moment. That drunken husband of hers had better not be beating her up again, she thought.

"Good evening, Cuquita."

"Evening."

"Is something wrong?"

"No, I'm just watching *The Right to Live*."

Azucena had totally forgotten Cuquita never did anything while her favorite soap was on.

"I'm sorry, it slipped my mind completely. I just wanted to ask who came to repair my aerophone . . ."

"Who do you think? The men from the Aerophone Company."

"Do you remember if they had a work order?"

"Of course! I don't let just anybody waltz in here."

"Did they mention if they'd be back?"

"Yes, they said they had to finish up tomorrow. So if you don't have any more questions, I'd like to get back to my show . . ."

"Of course, Cuquita. I'm sorry to bother you. See you tomorrow."

"Hmmmpf!"

The sound of Cuquita's door slamming shut in her face stunned Azucena with the same impact as the word "Danger!" ringing in her head. The supposed aerophone workmen would suppose she was dead, and would expect to collect her corpse the next day, supposedly without any problem. Supposing sons of bitches! Coming back tomorrow, but what time? Cuquita hadn't said, but if she knocked at that door again, Cuquita would be the one to kill her. Most likely they'd come by during regular working hours, since they were passing themselves off as repairmen from the Aerophone Company. That meant Azucena still had all night to organize her thoughts and devise a defense strategy. But right now, what she had to do was get rid of the man with the mustache.

Azucena hurried back to her apartment and searched the cuckold's pants pockets for his ID card. Then she keyed in the aerophone number on the card, dragged the man into the booth, and sent him home. It was safe to assume two things: that this had not been the man's lucky day, and that it was turning out to be a day of unpleasant surprises for his wife as well. Azucena could just imagine her face when she saw her husband's corpse. But she didn't want to think about the guilt the woman would suffer later on. Azucena had to remind herself not to get mixed up in other people's affairs. It was an occupational reflex of hers to be always worrying about the traumatic effects of any tragedy upon people.

She felt very sorry for the man who had exchanged fates with her. She would be forever grateful to him. After all, he had saved her from certain death. But who was going to save her now from the dangers she still faced? If only the man had exchanged bodies with her as well, the favor would have been complete, because then the workmen would arrive, find a lifeless body, and take Azucena for dead, thus allowing her to keep on looking for Rodrigo, even if she was in the body of a mustached stranger. Changing bodies . . . that was it! All she had to do was show up early the next morning at the Consumer Protection Agency and she'd be sure to bump into the *coyote* who dealt in soul transplants to unregistered bodies. She knew that this would mean crossing the line into illegal territory, thereby running the risk that the Office of Astral Ascension would find out and cancel her authorization to live with her twin soul. But Azucena could see no other way out. She was ready to try anything.

While on the lookout for the *coyote* the next morning, Azucena joined the line of people waiting for the Consumer Protection offices to open. She couldn't stop thinking about who might want to kill her, and why. She had already worked off her bad karma; she didn't have any enemies, and hadn't committed any crimes. The only person who seemed to hate her was Cuquita, but Azucena didn't think her capable of plotting such a convoluted murder. If she had meant to kill Azucena, she would have buried a kitchen knife in her back long ago. Then who could it be? The ugly sight of the *coyote* rounding the corner interrupted her thoughts. Azucena walked over to meet him. As soon as he saw her approaching, he smiled maliciously.

"So? Changed your mind?"

"Yes."

"Follow me."

Azucena followed him for several blocks as gradually they made their way into the oldest, most run-down part of town. After entering what appeared to be a clothing factory they descended a hidden stairway to the cellar. Azucena was terrified to find herself in the midst of the black-market body trade.

This business owed its inadvertent beginnings to a group of late-twentieth-century scientists who had been experimenting with the artificial insemination of barren women. The procedure worked in the following manner: first an operation was performed to remove an egg from the woman. This egg was then fertilized with the husband's sperm in a test tube. When this test-tube fetus was several weeks old, it was implanted in the woman's womb. Sometimes the woman's body rejected the fetus and spontaneous abortion occurred, in which case the entire process had to be repeated. As the surgical procedure was uncomfortable, the scientists decided that instead of extracting one egg at a time, they would extract several. They would then fertilize them all, so that if for some reason the first attempt at insemination failed, they would have a replacement fetus from the same mother and father ready to be introduced into the uterus. As it was not always necessary to utilize a second fetus, much less a third, the extras were frozen, thus creating the first fetus bank. The fetuses were used for all manner of inhuman experiments up until the time of the Great Earthquake, when the laboratory and fetus bank were buried beneath the rubble. It was not until this century, during the process of remodeling a store, that the frozen fetuses had been discovered. An unscrupulous scientist had immediately purchased them, and with modern techniques succeeded in developing each fetus into an adult body. It seemed an ideal venture. The only person capable of implanting a soul in a human body is the mother. These bodies had no mother and, therefore, possessed no soul. Nor had they ever been registered, for they had not been born at any institution regulated by the government. In other words, they were merely awaiting a transplanted soul in order to exist. And the *coyote* relished playing his part in these good works.

Azucena followed him through the gloomy corridors, not knowing which body to choose. They came in every size, color, and scent. She stopped in front of the body of a woman with beautiful legs. Azucena had always dreamed of having a great pair of legs. Her own were rather spindly, and though she had any number of intellectual and spiritual virtues to compensate for this defect, she had always yearned for shapely legs. Hesitating a moment, but realizing she had no time to waste since the aerophone workmen would soon arrive at her house, she pointed quickly to the woman's body, saying, "That one!" Her choice now made, she requested an immediate transplant. This raised the price, but what could she do? Some things in life you just don't quibble over.

In a matter of seconds, Azucena was installed in the body of a blonde woman with blue eyes and to-die-for legs. She felt very strange, but didn't have time to reflect on her new state. She paid for the transplant and, without even a moment to say goodbye to her old body, was led to a secret aerophone booth from which her old body was transflashed to her apartment. Immediately after, she transflashed to the aerophone booth nearest her home. She wanted to arrive at approximately the same time as her body, because she needed to be there to see the faces of her enemies when they came to pick up her corpse. She had been careful to leave the wires connected just as she had found them. That way, as her old body crossed through the barrier, it would "die," just as her assassins had expected, and they wouldn't bother her anymore.

Standing on the corner near her house, Azucena could observe everything going on in the vicinity of her building. However, she too was being observed, the object of constant whistles and remarks about her legs. How could it be that humanity had evolved so little through all the millennia? Why was it still possible for a pair of shapely legs to derange seemingly rational men? She was the same person she'd been the day before: she felt exactly the same, thought exactly the same, and yet yesterday no one had given her a second look. Who knew how much more time would go by before men rhapsodized over the brilliance of a woman's aura?

Azucena only knew that if she stood on that corner much longer she'd be propositioned outright. She decided to repair to the small café across the street where she could continue her observations while treating herself to one of their delicious sandwiches. Suddenly she felt ravenous. Perhaps it was due to anxiety, perhaps to this new body that needed nourishment, but the fact was, she was dying for a sandwich.

As soon as she entered the café, she was annoyed to find that all the men's eyes were drawn to her. She made her way swiftly among the tables, taking a seat by the window so she could see what was happening outside. As soon as her legs were hidden from view, the café resumed its routine. Most of its regulars were workers from the Moon, who had to begin their commute long before the first newscast of the day. This café provided them not only breakfast, but also an easy way of keeping up with the world. The owners had an ancient television there, as opposed to a Televirtual. This was always a great relief, but especially so in these convulsive times when there had been nothing on the news but replays of Mr. Bush's assassination. Whenever you were watching Televirtual you necessarily found yourself in the middle of the crime scene over and over again, hearing the shot ring out, seeing the bullet enter and then exit the candidate's head carrying part of his brain along with it, seeing Mr. Bush collapse, hearing the screams and confusion, reliving the horror. Most restaurants had their Televirtuals on all day long at the request of a frightened populace who wanted to know what was happening minute by minute. Azucena didn't know how people could stand it, or how they could eat amid all the blood, pain, and smell of gunpowder. At least here, where the owners had refused to install a Televirtual, the customers could make their own decisions about whether or not to watch. Azucena had plenty of reasons for feeling sad and anxious without having to relive all this other suffering.

She decided to concentrate instead on what was happening across the street, while her fellow diners stared blankly at the screen. The broadcast had nothing new to say about Mr. Bush's assassination.

"Police continue to search for evidence at the scene of the crime . . ."

"This cowardly act has jolted the conscience of the world . . ."

"The Planetary Attorney General has issued instructions to all police bureaus to coordinate efforts in locating the assassin . . ."

"The Planetary President condemns this affront to peace and democracy, and promises citizens that every effort is being made to determine as swiftly as possible the motivation for this reprehensible act, as well as the identity of the masterminds behind it . . ."

Azucena listened to the frightened whispering of the other customers. Everyone seemed extremely alarmed, but as soon as the sportscast came on they came to life again. The soccer championships made them forget that there had been any assassination, and their greatest concern became whether or not the young athlete who was the incarnation of Hugo Sánchez would be playing. As far as Azucena could see, the assassin or assassins had planned everything to coincide with the Interplanetary Soccer Championship. Amazing how soccer could distract an entire populace!

Now the Governor of the Federal District was being interviewed, warning people that no rowdy celebrations would be allowed at the Angel de la Independencia monument. For the Earth–Venus match, they planned to disintegrate the monument for an entire week in order to avoid disturbances. Loud protests erupted from the diners at that announcement. Between their whistling and catcalls, it was almost impossible to hear the interview Abel Zabludowsky was conducting from the home of Isabel González, the new candidate for Planetary President, who was bragging about the Nobel Prize she had received in her twentieth-century incarnation as Mother Teresa.

At the end of the interview, the camera focused on an obese young woman whose image filled the screen. Everyone asked who this fat girl was, but no one found out because the interview was abruptly cut off. The only person who didn't seem to mind was Azucena. She was watching the Aerophone Company's spacecraft, which had just landed in front of her building. Two men were emerging from it, but just as they turned and she prepared to scrutinize their faces, her neighbor Julito's spaceship, the *Interplanetary Cockfight*, landed, obstructing her view. Azucena was frantic. Why did he have to land now? One by one, a group of mariachis who provided accompaniment for Julito's cockfights descended from the spacecraft. Their enormous sombreros blocked everything from view.

Azucena quickly paid her bill and ran outside. All she could do now was move closer to the building so she'd be able to see the murderers as they came out, even at the risk of being recognized. But no—how stupid could she be? They couldn't recognize her: she was in a different body. Azucena laughed at herself. She had changed bodies so fast that her mind hadn't taken it in.

Azucena sat on the stairs outside her building to wait. Minutes later, she saw the aerophone workmen coming, accompanied by Cuquita, who was sobbing loudly. They were saying good-bye to her in the doorway, telling her how sorry they were. Azucena remained frozen in place, not so much because her supposed death had moved Cuquita to tears, but because one of these two murderers was none other than the former ballerina in line behind her at the Consumer Protection Agency, the one who had wanted a woman's body so badly. My God! Had they killed her for her body? But if that was the case, why hadn't they taken it with them? Apparently, to continue the pretense. Now Azucena was thoroughly confused, because the spacehearse from the Gayosso Funeral Home would pick up her body and disintegrate it in outer space. So if the men from Gayosso took the body, how would the ex-ballerina get possession of it? Did he have contacts at the funeral home?

Her friend Julito meanwhile was warming up his mariachi group with the song "Sabor a mí." The music interrupted Azucena's train of thought and made her cry. She had been abnormally sensitive to music lately. Music! She really was stupid! In all the confusion, she had forgotten to take the compact disc from her apartment. If she was lucky, the opera that had been playing during her examination for the job at COPE would be on that CD.

Now she was on the right track. She had to get into her apartment, but her new body wasn't registered in the master control. She had to have that CD! So without a second thought she rang Cuquita's doorbell. Cuquita answered on the videophone.

"Yes?"

"Cuquita, it's me. Please let me in."

"What do you mean, 'me'? I don't know you."

"Cuquita, you're not going to believe this, but it's me—Azucena."

"What? Yeah, right!"

With that Cuquita hung up. Her image disappeared from the video screen. Azucena rang again.

"You, again? Look, if you don't leave, I'm calling the police."

"All right, call them. I think they'll be very interested to learn where you bought those VRBs for your grandmother."

Cuquita didn't answer. She was left speechless. Who the hell *was* this woman, and how did she know about those books for the blind? There was only one other person in the world who knew about the VRBs, and that was Azucena.

"Cuquita, please let me in and I'll explain everything. Okay?"

Cuquita finally gave in.

❖

As Azucena told her story, Cuquita began to feel closer to her. She no longer looked on Azucena as an enemy, nor as some superior creature to be envied. For the first time, she saw Azucena as someone she could be friends with, even though Azucena belonged to the political party of the Evos, who were highly evolved. The class conflict between them had always been a great barrier, and had been recently intensified due to a new government regulation stating that all Evos should display a visible sign on their aura: a six-pointed star at forehead level. The purpose was the immediate identification of Evos, so that they would be given preferential treatment wherever they went. Evos enjoyed a wide variety of advantages, including the best accommodations in spaceships, hotels, and resorts. More important, only they were eligible to fill positions of trust. That was only logical; after all, it would never occur to anybody to place the nation's resources in the hands of a Non-Evo. On the contrary, it was almost a given that because of their criminal past and their lack of spiritual enlightenment, they would inevitably loot the nation's coffers.

To Cuquita, this situation was highly unjust. How were the Non-Evos ever going to be able to work their way out of their low spiritual rating if no one gave them the chance to demonstrate they were evolving? It wasn't fair that just because they had raised a little hell in one life, they were branded as riffraff in this one. They had to fight for the right to exercise their free will, and this was why the Party for the Retribution of Inequities had been founded.

Cuquita was an enthusiastic party activist, and her greatest aspiration was to win the right to meet her twin soul, just like her Evo neighbor had done. How she had envied Azucena on that day when she found out she and Rodrigo had met! But just look how fate could play out. Here they were, both in the same boat: anxious, abandoned, and desperate.

Cuquita's expression softened now, and she was moved to tears as Azucena shared her love story with her. The two women hugged each other like old friends and promised to keep each other's secrets. Cuquita would not reveal any information about Azucena's true identity, and Azucena would not tell anyone about the VRBs Cuquita had bought for her grandmother.

And now that they were beginning to trust each other, Cuquita allowed herself to ask Azucena a question: what was Azucena going to do on Monday when she was supposed to turn in her papers at COPE, because the aurograph they'd taken of her wouldn't correspond to her new body? Azucena's jaw dropped. She'd never thought of that. When you focus on pure survival, you're bound to lose overall perspective. How was she going to handle this? Then she remembered that they had closed the window before she handed in her papers. This would allow her to have an aurograph of her new body taken somewhere to substitute for the one taken at COPE and . . . Suddenly all the color drained from Azucena's face. She had a new body! When she had had her soul transplant, she hadn't considered that the microcomputer would be left behind in her old body. Now there was a *real* problem. Without that microcomputer she couldn't go anywhere near COPE, because they photographed the thoughts of everyone within a block's radius of the building. She'd have to find Dr. Díez right away so that he could install another microcomputer in her head.

⸎

Azucena took a deep breath before knocking at the door of Dr. Díez's consulting room. She had had to climb up the fifteen floors because the Doctor's aerophone kept ringing busy. It must have been out of order. And since she could not use the aerophone in her own office because her new body wasn't registered in its electromagnetic protective field, she had made the climb on foot. When she had more or less recovered her breath, she knocked at her good friend's door. It was slightly ajar. Azucena pushed it and discovered instantly why Dr. Díez's line kept ringing busy: because as the doctor had died, his body had fallen right across the doorway of the aerophone booth, obstructing the mechanism that closed it. The doctor had perished in the same way as the mustached stranger.

Azucena felt she couldn't breathe. What was going on? A second crime in less than a week. She began to shake. And that was when she heard Dr. Díez's African violet quietly weeping. Dr. Díez had the same habit as Azucena of leaving his plants connected to the Plantspeaker. Azucena felt sick and ran into the bathroom to vomit. She had to get out of the building. She fled from the office, taking the African violet with her. If she left it behind, it would die of grief.

⋅⋇⋅

Azucena was lying on her bed. She felt lonely, so very lonely. Sadness does not make good company; it numbs the soul. Azucena turned on the Televirtual, more to feel someone next to her than to watch any particular program. Immediately, Abel Zabludowsky appeared at her side. Azucena snuggled next to him. As a Televirtual image, Abel did not feel Azucena's presence, since he was not really there but in the Televirtual broadcasting studio. The body in Azucena's bedroom was an illusion, a chimera, but still it made Azucena feel that she was not alone.

Abel was discussing the long career of the former candidate for Planetary President. Mr. Bush had been a man of color born into one of the most prominent families in the Bronx. He had spent his early life there, attending the best schools. Since childhood he had shown a natural inclination for public service, performing countless humanitarian acts, and so on and so on. But Azucena heard none of it. She didn't care what Abel was saying at the moment. All she wanted to know was who had killed Dr. Díez, and why. His death affected her deeply, not only because he was a good friend, but also because without his help she'd never be able to work at COPE, and that meant the end of any hope of finding Rodrigo.

Oh, Rodrigo! How long ago it seemed that she had shared this bed with him. Now she was lying there with Abel Zabludowsky, who was only a pathetic and illusory substitute. Rodrigo was so different. He had the most profound eyes she had ever known, the most protective arms, the most delicate touch, the firmest, most sensual muscles. During the time she had spent in his arms, she had felt protected, loved, alive! Desire flooded every cell in her body, her blood hammered at her temples in passion, warmth invaded her body just as it had . . . just as it was doing right now—in Abel Zabludowsky's arms! Azucena opened her eyes in alarm. Could she really be such a horny bitch? What was going on? The incredible answer to that question was that she was cuddled against *Rodrigo's* body; Abel Zabludowsky had disappeared. Only his voice could be heard alerting the public:

"The man you are now viewing is the alleged accomplice of Mr. Bush's assassin and is being sought by the police."

An aerophone number appeared on the screen so that anyone who might have seen the suspect could immediately contact the Planetary Prosecutor General's office. Azucena leapt up. Impossible! That was a lie, a filthy lie! Rodrigo had been with her on the day of the assassination. He had had nothing to do with that crime. Even so, she was grateful they had confused Rodrigo with the accused criminal, because it had allowed her to be with him. Gently, she began caressing his body, but her pleasure was short-lived.

For the beloved image of Rodrigo slowly faded, to be replaced by that of her companion from the line at the Consumer Protection Agency. It appeared that the frustrated former ballerina who had intended to kill her had also murdered Dr. Díez.

What was going on? Who was this man? What was he after? Was he a psychopath? Abel Zabludowsky's voice was now answering those very questions, explaining that this was in fact the man who had assassinated Mr. Bush. Aurographic tests had proved it. He had been found dead at his home from an overdose of pills. Why had he committed suicide? And now, who would be able to prove that Rodrigo had had nothing to do with the murder? Azucena had too many questions to deal with at once. What she needed was answers, urgently. The only one who could give them to her, however, was Anacreonte. She was sorely tempted to reestablish communication with him, but her pride got in the way. She wasn't going to reach out to him, only to have her arm twisted. She had told him she could manage her own life, and that was exactly what she was going to do, whatever the cost.

CD
Track 3

Zongo took a crack at Borondongo,
Borondongo then whacked Bernabé
Bernabé started beating Muchilanga
Who, kicking Burundanga,
Got two swollen feet.

Why did Zongo take a crack at Borondongo?
'Cause Borondongo took a whack at Bernabé.

Why did Borondongo take a whack at Bernabé?
'Cause Bernabé started beating Muchilanga.

Why did Bernabé try to beat Muchilanga?
'Cause Muchilanga kicked Burundanga.

Why did Muchilanga kick Burundanga?
'Cause Burundanga got him two swollen feet.

O. BOUFFARTIQUE

8

That Azucena is stubborn as a mule. Ever since she stopped speaking to me, and got it into her head to act on her own, all she's done is screw things up. It's exasperating to watch her do one stupid thing after another, and not be able to intervene. I've said it before: that little brat is used to getting her own blessed way. I've had it!

And the worst of it is that when she goes into a depression, no one can snap her out of it. I've been monitoring her insomnia for a while. She couldn't sleep because, among other things, her new body doesn't fit in the hollow her old one left in the mattress. So she ended up sitting on the edge of the bed for a long time. Then she cried for about twenty minutes. And blew her nose fifteen times while she was at it. Then she stared at the ceiling for thirty minutes. After that, she studied herself in the mirror of the antique armoire facing her bed. She slipped her hand beneath her night-gown and stroked herself, slowly, very slowly. Then, perhaps to take absolute possession of her new body, she masturbated. Then she cried again for another twenty minutes. Next she compulsively wolfed down four sopes, three tamales, and five custard-filled cornucopias. Ten minutes later, she vomited everything she'd eaten, soiling her nightgown. She took it off. And washed it. And hung it up to dry. Next, she took a shower. And, as she shampooed her head, she ached for the long hair she used to have. Then she went back to bed, where she tossed and turned like a top.

She's been lying there in a catatonic haze for five hours. But at no time, not one single instant, has it occurred to her to listen to my advice. If only she'd let me talk to her, I'd tell her that the first thing she has to do is listen to the compact disc; that's her ticket to the past. That's where she'll find the key to everything, but she hasn't done that because she feels she's not in the mood to cry! Talk about depression!

No question about it: waiting does erode hope. Azucena is waiting for Rodrigo to come back. I'm waiting for her to find a way out of the state she's in. Pavana, Rodrigo's Guardian Angel, is waiting for me to work with her. My sweetheart Lilith is waiting for me to complete Azucena's education so we can go away on vacation. We're all spinning our wheels because of her stupidity!

She doesn't understand that everything that happens in this world happens for a reason, and not just randomly. One act, however minimal, unleashes a chain reaction in the world around us. Creation has a perfect operating mechanism, but to run smoothly it requires that each being who is a part of it carry out his or her appointed role correctly. If we don't, the rhythm of the entire Universe is disrupted. It is impossible, therefore, for Azucena even to consider acting on her own! For even the smallest particle of an atom knows it must receive orders from above; that it cannot make its own decisions. If one of the cells in the body were to decide it was guide and mistress of its destiny, and opt to do whatever its whim might be, it would become a cancer that would completely alter the healthy functioning of the organism. When one forgets one is a part of the whole, that one bears the Divine Essence within; when one ignores the fact one is connected with the Cosmos—like it or not—one ends up foolishly lying in bed dwelling on sheer nonsense.

Azucena is not isolated, as she believes she is. Nor is she disconnected, as she imagines. Damn, how can she be so stupid! She thinks she has nothing. She doesn't realize that this Nothing that surrounds her is sustaining her, and will always sustain her wherever she is; this Nothing will keep her in harmony wherever she may go; this Nothing will always choose the proper moment to communicate with her, so that she can hear its message. Every cell of the human body bears a message, sent from the brain. And where does the brain get it? From the human being in command of that body. And where did that human being get the message? Her Guardian Angel dictated it to her, and so on. There is a Supreme Intelligence that directs us to foster the balance between creation and destruction. Activity and rest regulate the battle between these two forces. The force of creation imposes order on chaos. Then comes the period of rest before a new effort required to control disorder. If this rest is overly prolonged, creation is endangered, for destruction, sensing that creation has lost its force, springs into action again. It's as if a plant that had grown in sunlight were suddenly placed in the shade; it is deprived of the strength to sustain itself, and so the destructive force sees to its death. That is precisely the danger Azucena finds herself in as a result of her paralysis.

One person's inaction paralyzes the world. The rhythm of the Universe is broken. If one day the moon stopped still in its orbit, a catastrophe would result. If one day the clouds went on strike and refused to rain, a widespread drought would follow. The drought would cause famine, and a severe enough famine, the end of the human race. The greater the paralysis, the greater the depression, and the greater the depression, the greater the calamities to follow.

Sometimes a person seems to be paralyzed but really isn't; she is merely rearranging things inside, which eventually will put her in harmony with the Cosmos. The real problem arrives when total paralysis occurs. Precisely what Azucena is suffering. It's not so bad that she is doing nothing about it outwardly; what's bad is that she's doing nothing about it inwardly. Not only does she not want to listen to me; she does not want to listen to herself. And since she's not allowing herself to hear her inner voice, she doesn't know what action she should take. She doesn't get the message because her mind isn't allowing it in. She's keeping it filled with negative thoughts. She's going to have to let them out, because they're jamming her line of communication.

The Supreme Intelligence uses a direct line, which, if it encounters interference, veers off in a different direction, with the result that its message either is heard only faintly or is misinterpreted. The solution for this problem is a spiritual alignment. This kind of alignment has nothing to do with the kind that operates on Earth. The latter is like a pyramid in which those at the bottom do what those on top command, and nothing else; and that's when human beings lose responsibility for their actions and submit to what others tell them. No, that is to append, not align, oneself.

The kind of alignment I'm talking about consists of getting oneself in syntony with the loving energy circulating throughout the Cosmos. This is achieved by relaxing and letting life flow among all the cells of the body. Then Love, the cosmic DNA, will remember its genetic message, its origins, the mission assigned it. That mission is unique and personal—not collective, as is avowed in one kind of earthly alignment. The moment Azucena can do that, her entire being will breathe cosmic energy, and will remember it is not alone—much less, without Love.

It isn't so easy to understand Love. Usually people think they find it through a partner. But the love we experience while making love with another is only a pale reflection of what is truly Love. One's partner is only the intermediary through whom we receive Divine Love. Through the kiss, the embrace, the soul receives all the peace necessary to align itself and make the connection with Divine Love. But be warned: that does not mean that our partner possesses that Love, nor is he or she the only one who can bestow it. Nor is it true that if that person leaves, he will take Love with him, leaving us unprotected. Divine Love is infinite. It is everywhere and entirely within reach at every moment. It is foolish of Azucena to limit it to the small space of Rodrigo's arms. If she only realized that all she has to do is learn to open her consciousness to energy on other planes to receive the Love she needs in full store. If she only realized that at this very moment she is surrounded by Love, that it is circulating about her, despite the fact no one is kissing or caressing or embracing her. If she only realized that she is a beloved daughter of the Universe, she would no longer feel lost.

Azucena blames me for everything that is happening to her; she fails to realize that losing Rodrigo is something she had to go through, because the moment she throws herself into the search she will find, in the process, the solution to a problem that has been plaguing humanity for thousands of years. That is the real reason behind all the doubts she is experiencing.

There is a problem of cosmic origin affecting all inhabitants of the planet, and she is the one charged with resolving it. Although it is a mission that actually involves every one of us, Azucena's ego has minimized and converted it into a question of a personal nature. Her bruised and battered self-esteem makes her believe that the whole world is against her, and that everything that is happening affects her alone. But she is a part of this world, and anything that affects her also affects the world. And the world has much more important things to think about than destroying Azucena. That would be absurd, anyway, because in destroying a human being it would be destroying itself, and the Universe has no inclination toward self-destruction.

If only she could be here beside me in space! She would see her past and her future at the same time, and thus understand why I allowed Rodrigo to disappear. If only she could see that all her possibilities did not die with Dr. Díez. If only she could see that she has much better alternatives at hand than those the doctor offered her. If only she would exercise her free will in the right way. Hell, it isn't that difficult to do! Life will never place us at a crossroads where one way leads to perdition. It places us only in circumstances we are able to handle. What usually happens is that people allow themselves to be defeated by circumstances that they perceive as insurmountable obstacles—but nothing could be farther from the truth.

The Universe will place us in situations that correspond to our degree of evolution. That's why in Azucena's particular case, I always opposed rushing her meeting with Rodrigo. Not because she wasn't sufficiently evolved, and not because Rodrigo still had outstanding debts, but because Azucena needed to learn to exercise more control over her impulsiveness and rebelliousness before confronting her present situation. I knew very well that she was going to fly off the handle, and I certainly got that part right! Her confused state of mind prevents her from seeing the truth.

On Earth, truth always exists amid confusion and lies. Confusion comes from our taking as truth things that are not. Truth never is found outside oneself. Each of us has the capacity, if we communicate with ourselves, to find truth. It is only logical that Azucena is confused at this moment, for externally she has encountered nothing but chaos, lies, murder, fear, and indecision. She believes that truth is solid as a rock, but that is not the case. In the face of the general despair that characterizes the outside world, she should be able to say: I don't have to participate in this chaos, even though I realize it is all around me, because I AM NOT CHAOS. At the moment she denies as truth the reality surrounding her, she will find her own truth, and with it, peace. Since what is internal becomes external, individual peace will lead to universal peace. But since Azucena is in no condition to recognize this at the moment, I must arrange for her to be able to help someone else. By helping another, she will be helping herself.

9

Azucena was startled out of bed by a series of loud knocks at the door. She opened it to find Cuquita, Cuquita's grandmother, Cuquita's suitcases, and Cuquita's parrot staring her in the face. The parrot looked well enough, but Cuquita and her grandmother were all black and blue.

Azucena didn't know what to say; she could only ask them in. Cuquita then proceeded to explain her problems. Her husband was beating her more each day. She couldn't take any more. But the last straw was that today he had beat up her grandmother, and that was something she wouldn't stand for. She asked Azucena if they could stay a few days with her. Azucena said that would be all right. What else could she do? Cuquita knew about the body exchange and Azucena didn't want her to inform the authorities. Of course, she could do the same thing, report how Cuquita had illegally obtained the VRBs, but she didn't want to do that. She had much more to lose than Cuquita. So Azucena decided to put her misery aside and share her apartment with them. After all, it would only be for a few days.

As soon as Cuquita took over the kitchen, Azucena began to feel she'd been invaded. True, the grandmother urgently needed a linden-flower tea to calm her down, but what annoyed Azucena was that Cuquita hung the parrot's cage right over the breakfast table. No one could see past it, and besides, that meant from now on they'd all be eating with bird feathers up their nostrils.

Her sense of being displaced was intensified when Cuquita installed her grandmother on the living room sofa bed. The old woman was very docile and quiet, but still she was in the way. Now every time Azucena went to the kitchen for a glass of water, she had to climb over her. But the crowning blow came when Cuquita took over Azucena's bedroom. She dropped her things everywhere. Azucena followed behind, trying to reestablish order. For example, she suggested in a friendly way that Cuquita might keep her suitcase of Avon samples in the closet. Azucena did not want to think how Rodrigo would react the day he returned and found the damn thing in the middle of the bedroom. But Cuquita categorically refused, saying she had to give a demonstration the next day and the only way she'd remember was if she kept it out.

Azucena could scarcely believe her eyes. Cuquita was the proud owner of a stupefying collection of horrible, tasteless bric-a-brac. Most outrageous was a strange apparatus that resembled a primitive typewriter. Cuquita handled it with special care. When Azucena asked her what it was, Cuquita replied with great pride:

"One of my inventions."

"Oh? It is? What does it do?"

"It's a cybernetic Ouija."

Cuquita set the apparatus on the night table, and gave a demonstration as if she were selling an Avon product. The apparatus was put together from an ancient computer, a fax, a Stone Age record player, a telegraph, a scale, and an apothecary flask connected to a strange assortment of tubes, a clay tortilla platter edged with quartz crystals, and a wooden New Year's Eve party clacker. In the center of the platter was the outline of two hands, indicating the position where the subject's hands should be placed.

"Uhhh . . . very . . . striking! What's it for?"

"What do you mean? You never used a Ouija?"

"No."

"Oh yeah, I forgot, you Evos are so high and mighty you don't need any gadgets to get in touch with your Guardian Angels. But we don't have your superiority complexion. No one does anything for us, we have to scratch our own backs. And if we want to find out anything about our past lives, we have to rig up some lousy contraption like this."

Azucena was moved by Cuquita's complaint. You could see a mile away that she was boiling over with resentment and pain. As an astroanalyst, she knew she couldn't let Cuquita's negative emotions keep resonating that way without treatment, so she tried to give her some confidence and buck her up.

"Don't be angry, Cuquita. The reason I asked you what it's for wasn't because I never used a Ouija, but because I'd never seen one that was so . . . uh, complex, so . . . different, so . . . inventive! Show me how it works, will you?" Cuquita, feeling more secure, immediately calmed down and began talking in a less strident tone.

"Oh! Well, you see, it's real simple. If you want to go and communicate with your Guardian Angel, you put your hands here on the platter like this and think your question, and presto, you get your answer back on this facts machine. Now, if you want to talk with loved ones who've already passed on, you fix it so no one can pick up what they say—you know, in case they bring up secret treasures and stuff like that—so what you do is telegraph your question, and you get your answer back right here."

"Wow, that's fantastic!"

Cuquita's face glowed from the feeling that she was appreciated, and there was a flush in her cheeks that competed with her purple bruises.

"Hey, that's not all! Let's say someone wants to sell you something, like a record or some antiquary that might have belonged to, let's say, a famous singer like Pedro Infante, and you want to know if it's the genuine article, or maybe somebody's trying to put one over on you. So, let's say it's a record, right? Well, you'd put it right here," she said, pointing to the record player, "or, if it's some other kind of hairloom, we put it in this thing here," pointing to the flask, "with this special fluid that breaks it down like it was mushed ice, and then this computer prints out its whole history, told by the hairloom itself, and over here on the facts machine out come color pictures of all the people who ever touched it. Or, put it another way, you kill two birds with one, because on the one hand you make sure you're not being sold a pill of goods, and at the same time you're getting a free picture of your favorite star. How's that?"

Azucena was truly dumbfounded. How was it possible that this woman who had never finished elementary school was capable of inventing such a sophisticated apparatus? Of course, it remained to be seen what it could actually do, but, in any case, her initiative was remarkable. Cuquita was beside herself with pleasure when she saw that Azucena was truly interested in her invention.

"Listen, Cuquita. I have only one question. What if I wanted to know, for example, whom a bed had belonged to? How would you find out?"

"Well, you take a splinter from it and we put it in the flask."

"But what if it's a brass bed?"

"Then, hey, don't buy it! Come on, I can't go around thinking of everything. You know what? Maybe we'd better stop right here, because I'm beginning to get paranotic."

Cuquita was starting to heat up, and Azucena wanted to avoid that, especially now that they were sharing an apartment.

"Oh, you haven't told me what that party favor's for."

"Oh, that clacker thing is the most important part. You whirl it around, and the sound it makes changes the energy in the room where you're going to receive shortwave messages. It's to prevent interference from demons."

"I see . . ."

Azucena could not avoid feeling an enormous curiosity about communicating with the beyond. Ever since breaking off with Anacreonte, she had had no idea of what was happening or what was going to happen. This might be her opportunity to find out about Rodrigo without having to submit to Anacreonte.

"Listen, could I ask it a question?"

"Sure, go ahead!"

Cuquita felt greatly flattered by Azucena's request, and immediately began whirling the wooden clacker all around the bedroom. Then she gave Azucena instructions about how to place her hands on the platter and how to concentrate when she asked her question. Azucena followed Cuquita's instructions to the letter, and, in a few seconds, the fax began printing out a reply: *My dear child, you are going to see him much sooner than you think.*

Azucena's eyes filled with tears. Cuquita put an arm around her protectively.

"You see? It's all going to work out."

Azucena nodded. She could not find words, she was so happy. And Cuquita felt completely vindicated. This was the first time anyone had used her invention, and now she knew that it worked. The atmosphere in the house immediately felt different. Azucena realized that the small attention she had given Cuquita was paying substantial rewards. She began to see the brighter side of her present circumstances. After all, it could be very entertaining and beneficial to have Cuquita with her for a few days. The news that she would soon be seeing Rodrigo had so greatly improved her spirits that it drove all the black clouds from her head. For the first time in many days, her heart was not oppressed. She thought that this might be a good moment to listen to her CD. Once she relaxed, she realized how tired she was. She suggested to Cuquita that they turn in, and Cuquita agreed. It was three o'clock in the morning, and it had been a long day. Azucena put on her headphones, lay down on her side of the bed, and closed her eyes.

While Cuquita was making her own preparations for bed, she suddenly spied the remote control of the Televirtual. She felt a surge of pleasure and forgot about her exhaustion and her bruises. All her life she had longed for a Televirtual, but had never had the money to buy one. The closest she had come was a run-of-the-mill 3-D set. Cuquita sat down on her side of the bed, pressed the ON button, and started cruising the channels like a five-year-old. Azucena didn't even notice. She was quietly listening to her CD with her eyes closed.

Cuquita, like any worthy representative of the party of the Non-Evos, was lapping up the talk show *Cristina* with morbid pleasure. That night they were broadcasting live from a penal planet prison. Through the device of a photomental camera, the thoughts of the worst criminals were being converted into virtual-reality images. Televirtual viewers were transported to bedrooms where incest, rapes, and murders had occurred. Cuquita was delighted. She hadn't felt such strong emotions since her school days, when the same pedagogical methods had been used to teach students about the horrors of war. Students were set down in the midst of a battle, so they could smell death, so they could feel in the flesh all its pain, anguish, and horror. It was well known that the only way human beings learned anything was by perceiving experiences through the senses. It was hoped that after this direct exposure, no one would dream of starting a war or torturing anyone or committing any kind of illegal act, since they would know how it felt.

It hadn't worked out that way, however. Admittedly, crime had been brought under control, but not so much because people had learned their lesson, as because of advances in technology. Until Mr. Bush's assassination, no one in ages had dared commit a murder. Again, not because they didn't have the desire, but because of their fear of punishment. New devices meant that no one escaped capture. Human beings, then, had no choice but to learn to repress their criminal instincts. That did not mean they didn't have them. Not in the least: witness the sensational ratings of shows like *Cristina*, *Oprah*, *Donahue*, *Sally*, and others, in which the Televirtual audience vicariously experienced all manner of base emotions. The government allowed these shows to be broadcast because they channeled murderous urges, making it easier to keep them under control.

Cuquita couldn't believe how wonderful it was to be in the thick of the action. She felt thrilled to be present at the murder of Sharon Tate. She loved the sensation of fear coursing through her, causing goose bumps, making her hair stand on end, paralyzing her voice. The violence nauseated her, but, like any good masochist, she thought that was part of the fun. Then came the commercials, right in the midst of her sufferings. Cuquita was furious. She frantically began switching channels, searching for a similar program. Suddenly her eyes were caught by a burning red glow: lava had always exercised a hypnotic power over her.

The station was broadcasting live from the planet Korma. Isabel González was walking among the survivors of the eruption, having traveled there with a group bringing disaster relief. She wanted this to be the kickoff for her campaign. Thanks to Televirtual transmission, Cuquita was suddenly in an ideal spot to savor everything: right between Isabel and Abel Zabludowsky, who kept commenting on how incredibly well Isabel carried off her 150 years. "And, why shouldn't she!" thought Cuquita. Isabel had spent years as an interplanetary ambassador. On each journey she had shaved off a large number of years because of the difference in time between planets. When she returned from a voyage that for her had lasted a week, she found that on Earth five years had gone by. But Cuquita wouldn't have traded places with Isabel, even if she did look so young. All she could think of was how many burritos Isabel could have eaten during those lost years. How many New Year's Eve parties she must have missed!

As Isabel began distributing sandwiches among the victims of the eruption, all the primitives rushed toward her to receive their share. Isabel's bodyguards stepped forward to protect her, lashing out indiscriminately.

Cuquita jumped up from the bed and began screaming, "Azucena, Azucena! Look!"

Isabel's two bodyguards turned out to be: one, the supposed Aerophone Company workman, and two . . . Azucena! Well, that is, the once and former Azucena, because a different person was occupying her body now. In a daze, Azucena opened her eyes to see what was going on. She watched as Isabel's guards moved her away from the mob of starving savages. Azucena was stupefied to see that one of the guards had her former body, and that standing beside it was the supposed aerophone repairman. But she nearly fainted as she saw Isabel approach a man sitting apart from the others. *Rodrigo!* Azucena had been dreaming about him when Cuquita awakened her, and now she didn't know whether what she was seeing was still part of her fantasy, or was real.

Rodrigo was painstakingly carving a wooden spoon with a stone. As soon as he saw Isabel approach, he stood up. She offered him a sandwich, but instead of taking it, Rodrigo walked toward Ex-Azucena and stroked her face, trying to place her. Ex-Azucena was getting nervous. Isabel was intrigued. Cuquita was outraged. And Azucena, with all her heart, devoted herself to caressing Rodrigo for a few brief moments. It wasn't much time, but it was long enough to make her despair boundless as she watched him vanish into thin air. The images from Korma were replaced by those of soccer players on a practice field. The news had shifted to the sports segment. Cuquita and Azucena turned to each other. Azucena was weeping hopelessly.

"That was Rodrigo!"

"That man?" Cuquita was shocked at the pathetic state he was in.

"Yes."

"And that was *you!*"

"Yes."

"What's your financé doing on Korma?"

Azucena had no idea. All she knew was that she was in one hell of a mess. If the men who tried to murder her, and who stole her body, were Isabel's private bodyguards, then Isabel had had a hand in all this. If Isabel was involved, then she had a huge advantage: power. And since she had the power, going head to head with her was going to be a real nightmare.

Azucena quickly tried to list reasons why Isabel might have wanted to have her killed. Could Isabel have been behind the assassination of Mr. Bush? But then why had she chosen Rodrigo to be the fall guy? Who knows? Also, she must have found out somehow that Rodrigo had been making love to Azucena the entire night of the crime, so the next logical step was to order the elimination of his alibi, that is, Azucena.

All right, but what would Isabel's next move be? Granted it was expedient for Isabel to have Rodrigo as assassin, but how was she going to keep him from protesting his innocence to the authorities? Maybe it wasn't in her plans for him even to make a statement. Maybe that's why she had him taken to Korma: to leave him there forever. Maybe . . . maybe. What Azucena couldn't understand was how Isabel could risk having everything unravel. What if one of the Televirtual viewers watching the news at that very moment recognized Rodrigo and turned him in? What would happen then? That was the question. Azucena couldn't see any way out of her dilemma, but Cuquita, without the same analytical powers, took the situation in hand immediately.

"We'll just have to go after your financé and bring him back."

"We can't, the police are looking for him. They say he's implicated in Mr. Bush's assassination. But it isn't true, he was with me that night."

"I can swear to that, all right. I couldn't sleep for all the squeaking the bed was making."

Azucena thought back to their night of love, and sobbed even louder.

"Don't cry, it doesn't matter that the police are searching for him. We'll just get him a different body, and that'll be the end of the problem. We're not living in my grandmother's times anymore, when they used to say, 'The house is on fire, the children have gone, O woe is me!' No, in times like this you have to put your best face forward. Dry your tears, and to battle!"

Azucena stopped her crying and yielded meekly to Cuquita's guidance. She couldn't take any more. She had received too many blows in too short a time. She had lost her twin soul, had been on the verge of being murdered, had been forced to undergo a soul transplant, had discovered the murder of a close friend, had witnessed her beloved body occupied by an assassin, and, finally, had found Rodrigo but under terrible circumstances, in grave danger and in a place that was for all practical purposes out of her reach. It was more than she could take. She felt profoundly fragile, isolated, drained, incapable of making a decision.

"We'll have to leave first thing tomorrow."

"How can we? I don't have any money. And you have less! And interplanetary flights are so expensive."

"Yeah, they're not exactly bargain basement, but we'll find a way."

Cuquita and Azucena stared at each other for a moment. Then suddenly there was a brilliant spark in Cuquita's eyes, a stroke of inspiration that she transmitted to Azucena. Azucena grasped it instantly, and they both shouted together:

"Good old Julito!"

Azucena was beginning to give up hope. Julito's interplanetary spaceship was more like a milk train, stopping at every planet between Earth and Korma. Every time it landed, Azucena felt as if the Universe had ground to a halt. She had approached Julito to ask about the possibility of a direct flight, but her old pal had flatly refused and, as subtly as possible, had reminded Azucena that she was in no position to demand anything, since she was traveling free. Besides, Julito had to make the stops because, in addition to the *Interplanetary Cockfight*'s routine flights to underevolved planets, he had two sidelines that brought in a major portion of his income: home-delivery grandchildren, and express-mates.

In the most distant space colonies there were elderly men and women who had never been able to marry or have grandchildren and were, as a result, subject to terrible depressions. Julito had been struck with the brilliant idea of renting out grandchildren, and this was his peak season, since vacation time was just beginning at the orphanages. Another of his enterprises much in demand was that of express-delivery husbands and wives. When young adults were assigned special missions for long periods of time on very distant planets, they often suffered inflamed hormones. As it was highly undesirable for them to have sexual relations with the aborigines, their earthmates would often send them a substitute husband or wife to satisfy their appetites. And that wasn't all. At the specific request of the partner, the surrogate lover learned prose passages and poems by memory and recited them in the client's ear while they were making love.

All of which was why the spaceship—besides carrying game cocks, mariachis, starlets, and entertainers for the cockfights—was stuffed with children and surrogate husbands and wives. Azucena thought she was going insane. She needed silence and calm to organize her thoughts, and the chaos that reigned in the ship was just too much for her. Children were running everywhere, the mariachis were practicing "Amorcito corazón" with a singer who was the incarnation of the great Pedro Infante, the surrogate partners were practicing their routines on the starlets, Cuquita's blind grandmother was practicing her crochet, Cuquita's drunken husband was practicing his vomiting, the cocks were practicing their cockadoodledoos—and the *coyote* who had sold Azucena her body was practicing, unsuccessfully, an exchange of souls between a starlet and a rooster.

Given these circumstances, Azucena had only two options: to go completely round the bend, crazed by the chaos, or to give in and practice something herself. She decided to rehearse the kiss she was going to give Rodrigo the minute she saw him. So with great eagerness, placing her index finger between her lips, she practiced again and again the best sensations she could evoke with a succulent kiss. She stopped, however, when one of the surrogates offered to rehearse with her. She was embarrassed to have been discovered, and concluded that she'd better keep her distance from all the crazies on board.

Like all lovers throughout the ages, Azucena wanted to be alone, to be able to think about Rodrigo with more serenity. She was distracted and annoyed by the company of her fellow passengers. Since she couldn't make them vanish from the ship, she closed her eyes to retreat into her memories. She needed to reconstruct her image of Rodrigo, to give him shape, to remember the magic of being one with her twin soul, to relive those sensations of self-sufficiency, fullness, boundlessness. Only Rodrigo's presence could give meaning to her reality, only the light that illuminated his smile could free her from the sadness withering her soul. The idea that she would soon see him gave her new life.

She put on her earphones and began to listen to the compact disc. All she wanted was to be in a world different from the one in which she was living. She had already lost hope that the music would trigger a regression to the life she had lived with Rodrigo in the past. The night before, she had listened all the way through, hoping to hear the music she had heard while taking her examination at COPE, but nothing. Now that she knew in advance that the music on this CD was not what she was looking for, she was able to relax and lose herself in the melody. Oddly enough, it was in relinquishing her obsession about having a regression that she was able to let the music flow freely into her subconscious. Easily, spontaneously, she was borne to the former life she was so curious about.

CD
Track 4

Cuquita shook Azucena awake, abruptly interrupting her reverie. Azucena's heart was pounding and she could scarcely catch her breath. When Cuquita saw Azucena's expression, she felt awful about having disturbed her. But she'd had no choice, as they were about to land on Korma. Cuquita could have kicked herself. Azucena's face was deeply flushed, with sweat dripping from her temples. Cuquita was sure Azucena must have been having some erotic dream about Rodrigo. She begged Azucena to forgive her, but Azucena neither saw nor heard her, as she was completely absorbed in her own thoughts.

So, she and Isabel had known each other in their past lives! How could that be? Many years had gone by, yet Isabel looked exactly the same. Things were getting more and more complicated. In that past life, wasn't Isabel supposed to have been Mother Teresa? And how could this "saint" have killed Azucena when she was just a baby? Easy. Because Isabel was no saint. She was a lying bitch who'd deceived everyone, making them believe she'd been Mother Teresa when in fact the Isabel of 1985 was no different from the Isabel of 2200.

Azucena made some quick calculations. If this was the same woman she'd seen during the Mexico City earthquake of 1985 in which her parents had died, then instead of being a hundred fifty years old, Isabel was *two* hundred fifty. Who could have fabricated the life of Mother Teresa for her? Only one person: Dr. Díez! He must have falsified a life for her and recorded it in a microcomputer like the one he'd implanted in Azucena. Things were beginning to fall into place!

Obviously, as soon as Dr. Díez had done what she wanted, Isabel had had him eliminated to keep him from ever telling what he knew. That might in fact be why she had ordered Azucena killed. In addition to being Rodrigo's alibi, Azucena had been witness to Isabel's having lived, as Isabel, in 1985. And something else! She could also testify to Isabel's having murdered her as a baby. No one was allowed to run for Planetary President if he or she had a criminal record, at least in any of the ten lives preceding the candidacy. If anyone ever learned of the murder she had committed in 1985, Isabel would automatically be disqualified.

But something didn't fit. If Isabel had murdered Azucena when she was a baby, then Isabel should know Rodrigo, because in that life Rodrigo had been Azucena's father. And if she knew Rodrigo, why hadn't she just had him killed? Possibly because when she committed the murder, Rodrigo was already dead, and couldn't have seen her. Who knows? And another thing, to what extent was Rodrigo's life in danger now that Isabel had run into him on Korma? One thing was certain: Isabel was extremely dangerous, and Azucena was going to have to keep out of her way.

Azucena took a sip of the warm cornmeal porridge Cuquita was offering her, and immediately felt comforted by it. As an orphan, Azucena had never had anyone who fussed over her. This was the first time anybody had ever done something for her with the sole purpose of making her feel better. She was deeply moved that Cuquita had gone to so much trouble, and from that moment on, she began to love her.

10

Just as a hot glass shatters when filled with an icy liquid, so Azucena's heart burst when she saw Rodrigo. Her soul had not been tempered to receive such a chilling stare. His cold eyes bored into her as if she were a stranger, freezing all her hopes for this reunion.

Finding Rodrigo had not been easy because he kept his distance from the tribe. His constant need to put things in order made him wait to begin his day until the primitives had already performed their slovenly rituals and gone off to hunt. When Azucena found him, he was still inside the cave picking up the discarded sandwich wrappers and folding them one on top of the other. The cave's appearance had changed drastically since his arrival. It was no longer littered with excrement or scraps of food rotting in corners, and the firewood was neatly stacked. At the sight of Azucena, Rodrigo interrupted his work, his attention now fixed on this blonde woman smiling before him with her arms opened wide. He had no idea who she was or where she came from. Clearly she was not from some Kormian cave. It was obvious that, like him, she did not belong there.

Rodrigo's passivity disconcerted Azucena. She could only attribute it to the fact that he had no way of recognizing her in her new body. Pulling herself together, she quickly explained that despite the different body, she was still Azucena.

Rodrigo stared at her vacantly and repeated, "Azucena?"

Now Azucena was truly at a loss. She had dreamed of a romantic meeting in the best movie tradition, where Rodrigo, seeing her from a distance, would run toward her in slow motion: she, in a white chiffon gown undulating in the wind; he, dressed like a twentieth-century heartthrob in elegant linen slacks and a silk shirt half unbuttoned to reveal his strong muscular chest. The background music could only be the theme from "Gone With the Wind." As they met, they would throw themselves into each other's arms, like Romeo and Juliet, Tristan and Isolde, Paolo and Francesca. And then the music of their bodies would become one with the music of the spheres, turning their encounter into an unforgettable moment in the lore of famous lovers.

Instead, there she stood, facing a man who showed not the slightest flicker of life, who had no intention of touching her, who could not stir himself to speak a single word, who refused her the luxury of gazing into his eyes, who was killing her with his indifference and making her feel like a living anachronism. She felt as ridiculous as the sequins on the peasant skirt she'd used on the spaceship to disguise herself as one of the performers at the cockfights: as forced as a beauty contestant's smile, as unwelcome as a cockroach in a wedding cake.

How could this be happening? Had she spent all those sleepless nights waiting for *this?* How could she hold back the kisses longing to escape her lips? To whom could she give her passionate embrace? What could she do with the sweet murmurings stifled in her throat? Azucena turned away from Rodrigo and began running. At the cave's entrance, she bumped into Cuquita, Cuquita's husband, and the body-trafficking *coyote*. She shoved them aside and kept running. Cuquita left the men behind in the cave, and went to look for Azucena. She found her in tears beside a charred tree trunk.

"What's wrong, you feel sick? Me, too. I already threw up. That Julito must think he's a test pilot the way he zooms around in that ship of his. But what's wrong with you? You're crying."

Azucena was weeping bitterly. Cuquita put her big soft arms around Azucena, and hugged her against her pillowy breasts. Azucena sank into them, and for the first time knew how it felt to be cradled in a mother's arms. Unconsciously, she returned to her childhood, and in a childlike voice whimpered all her disappointment to Cuquita, who cuddled and reassured her, as any good mother would.

"So, you scrapped with your financé?"

Azucena shook her head.

"Then why are you crying?"

"Oh, Cuquita," Azucena sobbed inconsolably, as Cuquita kept wiping her tears.

"Men are all alike, they should all be pickled by now from the salt of our tears. The philaundering bastards! He got himself another sweetheart, right?"

"No, Cuquita, he doesn't even remember me."

"Doesn't remember you?"

"No, he doesn't know who I am. He didn't recognize me."

"Well, why not! You think they laid some *burundanga* spell on him?"

"*Burundanga?!* No, it's nothing like *that!* It's that God doesn't love me. He hates me, He tricks me, He makes me believe in love just so I'd get screwed over like this, but, the truth is, love doesn't exist."

"No, no, don't say that. God's gonna get mad if He hears you."

"Well, let Him. Then maybe He'll leave me alone. I'm sick and tired of Him and His whole choir of Guardian Angels—all they do is crap up my life!"

"Look, haven't you ever thought that what's happening to you maybe *has* to happen?"

"But why, Cuquita? I haven't done anything to anyone."

"Maybe not in this life, but what about the others? You never know!"

"I do so know! And I swear to you, I've already paid off everything I did in the others. This is just plain unfair."

"I can't believe that: in this life, nothing's just plain unfair."

"That's not true!"

"All right, but instead of us fighting over it, why don't you ask your Guardian Angel what he thinks?"

"I don't want to hear anything from him. The reason I am where I am is because he didn't help me, he just let them wreck my life. He abandoned me just when I needed him most. I'm never going to talk to him again. In fact, he'd better not show up, or I'll beat him to a pulp!"

"Hmmm . . . Then we're really in a jam, aren't we?"

"No, we're not! I'm not some helpless idiot!"

"I didn't say you were, and besides, it's completely irreverent to me what you do with your life, but I know there's a reason for everything that happens. Or do you think my grandma's gotta try this in her bones for no reason at all?"

"Gotta try? Gotta . . . *Got arthritis!*"

"Yeah, in her hips! She can hardly walk, and that's from a karma she earned when she was one of Pinochet's generals. But as for you, you need to go way back in your past to find out why all these terrible things are happening to you."

"But I can't. As long as I'm depressed, I can't regress to my past lives."

"Well, then get *un*depressed, because if you don't . . ."

Cuquita's desire to help Azucena was so strong that she became the ideal medium for Anacreonte to convey a message to his protégée. So without any warning, words that were not her own began issuing from Cuquita's lips.

"Because if you don't . . . because . . . what you still haven't realized is that you are living a privileged moment. Caught up in great suffering, true, but it is at moments like these that one can acknowledge that one feels awful. The moment you do, a very real, a very palpable, door is going to open to the possibility of your being able to find inner harmony.

"In this state of openness, you will realize that you can be truly happy on Earth. It is only logical that you don't feel that way now; you have suffered a lot, but soon you will begin to see clearly. You will begin to feel that everything that happens is part of a world in equilibrium. From the rose that comes as a gift, to the stick that is used to beat you. Everything has a reason for being. Why then must people always respond to the stick? The world has become an unending chain of 'He did it to me, so I'll do it to him.' This chain will be broken when one person stops and, instead of responding with hatred, acts with love. That day, you will understand that one can love one's enemy. Countless prophets have told us that. And that day, you are going to laugh at everything that happens to you. You will accept it as part of the whole, and will allow your mind to lead you where it will. Toward the unknown. Toward the beginning.

"Not the beginning of the Earth, which is difficult enough; but toward *the* beginning, which no one yet has reached. For even though man has spoken and written and philosophized so much, he has still not found sufficient strength to go back to the beginning of the beginning. When I met you, I knew you possessed this strength. You are trying to find inner peace and equilibrium by being reunited with your twin soul. You are struggling to find yourself in Rodrigo, which is good. But let me tell you one thing. During that struggle, the person you will truly discover is yourself. That sounds as if it is the same thing, but it isn't.

"It is not the same to recover equilibrium through inner harmony as through union with another person, even if that person is your twin soul. So how will you achieve it? By expanding your consciousness, so that it encompasses everything around you. For example, at this moment you are sad: sadness surrounds you. The external world offers you only pain and suffering. What can you do? Enlarge your consciousness! Appropriate your sadness by drinking it in, sip by sip, inhaling it, capturing it within you, allowing it to spread to the farthest corner of your body until none is left outside. And at that moment, what is going to surround you, once you've let in all that sadness?"

"What?" asked Azucena.

"Happiness, of course! And that is why you must not fear sorrow or pain. You must learn to rejoice in them, to accept them. Whatever you resist, persists. If we resist suffering, it will always be there, surrounding us. If we accept it as part of life, of the whole, and let it enter us until it has run its course, we will be left surrounded with happiness and joy. So go ahead, I wish you well, my child, enjoy it all to the fullest!

"And one thing more before I finish. If you enlarge your consciousness enough to encompass Rodrigo completely, you'll be able to see beyond his rejection and discover why he didn't know who you were."

Cuquita broke off her soliloquy, so impressed she was speechless. She knew all too well that every word she had uttered had been dictated to her. It was the first time she had ever experienced anything like it. Azucena had stopped crying and was staring at Cuquita in astonishment and gratitude. Then she closed her eyes for a moment, and in a quiet, nearly inaudible, voice said, "Because they erased his memory."

"What?"

"Rodrigo didn't know who I was because they erased his memory!"

Azucena was ecstatic. She hugged and kissed Cuquita. Cuquita also celebrated the discovery, but their excitement was short-lived because at the moment Isabel's entourage was heading straight for the cave. Cuquita and Azucena ran to spirit Rodrigo away before anyone realized they were on Korma.

✛

Azucena could not stop staring at Cuquita's drunken husband. It was incredible to think that inside that fat, gross, filthy, alcohol-wasted body was the soul of Rodrigo. The *coyote* had done a superb job. The exchange between Cuquita's husband and Rodrigo could not have been more successful, especially considering he'd had to work under highly unfavorable conditions.

Cuquita was equally amazed as she regarded Ex-Rodrigo from the window of the spaceship. He was wandering among the members of the tribe, completely bewildered. She couldn't believe that she was finally rid of her husband. From this day on, she could sleep in peace. The body exchange had been a terrific idea. For one thing, it allowed Azucena to bring her beloved—or at least, the soul of her beloved—back to Earth with no danger of having the police arrest him for his involvement in Mr. Bush's assassination; and for another, she herself got back her freedom! The sooner the ship left Korma, the happier she'd be.

In the meantime, she watched with glee as a hairy-chested female primitive came up behind Ex-Rodrigo to embrace him. Her husband, thinking it was Cuquita, automatically gave her a whack, to which the female responded by walloping him. Cuquita clapped and cheered, tears rolling down her cheeks. If this was not divine justice, she didn't know what was. For once, someone was giving him a dose of his own medicine. Ex-Rodrigo was laid out on the ground, not knowing what was going on.

He wasn't the only one. On board the spaceship Cuquita's grandmother hadn't a clue as to why they'd seated her beside that "drunken shithead," as she called Cuquita's husband, and no one could convince her that the man she was sitting next to was Rodrigo, not her granddaughter's husband. Being blind, she was guided by smell and sound, and the body beside her, which reeked of alcohol and urine, could only belong to Cuquita's husband Ricardo. They explained the soul exchange to her over and over again, insisting that Rodrigo's soul, which now occupied that body, was very pure. To prove it, they gave him a good sock in the nose. When Rodrigo did not respond in kind, that was all Cuquita's grandmother needed; she began pummeling him for all she was worth to avenge herself for the beating he'd recently given her. She shouted in his face that it was all his fault how sick she was, informing him that to her, he always was and always would be nothing but a "drunken shithead." After venting all her rage, she relaxed into a deep sleep. Finally she could rest in peace.

Rodrigo felt greatly mistreated, emotionally more than physically. Once again he couldn't understand what was going on. The stench coming from his body disgusted him. He was filthy and itched all over. He had a terrible thirst for alcohol and couldn't imagine why, since he himself had never been much of a drinker. He didn't remember ever having seen this old lady who had just beaten him up because he supposedly had mistreated her, and he felt as if he were surrounded by a horde of lunatics on this bizarre spaceship. He did not know where they were taking him, or why.

The only thing he did know was that he had a knot in his throat and a terrible need to urinate. He got up to look for the men's room, but his legs would not support him. The left one buckled completely, as if it were dislocated. Azucena rushed to his aid, telling him to lie down on the floor and asking him if he was hurt. Rodrigo complained of an intense pain in his hip. When Azucena touched him where he was pointing, he flinched. He couldn't stand anyone touching him.

As an experienced astroanalyst, Azucena realized immediately that Rodrigo's pain had its origin in a past life. It came from a hidden fear activated by Cuquita's grandmother's aggression. Azucena spoke to him in a soothing voice, explaining that they were friends who had come to rescue him, and that they wanted to help, not to harm him. They knew about his loss of memory, and they were in a good position to help him recover it, since she was an astroanalyst as well as his . . . his best friend. Rodrigo stared at Azucena for a long time, trying to recognize her, but her face was the face of a stranger.

"I'm sorry, but I don't remember you."

"I know that. Don't worry about it."

"Can you really help me recover my memory?"

"Yes, I can. If you want, we can begin today."

Rodrigo did not want to waste a minute. Without hesitation he nodded yes. The face of the woman who said she was his friend made him feel good. Her voice made him feel safe.

Azucena asked Rodrigo to relax and breathe deeply. Then she directed him to take a series of short, panting breaths. After that she told him to repeat several times in a loud voice, "I'm afraid!" Rodrigo followed all her instructions faithfully. At a certain point, his face and breathing changed. Azucena saw that he was in contact with memories from his past life.

"Where are you?"

"In the dining room of my home . . ."

"What is happening there?"

"I don't want to see . . ."

Rodrigo began sobbing. His face showed great anguish.

"Repeat after me: I don't want to see what's going on here because it's too painful."

"No, I don't want to . . ."

"In that life, are you a man or a woman?"

"A woman . . ."

"And what were they doing to you that makes you so afraid? Who hurt you?"

"My husband's brother . . ."

"What did he do to you?"

"I didn't want . . . I didn't want . . ."

"You didn't want what?"

"For him to . . . rape me."

"Let's go to that moment. What's happening?"

"It was horrible . . . I don't want to see it . . ."

"I know this is painful, but if we don't look at it, we won't get anywhere and you won't be cured. It's good to talk about it, no matter how bad it was."

"I'd just learned I was pregnant and . . ."

Rodrigo's sobbing grew more and more anguished.

"And . . . for me, being pregnant was something so sacred . . . and he destroyed it all."

"How?"

"My husband was drunk, and had fallen asleep. I was clearing the table and . . ."

"Then what?"

"I don't see . . . I can't see anything . . ."

"Say it again: I don't want to see because it's too painful . . ."

"I don't want to see because it's too painful."

"What do you see now?"

"Nothing, everything is black . . ."

Cuquita hadn't been able to hear anything of their conversation, but no detail of their posture escaped her. She was straining so hard to catch a word or two of what they were saying that she began hearing what Anacreonte was trying in vain to transmit to Azucena. Rodrigo couldn't speak for two reasons. First, he had an emotional block not unlike Azucena's, and second, there was an even more serious block caused by a cutoff in the flow of his memory. But if Azucena was able to break through by listening to the music played during her COPE exam, the same might work with Rodrigo, since twin souls react to the same stimuli.

Cuquita waited a minute to see whether Azucena was paying any attention to her spiritual guide, but seeing that she wasn't, decided to offer her services as a professional go-between by passing along the Guardian Angel's message to her: that Rodrigo needed to listen to one of the arias on her compact disc while she recorded his regression with a photomental camera. Azucena didn't know where they could find one, but Cuquita remembered that Julito always traveled with a camera in order to detect potential troublemakers on board. Azucena grew more and more amazed by Cuquita each day. Here was someone she'd looked down upon solving all her problems. The woman was a genius. The two of them lost no time in borrowing Julito's photomental camera, and set it up in front of Rodrigo. In an instant, they had the Discman earphones on Rodrigo's head and began playing him one of the love arias.

CD
Track 5

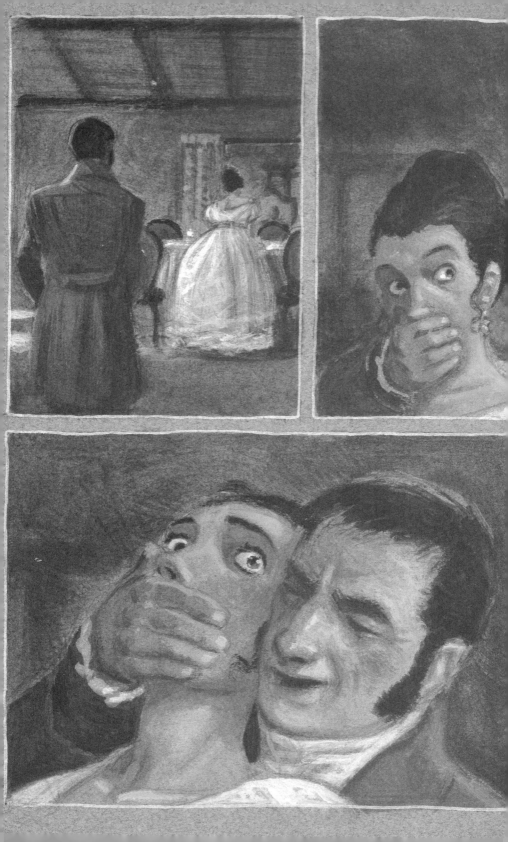

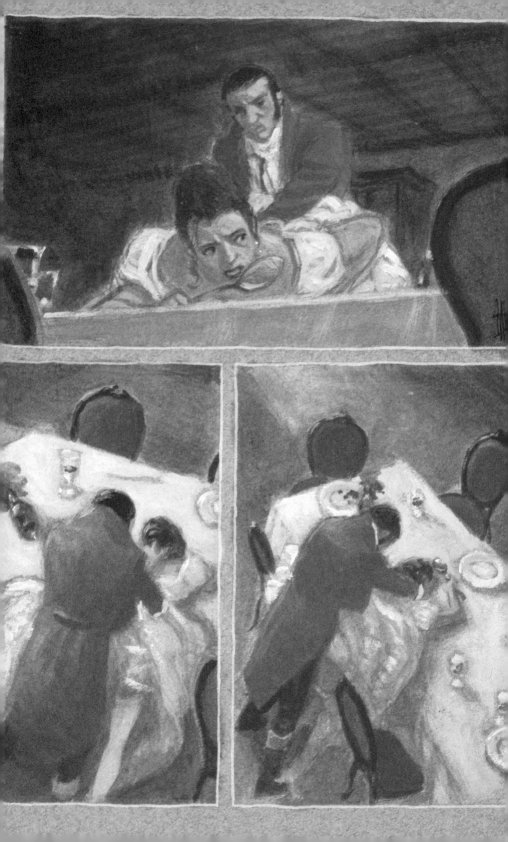

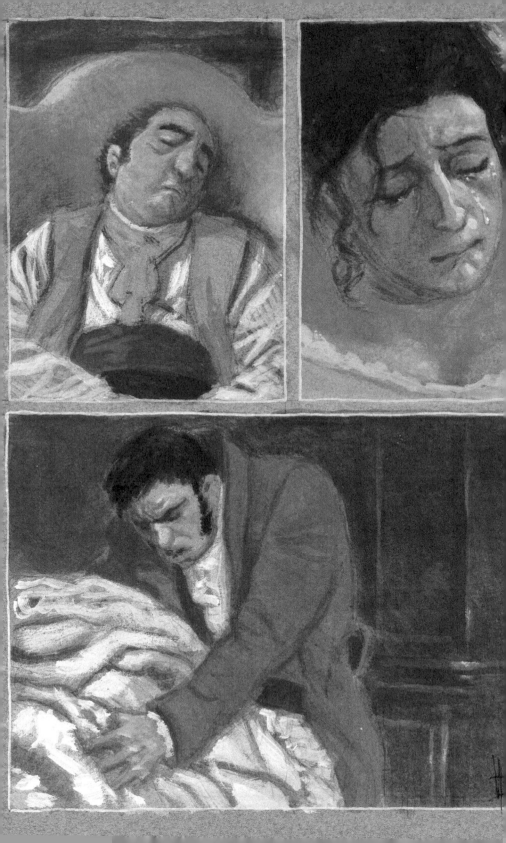

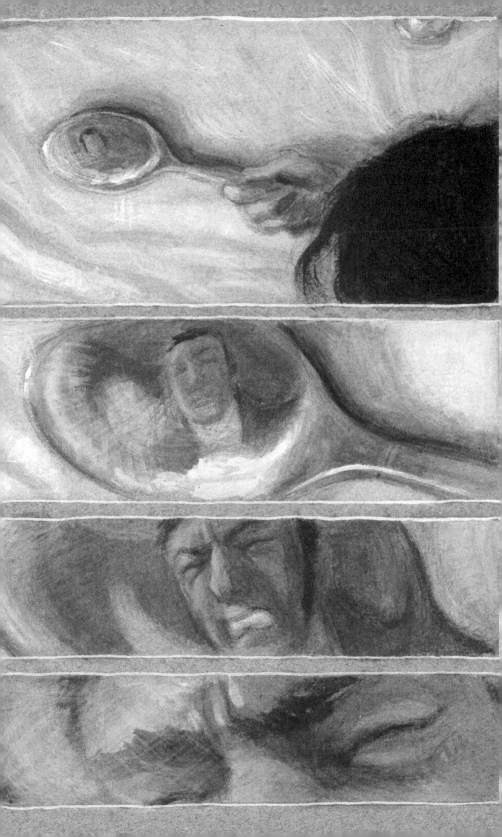

After the last image, horizontal wavy lines filled the camera screen. As a means of escape, Rodrigo had fallen asleep. Apparently, his block was much more powerful than Azucena's had been. Even so, the photomentals she was now holding were going to be extremely helpful. Rather reluctantly, she began leafing through them to see what Rodrigo had recalled. Her first jolt came with the recognition that the dining room he had pictured was the same room that had been her bedroom in her life in 1985. She had recognized the stained glass from the window that had nearly fallen on her the day of the earthquake. With that exception, the difference between the dining room of Rodrigo's life and the bedroom of hers was like night and day. His room belonged to the age of the house's splendor and hers to the time of its decadence.

Suddenly she interrupted her comparisons and held the photomental closer so she could study it in detail. She discovered that the spoon the female Rodrigo had held in her hand throughout the rape was the same one she herself had seen in Tepito, the one purchased by Teo's friend. As soon as they returned to Earth, Azucena would look up Teo and have him take her to his friend. She only hoped the woman still had the spoon. But for now, she had to complete Rodrigo's session and restore him to a state of harmony. She couldn't let him remain in his present condition. Placing her hand on his forehead, Azucena commanded Rodrigo to wake up, so that they could continue the regression. Rodrigo did exactly as he was instructed.

"Let's proceed now to the moment of your death. We're going there so you can understand why you had to have the experience you did. Where are you?"

"I just died."

"Ask your spiritual guide what you needed to learn."

"What it is to be raped . . ."

"Why? Had you raped someone in another life?"

"Yes."

"And how does one feel, being raped?"

"Powerless . . . enraged . . ."

"Call your brother-in-law by name, and tell him how you felt when he raped you."

"Pablo . . ."

"Louder."

"Pablo!"

"He's there now, in front of you, tell him everything . . ."

"Pablo, you made me feel awful . . . you caused me so much pain . . ."

"Tell him how you feel about him."

"I hate you . . ."

"Say it louder. Tell him to his face."

"I hate you, I hate you!"

"How do you feel?"

"Rage, total rage . . . my arms are bursting with rage!"

Rodrigo's face was completely contorted. His veins were bulging, his arms tensed, his fists clenched. His voice was hoarse, unrecognizable, and he wept uncontrollably. Azucena told him he had to scream until he let out all of his buried rage. To facilitate this release she got him a cushion and told him to punch it with all his might. The cushion, however, could not withstand the fury contained in the memory of a rape. After only a few minutes, Rodrigo had pounded it to shreds. The good effect was that his face began to show relief. The bad effect was that everyone aboard the spaceship had moved to one side to avoid being the accidental target of his blows, and the ship, which was not, shall we say, in the very best condition, was destabilized and began to pitch and shudder. Cuquita's grandmother, who had been fast asleep, was awakened by all the commotion. Rodrigo's yelling had pierced her very soul and, still half asleep, she managed to mutter, "I told you, he's still the same drunken shithead!"

Azucena succeeded in calming everyone down, explaining that Rodrigo had discharged all his negative energy and would cause no further problems. They had nothing to fear. All the passengers returned to their seats, and Azucena was able to continue.

"Good, Rodrigo. Very good. Now we must go to the moment when the trouble between you and your brother-in-law began. Because I'm sure that the cause is to be found in still another lifetime. Tell me if you knew him before that."

"Yes . . . a long time ago . . ."

"Where were you living, and what was your relationship to him?"

"He was a woman . . . I was a man. . . . We lived in Mexico City . . ."

"What year was it?"

"Fifteen twenty-one. She was an Indian in my service . . ."

"Now let's go to the moment when the problem surfaced. What's happening?"

"I'm standing atop a pyramid—they call it the Temple of Love—and she comes there, and I . . . I rape her, right there."

"Hmmm . . . That's interesting. Now that you know how it feels to be raped, what do you feel toward her?"

"I feel very guilty at having caused her such pain."

"Tell her that. Summon her. Do you know her in this present life?"

"No, not in this one, but I do in the other one. She was the brother-in-law who raped me."

"I see . . . And now that you know this, do you still hate him?"

"No."

"Then summon your brother-in-law and tell him. Do you know his name in that earlier life?"

152

"Yes. Citlali . . . Citlali, I ask your forgiveness for having raped you . . . I didn't know how much I was hurting you . . . forgive me, please . . . I'm so sorry for what I did to you . . . I didn't want to harm you . . . I only wanted to love you, but I didn't know how . . ."

"Tell her how you paid for having raped her. . . . Now, move forward in time. . . . Let's go to the life immediately following that one. . . . Where are you?"

"In Spain . . ."

"What year?"

"Around 1600 I think . . . I'm a monk . . . I have a beard and a tonsure . . . I'm trying to subdue my body . . . I'm half naked and waist deep in snow . . . there's a blizzard . . . I'm freezing . . . but I must dominate my body . . ."

Rodrigo was trembling from head to foot; he looked exhausted, anguished, but Azucena had to continue her questioning.

"And are you learning to?"

"Yes. . . . A nun is coming toward me . . . she's taking off her clothes, but I resist . . ."

"What is she like?"

"Pretty. . . . She has a beautiful body . . . but . . . she's a hallucination . . . she doesn't exist . . . my mind has invented her because I haven't eaten in days so that I can conquer my appetites . . . I'm very weak . . . I'm dying . . . I regret having mortified my body . . . wasted my life . . ."

"Why? What did you devote yourself to in that life?"

"Nothing. . . . To controlling my body and my desires . . . but it was so hard, so hard . . ."

"But you must have done something good. . . . Search for a moment that gave you some satisfaction."

"I can't find one . . . nothing. . . . Well, the one useful thing I did was to invent profanities . . ."

"Tell me about it."

"The monks in New Spain did not want the Indians to learn to curse the way the Spaniards did, always saying, 'I shit on God,' and they asked us to invent some new curses."

"Hmmm . . . interesting. Well then, your life wasn't a total waste, was it?"

"Maybe not, but I suffered a great deal."

"Tell Citlali that, back in the life when you raped her. Tell her you had to endure great pain to atone for your guilt. Tell her how hard it was to learn to control your desires. Tell her how you suffered."

Azucena allowed a period of time for Rodrigo to speak mentally with Pablo-Citlali, and then decided it was time to end the session.

"All right. Now repeat after me: I release you from my passion, from my desires. . . . I release myself from your thoughts of vengeance, for I have paid for what I did to you. . . . I release you and I release myself. . . . I pardon you and I pardon myself. . . . I'm letting go of all the rage that bound me to you. . . . I'm letting it circulate freely once again. . . . I release it and allow nature to purify it and utilize it—in regenerating life, in harmonizing the Cosmos, in disseminating love. . . ."

Phrase by phrase, Rodrigo repeated Azucena's words, and as he did so his face reflected his growing relief. He discovered that the pain in his hip had disappeared, and when he opened his eyes, swollen from crying, he had the look of a different person. The atmosphere in the spaceship improved immediately, and everyone was in great spirits for the remainder of the journey.

11

Bells and rattles ring out,
Dust rises as if it were smoke:
The Giver of Life rejoices.
The flowers on the shield unfold their petals,
Glory spreads far and wide,
Binding all the Earth.
There is death here among the flowers,
Here in the middle of the plain!
On the field of battle,
As the war begins,
In the middle of the plain,
Dust rises as if it were smoke,
Turns and curls about
In flowered wreaths of death.
O Chichimec princes!
Heart, be not afraid!
In the middle of the plain
My heart desires
Death by the obsidian blade.
Only this my heart desires:
To die in battle . . .

"Cantares mexicanos," fol. 9 r.
Trece Poetas del Mundo Azteca
MIGUEL LEÓN-PORTILLA

As fast as the Kormian volcano was spewing lava, Isabel's heart was pumping blood. It was in emergency mode, because the moment Isabel had felt that the lava might overtake her she had begun running like a madwoman, leaving her bodyguards far behind. No one could keep up with her. She ran and ran until finally she passed out. The fear of being burned alive in the seething lava had swept through her body with the force of a hurricane, hurling her soul outward into space. Her body, trying to recover her soul, had raced after it futilely, until it could go no farther and collapsed on the ground.

This was not the first time Isabel had lost consciousness. As a young girl, she had been an accomplished runner, but she had stopped participating in the sport when she realized she no longer had control of her body. Frequently while training, her body, like an untamed horse, would run away with her and not stop until it had used up all her strength. It seemed to happen for no special reason. Of course escaping from the burning lava was reason enough, but generally the impetus wasn't so clear. She seemed to have an inexplicable need to flee, which welled up from the depths of her soul. And now her body, spent by her sudden flight, had fallen not far from Ex-Rodrigo, who himself had lost consciousness at the hands of the primitive woman who had knocked him out with a single blow.

When Isabel's bodyguards Agapito and Ex-Azucena reached her side, they were extremely alarmed by what they saw. Isabel gave every appearance of being dead. What in the world would they tell the Party if that was true?

Ex-Azucena quickly suggested they find someone to blame for Isabel's apparent murder. They thought it expedient to choose a suspect from among the Kormians, who, speaking only that primitive tongue, would be unable to defend himself against the charge.

"How does this one strike you?" asked Agapito, pointing to Ex-Rodrigo.

"Perfect," replied Ex-Azucena, and forthwith initiated Operation Fist.

They were still at it when Isabel came to. The sight of her guards savagely beating the person she believed to be Rodrigo threw her into a fury.

"What the hell are you doing?" she screamed.

"We're interrogating this suspect, boss," was Agapito's quick reply.

"Idiots! Leave him alone!" Isabel struggled to her feet and rushed to Ex-Rodrigo's side where, to her bodyguards' amazement, she began wiping the blood from his nose.

"Are you badly hurt?" she asked.

Ex-Rodrigo, who by then had emerged from the combined fog of his drunkenness and the knockout punch, immediately recognized Isabel as the candidate for Planetary President and clung to her desperately. Tears flowing from his eyes, he implored her: "Señora Isabel, I'm so glad you're here! Help me, please! I don't know what I'm doing here. I live on Earth, my name is Ricardo Rodríguez. My wife brought me here in a spaceship, and . . ."

But Ex-Rodrigo's words were no longer of any interest to her. Leaning back slightly from him to look into his eyes, Isabel realized that this man was not Rodrigo. She shoved him aside and began brushing his filth off her clothing in disgust. Then, to confirm her discovery, she demanded, pointing to Ex-Azucena, "Do you know this woman?"

As soon as he looked at her, Ex-Rodrigo went into a frenzy. "You bet I do! That stinking bitch kicked my balls up my ass. I thought you were dead, bitch! Am I happy to see you again—now you're really going to get it!" Ex-Rodrigo lunged at Ex-Azucena, but he was restrained by Agapito.

"Cool it, sport. You touch this woman and I'll bust what little balls you have left!"

Isabel was deep in thought. She knew that even though she had effectively erased Rodrigo's memory, Azucena's image—the image of his twin soul—must still be embedded somewhere in his mind. However, this man had reacted with total rage, exactly the opposite of what might be expected from a twin soul. That was all Isabel needed to prove to her satisfaction that this "Rodrigo" was indeed someone else. But who? And more important, where was Rodrigo's soul? To find out, she handed Ex-Rodrigo back to her guards, saying, "Proceed with your interrogation!"

It was imperative that Isabel learn who was behind this sinister act that placed her in such danger. She began to tremble. Cold sweat was running down her neck. She could not allow anyone to stand in her way. She *had* to occupy the presidential office, no matter what it took. If not, the era of peace everyone so eagerly awaited would never be achieved. This evidence that she had hidden enemies forced her into the realization that this was war. If she was to win the peace, she had no choice but to do battle.

Unfortunately, her bodyguards didn't have time to extract much information from Ex-Rodrigo because the remaining members of Isabel's entourage were now approaching. It would not be a good idea for them to witness her guards' methods of interrogation. They had only managed to get out of him the names of his wife, her grandmother, Julito, and Chonita, their "new neighbor"—that is, Azucena. Isabel jumped at the mention of a new neighbor.

"This Chonita, did she arrive the same day Azucena died?"

Ex-Rodrigo's reply was a loud affirmative. The fact that the new tenant had arrived the same day they took away Azucena's body couldn't be a mere coincidence, nor could the fact that someone had made away with Rodrigo's soul. Isabel quickly surmised that, before dying, Azucena must have changed bodies. Then she was still alive! And she had somehow come into possession of Rodrigo's soul. Isabel would have to get rid of Azucena at the first opportunity. That was as far as her plans for the future went for the moment. She couldn't determine how to do it just yet, because right now she had to go back to playing her role as saint in front of her entourage.

Everyone was very concerned about her. They had watched her disappear at top speed, running like a soul in torment, but none of them could catch up with her. The attention of one of the female reporters in the group now focused on Ex-Rodrigo. Within seconds, she had recognized him as the alleged accomplice of Mr. Bush's assassin. Isabel immediately intervened to prevent any speculation. She informed everybody present that this was precisely why she had left them so abruptly. She, like the reporter, had a very good eye for faces, and, recognizing this man on sight, she had run after him. He had already confessed to her that he'd been attempting to hide on Korma, but fortunately she had discovered him, and soon he'd be in the hands of the authorities. As a finishing touch, she explained that the bruises visible on his body were the result of a beating inflicted on him by the tribe, who considered him an intruder.

Everyone congratulated Isabel for her bravery, and a series of photographs was taken with her standing beside the "criminal." When Ex-Rodrigo realized that this "dangerous suspect" they kept referring to was himself, he tried to protest and declare his innocence, but with a quick, nearly imperceptible knee to his battered balls, Isabel quieted him. She then ordered her bodyguards to escort the alleged accomplice of Mr. Bush's murderer inside their spacecraft, where he could receive medical attention.

The reporter wanted to beam back to Earth a report on everything that had happened, but Isabel convinced her not to, saying it would hinder the investigation. Any sensational news about the case might alert the other members of this fellow's urban guerrilla gang. The best thing would be to keep it all quiet for the moment, however difficult that might be, and to hand over the suspect to the Planetary Attorney General. His office would conduct a proper investigation and see to the apprehension of the man's accomplices, who were already known to be Cuquita, Cuquita's grandmother, Julito, and Azucena. The reporter willingly accepted Isabel's suggestion, and agreed to delay her story, not realizing she was giving Isabel free rein to act in her own best interests and eliminate the "accomplices" before they were ever arrested.

Who knows whether it was due to the heat, or to their having met with so many obstacles on their return to the ship, but the fact was Ex-Azucena fainted as he boarded the interplanetary spacecraft. Ex-Rodrigo tried to take advantage of his momentary lapse in order to escape, which only brought him another walloping at the hands of Agapito.

✦

Isabel had taken it upon herself to convince everyone that Ex-Rodrigo was an extremely dangerous person and that the wisest course would be to keep him sedated until they returned to Earth. Currying her favor, they had all agreed with her. Knowing that the man could not communicate with anyone had given her a little breathing room. She withdrew, along with her bodyguards, to the conference room of the spacecraft, ostensibly to get some work done.

The truth, however, was that Isabel was playing solitaire, and her much-put-upon guards were reduced to doing nothing but watch. Solitaire was Isabel's passion. She would spend hours and hours shifting the cards around on the computer, especially when she had a lot on her mind. It was as if in arranging the cards she were constructing a dike between the sea and the sand. Or as if in mastering the cards she were mastering her thoughts. Through her game of solitaire, Isabel felt she was transforming confusion into order, chaos into harmony and normality. If only it were as easy to find a suspect as it was to turn over a card. That there was a plan to destroy her, she had no doubt. She had to discover who was behind it before her enemies succeeded in tearing down the image she had labored so hard to construct.

Too bad they weren't traveling directly back to Earth, but she had committed to a stopover on Jupiter. Since the President of that planet was very powerful, it would be greatly to her advantage if they could work out an interplanetary free trade agreement. That would give her enormous credibility and place her far ahead of her opponent in the upcoming election. She couldn't imagine that the negotiations would take more than a day, and as long as Ex-Rodrigo was kept asleep she had nothing to fear. Isabel was confident that no information could be gotten out of the real Rodrigo either, wherever he was. He couldn't possibly recover his memory. At least she hoped not!

What a black day it had been when she fell in love with him. Rodrigo was the one person she had been unable to bring herself to eliminate. And now she was paying the price. She had only herself to blame for being up to her ass in this mess, and it wasn't going to be easy to get out of it clean. She tried to calm herself down, thinking it wouldn't make that much difference if she returned a day late. What *was* certain in her mind, however, was that as soon as she reached Earth she was going to settle accounts with everyone plotting against her. She had already made countless calls from the spacecraft trying to determine who else was in on the plot, but had uncovered nothing. Apparently, Azucena and her co-conspirators were working on their own. Even so, Isabel did not rule out a political plot of wider scope.

Isabel felt fear wrenching her stomach, churning her gastric juices, boring into her intestines. She knew she'd better control herself, but she couldn't. Her thoughts raced on with a will of their own. Unable to restrain them, she continued playing solitaire: to stop thinking; to make order out of something, even if it was only a bunch of lousy cards. Still, they were the only things remaining under her control. Although, now that she thought of it, she did have her bodyguards. She had forbidden the poor creatures to budge or make a sound that might interrupt her concentration, and they were obeying her orders exactly.

This was not the case, however, with Isabel's computer. It had already given her a callus on her finger as she attempted to break her speed record in order to get into the *Guinness Book of World Records*, but the damn thing wouldn't oblige. It just plodded along and couldn't—or wouldn't—follow her rhythm. Isabel was beside herself. She had played several games without winning one. Her heart was pounding, occasionally skipping a beat. If she didn't win she was going to have a heart attack. If only she had a three of hearts! Then she could get rid of the four and work on the next column.

At precisely that moment, Ex-Azucena keeled over with a thud. Isabel leapt from her chair and threw herself down on the floor. She was shaking with fear, convinced that someone had kicked in the door with the intention of assassinating her. Not hearing any shot, she looked up and realized what had happened. Agapito was at Ex-Azucena's side, trying to revive him. Furious, Isabel got to her feet and brushed off her clothing.

"What's got into that moron? Ever since he got that woman's body, he keeps fainting on me."

"I don't know, boss."

"Well, get him out of here. Have the doctor look at him, and then come straight back. Oh, and while you're at it, make sure that our impostor stays sleeping."

Agapito took Ex-Azucena up in his arms and left the conference room.

Isabel sat cursing under her breath. She had been so close to breaking her record, and then that stupid guard had to swoon and screw up everything. Now, even if she played it out, the game would not qualify for the *Guinness Book* because it had been interrupted. It seemed as if lately everything was going wrong, nothing was working out, everything stank. Everything! Even herself. Herself? Yes! That was when she realized that her scare had caused her to fart. It was one of the foulest she'd ever passed. Her colitis was to blame. And the colitis was all Azucena's fault. And Azucena was all . . . whose fault? No matter. The main thing was to get rid of the overpowering stench, or else when Agapito returned he'd find someone else passed out. Opening her purse, she took out an air freshener she carried with her for just such emergencies, and began spraying it around the room. She was still at it when Agapito returned with a troubled look on his face. As he came into the room, his frown deepened; the stench of perfumed fart was nauseating. But being a conscientious bodyguard, he made a superhuman effort and put on a "Me? I don't smell anything" expression. Isabel was relieved, and proceeded to question him.

"What was it? What's the matter with him?"

"Well, he . . . had a microcomputer implanted in his head."

"I thought so! That Azucena is someone to be feared. I wonder what she was up to with that microcomputer? Nothing good, I'll tell you. Well, what's the doctor going to do now, take it out?"

"No, no, he can't."

"Why not?"

"Uh . . . because, well, it might affect . . . uh, because . . . he's pregnant."

"He's what? That lousy hustler? Now he turns into a hooker on me? Get him in here! I have a few things I want to say to him."

"He's right outside, boss."

"Well, what are you waiting for? Bring him in."

Agapito opened the door, and Ex-Azucena entered the room sheepishly. He already knew what awaited him, having heard Isabel's screams all too clearly. When Isabel threw a temper tantrum, no room could contain that voice of an amplified screech owl.

"What's going on, Rosalío? What's all this about your being pregnant?"

"I'm not sure, chief."

"What do you mean, you're not sure? I can't believe you can be so goddamn stupid! Don't you know if you go screwing around like a whore you can end up pregnant? Couldn't you have waited just a few months till I finished my campaign?"

"I swear to you, chief, I haven't had any time for that kind of thing. The only one who I . . ."

Ex-Azucena paused, throwing a frightened glance at Agapito. He was not eager to confess that his cohort was the only person who'd laid a hand on him. Agapito deftly cut in before Ex-Azucena could get the words out.

"Well now, Doña Isabel. Allow me to stick my nose in where it doesn't belong, but I have to say that I don't see how this pregnancy is going to interfere with anything, 'cause it takes nine months for a baby to be born."

"Yes, of course. But how much time is left in the campaign?"

"Just six months."

"And what good is this lousy whore to me for the next half year?

164

Who's going to respect or fear a bodyguard who runs around fainting and vomiting, let alone when his belly starts sticking out!"

Ex-Azucena felt extremely wounded by Isabel's words and tone of voice. After all, this was no way to treat an expectant mother. Unable to hold back any longer, he burst into tears.

"That's just what I needed—for you to start bawling! Get out of here! You're fired, as of right this minute, and I never want to see you anywhere near me again. Understood?"

Ex-Azucena nodded and ran from the conference room.

At the door, he bumped into one of the thought analysts who were part of Isabel's entourage. The analyst regarded the retreating figure with pitying eyes. He didn't even want to imagine what the fate of that guard would be once Isabel saw the photomental shots he'd just taken of him. The whole time Isabel was berating him, Ex-Azucena had been wishing for her to turn into a diseased rat. The photomentals showed, in excruciating detail, Isabel's face on the body of a rat swollen with worms, drinking water from a toilet. Another of the images showed her scurrying through a garbage dump when suddenly a satellite fell on her and she burst into smithereens, releasing a putrid gas. And now as he entered the room, the analyst was astounded, for he believed the bodyguard possessed supernatural powers. It seemed that the fleeing guard could actually produce the same physical phenomena his mind had projected so clearly onto the film. The room really did smell like a dead rat.

CD
Track 6

What kind of thing is love, it seems so much
   like pain,
It never touched me, never touched you,
Never knew how to, or wished to, or tried to.
That's why you aren't with me . . .

Because we never even met
And in all the time we lost
Each one of us lived his part
But each one always apart.
Because you can't extinguish
What has never been ignited,
Because you can't restore to health
Something that never has languished.
Because you'd never understand
My weariness, my manias,
Because to you it'd be just the same
If I fell into the abyss.
This love you've scorned so long
Because you never even looked for me
Where I wouldn't have been anyway,
Nor would you have loved me.

That's why you aren't with me.
That's why I'm not with you.

LILIANA FELIPE

12

How it pains me not to be able to calm Isabel's agitated state of mind. She urgently needs a rest. She's been working like a maniac these last few hours, flashing negative thoughts in all directions; so busy suspecting, plotting, and planning revenge, that for the first time she has rendered herself incapable of following my advice. All that thinking has clouded her mind. Nergal, the chief of Hell's secret police, just paid a visit to bawl me out. He says I have to find a way to tranquilize her as soon as possible. Her rash actions are liable to ruin everything.

I suggested that she take a nice hot bath to relax, but she can't. For some time now, she's been sitting naked on the edge of the tub, too afraid to get into the water. She has never felt secure without her clothes on, anyway. Her love for the movies has merely exacerbated this phobia, because she's seen how as soon as the heroine steps into the shower some calamity befalls her. So that now, when she has real reason to fear an attack, stepping into the tub is the last thing she wants to do. And it would do her so much good! I mean, to relax a little. And that's how I need her, nice and relaxed.

Before any act of destruction there is a period of calm during which the mind becomes clear and decisions can be made. If Isabel does not put a stop to all this activity, that peace will not come to her, and we'll never be able to spring into action. Unthinkable, considering all the things we have to savage and destroy! It doesn't seem possible that Isabel could have forgotten that her mission on Earth is to foster chaos as part of the Universal Order. The Universe cannot allow order to become a permanent condition. To do so would mean its death. Life emerged as a need to balance chaos. Thus if chaos ends, so does life itself.

If all human beings possessed a soul filled with Love, and all were occupying their rightful places, that would be the end of the Universe.

That is why it has been necessary to create such a variety of wars and social conflicts: to distract the human race in its search for order, peace, and harmony. That is why we must fill their hearts with hatred; confuse, torment, exploit them; keep them continually on the run. And that is why we situate them within a pyramidal power structure, so that they cannot think for themselves, so that they always have orders to carry out, a superior above them telling them what to do.

On the day that the cells of Isabel's body are liberated from negative energy, she will be in syntony with positive energy, and will, therefore, be in the proper state to receive Divine Light—which would be disastrous. I will never allow that to happen. And I say that only for Isabel's own good. The human soul is impure. It is in no condition to receive the luminous reflection of God. If that happened in her present state, she would be blinded. And no one wants that, right? Then all of you will agree with me that it is something to be avoided. Generally, the best way of achieving this is to cloud the eyes with that smokescreen the ego, so the individual cannot see beyond himself, nor see any reflection other than that of his own ego projected onto the pupils of his eyes. And if somehow he manages to perceive any glimmer of external light, he will see it as a simple reflector placed there to lend brilliance and glitter to his own person—he will never recognize it as the True Light. That is why it is next to impossible for man to recall where he comes from and what he has to do on Earth. In that state of darkness, it is very simple to align him within an earthly power structure. He will subjugate his will to the service of his superior, and will not offer the least resistance in carrying out his orders.

Orders are transmitted from top to bottom. And who is atop the pyramid? The rulers, of course. And who tells them what to do? We Demons, of course. And who gives us the word? The Prince of Darkness, he who is charged with ensuring that hatred lives on in the Universe. Without hatred, there could be no wish for destruction. And without destruction—I will repeat it a thousand and one times, until all of you learn it—there . . . is . . . no . . . . life! Destruction is an essential element in the truly perfect plan for the functioning of the Universe—the very plan Isabel is about to ruin!

I never would have expected it. In numerous lives she has been chosen to occupy the highest position in the power pyramid, and not once has she failed us. She knows how to make people respect her and follow the rule of force. Availing herself of the luxury of cruelty, she imposes her law. She knows how to scheme and intrigue to keep her place on the throne. She knows how to lie, deceive, torture, compromise, deal, and bend the law. Her virtues are beyond number, but the most important may be that she knows how to keep people physically and intellectually occupied, with no time to merge harmoniously with their superior being or to remember their true mission on Earth. And now she's gone and fallen in love! At the worst possible moment, just when we have to engage in the final battle. And God knows what surprise Azucena has in store for us next. I am honestly worried.

When human beings are in love, their minds and thoughts resonate with those of the beloved. And when they settle into that harmonious relationship with love, the door opens to Divine Love, and if this Love filters into their soul, we're lost, since the same will be true for the beloved: once people know Divine Love they want nothing but to experience its presence within them.

Should that happen to Isabel, she would forget she was born to be a destroyer. She would stop working for us and go over to the other camp, to the side of creation, of harmony, of order. The only time we can allow Isabel to put things in order is in her games of solitaire, because when she's occupied with her cards, she slides into a state of mental tranquillity that gives us the perfect opportunity to communicate our instructions. Now, however, not even the solitaire seems to be calming her mind.

After playing for hours and hours, all she has to show for it is a blinding headache. The thought that someone on her team is betraying her is driving her out of her mind. She knows that there must be a traitor somewhere around her; she can't explain how Azucena could still be alive. Someone must have warned Azucena about the plan to kill her, and proposed the solution of a body exchange. So now Isabel has begun to distance herself from all her collaborators, because she sees a traitor in each one of them. She is obsessively studying them in hopes that they will slip up and expose themselves. All this focus on others is preventing her from concentrating on her inner state. She has never liked looking at herself. Not ever. Not even in the mirror. This is logical, because mirrors present the image of what she really is. Usually when people don't like their image, or simply refuse to look at it, they create a reflection of the person they would like to be instead, and by assuming the fictitious image, they no longer see themselves at all.

Wishes act as mirrors. When Isabel says she is determined to destroy Azucena, what she really wants to destroy is herself. That seems fine to me, because I have nothing at all against destruction, but I have to ask myself whether Isabel would agree. Recently it seems that she has forgotten all my teaching and is so filled with fear and remorse that she's afraid to destroy anything. She does not want to accept that it was a mistake to let Rodrigo live—the one weakness she has shown in an entire lifetime. Now she has no choice but to eliminate him, and she doesn't want to.

Her judgment on this and other matters has isolated her from me. Decisions invariably isolate a person from life. Thinking whether I should do this or that, or go from here to there, causes great anxiety. The correct response is always within us, but in order to hear it there must be silence, calm, paralysis. I hope to heaven that Isabel can settle down soon and get over her fear. No one should have any trepidation about what she has done, since the energy of the Universe is always twofold: masculine and feminine, negative and positive. In that energy, Good and Evil are always linked, as are fear and aggression, success and envy, faith and doubt. And that is why no one can ever make the wrong decision. Nothing we ever did can be considered bad if we acted by following our emotions. It will be bad in our eyes only if we allowed judgments to interfere, if our mind makes guilt feel at home. Because if one has set aside reason and connected directly with life, one will discover that there is nothing bad in the Universe, that every particle carries within it an equal capacity for creation and destruction. And more immediately, I, Mammon, exist only because of Isabel's self-destruction. This limits me considerably, for it means that should Isabel lose this capacity, I would automatically disappear from her life. Now *that* would really be a shame!

13

Order was being restored to Azucena's apartment. Cuquita was in the midst of moving back to her own apartment now that there was no obstacle to her living there in peace with her grandmother. Azucena had offered to let them stay with her a few more days, but Cuquita had refused. Azucena kept insisting, but could not persuade her. Azucena's obstinacy was not so much due to a feeling that she'd miss her neighbor as to the fact that Cuquita was planning to take Rodrigo with her.

As for Cuquita, she was making a virtue of her own stubbornness, offering Azucena thousands of reasons why she had to move back and take Rodrigo with her. The most convincing was that as far as everyone in the neighborhood was concerned Rodrigo—or rather the body Rodrigo was occupying—was Cuquita's husband. No one else knew that this big slob of a body housed a good and evolved soul. And it wouldn't be a good idea if people got wind of it, so in order not to arouse suspicion, they'd better have Rodrigo move into the super's apartment with her.

"Honest, you don't have anything to worry about, he's just pure window dressing," Cuquita told Azucena. Naturally, she said it with her fingers crossed behind her back, because beneath that facade Cuquita was nobody's fool and she wanted Rodrigo all to herself. More than anything, she wanted to impress on her neighbors that finally her husband had turned over a new leaf.

Poor Rodrigo. In addition to living in total confusion, he was also the one bearing the brunt of their decisions. The women had told him that he'd have to pretend to be Cuquita's husband, and that although she was not his real wife, she was indeed the wife of the body he was occupying and so it was in his interest to put on the best show possible, since if people learned his true identity his life would be in danger. They had not allowed him to raise any questions, and his amnesia made it impossible for him to pull any weight. The one thing he begged of them was that they explain the situation thoroughly to Cuquita's grandmother, for she still had him confused with Ricardo Rodríguez and consequently would sneak in a passing kick whenever she got the chance.

Rodrigo felt totally out of place. He was not at all pleased with the idea of living with these women who were not his family and who meant nothing to him, and, to top everything off, were making him pay dearly for the favor of hiding him in their house. They were having him pack all their things while they sat back and took it easy. How he longed to have his memory back and to be able to return to his real family; but before that could happen, he needed to work on his subconscious. He desperately needed an astro-analysis session with Azucena! But Azucena kept putting it off, with the excuse that first he had to get all of Cuquita's belongings moved out, so that he could concentrate on the session without feeling any pressure. Well, that was the excuse, but the real reason was that Azucena was waiting for Cuquita and her grandmother to get out of her apartment so she could hold the session alone with Rodrigo, with no busybodies hanging around.

Meanwhile everyone was taking advantage of their last moments together. Cuquita was sprawled out on the bed, enjoying the Televirtual; her grandmother was dozing in the sunlight on the terrace before returning to their cold, damp apartment; and Azucena was using the cybernetic Ouija one last time before its owner left with it. She had put one of the African violet leaves into the flask along with Cuquita's special liquid formula, and she immediately began receiving on the fax images of everything the plant had witnessed during its lifetime. Most of them were totally insignificant, and Azucena was getting glassy-eyed by the time a photo appeared that brought her right out of her chair. It showed the dexterous fingers of Dr. Díez introducing a microcomputer into the ear of . . . none other than ISABEL GONZÁLEZ!

That photograph confirmed several suspicions. First, that that bitch Isabel was no saint! Second, that Dr. Díez had programmed one, if not several, fictitious lives into the microcomputer. Third, that if Isabel had needed a fictitious life, it was because she had a dark past that, were it known, would prevent her from becoming President. And fourth, that the African violet had witnessed the implant. And that wasn't all! It seems it had also witnessed the doctor's murder!

Now the fax was producing highly detailed photographs in which Isabel's bodyguards could be seen altering the cables of the protective alarm system wired to the aerophone booth in Dr. Díez's office, with the express purpose of killing him. Bless Cuquita and her cybernetic Ouija! Thanks to her, Azucena had discovered what seemed to be just the tip of an iceberg. She now had sufficient evidence at hand to incriminate Isabel. She had to put these photos in a safe place.

But first, she wanted to give the African violet a drink. The poor thing was drooping because no one had watered it while she was away on her journey to Korma. She couldn't let it die, the plant was her key witness. Where had it gone? She had last seen it on the table, but it had mysteriously disappeared. Azucena began searching frantically through Cuquita's suitcases. Rodrigo, seeing that Azucena was undoing his morning's work, became enraged, and a terrible row ensued, ending only when Rodrigo finally confessed he had put the plant in the bathtub. Azucena ran to rescue it, leaving Rodrigo muttering to himself.

At that exact moment, the aerophone door opened, and Teo and Citlali walked into the room. Rodrigo was dumbstruck at the sight of Citlali; his face took on the same expression it had the first time he had set eyes on her.

Sometimes, it is a real advantage not to have a memory, because by not remembering the bad things others have done to us, we can look at those people without prejudice. If that were not so, memory would become a powerful barrier to communication. When we see a person who once harmed us, we say: this person is bad because he did such and such to me. We should ignore the past in order to establish healthy ties, and create an opportunity for relationships to develop to the point they are intended. Without memory, prejudices do not exist. Because opinions inevitably draw us toward or away from others, we must know how to set them aside if we are to capture the real essence of a person.

This sounds rather easy, but it isn't. Most people are constantly forming opinions to hide their inability to capture this subtle energy. "She's very high up, you know." "He belongs to the opposition party." "They're not from around here." This creates an insurmountable barrier and we find ourselves dominated by intolerance. As soon as we meet a person, we immediately set out our opinions before him to see how he reacts; if he shares them, we accept him. If not, we try to tear down his opinions in order to impose our own, convinced that the other person is bad because he thinks differently from us. We become narrow-minded inquisitors who in the name of truth put to death anybody whose ideas do not coincide with our own.

We should respect and welcome the opinions of others, even those not in agreement with our own, because ideas are capricious. From one day to the next, our world of beliefs can change, making us aware of all the time we wasted arguing and fighting to the death with someone who—curiously enough—believed what we ourselves now believe. The one constant is Love, unique and eternal. Life would be so easy to bear if only we could look into one another's eyes with the same innocence and vulnerability Citlali and Rodrigo now experienced gazing at each other.

When Azucena returned, African violet in hand, she was paralyzed with jealousy. Tears welled in her eyes as she realized that she, Rodrigo's twin soul, had never inspired such a gaze of perfect love. Teo, gifted with extreme sensitivity, took in the situation at a glance and, trying to ease the tension, hurried to make the formal introductions among Rodrigo, Citlali, and Azucena. Then he quickly explained to Azucena that he had spoken with Citlali as promised and she had agreed to lend her spoon for analysis.

As Citlali handed Azucena the spoon, Cuquita rushed into the room yelling at the top of her voice. Her grandmother snapped awake, cutting short a rumbling snore; Rodrigo and Citlali were shocked back to reality; and Teo and Azucena turned toward Cuquita with expressions of What's going on?

Cuquita motioned for everyone to follow her to the bedroom, where they received the surprise of their lives. There in the room were their televirtualized images. They were being identified as suspects belonging to an urban guerrilla group whose goal was to destabilize universal peace. Strangely enough, the only figure that was not included, the very one responsible for their plight, was Azucena, who possessed an unregistered body that could not be traced.

Abel Zabludowsky was reading a special bulletin:

"Today the Planetary Attorney General released the names of persons belonging to the guerrilla group that has been striking fear into the hearts of the public with its terrorist attacks." The camera zoomed in on Cuquita's husband: "Orders have been issued for the immediate apprehension of Ricardo Rodríguez, alias 'Iguana.'" The camera then focused on Cuquita: "Cuquita Pérez de Rodríguez, alias 'Jalapeña.'" After Cuquita's image came a close-up of her grandmother: "Doña Asunción Pérez, alias 'The Mad Madam.'" And finally the camera showed a still of their old pal Julito: "And Julio Chávez, alias 'Snotnose.'" Zabludowsky continued: "The Planetary Government cannot, and should not, ignore this violation of the Constitution. In order to protect the public and prevent further acts of violence by this guerrilla group, which is a menace to public order, there will be . . ."

Citlali didn't wait to hear more. Grabbing the spoon from Azucena's hand, she apologized, saying she had left beans cooking on the stove, and headed for the door. Teo, defending the accused, tried to convince her to stay a little longer. He did not believe these people were guilty of any offense. This sign of Teo's trust touched Azucena's heart. Every day she had more reason to appreciate this man. Citlali insisted on leaving, promising that she would not tell anyone that she had met them.

"Who did they say the terrorists are?" Cuquita's grandmother asked several times.

"They say it's us, Granny," Cuquita replied.

"You people?"

"Yes, and you, too."

"Me? Go on, you must be kidding! How? When?"

A suitable answer was never given, for at that instant a blast from a bazooka blew out the entry gate to the building. The enemy was literally at their doorstep.

A band of policemen stormed into the building, led by Agapito. With one kick, the door to the super's apartment flew open. Finding it empty, Agapito gave his men orders to comb the building. They rushed toward the stairs. Anyone in their way quickly stepped aside, terrified. Agapito and his men struck out at anybody blocking their path. Suddenly, however, their blows began missing the mark. It took only a few seconds for them to realize that an earthquake was spoiling their aim. Nature is the great leveler, making all humans equal. It has its way with police and civilians alike. Hysterical tenants trying to escape first the officers, and then the earthquake, were scattering down the stairs. Agapito fired a shot in the air. Everyone screamed and fell to the ground. Agapito ordered his men to ignore the tremor and continue up the stairway.

At the first tremor, Julito had bolted from his apartment, not wanting to be crushed inside the building. On the stairs, however, he ran into Agapito and his men. His first thought was that these men had come looking for him. But why? It could have been for any number of reasons. All his life, Julito had been involved in one shady deal after another. His first thought was that it might be best to surrender. The time to settle accounts had finally arrived. Too bad!

He took one step forward, but immediately changed his mind. On second thought, his crimes weren't that serious. Besides, those police were carrying enough weapons to subdue an army, not a poor promoter. He was just being paranoid, they didn't mean him any harm. A rocket from a bazooka passing only centimeters from his head quickly clarified his situation. They hadn't come to arrest him, they'd come to *kill* him!

He had to get out of there, fast. In his desperation, he began running *up* the stairs. On the landing of the third floor he caught up to Azucena, Cuquita, Cuquita's grandmother, Rodrigo, Citlali, and Teo, all of whom, like him, were trying to escape. The first person he overtook was Cuquita's grandmother, who because of her blindness and advanced years was bringing up the rear. Then he passed Cuquita, who was slowed by the cybernetic Ouija she was carrying. Then came Citlali, being forcibly dragged by Teo because she clearly did not want to be caught fleeing in the company of accused criminals. Next was Azucena, who stopped from time to time to wait for the others to catch up. And finally Julito passed Rodrigo, who, since he had no responsibility for anyone but himself, was in the lead.

The stairs were swaying from side to side. The walls seemed to be imitating The Wave undulating around a soccer stadium. At first it seemed as if the tremor was working in favor of the escapees, since it was preventing the police from reaching them, but then it suddenly turned against them. Bricks began to rain down, and steel beams fell across their path. Cuquita cried out for help. Her grandmother couldn't go any farther, and Cuquita couldn't help her because she was carrying the Ouija, which contained their evidence against Isabel. Azucena went back to help. Cuquita's grandmother grasped Azucena's arm and hung on tight. She was terribly unsteady. The stairway, so familiar in memory, was now littered with obstacles. It was terrifying to take a step and find the stair missing, or stumble over a chunk of debris.

Azucena's arm provided firm support. She knew the way well enough to lead the grandmother through the darkness. The old woman, in turn, held on to Azucena and would not let go—not even when her will to live gave out. Azucena did not notice that the grandmother had died, because the aged hand was still gripping her arm with the tenacity of a bureaucrat squeezing a budget.

Neither did she notice when three bullets pierced her own body. The only thing she perceived was that the darkness grew more intense. Everyone vanished from her sight. Her only reality was the tunnel of the dark kaleidoscope she and Cuquita's grandmother were walking through. At the end, she could see a faint glow of light and a few waiting figures.

Azucena began to suspect something strange was happening to her when among those figures she recognized Anacreonte. He received her with open arms. Azucena, dazzled by his light, forgot her old quarrels with him and melted into his embrace. She felt loved, accepted, light as air. The weight of all her problems, her loneliness, and even Cuquita's grandmother, instantly lifted from her.

The grandmother had finally let go of her and was walking toward the light. And not until that moment did Azucena understand that she had died, and she was saddened to know that she had not fulfilled her mission. At last she had remembered what that mission was. When a human being is aligned with Divine Love, knowledge is easily recaptured. What is difficult is to retain that lucidity on Earth, on the field of battle.

To begin with, as soon as one descends to Earth, one loses cosmic memory and can recover it only gradually, in the midst of the daily struggle, with all its problems, necessities, and demands. What happens most frequently is that one loses the way. Just like the general who plans his strategy brilliantly on paper but forgets it all in the heat of battle, when the one thing that interests him is coming out of it intact. Only the initiated know exactly what they have to do on Earth. What a pity that everyone else remembers only when there is nothing they can do about it. What good was it for Azucena to have remembered what her mission was? She had no available body in which to carry it out.

Alarmed, she turned to Anacreonte and begged him to help her.

She couldn't die. Not now! She had to go on living, whatever it took. Anacreonte told her there was nothing he could do. One of the bullets had destroyed part of her brain. Azucena's despair was boundless. Anacreonte told her that the only possible solution was for her to seek authorization to take the body Cuquita's grandmother had just vacated. The drawback, of course, was that the body had a lot of years on it, was not gifted with sight, was racked with aches and pains, and would not be much use in general.

Azucena didn't care. She was truly repentant for having been so foolish, for having broken off communication with Anacreonte, for not having allowed herself to be guided, and for not having cooperated in the important mission of peace to which she had been assigned. She promised to behave properly and to mend her ways if they allowed her to return to Earth. The Gods were moved by her sincere repentance and issued instructions to Anacreonte to give Azucena a speedy review of the Law of Love before they permitted her to be reincarnated.

Anacreonte led Azucena to a glass chamber where he placed in her forehead a brilliant diamond that sparked iridescence as the light struck it. This was a precautionary measure, since Anacreonte was all too aware that tigers do not change their stripes. At this moment, Azucena was feeling very contrite, and willing to do anything, but as soon as she was back on Earth, there was every chance that she would once again forget her obligations and at the least provocation allow the dark veil of obstinacy to settle over her soul, obscuring the way. Now, in case that did happen, the diamond was charged to capture and disseminate Divine Light to the deepest crevice of Azucena's soul, so that there could not be the remotest possibility she would lose her way.

Once the diamond was in place, Anacreonte began—in simple terms and taking the least possible time—to run through the Law of Love, approaching it as a review, not a rebuke.

"My dear Azucena," he began, "every action we take has repercussions in the Cosmos. It would be infinitely arrogant to believe that we are the be-all and end-all, and that we can do whatever occurs to us. We *are* that all and everything that vibrates with the sun, the moon, the wind, water, fire, and earth, with everything visible and invisible. And therefore, in the same way that everything outside us determines what we are, so, too, everything we think and feel has its effect on the external world. When a person accumulates hatred, resentment, envy, and anger within, her surrounding aura becomes black, dense, heavy. As she loses the ability to capture Divine Light, her personal energy goes down, as does—logically—the energy of everything around her. To build up her energy level, and, with it, the level of her life, that negative energy must be released. And how?

"That part is simple. Energy throughout the Universe is one: always the same, yet in constant movement and transformation. The movement of one energy produces displacement of another. For instance, when an idea emerges from the brain, its movement opens a path through the ether and leaves behind it, following the Law of Correspondence, an empty space that must—without exception—be occupied by an energy identical to that creating the vacuum, for it was displaced at that level.

"To give you an illustration, if a thought leaves our brain on the level of a shortwave, we will receive the same energy in return, because the original impulse utilized that level of vibration. This is the same way that a consistent syntony is maintained on a radio station: if what is broadcast, syntonized, is a program of country music, then what you will hear if you are tuned to that frequency is country music. If you want to hear a different station, you have to change the frequency—the syntony. Therefore, if what we send out is negative energy, negative waves of energy is what we will receive.

"All right so far.

"Now, another law says that energy that remains static weakens; and energy that flows grows stronger. Perhaps the best example of this is water in a river and water in a pond. The water of a pond is relatively static, and consequently is restricted in its potential to expand. The water in a river flows and increases to the degree that it is fed by the streams that empty into it along its course. It grows and grows until it reaches the sea. The water in a pond can never become part of the sea; water in a river can. Stagnant water grows foul; flowing water is purified. The same is true of an idea that issues from our mind. As it flows, it increases and will return to us in greater volume. That is why we say that when a person does good, good will be returned to him sevenfold. And the reason is that along the way his goodness will be fed by energy of the same affinity. This is exactly why we should be very careful with negative thoughts, for the same is true of them.

"If people only knew how this law functions, they would not be so driven to accumulate worldly goods. Let me give you a very clumsy example. Let's say a woman has her closet filled with clothes, but she wants to change her wardrobe. First she has to throw out the old clothes or give them away, before she can get new ones, because there's only so much room in the closet. This is precisely what happens in the Universe. The energy moving through it is always the same, but always in constant movement. We are the ones who determine what kind of energy we will allow into our bodies to circulate there. If we store up hatred inside us, like the old clothes, there will be no room for love. If we want love to come into our lives, we must use any means we can to rid ourselves of hatred. The problem lies in the fact that according to the Law of Affinity, as we displace hatred, we receive hatred in return. The only way around this is to transmute the energy of hatred into love before it leaves our body.

"The Pyramid of Love was at one time charged with these functions, and this is why it must be restored. What we are asking of you is a mission that is very nearly impossible, but I know that you can do it. And to make sure, I am going to be at your side at all times. You are not alone. Remember that. You have all of us with you. I wish you well."

With these words, Anacreonte ended what he had thought would be a brief, but turned out to be a lengthy, review of the Law of Love. He gave Azucena an affectionate hug, then accompanied her on the journey back to Earth.

✦

Azucena never really knew how it was that she had managed to escape from Agapito and his accomplices. Her return to Earth in the body of an aged blind woman was truly dramatic—not only because it came at a critical moment, but because it was so complicated to manage this unfamiliar body. The first time she had changed bodies, she had been given a nice new one, and had not encountered any great difficulties. Now, however, the one she had was old and defective. She would have to learn to control it gradually, until she became familiar with its stimuli, its quirks, its pleasures, and its irritations.

She would have to begin by learning to walk without relying on the sense of sight, and to do it on rheumatic old legs. Not at all easy. Not being able to see made her feel absolutely lost. And she had no idea how it was they had escaped Isabel's thugs. The one thing she could be sure of was that a man's hands had pulled her along, helped her to keep climbing the stairs amid the ricocheting bullets and over the countless obstacles in their path. There was a moment when she had collapsed, her body no longer responding to her will. Everything hurt, right down to her soul. Excruciating stabbing pains in her knees had prevented her from getting up again.

The man's hands had lifted her up and carried her to Julito's spaceship, which was docked on the rooftop of the apartment building. She had been blessed with such incredible luck that not a single bullet fired at her hit its mark. Just as they climbed aboard and the door was being shut, a hail of bullets sprayed across the hull. Theirs had been an extremely fortunate getaway. As they reviewed the damage, they found nothing more than a few scrapes and an occasional bruise. With the one exception of Azucena's former body, which was dead, everyone was safe and sound. As the ship lifted rapidly, its passengers let out a cheer.

It was not until the immediate scare was behind them that Azucena began to be aware of what had happened. She was alive! In the body of an aged blind woman, but alive nonetheless. Everyone had welcomed her, and all were happy to know she was still with them. Azucena was deeply moved. Even Cuquita, who had lost her grandmother, was happy for Azucena. She understood perfectly that the old woman had lived her time on Earth, and it seemed only fair that her neighbor should occupy the body her beloved Granny had left behind.

Azucena felt elated. Now all she had to do was learn to get along in the dark. She was so grateful that the Gods had allowed her to return to Earth that she couldn't see the negative side of the state she was in. What's more, she was finding that blindness had its advantages. Forms and colors are very distracting when you want to focus your attention. Her new situation would force her to concentrate on herself, to look inward, to seek images from her past. Besides, out of sight, out of mind: now she wouldn't have to witness the looks of infatuation exchanged between Rodrigo and Citlali. But she had forgotten one small detail. The blind compensate for lack of vision with sharper hearing. To her horror Azucena discovered that, without even trying, she could hear something as delicate as the fluttering wings of a fly—to say nothing of conversations between Rodrigo and Citlali. She could hear all too clearly their flirtation unfolding: the laughter, the come-hithers, the insinuations.

Azucena's optimism ebbed. Like an evil spell, jealousy came back to haunt her once again. Her peace of mind had lasted but a few minutes. Insecurity and doubts returned, taking hold of her mind and plummeting her into depression. She feared she might lose Rodrigo forever. But most depressing of all was discovering that Rodrigo was even more blind than she. Hearing his words, she could tell he was crazy about Citlali. How was that possible? What could Citlali have to offer him? A beautiful body, yes, but no matter how great Citlali's attraction, it could never compare to what she—his twin soul!—could give him. How could Rodrigo waste his time in such petty flirtations? How could he fail to realize that she, Azucena, loved him more than anyone, and could make him the happiest man in the world? From the moment she met him she had done nothing but help him, understand him, lend him her support, try to make him feel good; yet instead of appreciating her, he was letting himself be carried away by Citlali's swaying hips.

Azucena was sure Rodrigo's eyes never strayed from those sensuous buttocks. She had seen him devouring them with his eyes the first moment he met her. That would not have surprised Azucena in any other man. They're all like that, she thought. They can never recognize an ideal woman, they're all blinded by a beautiful ass. She had not expected that, however, from her twin soul, erased memory or not. And what made her angriest of all was that this feeling of being underrated, along with her growing insecurity, was preventing her from dealing with the mess they were all in.

She felt bad for the others. Because of her, Cuquita, Julito, even Citlali, were in up to their necks. Things were getting worse and worse, and she asked herself whether they would ever improve. Even the volcano Popocatépetl exploded in anger. She didn't know for sure, but she suspected that this earthquake had been provoked by the snow-topped volcano. Popocatépetl had done that on previous occasions. It was his way of showing his disgust over the current political situation, a warning that events were not going well.

The one thing that calmed Azucena was to think that his spouse, the volcano Iztaccíhuatl, had not been infected by her mate's anger, for she was the one who was truly in charge of the destiny of the nation, and of every Mexican in it. Popocatépetl had always acted as her prince consort. It was she who reigned. Her enormous responsibilities kept her very busy and distracted her from the small pleasures couples normally share. She could not allow herself the luxury of yielding to the gratifications of the flesh, because she had to watch over all her children.

One of the legends of the Indian past recounts the relationship between the two volcanos. Iztaccíhuatl's husband Popocatépetl looks upon her as a great lady, and respects her enormously, but as he needs to vent his passion from time to time, he has taken a lover, Malintzín. She is very seductive and sweet, and he passes many happy moments in her company. Iztaccíhuatl of course knows about their love trysts, but does not take much notice of them. She has more important matters to attend to. The fate of a nation is a serious burden. She has no interest in punishing Malintzín. Actually, she is grateful to Malintzín for keeping her husband happy, since she herself can't. Well, it isn't that she can't. Obviously she can, and would do a better job than anyone else! She simply isn't interested. She prefers to maintain her grandeur, her power, and her dominion, letting Malintzín tend to lesser matters, those appropriate to her station. In Iztaccíhuatl's eyes, Malintzín's talent is limited to the bedroom. She makes sure that Malintzín remains in that category, and otherwise ignores her completely.

It seemed to Azucena that if Rodrigo was to have his Popocatépetl syndrome, and entertain himself with his Malintzín, it was only fair that she should enjoy the Iztaccíhuatl syndrome. After all, at this moment she was responsible for several people's fates. She had major problems to resolve, but all she could think of was losing Rodrigo's love. With all her heart and soul, she appealed to the great Lady Iztaccíhuatl for help. How she wished for a little of that lady's loftiness. It would be such a relief not to feel that passion tormenting her, burning her up inside. How she wished to be free of the anguish of hearing the flirtatious tone in Rodrigo's voice, and to find the inner peace she so desperately needed. How she longed to feel a man's arms around her. To feel a little love!

Teo walked over to Azucena and very tenderly embraced her. He seemed to have divined her thought, but that was not quite the case. In fact, Teo was acting under Anacreonte's orders. He was one of the undercover Guardian Angels Anacreonte had assigned to Earth. He called on them in cases of extreme necessity, and this was certainly one of those! They could not allow Azucena to become depressed again.

Azucena did not resist Teo's embrace. At first it communicated protection and shelter. She leaned her head against Teo's shoulder. With great tenderness, he stroked her hair, and kissed her softly on the forehead and cheeks. Azucena lifted her face to make it easier for him to kiss her. Her soul began to feel soothed.

Timidly, Azucena returned Teo's embrace with another, his kisses with her own. The caresses between the two gradually increased in intensity. Azucena was madly sucking in the male energy Teo was supplying her and that she had such need for. Teo took Azucena by the hand and gently led her to the ship's bathroom. There they closed the door and gave free rein to the mingling of their energies.

Teo, being the undercover Guardian Angel he was, had achieved a very high degree of evolution. His eyes were conditioned to see and to take pleasure from the surrender of a soul like Azucena's, even one inside a body as decrepit as that of Cuquita's grandmother. Slowly, Azucena took possession of that aged body, and pushed it to work harder than it had in many, many years. To start with, Azucena's jaws had to open much farther than usual to receive Teo's tongue in her mouth. Her dry, wrinkled lips had to stretch, though they were aided in this by saliva from her astral companion. Her leg muscles had neither the strength nor the flexibility required for the act of love, but nearly miraculously, they acquired them in short order. At first she had leg cramps, but once they warmed up, they worked quite well, like those of somebody much younger. The inner core of her body, moistened by desire, permitted penetration to occur not only comfortably but indeed pleasurably. Her body remembered once again the agreeable sensation of being caressed inside, over and over.

The enjoyment Azucena was experiencing so opened her senses that she was able to perceive Divine Light. The diamond Anacreonte had placed in Azucena's forehead was working perfectly as planned, magnifying the light that blazed at the moment of orgasm. Azucena's barren soul was left radiant, refreshed, budding with love. Its desert-like thirst had been finally assuaged. It was not until she was loved that she knew peace . . . And it was not until she heard the desperate banging on the door—Cuquita needed to use the bathroom—that Azucena returned to reality.

When the door opened, and Teo and Azucena walked out

together, all eyes were turned to them. Azucena couldn't conceal her happiness. It was visible a mile away. Her cheeks were rosy and her expression full of contentment. She actually looked lovely, imagine! But naturally, despite how well her body had performed during the heat of passion, nothing was going to help her the next day. Every inch of her body would ache—even her eyelashes. No matter, making love had fulfilled its purpose. For a moment, Azucena had been aligned with Divine Love. That was enough to give her the urge to work on her subconscious once more.

Whistling a tune, she strolled down the aisle of the spaceship on Teo's arm. As soon as she reached her seat, she sank down with a deep sigh, got out her Discman, and awaited her regression in a state of total bliss.

CD
Track 7

Azucena opened her eyes too soon. She was breathing fast, and had emerged from the regression in a disturbed state of mind. She realized that the woman who screamed so desperately over the death of her child was none other than Citlali, and that the baby boy who lived but a few minutes was none other than herself in another life. She was deeply moved to learn that this woman she was so jealous of in her present life had been her mother then. She could no longer look at her in the same way. Or at Rodrigo. It was truly a shock to learn that Rodrigo, her adored Rodrigo, the man she was prepared to do anything for, was the Conquistador who had killed her in cold blood.

It had taken a moment for her mind to connect the image of Citlali with that of the Indian woman Rodrigo had raped. They were one and the same! She was certain, because she had examined the photomental of the rape countless times. She knew that face by heart. The photomental had been part of Rodrigo's regression, and Azucena had morbidly held on to it. How many times had she succumbed to the torment of seeing Rodrigo possessing another woman, seeing the lust in his eyes. Now she would consider that image from a different perspective. It must have been traumatic for Citlali to have been raped by the same man who murdered her son. What a horrendous experience! Azucena felt a deep sympathy for her.

Teo immediately understood what Azucena was feeling. Putting his arm around her, he quietly consoled her, and his gentle words had their effect. Azucena relaxed and slipped back into the Alpha state. He suggested that Azucena ask what her mission had been in that life. Meekly Azucena followed his instructions. After a pause she replied that it had been to inform the Aztecs of the importance of the Law of Love, because in breaking it, they were courting danger and could suffer the consequences of the Law of Correspondence. Teo asked Azucena if she had been able to deliver that message. She shook her head, explaining that she'd been murdered before she could pass it on. She spoke of having had another occasion to deliver that message, in 1985, but again she was prevented from doing so. Now Azucena understood that she was being given another opportunity to say what must be said.

At that moment Azucena began to comprehend the reason for everything that had happened. She discovered that there is a logic to all events; everything that happens is the result of some prior occurrence. Following that logic, there is no such thing as injustice. For her, the only question that remained was, why me? Why hadn't they chosen someone else to deliver such an all-important message? She could find no answer, but at least she was now aware of her mission, and had regained her enthusiasm for carrying it out.

But now, too, she had the bad luck of having a new impediment: she could not return to Earth because she, along with everyone else on board the spaceship, was being sought by the police. She was mulling over that problem when Cuquita brought some important news. She had just heard on the radio aboard that a group from several planets was making a pilgrimage to La Villa, in Mexico City, to worship at the shrine of the Virgin of Guadalupe. If they could somehow infiltrate that crowd, it would be impossible for anyone to detect their return to Earth. Azucena was thrilled by this news. She consulted with her companions, and they all agreed to abandon the *Interplanetary Cockfight* on the nearest planet, and travel on the huge spacebus carrying the pilgrims.

CD
Track 8

San Miguel Archangel, little saint,
Don't be so hard, so silent,
Don't go on rejoicing in your past
When it's now I really need you.

Now's when the devil's heating up,
Now's when the saints, there ain't so many,
Now's when the gods are all good-byes,
And sin strolls around so easy.

San Miguel Archangel, little saint, little saint,
San Miguel Archangel, little saint,
Don't stand there like you're made of stone,
While I'm dragged down by disillusion.
I cry cry cry, can't sing anymore.

Now's when Mephisto's ringing my bell.
Now's when the fat cows are growing skinny.
Now's when bribes are a dime a dozen.
And life's pushing me over the edge.

San Miguel, little saint, little saint . . .

LILIANA FELIPE

14

Really, there's nothing I can do about Azucena. No matter how much help you give that woman she always goes and craps things up!

I swore to abide by the Law of Love, and to see that others did the same, and here I am on the verge of breaking it. I'm no longer capable of administering justice. I'm running short on ethics and, what's worse, I feel like the ultimate cynic, sitting on a Guardian Angel throne when in my heart all I want is to be done with the whole lot of those bastards—beginning with Isabel and ending with Nergal, the chief of Hell's secret police!

I thought that with the help of Teo, Azucena would pull herself together and carry out her mission. But no! All she's done is go and fall head over heels in love with him like some teenager, and she can do nothing now but think about him. No, there's no doubt that everyone is playing their part very well—except me! Teo, our undercover Guardian Angel, is *too* efficient, the rascal! He's having the time of his life backing Azucena into corners and pawing at her. His excuse is that he's doing it to keep her pointed toward Divine Love, but the pointer he's using is something else again.

And I'm stuck here like an idiot, while Nergal removes Mammon from his post as Isabel's Devil; and Mammon, who now has all the free time in the world, starts flirting with my sweetheart Lilith. Meanwhile, Azucena, full of romantic ardor, is plotting an armed revolution with Julito that will put an end to Isabel once and for all. God help us!

Since Azucena refuses to look inside herself for answers, she is centering all her attention on finding solutions to other people's problems. Why not! It's a lot easier to see the speck in someone else's eye. Fear of having to plunge right into her own gut, a real terror of mucking around in the shit, has pushed her to look for a collective solution to her problem—forgetting that collective solutions don't always work, because every person must attend to his or her own spiritual evolution. No social organization will ever be able to find the one road that's good for everybody, because Azucena's everyday problems—like those of the rest of humanity—are the result of errors that were left unresolved in the past. Each case is unique. Of course, such errors affect the person's participation in the outside world, but it's not by changing the social order that one's problems are resolved. It's by changing ourselves. When that happens, society is automatically modified. Every internal change has repercussions in the external world.

So what must be changed internally? The answer is found in the past. If we are to overcome them in this lifetime, each person must discover which problems could not be solved in other lives. If not, these problems will remain bound to the past with ties that sooner or later will be converted into chains that will prevent us from carrying out the mission in our present lives. Knowledge of the past is the only way to free ourselves from those chains and to fulfill our mission—our unique, our untransferable, our personal mission. Who the devil told Azucena that organizing a guerrilla war is going to solve all her problems? Wars or revolutions, even though they are sometimes needed and sometimes attain their objective of benefiting society, can also adversely affect individual evolution. Such is the case with Azucena at this particular moment: any activity of that sort will only distract her from her mission.

There are other obstacles to the fulfillment of Divine Will. The most common, and the most damaging, is the Ego. Everyone in the world likes to feel important and appreciated, recognized and honored. To achieve that, they usually make use of the gifts nature has given them. The praise they receive from their writing, their singing, their dancing, their national leadership, makes them forget the reason they were granted those gifts. If they were born with special talents, it was not for personal glory, but because with those gifts they were to serve Divine Will.

Azucena's gift for organization is the primary weapon she can count on if she is to succeed in her mission, but, paradoxically, the way she's going, it'll turn out to be her worst enemy. She's so full of herself right now—caught up in Julito's praise of her skills and intelligence—that she is directing all her free will toward making decisions that will lead to a victory over Isabel. A victory that obviously will mean additional praise for Azucena, but one that will divert her more and more from her mission.

Why is that? Because if she triumphs, she will then be a government politician. Power will convince her that she is a very important woman. Feeling important, she will believe that she is deserving of all kinds of honors and recognition. If she doesn't obtain them immediately, she will feel offended, hurt, and diminished, and will hate the person or persons who've denied her recognition. Why? Because to this day, no one in power has ever reacted differently. That's why. And afterward? She will try to hold on to power any way she can. By scheming, murdering, and—in a word—hating! Resentment will coat her aura with a thick layer of negativity.

The more resentment that accumulates, the less able she will be to hear my counsel, because such messages travel on very subtle vibrations of energy that will be blocked by the curtain of praise that keeps her trapped in self-delusion. Then what? Then we will never exchange another word. That curtain will seal off relations of any kind, and I'll be out in the cold. Me, her Guardian Angel! The one she should in fact be seeking recognition from, not that jackass Julito! What a jerk!

But what am I saying! Here I am insulting an innocent man. It's just that Azucena is beginning to push me over the edge. If she doesn't come around soon, I'm afraid I'm going to end up losing my mind. What I most resent is that because of her I'm losing Lilith. That I can't take! Oh, I know that this, too, is a vulgar problem of ego, and that it's best to set it aside so that it doesn't prevent me from accomplishing my mission with Azucena, but what can I say? I can't control myself. How embarrassing! I know what a pitiful spectacle I must make. A Guardian Angel sick with jealousy— what a perfect story for the tabloids! What makes it even more incredible is that I wrote my doctoral thesis on how a deformed ego can ruin a relationship. Believe me, I know it all by heart.

A person with an ego problem will want as a partner someone who is a prized and valuable object. The most handsome or beautiful, the most intelligent, and so on. An object that only he possesses, because if everybody had the object, it would lose its value. Once he has acquired it, he will take meticulous care of his property to make sure that no one else touches it, that no one steals it, because if it is lost, his ego will feel diminished. The partner is thereby converted into a mere article that confers status and evokes admiration. The egoist will never for a minute wonder whether the object-partner was the one indicated in the Divine Plan. The perfect partner could have walked right by the egoist without even provoking a second look, because he did not possess an observable talent, or muscles, or she was not sufficiently beautiful, or intelligent. This inability to probe the depths of the human soul prevents the egoist from recognizing that partner; instead, the voice of the ego urges him to choose someone not meant for him.

The only way to resolve such mistakes is to convert a negative ego to a positive one through self-awareness. When we know ourselves truly well, we learn to love ourselves and to value ourselves for who we are, not for who our partner is. This love will change the polarity of an aura from negative to positive, and then, thanks to the Law of Correspondence, we can attract the person we were meant to be with in our lifetime. We'll no longer feel unhappy if someone rejects us, because we'll understand that attractions and rejections have to do with karmic law, and not with our value as human beings. Our ego suffers if somebody rejects us, but if we overcome that rejection through knowledge, we will realize that we ourselves are responsible for having broken the Law of Love, and that the only way to restore balance is through Love.

You see? I know it by heart. But that doesn't stop me from being all screwed up.

Shit! Here comes *my* Guardian Angel. That's all I need. He always shows up when our line of communication is fouled, and when I'm behaving like an idiot. But what is it I'm doing wrong? The one who's pissing outside the pot is Azucena, not me. Or *is* it? Maybe I have it backwards and I'm being as big a fool as she is. Maybe I've been waiting for her to change and make everything all right, when the one who needs to change is me. What a fool I am!

So now what do I do?

15

The prayers of the thousands of people traveling in the enormous spacebus filled Azucena's heart with hope. So much faith concentrated in such a relatively small space was contagious. The heat of the votive candles and the smell of incense generated a feeling of warmth, innocence, purity. Azucena felt younger than ever. Her cheeks had taken on a rosy color; her aches and pains had disappeared, and she had completely forgotten her blindness, her arthritic hands, her sciatica. Her relationship with Teo made her feel secure, loved, and desired. She knew it did not matter to him that her skin was wrinkled, that her hair was gray and her teeth not her own. He loved her just the same.

No one can deny that this business of being in love does wonders for a person. Life changes completely. Azucena, cuddled in Teo's arms, felt like the youngest, most beautiful woman in the world. She asked herself whether her emotions were unique, or whether this often happened with people of advanced age. What did it matter if the body was old? The person was the same inside. The desires were the same.

But at the thought of her desires, Azucena suddenly remembered Rodrigo. She had completely forgotten him! That was logical, because with all the kissing she'd been doing, it wasn't easy to remember anything. Besides, Teo had taken it upon himself to convince her that Rodrigo truly loved her more than anyone in the world, and that the only problem was he didn't remember that. Like any other woman, once she accepted that her lover loved no one but her, Azucena was able to tolerate his infidelity. She understood that if Rodrigo felt attracted by Citlali it was because of a fleeting passion in a different life, and that as soon as his reason returned, he would come back to her forever.

Meanwhile, she was getting along famously with Teo, and had no guilt about doing so. Teo had a very interesting theory about fidelity, which she had come to share. He said that a partner is good for someone as long as one's heart is inflamed with love. However, the day the relationship produces hatred, resentment, or any kind of negative emotion, rather than being advantageous, it holds back individual evolution. The soul fills with darkness, and that person can no longer see the path that ultimately will lead to the twin soul, and the recovery of Paradise.

It certainly suited Azucena for Citlali and Rodrigo to be in love, because Rodrigo's infidelity would bring him back to her sooner. In the end, a person spends fourteen thousand lives in which he is unfaithful to his original mate, but, paradoxically, infidelity is the one way to return to her. Of course, this is not infidelity for the sake of infidelity. The love that makes us evolve is the product of a total surrender between two parties. This is the love that grows within a closed circle containing male and female, *yin* and *yang*, the two indispensable elements for the generation of life, pleasure, and equilibrium. When we are in love, we should devote ourselves only to that person, and the more in love we are, and giving of ourselves, the more energy will circulate and the more quickly we will evolve.

But if, say, the man decides to break his circle of energy to make a connection with a new lover, a large part of the energy he had generated will, unavoidably, escape. In those instances, infidelity is damaging. Nevertheless, that does not mean that one must remain faithful to one partner for a lifetime. No, the union should last only as long as loving energy flows between the two partners: once it is no longer present, we should search for a different partner. In sum, the solution is infidelity, but a qualified infidelity. The objective is to keep oneself filled with the energy of love, just as Teo and Azucena were.

Teo, after having spent the night consoling Azucena, was near exhaustion and had fallen asleep. Azucena, on the other hand, was brimming with energy. She jumped out of bed and went to look for Julito, so that they could continue their work on the plan to remove Isabel from power. Azucena was worried that she would never be able to return the capstone of the Pyramid of Love to its rightful place as long as Isabel stood in the way. Why? Simply because Isabel was a total bitch, and only by getting her out of the way would Azucena be free to act.

She found Julito in a remote corner of the ship, working on a bottle of tequila. Azucena sat down beside him. His choice of location was perfect: as far as possible from all the others—the farther the better. That way they could work on their plan without being overheard. Well, that wasn't the only reason. The truth was that Azucena never felt comfortable in crowds. She preferred intimate spaces. Exactly the opposite of Cuquita, who was like a fish in water when surrounded with people. The more there were, the better she liked it.

Azucena was convinced that the great majority of Non-Evos shared this trait. It didn't matter how different they might be in physical appearance, they behaved in a similar way throughout the Cosmos. They understood each other. Azucena was always amazed at the quick ease with which Cuquita related to everyone. In the short space of time they had been traveling with the shipload of pilgrims, she already knew nearly all their life stories. It was incredible how she had been able to put her grandmother's death behind her. Azucena believed that part of it might be that Cuquita could still see her grandmother. She hadn't had time to feel she'd lost her, because in fact she hadn't. Her grandmother wasn't exactly there, but in a way she was; bearing Azucena's soul, but still alive.

Whatever the reason, it was fortunate that after everything that had happened, Cuquita hadn't lost her sense of humor. She wandered around from group to group, poking into all the conversations. One of the groups was arguing over whether someone had taken a shot before or after . . . the other was struck in the head? Cuquita thought they were talking about the Bush assassination and ran over to hear the latest bit of gossip, but she was disappointed to discover they were arguing about the finals of the Interplanetary Soccer Championship between Earth and Jupiter—in which Earth had lost. Cuquita was of the opinion that the person responsible for the loss was the trainer, because he hadn't played Hugo Sánchez. They should have paid attention to his wife, who kept screaming from the stands, "Put him in, put him in!"

That was the tenor of the conversation when someone asked Cuquita whether she knew anything about Mr. Bush's murder. That made her a little nervous, but as she didn't want to arouse their suspicion, she took a deep breath and prepared to give a suitable answer. As was her way, her comments began normally enough. In a loud voice, she warned everyone present not to let themselves be swayed by the news programs, because the people who had been accused of the crime were nothing more than the sacrificial limbs of the system. Everyone was satisfied with that explanation and apparently no one noticed that Cuquita got her words mixed up, or, if they did, they didn't seem to mind. Well, Azucena thought, "Birds of a feather . . ."

Once the pilgrims saw how well informed Cuquita was, they asked her opinion about the direction things were taking in Mexico. What worried them most was all the recent violence. Cuquita agreed, saying she hoped that soon they would discover whose Macrobellian mind had planned those horrible murders.

"Murders? We thought there had only been one—Mr. Bush's. Were there others?"

Azucena was getting upset. She was going to have to find a way to silence Cuquita, or else she'd spill everything and sink them all. So Azucena asked Julito to lead her over to Cuquita in order to defuse the conversation, but by the time she reached her side, it was no longer necessary: Cuquita had smoothly switched to a different topic and was entertaining her audience with a theory about why Popocatépetl had vomited. She told them that in case they didn't know, the volcano absorbed the energy and thoughts of everyone who lived on Earth, and that recently he had been feeding on a diet of shock and violence, which was why he'd developed indigestion and belched up the sulfurous blasts that accompanied the earthquake they already knew about. The pilgrims were astounded by Cuquita's explanation, which made them even more convinced that things in Mexico were growing worse. If Popocatépetl was that steamed up he might set loose a chain reaction among all the volcanoes connected to him through underground channels, thereby provoking a world catastrophe that would affect not only the inhabitants of Earth but everyone in the Solar System.

If only Rodrigo hadn't gone off with Citlali, Azucena might have been less sensitive to the pain of the gravel digging into her knees. She and her companions had been on their knees a long time, still masquerading as pilgrims, inching forward with the thousands trying to enter the Basilica of the Virgin of Guadalupe. So as not to awaken suspicion, they had decided to wait until after the Mass to break away from the worshipers. The only ones who had risked leaving were Rodrigo and Citlali: Citlali because she urgently needed to get back to her house; and Rodrigo, to follow her. In addition, Citlali could not see any reason why she should remain with this dangerous group, since neither Rodrigo, in the body of Cuquita's former husband, nor she, was being sought by the police.

Before they left, Azucena, feigning indifference, had quickly bid them farewell. Teo knew very well, however, that she was torn up inside. Supportive as always, he had not left her side, lending his great physical and spiritual support. Had it not been for Teo, who knows how Azucena could have borne the loss of Rodrigo. She was able to tolerate his infidelity as long as he was near her, but not when he was gone.

With great tenderness, Teo attempted to make up for Rodrigo's absence, guiding Azucena along the easiest route to El Pocito. This was a natural spring where from time immemorial the Aztecs had purified themselves before offering tribute to the goddess Tonantzin. The ritual had continued, uninterrupted, from the time of the Conquest, but for some time it had been performed in honor of the Virgin of Guadalupe. The purpose of this ceremony was to remove all impurities of thought, word, and deed before entering the Basilica, by washing one's face, hands, and feet in the pool. Teo, the perfect guide, avoided obstacles of every kind as he led Azucena to the edge of El Pocito. She leaned over and cupped water in her hands, but before she could splash it on her face to purify herself, Cuquita hurried up to her and whispered:

"Don't turn around, but right behind us is that guy who's been using your ex-body."

Azucena's heart jumped. That could only mean that Isabel's men had already caught up with them.

A split second later, Cuquita, Azucena, and Teo were on their feet and moving through the crowds, with Ex-Azucena hot on their heels. It was nearly impossible to push through the oncoming throngs, especially for the blind Azucena. Teo decided to pick her up and carry her, since she had already stepped on at least six people moving toward the shrine on their knees. After only a few minutes of pushing through the masses of people pressing toward them, they had lost Ex-Azucena, but then bumped into two policemen who regarded them suspiciously and began following them. Teo, still carrying Azucena, who had fainted, picked up speed and told Cuquita to follow as he zigzagged through the crowds. He knew his way around this part of the city because he had grown up here. When they came to a certain corner, he beckoned Cuquita into an abandoned building. Laying Azucena down on the floor, he softly began to kiss her forehead. Azucena regained consciousness. Teo put his hand over her mouth to keep her from making a sound that might betray their whereabouts to the two policemen, who had stopped in front of the door to the building. Cuquita, contrary to her nature, also kept quiet. The only thing they could hear was the pounding of their hearts, the loudspeaker of a spacecraft announcing the Televirtual debate between the European and American candidates for Planetary President . . . and Ex-Azucena's sobs.

Teo and Cuquita whirled around and spotted him hiding there in the shadows of the ruined building. He looked bedraggled and terrified. As soon as he saw that he had been discovered, he motioned for them to remain quiet. Teo whispered to Azucena what was happening. She was shocked to learn that the bodyguard seemed to be in the same predicament they were.

As soon as the police moved on, Cuquita gave Ex-Azucena a piece of her mind.

"So now it's the big crybaby, eh? Well, what about when you were going around liquefying everybody? So you thought the police were never going to find you! Hey, wait a minute. If the police know you're the one who had a body change after you killed Bush, then they also know that we're innocent. So, now *you'll* see, I'm turning you in!"

Cuquita began heading for the doorway to call the police, but Ex-Azucena pulled her back.

"Hang on a minute! The cops still believe you're the ones who killed Mr. Bush, and if they see you here, they're going to drag you off to the slammer, I can tell you . . . Honest, it won't help you to turn me in—it's not the police I'm hiding from."

"Well, who *are* you hiding from?" asked Azucena.

"Isabel González."

"But isn't she your boss?" Cuquita wanted to know.

"She was, but she fired me. Oh, it was just horrible—and all because I'm pregnant."

Azucena was livid. This ex-ballerina bodyguard, thanks to having *her* body, was now going to have a baby. The lousy bitch! Envy flooded Azucena's soul. How she longed to have her own body back, to experience pregnancy, which was forbidden to her as long as she was in the body of Cuquita's grandmother. Anger shot straight to her head, like wine, and before Teo could stop her, Azucena leapt upon Ex-Azucena and began scratching and clawing.

"You slut! How dare you get pregnant in a body that doesn't belong to you!"

Ex-Azucena bent over to protect his belly. It was all he could do. There was no hope that he could fight back against the pummeling he was taking from the crazed old woman.

"I didn't get it pregnant, it was already that way!"

Azucena stopped dead. "Already that way?"

"Yes."

Blood pounded in Azucena's temples, and for a moment she was as deaf as she was blind. If that body was already pregnant before the bodyguard took it over, then the baby this man was expecting was hers—she had conceived the child with Rodrigo during that one marvelous night of their honeymoon. Azucena grabbed hold of his belly as though she were trying to snatch away the child that did not belong to him; to feel through his skin the least sign of movement, of life . . . of love; to communicate to the baby that she was its mother; to bring back the memory of Rodrigo on that day he had made love to her. She seemed as though she were begging forgiveness of this baby she had unknowingly abandoned. Had she known she was pregnant, she never would have given up that body. Never! And now she would give anything, everything, to have the baby in her own womb, to feel it grow, to nurse it, to see it! But it was too late for all that. Now she was in the body of a blind old woman with dried-up breasts and arthritic arms, someone who had nothing to offer the baby but love. Feeling Teo's arm around her shoulder brought Azucena back to reality. She buried her head in his chest, weeping disconsolately. Her sobs blended with those of Ex-Azucena.

"None of you knows what it means for me to have this baby. Don't turn me in. You wouldn't be that cruel. Help me, please, they want to kill me!"

"But why?" asked Azucena, interrupting her own tears. She was concerned now for the future of her child.

"Because you're pregnant?" asked Cuquita.

"No! Don't be silly. That was why they fired me. No, they're going to kill me because that Jezebel doesn't know the meaning of gratitude. Look how she treated me—and after all the years I've slaved for her! What I didn't do for that woman! I anticipated her every whim. I worked thousands of hours overtime. There was no job she gave me that I didn't immediately take care of. . . . Well, there was one I never had the heart for, and that was to kill her daughter."

"That fat girl?" Cuquita interrupted.

"No, the other one, the one she had before her . . . a cute, skinny little thing. How could I ever kill a little baby girl, crazy as I was to have a kid myself. Imagine!"

"So then, who did kill the girl?" asked Azucena.

"No one. I would have liked to have kept her myself, but I couldn't. Working as close to Doña Isabel as I did, sooner or later she would have found out. What could I do! I took her to an orphanage . . ."

The word "orphanage" penetrated Azucena's heart with an icy blast that sent chills up and down her spine. It brought back memories of the cold institution where she had spent her childhood. She shivered, feeling a bond with the poor little girl who, like her, had grown up without a family.

"That's terrible! That must have been one of the most unhappiest satisfactions of your life," remarked Cuquita in her inimitable style.

"Uh, yes," said Ex-Azucena, not really understanding what Cuquita had meant to say.

"But why did Isabel want her killed!" asked Teo, intervening for the first time in the conversation.

"Well, because the little girl's astrological chart said she might topple Isabel from a position of power someday. But me, I think it was pure meanness. I don't know why God gave children to that woman when she never wanted them. You should see how she treats her other daughter, and only because the poor thing's a little heavy."

"Okay, okay, but you still haven't told us why they want to get rid of you," Cuquita insisted.

"Well, because when she told me she didn't want to see me around there a minute more, well, I felt really bad, you know? The witch was tossing me out, and I couldn't swallow that, could I? And so I began thinking about how I'd love to see the lousy bitch changed into a diseased rat, and then have a satellite fall on her and splatter her to kingdom come, and about then, in came one of those head analysts who are always recording what we're thinking, and he told her what was showing up on the screen, and you can imagine how she reacted!"

"But why didn't they kill you then and there!" Cuquita asked, half disappointed that they had let him get away.

"Well, because my buddy Agapito didn't have the nerve. He told the boss that he'd done it, that he'd disintegrated me, but it wasn't true. He hid me in his room until we reached Earth because . . . well, because he sort of likes me, and . . . sort of liked being with me, you know. Then he left me here so I could pray to the Virgin of Guadalupe for help, because he couldn't do anything more for me, but you saw what happened. I didn't even have time to ask for my miracle."

"Hmmm. One thing I'm not clear about. How was it that the photomental camera recorded your real thoughts?" asked Azucena.

"The way it always does, I guess."

"That can't be. My body, I mean, your body, has an implanted microcomputer programmed to emit positive thoughts. With that computer working, it would have been impossible to have photo-mentaled your real thoughts."

"Oh, really? Then maybe the computer you say I got up here failed . . . or had a nervous breakdown . . . I don't know. But what-ever it was, Isabel nearly had a stroke."

Azucena, remembering that Dr. Díez had told her that his invention was still in the experimental stages, got excited. That meant that the computer Isabel had in *her* head might act up during the debate that was scheduled to take place within a few hours. What the panel of reporters intended to do during that debate was dig into the candidates' past ten lives, according to the rules of qualification, to see which of the two had the cleanest record. Each one of them, separately, would have to submit to a music-induced regression. Naturally, the reporters had chosen musical themes that would trigger a direct connection with the dark and macabre in the subconscious. If only the apparatus Dr. Díez had fitted Isabel with would fail, as Ex-Azucena's had, Isabel would be revealed to the eyes of the world for the liar she was.

They had to see that debate! It was not something they could afford to miss, but first they had to find Julito, whom they had lost somewhere in the crowd. They finally came across him selling bogus tickets for the purifying waters of El Pocito. Before they had left the building where they had been hiding, Azucena stopped at the door and invited Ex-Azucena to come along with them. Ex-Azucena thanked her profusely.

"Don't thank me. I'm not doing it to be nice, but because I want to be near the man who's going to have my baby."

"Good heavens!" exclaimed Ex-Azucena. He couldn't believe that Azucena's soul was in the body of that little old lady.

"Yes, it's me, and you can get that idiotic look off your face. You didn't kill me, you bastard, just my body, but I'm not going to forget that you tried."

Just as Ex-Azucena was attempting to apologize to Azucena for having killed her, they heard the sound of running feet and ducked into a side street. In silence, they watched as Rodrigo and Citlali ran toward them. Citlali was terrified. Everywhere they'd gone, they'd seen posters with a picture of Citlali's aurograph. She and Rodrigo—more accurately, the body Rodrigo was currently occupying—were accused of being the masterminds behind the plot to assassinate Mr. Bush. As soon as Citlali saw Azucena, Teo, and

Cuquita, she ran to meet them, hugged them warmly, and begged them to help.

"Oh, right," scolded Cuquita. "We look good to you now, huh? But when we needed you, where was your royalty then?"

Azucena prevented the two women from becoming entangled in an endless string of mutual recriminations. She welcomed Rodrigo and Citlali warmly, blessing the "Wanted" posters that had sent the pair running back to them.

Teo's house looked like a substation of the Shrine of Guadalupe. It had, out of necessity, become a sanctuary for everybody. Azucena, Rodrigo, Cuquita, and Julito could not in a million years go back to their apartment building. Citlali's house had been searched by the police, and Ex-Azucena's—besides being watched—had been badly damaged by the earthquake. None of them, as a result, had any choice but to accept Teo's cordial offer. He lived in a small apartment in Tlatelolco. He felt at home in that part of Mexico City, as it had been his haunt in several previous incarnations.

It was the moment for the debate between the two candidates for Planetary President, and all of Teo's guests were sitting around his TV, ready to watch. Like Cuquita, Teo had only a 3-D set, but no one protested. All that interested them was to be able to witness the moment when Isabel made a fool of herself. Azucena was desperate at not being able to see the show. Since Teo was busy preparing dinner for them, Cuquita was charged with narrating to Azucena what was happening, an arrangement that turned out to be a real cross for Azucena. Cuquita couldn't chew gum and report at the same time; she had never been able to do two things simultaneously, so now she was either watching the screen or telling what had happened. She would become entranced by the interesting parts and her tongue would freeze while she gaped at the images. All Azucena could do was listen to the music being played during the regression and repeatedly ask Cuquita what was happening on the screen.

Azucena didn't have much of a choice. Rodrigo and Citlali were hugging and smooching at every opportunity and had no time for anything besides themselves. Ex-Azucena was a disaster; he freely embellished the picture, narrating more than he actually saw, and there was no way to shut him up once he began talking. Julito was already half drunk, and kept making stupid remarks, so Azucena's only option was Cuquita, however hopeless she seemed.

It was bad enough that she would suddenly fall silent; but in addition, she dozed during the boring parts, so that Azucena didn't know whether what was happening was incredibly interesting or incredibly dull. Right then, however, things were definitely dull. The European candidate's most recent ten lives were the most boring anyone could imagine. Cuquita had fallen into such a deep sleep that she wasn't even snoring. Azucena hated the silence, it left her in total darkness. She needed the sound of a voice in order to connect to the present, otherwise, her senses were left at the mercy of the same music the presidential candidates were hearing, and her mind would begin to wander. She became lost in the blackness to which she was condemned and ended up traveling through her own past lives. There was nothing terrible about that, but it wasn't what she wanted. She wanted to be the first to know whether or not Isabel's computer would fail her.

When Isabel's turn came to be regressed, the silence in the room was absolute. All of them had their fingers crossed, hoping the implanted computer would malfunction. Isabel's first three lives were reviewed without incident. Her problems began when they came to her life as Mother Teresa. At first it went very well. Images of her life as a saint appeared on the screen in meticulous detail. She was shown carrying an undernourished child in Ethiopia, distributing food among lepers, but then . . . the microcomputer finally fizzled out!

CD
Track 9

Rodrigo yelled, "That's my regression! That woman was me!"

Upon hearing this, Azucena was startled back to the present from where she had been wandering in memory. The silence of Cuquita, as well as the others, had left her at the mercy of the music and she herself had slipped into regression—not too far into the past, only to the beginning of her present lifetime. She learned that it had been an extremely difficult birth. The umbilical cord had been wrapped three times around her neck. Three times! She had barely escaped being stillborn. The doctors had revived her, but she had come very close to succeeding in strangling herself. And the reason she had wanted to kill herself was that she knew her mother was going to be none other than Isabel González. What a nightmare! And *she* was that daughter Isabel had ordered killed! To add to the complications, Ex-Azucena, the bodyguard she held such a grudge against for having killed her body and claimed it for his own, was the person who had saved her life when she was a baby. It seemed that on the one hand she owed him her life; and on the other hand, her death.

Rodrigo's shouting once again startled her from her thoughts.

"Azucena! Did you hear me? Isabel's life is the same one *I* saw!"

Azucena was so stunned by what she had just discovered about herself that it took a while to realize what Rodrigo—aided, of course, by that busybody Cuquita—was trying to tell her: that Isabel was a murderer of the worst kind, that in one lifetime she had impaled people, that in another she had stabbed and killed Rodrigo's brother-in-law, and that now everything was going to come out in the open, that she'd been hogtied and humiliated in front of the entire population of the planet, that she deserved it for being such a monster, that she was sure to be killed for having deceived everybody with the microcomputer she had implanted in her head, that it was only a matter of time until they themselves were going to be exonerated completely, and on and on.

That pipe dream ended when Teo made everyone quiet down and watch what was happening. The television screen was blank. An announcement was being made to viewers explaining that the station was experiencing technical difficulties. Abel Zabludowsky was reading a special bulletin from the Planetary Attorney General's office, informing the public of reported sabotage. In sum, what they were attempting to do was to convince viewers that the images they had just seen were faked, that they were transmitted by saboteurs who had taken over the Televirtual studio and whose objective was to smear Isabel.

"No!" they all shouted. "We saw it with our own eyes!"

Azucena was desperate. They had to prove somehow that Isabel was a liar. It was the only way to defeat her. Julito quickly began taking bets on whether or not they'd succeed. The pessimists among them were inclined toward failure, but not Azucena. She could not give up. She was ready to go to the final round, to do whatever it took to win, even if that meant all-out war. But it wasn't that simple. On Earth, no one had weapons. She and Julito had a plan to organize a guerrilla force, but to carry it off they needed money, contacts, and a spacecraft for transporting the arms—and they had none of those things.

The most direct action they could manage would be to present proof that the images the entire world had seen were authentic. They had to get their hands on them. But where? If only they still had the cybernetic Ouija! They'd had to leave it in Julito's spaceship, and the ship itself had been left behind on a very distant planet. Well, no use crying over that. They'd had no choice. Even worse was that, in leaving Azucena's apartment so abruptly, they'd lost the photos of Rodrigo's regression, the compact disc, the Discman, the African violet with its information, and all the photographs relating to the murder of Dr. Díez. And they had no way of recovering any of it.

Azucena didn't know where to begin. She went to look for Teo, and put her arms around him. She wanted him to flood her with peace. She was so exhausted from thinking, that she let her mind go blank, and, as she did, the diamond in her forehead filled her with Divine Light. She experienced a moment of incredible lucidity. She remembered that during the regression she had guided Rodrigo through on the spaceship, she had learned from him that Citlali, the Indian he had raped in 1521, had raped him in 1890, during his life as a woman. If the male Citlali was the brother-in-law who had raped Rodrigo, then she'd been Isabel's brother. And therefore, if they could perform a regression with Citlali, they would have access to the scene where Isabel the husband murdered Citlali, his brother.

It was exasperating not to have the music they needed at hand. Azucena tried to console herself by thinking that even if they could perform the regression and get new photomentals, the images wouldn't help in any case, since they couldn't very well take them to the police while they themselves were being sought. They'd have to get new proof somewhere else.

Citlali remembered that she still had the spoon Azucena had been so interested in at the flea market. Azucena brightened a moment, but her spirits fell once again as she realized that they didn't have the cybernetic Ouija to test it. It would have been extremely helpful to obtain an analysis of the spoon. Azucena remembered that in one of the photos in Rodrigo's regression the face of the rapist was reflected in the spoon, along with the face of the person who had stolen up behind him to stab him in the back—that is, the face of Isabel in her male incarnation. That would surely be convincing evidence to incriminate our sweet candidate!

What a nuisance not to be able to obtain that image! Cuquita suggested that they try to perform a regression on the spoon.

Everyone laughed at her but Azucena, who thought her suggestion made a lot of sense. All objects vibrate and are susceptible to music, possessing the additional advantage of not being afflicted with the emotional blocks that hamper human beings. But the plan was still stymied because they had no music to set the spoon vibrating, nor a photomental camera to register the memories. Cuquita came to the rescue, offering to sing a favorite *danzón*. She said she didn't need any accompaniment. So Teo pulled out a beat-up old photomental camera from a closet and everyone concentrated together to make the experiment work.

Rodrigo was to hold the spoon in his hand to activate memories of the life they wanted to revisit. And Cuquita, with absolute self-assurance, began to belt out the lyrics of "At Your Mercy," at the top of her lungs.

Intermission for Dancing

CD
Track 10

For everyone who enjoys
Vegetables and fruits
Comes this danzón *dedicated*
To Your Mercy Marketplace.

The mangoes all were chatting about how
The limes were so fresh,
And how the ordinary orange
Thinks she's such a tangerine.
And the prickly pears, led on
By the two-faced apple,
Grabbed the poor olives
For a midday snack.
Everything passes, everything passes,
Even . . . the prune passes.

Señoras, don't be so petty,
For all of us are tasty enough.
Some think they're fancy currants
But are only sour grapes.
"Ooh, what grand neighbors I have,"
Mocked the dark-skinned sapodilla,
Who later criticized the quince
For looking like a yellow gringo.
"Don't be so vulgar,"
Replied the pomegranate,
"You're just a swarthy sapodilla
And no one said anything to you."
Everything passes, everything passes,
Even . . . the prune passes.

LILIANA FELIPE

Cuquita lapped up the thunderous, ego-stroking applause. Her voice, more jolting than ammonia, shook out of the spoon every last drop of its rape scene. The fugitives were very pleased with themselves. The images were clear, although the reflections in the spoon were small and difficult to see. Teo had to go to his computer to make enlargements. Among them, he obtained a perfect reproduction of the male Isabel's face at the very moment she was murdering her brother, the male Citlali. But despite this, they could still not say that their problems were solved.

What they had was evidence that proved to them they were correct in their suppositions, but a good lawyer would discredit that photo in a second if they offered it as proof of Isabel's guilt. He could say, yes, that probably was the face of the murderer, but the photo in no way proved conclusively that the murderer was Isabel. And he would be correct, because the images revealed to the world on Televirtual as a part of Isabel's regression showed the scene not in the reflection in the spoon but from a different perspective: the murderer's, and in those images the killer was never seen. The fact that the crime was viewed through the murderer's eyes meant that his face was at no time visible, and therefore a photograph of it, though authentic, could not serve to implicate Isabel. The defense could allege that the image in the spoon had been computer enhanced. It was a shame, because the photograph was so good.

Azucena was totally frustrated that she herself could not examine the photo. Her only recourse was to recreate in her mind the description Rodrigo gave her. As she began visualizing it, Azucena felt as if she were close to retrieving some forgotten fact. Suddenly, she cried out: "I have it!" According to what Rodrigo had told her, Citlali's male face appeared in the foreground of the reflection in the spoon. In the middle distance was Isabel's male face. And in the background was the upper portion of a stained glass window. Azucena's pulse began beating more rapidly. The description of the stained glass was identical to that of the window she had watched fall toward her in 1985. The scene of the earthquake flashed before her mind with the same intensity she had felt the first time she'd viewed it. In a flash she again witnessed Rodrigo picking her up in his arms; saw the ceiling falling toward them; again experienced the confusion, pain, silence, dust, blood, debris; saw the legs of someone walking over to where she lay; and the hands lifting a stone that in an instant would thud down upon her head . . . and in the split second before the impact, she saw the hatred on Isabel's face. She remembered that at the precise moment she had turned her head, trying to avoid being crushed by the stone, and . . . her mind stopped, a blank. Her recollections froze into a single image: just before she died, as she turned away, her eyes—she was sure of it!—had caught a glimpse of the Pyramid of Love buried beneath the rubble of the house. Engraved in her mind was the scene in which Rodrigo had raped Citlali. Her mental masturbations had made her return to it again and again, but now she remembered that Rodrigo had told her that he'd raped Citlali on the Temple of Love. That was the same pyramid she had seen beneath her house as she died. So all she had to do was find out the exact location of the house and look for the Pyramid.

As long as she was having no luck in rejoining her twin soul, at least she could fulfill her mission in life. Azucena asked Teo to help her and quickly got to work. With the help of a pendulum and a map, she soon pinpointed the address of the house. Ex-Azucena nearly choked when he heard it—that was Isabel's address! This complicated everything. Ex-Azucena confirmed that in fact a pyramid had long been struggling to break through the patio of that house. Azucena realized they were in real trouble for sure now, because Isabel's house was an impregnable fortress and none of them could possibly gain entry. Ex-Azucena, however, gave them heart. He knew a way to get into the fortress, and that was through Carmela, Azucena's sister, Isabel's fat daughter. Carmela truly loved Ex-Azucena. He was the only person who had shown her any affection during her childhood, staying by her side when she was ill, helping her with homework, bringing her flowers on her birthday, taking her out Sunday afternoons, telling her she was pretty, and never neglecting to kiss her good night. He was absolutely sure, therefore, that if he asked her for help, she would not refuse him, because she had been like a daughter to him.

"And besides," he said, "she won't care if we're using her help to get at Isabel, because the truth is, she never loved her mother. The hatred between them has always been mutual."

Teo commented that it was precisely the smoldering resentment generated by such relationships that had given rise to revolutions throughout history. At any given moment, the outcasts, the forgotten, the mistreated banded together against the powerful. The sad part was that once the downtrodden had triumphed and replaced those in power, their only thought was revenge and they ended up being no better than the ones they'd unseated—until, in turn, a new group of malcontents seized power from them. That, unfortunately, was the way things went. Only when they are the oppressed do people see injustice for what it is. When they are in a position of power, they will rule without mercy, resorting to anything to avoid losing the throne.

It is extremely difficult to pass the test of power. Most people become possessed by demons, forgetting everything they've learned as one of the powerless and committing all manner of atrocities. The solution for humanity will come only on that day when those who assume power do so by acting in accordance with the Law of Love. Azucena was convinced that this would happen only at the moment when the Pyramid was restored to its proper function. All the others were in agreement with her, and so they resolved to get in contact with Carmela.

Unfortunately, at that very moment, just as they were nearing the point of solving their problem, just when they had all the necessary information at hand, the police arrived to arrest them.

16

No holds were barred during the trial of Isabel González. The Law of Love was at stake. Anacreonte advised Azucena, while Mammon defended Isabel. Nergal, chief of Hell's secret police, was special counsel to the defense, and the Archangel Michael, to the prosecutors. Devils and cherubim alike looked after the jurors. Mammon prayed. Anacreonte cursed. And they all tried every dirty trick in the book. The battle was bloody: only the strongest would survive. But it was impossible to predict the outcome. From the very beginning it was obvious that both sides had an equal chance at victory.

Isabel had trained hard. Since she knew she had to fight a clean fight, that is, without the aid of a microcomputer, she had enlisted the help of a shady guru. Well aware that the jury would be composed primarily of mediums, Isabel reasoned that to convince them of her innocence it was imperative that she master—by sheer willpower—the images her mind emitted. After months of intense training, she was able to impede her true thoughts and to project, strongly and clearly, whatever images she chose to have others observe. She had become extremely skillful in preventing mediums from gaining entry to her private thoughts. They were thoroughly perplexed. They did not trust her, yet they could find nothing false in her testimony. Thus in plain view Isabel managed to inflict a series of low blows, without anyone's realizing it.

ROUND ONE
Right Cross!

The first to come forward to testify on behalf of the defense had been Ricardo Rodríguez, Cuquita's husband. The dummy had accepted a bribe in return for confessing to Mr. Bush's murder. Isabel had promised him that as soon as she won her case and ascended to power, she would pardon him. Ricardo Rodríguez took her at her word, convinced he'd end up living like a king for the rest of his days. What he didn't know was that Isabel's word meant nothing, and that she couldn't have cared less about helping him. Ricardo had fastened the noose around his own neck and, in the process, entangled Cuquita, Azucena, Rodrigo, Citlali, Teo, and Julito, by accusing them of being his accomplices.

ROUND TWO
Jab to the Kidneys!

The prosecution answered that first blow with testimony from Ex-Azucena, who explained in minute detail his participation in the murders of Mr. Bush, Azucena, and Dr. Díez. He related how each had been killed and accused Isabel of being the mastermind. The jury was clearly moved, not only by the sincerity of his statements but by the angelic appearance of a woman nine months pregnant.

ROUND THREE
Below the Belt!

To counter the positive effect of Ex-Azucena's testimony, the defense called Agapito to the stand. Agapito claimed that while it was true Ex-Azucena had been involved with him in all the murders, Ex-Azucena had acted on his, Agapito's, orders—not Isabel's. He declared himself to be the mastermind of all the crimes, absolving Isabel of all responsibility. He stated that he alone had planned the murders. He could not provide a convincing motive for having committed the crimes, but the one fact he emphasized over and over was that he had acted completely on his own. Isabel gained a lot of ground with this testimony.

ROUND FOUR
Left Jab!

As the next witness, the prosecutor called Cuquita, but the lawyer for the defense attempted to disqualify her from testifying. Her past life as a film critic made her a witness of dubious credibility. It was not that she'd been a critic per se, but rather that her sole motivation as such had been envy. Innumerable venomous reviews had flowed from her pen. She had maliciously meddled in the private lives of everyone she wrote about. The few times she had written anything favorable, it had been merely the result of cronyism, never impartial analysis. Furthermore, in her curriculum vitae there was no evidence to show that she'd ever repaid that karma.

Cuquita claimed over and over that she had done so by living with her husband, who was a royal pain in the ass, but the defense lawyer countered that assertion with depositions that characterized Ricardo Rodríguez in highly favorable terms, referring to him as a saint and stating that the one with the checkered past was Cuquita. Cuquita was furious, but there was nothing she could do.

What annoyed her more than anything was that she had missed her opportunity to perform before the Televirtual cameras. All her life she had been preparing for the possibility that one day she would be a witness to a crime. In every trip she made to the market, she tried to memorize the features of all the customers, in case later she would need to describe one of them to the police. Or she would attempt to remember every detail of her expedition: how many people were at the vegetable stands, how many oranges her neighbor had bought, what denominations of coins she'd used to pay, whether she'd haggled with the vendor over the price, whether the vendor had threatened her with a knife. And that wasn't all.

Her tabloid mind-set made her think about the remote chance that she might end up as the victim rather than the witness, so she also prepared for that eventuality. She never left home with a hole in her underwear or stockings. She was terrified by the possibility that she'd be taken to the hospital, and the doctors, removing her outer clothing, would discover how slovenly she was. And now, all that preparation down the drain!

ROUND FIVE
Jolting Hook to the Kidneys!

The prosecutor, set back by the dismissal of his previous witness, called Citlali to the stand. Her testimony could prove damaging. While serving her sentence in the prison rehabilitation program, she had had more than enough time to work through her past lives. It had become very clear to her just what her connections to Isabel had been. Citlali began her testimony by recounting her life in 1521. In that incarnation, Citlali had murdered Isabel's newborn baby, and Isabel had died hating her. In their next parallel lives, Isabel and she had been brothers. Citlali had raped her brother's wife, and, in return, Isabel had murdered her.

Then the Law of Love had come into play to balance the relationship between them, causing them to be born as mother and daughter, to see whether those ties could ease the hatred Citlali felt for Isabel. All in vain. Isabel had never loved her daughter. She more or less tolerated her as a little girl, but as soon as Citlali reached adolescence, Isabel perceived her as an enemy. Isabel had been divorced in that life. As the years went by, she had met Rodrigo and had fallen in love with him. They had married when Citlali was still a girl, but when Citlali began to turn into a young woman, Rodrigo, to Isabel's horror, had begun looking at her with different eyes. Finally, the day came when what Isabel most feared happened. Rodrigo and Citlali ran away from Isabel's home and became lovers.

Isabel found them living in a run-down old mansion in the center of the city. Citlali was pregnant and madly in love. Isabel was furious. Jealousy drove her over the edge. The day of the earthquake in 1985, she had run to where the lovers lived, not to see if her daughter Citlali was still alive but because she wanted to know whether Rodrigo had survived the earthquake. She had found them both dead, but beneath the rubble she discovered Azucena— who in that life was her granddaughter—alive. Blind with hatred, she had crushed the infant's head with a stone.

ROUND SIX
Below the Belt!

Citlali's testimony had hurt Isabel but, as always, when it seemed she was down for the count, the defense attorney turned things around 180 degrees and seemed to make the facts favor Isabel.

First, he asked Citlali what proof she had to substantiate her testimony. Citlali had none. The reason was that several years back Isabel had tracked her down, taking advantage of a moment when Citlali was in the hospital, to program her mind so that Citlali would never remember the lives in which she witnessed Isabel's crimes. Who knows what techniques they had used in the rehabilitation program to allow her access to those lives; but the fact was that while she was able to gain entry into those memories, her mind was unable to project them as evidence, because Isabel had put a block on her ability to project images. The only person who knew the password to override that program was Isabel herself, and it would be a cold day in hell before she'd let that out. So Citlali's testimony ended up having about as much impact as a leaf in a storm.

In addition, the defense attorney insisted that in 1985 Isabel was not Isabel, but Mother Teresa. He reminded the jury that Isabel was a former saint who had achieved a very high degree of evolution and was absolutely truthful. He asked them to look her in the eye and satisfy themselves that she was innocent of the crimes she was charged with.

Isabel withstood the penetrating gaze of mediums without flinching. The jury could not detect the least sign of deception in her eyes. Isabel smiled. Everything was working out just as she'd planned. She was certain that no one would be able to prove anything against her. Immediately after the presidential debate, she had had the microcomputer removed from her head, and there was no proof she'd ever had one. She had ordered her house to be dynamited, to avoid the possibility of having its walls analyzed. They would have provided damning evidence. Fortunately for her, no trace of them remained.

The only thing she hadn't fully managed to control was the extent of the explosion. It had uncovered the pyramid in her patio. But that hadn't been much of a problem. Before the police arrived to investigate the apparent assassination attempt against her, she had had time to remove the apex of the Pyramid of Love from the rubble. This stone had been her only remaining concern. She had taken it to the shrine of Our Lady of Guadalupe, and dropped it into the waters of El Pocito. She felt sure that no one would ever find it again. As long as the Temple of Love was not functioning, people would concentrate their love on themselves, not being able to see beyond their own image in the water's reflection. There was no better place to hide it. It would never be found, and therefore no one could use it to prove her culpability. She felt calm and collected. The rose quartz stone she had used to murder Azucena in 1985 was certainly not about to float.

Carmela was next to give testimony as a witness for the defense. She was truly unrecognizable. The time that had passed since her mother's presidential debate had completely transformed her. The principal reason was that Carmela had met her sister, Azucena, and that had given Carmela a different view of the world. The meeting between the two had turned out to be more beneficial than anyone would have imagined. They had come to love each other so much that Carmela, from the pure pleasure of being accepted and appreciated, had lost five hundred and twenty-eight pounds.

The first meeting between the two had taken place in the visitors' room of the José López Guido Rehabilitation Facility. Azucena had been sentenced to spend several months there. Those months turned out to be the most pleasant of her entire life, since the first thing prison officials did with new inmates was give them an examination to determine how much rejection and love privation had accumulated in their hearts. Using that information as a base, a plan was elaborated to replace any and all lack of love, because the staff was aware that the absence of love is the source of criminal behavior, fault finding, aggression, and resentment.

Azucena did not suffer through her sentence; she enjoyed it. At this institution, the greater the lack of love in one's past lives, the greater the coddling one received as treatment. For it was through love and attention that criminals were reintegrated into society. Of course, if it was discovered during the examination that a criminal had not actually been deprived of love but had acted under a Demon's influence, then that person was sent to the Alphonse Capone Memorial Pavilion at Negro Durazo Prison, where they specialized in performing exorcisms.

This was in fact what had happened to Julito. They had sent him to prison there, arguing that he was possessed by the Devil, and that "an enormous arsenal of explosives" had been uncovered in his house. Nothing of the sort: the "arsenal" actually consisted of some fireworks Julito used in his Interplanetary Cockfight productions; but since there was no way he could convince the authorities of his innocence, he was carted off to the Pavilion. Rodrigo, Cuquita, Ex-Azucena, Citlali, and Teo, like Azucena, had been remanded to the López Guido rehab facility, but finally all of them, even their old pal Julito, did marvelously.

Both institutions included first-rate astroanalysts among their staff. Rodrigo had even begun the process of recovering his memory. Having Citlali with him was extremely beneficial. They had been installed in a matrimonial suite. There, between orgasms, his past was coming to light. Of course, he had made no progress in remembering the lives in which he'd witnessed Isabel's crimes. The astroanalysts did not have the correct password, and without it, they could never gain full access to his subconscious. Rodrigo knew that Isabel was the only person who had the key. But how to get it out of her? Isabel gave every sign of being invincible.

ROUND SEVEN
Staggering Blow to the Head!

Isabel knew she was winning the battle, and was calmly awaiting Carmela's testimony. Thank God the girl has lost weight, she thought. She no longer had to be embarrassed by her. Carmela looked quite lovely now, and provoked a lot of admiring glances. Isabel felt extremely proud of her daughter, and was even beginning to like her.

"What is your name?"

"Carmela González."

"What is your relationship to the accused?"

"I'm her daughter."

"How long have you lived with your mother?"

"Eighteen years."

"And during that time, have you ever known her to lie?"

"Yes."

A murmur rippled through the courtroom. Isabel's mouth tightened. The defense attorney was thrown completely off guard. This had not been in his plans.

"And on what occasion?"

"There were many."

"Could you be more specific? Give us an example."

"Certainly. She told me I was her only daughter."

"And isn't that the case?"

"No. I have a sister."

The defense attorney glanced at Isabel. He knew nothing about this information, but he didn't like the smell of it. This could turn out to be dangerous. Isabel's jaw had dropped. She couldn't imagine where Carmela had obtained that information.

"Why do you say that?"

"Rosalío Chávez told me."

"The bodyguard your mother recently dismissed?"

"Yes, that's the one."

"And you trusted information given you by a person who obviously was resentful for having been dismissed?"

"Objection!" shouted the prosecutor.

"Sustained," ruled the judge.

So Carmela did not have to answer the question. The defense attorney wiped his brow. He had no idea how to extricate himself from the mess he'd stumbled into.

"And do you think that this Mr. Rosalío Chávez is a person who can be trusted?"

"Not only that, I consider him my true mother."

Exclamations of surprise reverberated throughout the courtroom. Ex-Azucena wept with emotion. He had never expected such public recognition of his role as substitute mother. Isabel's composure was crumbling by the minute. Fucking little fat-ass, you'll pay for this! she thought. Isabel motioned to her attorney, who hurried over to confer with her. Isabel whispered a few words into his ear, and the attorney returned to the witness with a telling question on his lips.

"Is it true that you've suffered all your life from obesity?"

"Yes, that's true."

"And isn't it true that this problem caused many arguments and confrontations with your mother?"

"Yes, that's true."

"And isn't it true that you envied your mother terribly because she could eat anything she wanted without putting on weight?"

"That's correct."

"And isn't it also true that for this reason you determined to take your revenge by coming here to this court to testify against her, even though you have no way of proving what you say?"

"Objection!" cried the prosecutor.

"Sustained," said the judge.

Carmela realized that once again she did not have to respond to the question, but this time she wanted to do so.

"Your Honor, I'd like to answer that question. May I?"

"Go ahead."

"For one thing, what motivated me to testify is a desire to see justice done. I no longer have anything to envy, because now, as all of you can see, I'm thinner than she is. And I *do* have a way of proving the things I've said." Removing a piece of leaded glass from her handbag, Carmela handed it to the judge. "If I may, I'd like to present this piece of stained glass as evidence. If you have it analyzed you'll see that I'm not lying."

Carmela had been extremely clever. First, in managing to remove a section of stained glass from the window, as Ex-Azucena had asked, before Isabel had the house dynamited; and second, in presenting it as proof that Isabel had lied to her about the existence of her sister. To obtain images of the events the glass had witnessed, the court ordered a complete analysis of its history, from the day it was made up until the present.

In the course of that analysis, Isabel's crimes were revealed, one by one. The first to come to light was what had happened in 1890. From its vantage point, the stained glass had witnessed the male Isabel creep into the room where the male Citlali was raping the female Rodrigo, and offered a clear image of Isabel plunging the knife into Citlali's back. This image corresponded perfectly to the one that viewers around the world had seen on the day of the debate, the only discrepancy being merely that the scene was witnessed from a different perspective. Farther on, images of the 1985 crime against Azucena appeared. These shots were blurred since, like everything else in the house, the stained glass window was vibrating from the earthquake. From its high perspective, however, it had witnessed the moment Rodrigo ran into the bedroom and picked up his daughter. But before he could escape with her, a beam fell on him, killing him. And then there was dust and darkness. The next image showed Isabel entering the room to find Rodrigo and Citlali dead in the rubble. Next her attention was drawn to the crying baby. Isabel walked over to her and saw that she was unharmed. Then with both hands she lifted up a large stone of rose quartz and smashed it down brutally upon the little head. The image showed in excruciating detail the icy emotions on Isabel's face at that moment, when she looked just a few years younger than in her present life. No one could deny that Isabel was indeed the one who had murdered that baby!

Finally came images of Isabel in 2180, with a baby in her arms. Waiting for her in the room was Rosalío Chávez as he appeared before he'd obtained Azucena's body. Isabel handed him the little girl and ordered him to disintegrate her for one hundred years. Taking the child in his arms, Rosalío left the room.

ROUND EIGHT
Knockout!

Isabel was finished. The defense had run out of arguments. The prosecutor asked the judge's permission to question Azucena Martínez, explaining that Azucena was the girl Isabel had ordered killed but, fortunately, she had survived. She was now here to offer her testimony. The judge agreed. Azucena was led into the courtroom. Before reaching the witness stand, she paused as Carmela gave her an affectionate hug.

Isabel felt her strength draining from her. Her daughter was alive! So she had not prevailed over fate. Her teeth chattered like castanets. She heard disgrace knocking at her door and went numb with fear. She could not absorb the turn of events and did not want to see any more of what was going on. But curiosity made her turn to look at her daughter Azucena for the first time. She found it impossible to believe that the aged woman who had just entered the courtroom was her daughter. What was going on? Azucena was sworn in. The prosecutor began his questioning.

"What is your name?"

"Azucena Martínez."

"What is your profession?"

"I am an astroanalyst."

"That means that you're continually involved with other people's past lives, is that true?"

"Yes."

"Did you ever wish you had experienced some part of your patients' lives?"

"Objection!" shouted the defense attorney.

"Overruled," declared the judge.

"Yes."

"Could you tell us when that was?"

"Yes. Whenever they had lived a happy childhood with their mother."

"Why was that?"

"Because my mother abandoned me when I was a baby. I never knew her."

"And if you had ever met her, would you have complained to her about how she'd abandoned you?"

"I would have, before I served my term at the rehabilitation facility."

"And how did your stay there change your way of thinking?"

"I not only forgave my mother for having abandoned me, but also for twice trying to have me killed."

Azucena looked in Isabel's direction, her blind eyes shining brightly. Isabel shuddered at the intensity of her gaze. Azucena was telling the truth. There was no hatred in her. No one had ever gazed on Isabel with love. Everyone around her regarded her with fear, respect, or mistrust—never with love. Isabel could not take any more, and burst into tears. Her days of villainy were over.

━┼━

"I promise to abide by and to enforce the Law of Love from this day forward." Much against her will, Isabel had to speak those words, at which time her trial was declared ended. As part of her sentence, she had been named Consul in Korma. Her one mission from now on would be to teach the Kormian natives to understand the Law of Love.

Her words affected no one more greatly than Rodrigo and Citlali. The password to their memories was precisely the word "love," spoken by Isabel. When Rodrigo heard it, he felt like Noah, on the day the rains ceased. The oppression weighing on his mind vanished. The constant feeling that there was something he was supposed to put back where it belonged disappeared. He breathed a deep sigh and felt a profound sense of peace. His eyes fixed upon Azucena's, and light glowed between them. He immediately recognized her as his twin soul. They relived their first meeting in its entirety, except that this time they had an audience. When the music of the spheres faded, Rodrigo, inflamed with love, asked Azucena to marry him that very day. All their friends accompanied them to the shrine of Guadalupe. The first thing they did there was visit El Pocito to perform the rite. And the moment Rodrigo leaned over to take some water, he spotted the capstone to the Pyramid of Love.

The notes of a distant conch sounded as they set the rose quartz stone in place. The air was replete with the aroma of warm tortillas and newly baked bread. The city of Gran Tenochtitlán appeared before them and, superimposed on it, colonial Mexico City. Then, in a unique phenomenon, the two cities became fused.

The voices of Nahua poets chanted in unison with those of Spanish monks. The eyes of all present were able to look deep into the eyes of any other, without apprehension. No barrier existed. The other person was oneself. For a moment, all hearts harbored Divine Love equally. Everyone felt part of a whole. Love struck them like lightning, penetrating every space in their bodies. At times the flesh could not contain it, and its truth burst out in a tingling on the skin. As Cuquita said, it was an "awe-expiring" spectacle.

CD
Track 11

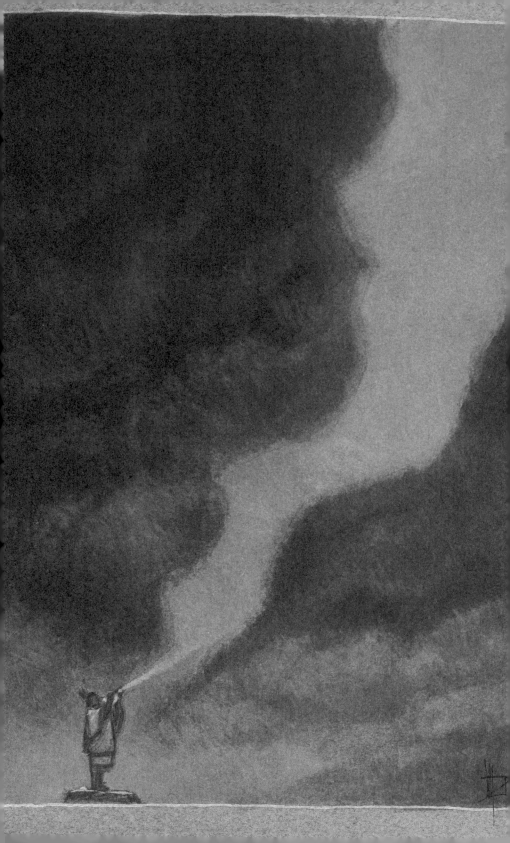

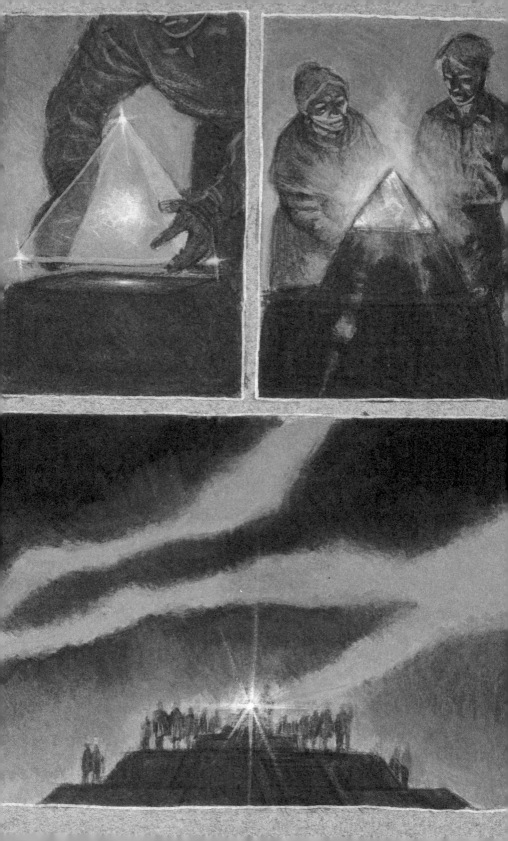

Like a mighty hurricane, love erased every vestige of rancor, of hatred. No one could remember why they'd ever grown apart from a loved one. The reincarnated Hugo Sánchez forgot that it was Dr. Mejía Barón who had not allowed him to play in the 1994 soccer World Cup. Cuquita forgot the beatings her husband had given her all those years. Carmela forgot that Isabel always called her a pig. Julito forgot that he liked only women with fat asses. Cats forgot that they despised mice. The Palestinians forgot their bitterness toward the Jews. Suddenly there were no more racists or torturers. Bodies forgot knife wounds, bullet wounds, gashes, kicks, torture, blows, and opened their pores to caresses and kisses. Tear ducts prepared to shed tears of joy; throats to sob with pleasure; mouth muscles to trace the broadest of smiles; heart muscles to expand and expand until they gave birth to pure love. Just like Ex-Azucena's womb.

His time had come. In the midst of the cacophony of love, he gave birth to a beautiful baby girl. She was born without a moment's pain, in absolute harmony. She came into a world that welcomed her with open arms and so had no reason to cry. Nor Ex-Azucena to remain on Earth: with the birth, his mission was fulfilled. Lovingly, he bid his daughter good-bye and died with a wink of his eye.

Rodrigo gave the baby to Azucena and she hugged her tenderly. She could not see her baby, but she knew exactly what she was like. Azucena wished with all her heart and soul to have a young body so that she could care for the child. The Gods took pity on her, allowing her to occupy her former body once again as a reward for all her efforts in carrying out her mission.

As soon as Azucena reentered her body, Anacreonte's mission was complete. He was at total liberty to go off and enjoy his honeymoon. During the trial, he had courted Pavana, and they had just been married. As for Lilith, she had married Mammon.

Within a few months, the former couple had a cuddly little cherub, and the latter, a dimpled little demon.

On Earth, all was happiness. Citlali had found her twin soul. Cuquita had found hers. Teo was promoted. Carmela discovered that she was hopelessly in love with Julito and they were married without delay. Order finally had been reestablished and all doubts resolved. Azucena learned that she had been assigned the mission of reinstating the Law of Love as part of a punishment. She had been the most foul murderer of all time, having blown up three planets with nuclear bombs. But the Law of Love, in its infinite generosity, had given her the opportunity to restore equilibrium. And to the benefit of all, she had succeeded.

⊹

I perceive the secret, the hidden,
O you, our lords!
Thus we are:
We are mortals,
And four by four we mortals
All must go away,
All must die on earth . . .
Like a painting, we shall go on fading.
Like a flower,
We shall wither
Here upon the earth.
Like the vestment of the zacuán,
Of the precious bird with the collar of blood,
We shall go on ending . . .

Think upon this, O lords:
Eagles and tigers,
Were you made of jade,
Were you made of gold,
There still would you go,
To the place of the uncarnate.
We must all disappear,
No one is to remain.

"Romances de los Señores de Nueva
España," fol. 36 r.
NEZAHUALCÓYOTL
Trece Poetas del Mundo Azteca
MIGUEL LEÓN-PORTILLA

CONTENTS OF CD

MUSIC CREDITS

WORKS OF GIACOMO PUCCINI

SOPRANO: REGINA OROZCO
TENOR: ARMANDO MORA

ORQUESTA DE BAJA CALIFORNIA
CONDUCTOR: EDUARDO GARCÍA BARRIOS

ORCHESTRATION: SERGIO RAMÍREZ*/DMITRI DUDIN**
ARTISTIC AND MUSICAL DIRECTION: EDUARDO GARCÍA BARRIOS

Concert Master: Igor Tchetchko
First Violins: Tatiana Freedland
Alyze Drelling
Second Violins: Jean Young
Heather Frank
Viola I: Sara Mullen
Viola II: Cynthia Saye
Cello: Omar Firestone
Double bass: Dean Ferrell
Flute: Sebastian Winston
Oboe: Boris Glouzman
Clarinet I: Vladimir Goltsman
Clarinet II: Alexandr Gurievich
Bassoon: Pavel Getman
French horn: Jane Zwerneman
Trumpet: Joe Dyke
Trombone: Loren Marsteller
Piano: Olena Getman
Harp: Elena Mashkovtseva
Percussion I: Andrei Thernishev
Percussion II: Alan Silverstein

Guest artists on *Senza Mamma:*
Viola II: Paula Simmons
Cello II: Renata Bratts

Chorus: Unidad Cristiana de México A.R.
and members of the choral workshop of the Orquesta de Baja California

Guest soloist: Laura Sosa

Conches and *tarahumera* drum: Ana Luisa Solís

Recording engineers: Luis Gil and Sergio Ramírez
Assistant engineer: Luis Cortés
Production assistant: Renata Ramos
Recorded in Tijuana B.C. in Autumn 1995

DANZONES

COMPOSER AND LEAD SINGER: LILIANA FELIPE

ORCHESTRA: DANZONERA DIMAS
CONDUCTOR: FELIPE PÉREZ
ARRANGEMENTS: LILIANA FELIPE AND DMITRI DUDIN

Tenor saxophone: Amador Pérez
Alto saxophone/clarinet II: Félix Guillén
Alto saxophone/clarinet I: Andrés Martínez
Alto saxophone/clarinet III: Eloy López
Trumpet III: Felipe Castillo
Trumpet II: Pepe Millar
Trumpet I: Abel García
Trombone: Pedro Deheza
Piano: Aurelio Galicia
Bass: David Pérez
Percussion: Hipólito González
Maracas: Paulino Rivero

BURUNDANGA

Lead singer: Eugenia León
Combo: La Rumbantela
Conductor: Osmani Paredes

Recording engineer: Luis Gil
Assistant to Annette Fradera: Renata Ramos

Recorded at Peerless's Pedro Infante studio and at El Cuarto de Máquinas
studio in Mexico City in Autumn 1995.

A production of Laura Esquivel under the direction of Annette Fradera

Musicomedia S.C./México
Fax (525) 513 40 17

Special thanks to CECUT (Tijuana)

Vocal fragment of Track 11 taken from "Versos de Pastorela" contained on
the LP *Tradiciones Musicales de la Laguna*, edited by the INAH.
(Excerpt from "Versos de Pastorela":
". . . Huélguense de ver al niño y acabado de nacer . . .")
Fieldwork, recording, and notes: Irene Vázquez Valle
Transfer, editing, and sound: Guillermo Pous
Postproduction and sound effects: Rogelio Villanueva

ABOUT THE ILLUSTRATOR

An award-winning illustrator, **Miguelanxo Prado** has collaborated in numerous animated film and television projects. He has a weekly comic strip, which is syndicated throughout Europe and Latin America, and he has published twelve books. Laura Esquivel saw his work in Mexico and asked him to collaborate with her on *The Law of Love*. Mr. Prado lives in Spain.

ABOUT THE JACKET ARTIST

Montserrat Pecanins was born in Barcelona and lives in New York and Mexico. Her theater boxes and miniature cabarets have been exhibited in Tiffany's windows and have adorned the Rockefeller Center skating rink at Christmas, as well as many other festive celebrations.

ABOUT THE AUTHOR

Originally published in 1990, *Like Water for Chocolate (Como agua para chocolate)* won **Laura Esquivel** international acclaim. The film based on the book, with a screenplay by Laura Esquivel, swept the Ariel Awards of the Mexican Academy of Motion Pictures, winning eleven in all, and went on to become the largest grossing foreign film ever released in the United States. In 1994 *Like Water for Chocolate* won the prestigious ABBY award, which is given annually by the American Booksellers Association to the book the members of the organization most enjoyed hand-selling. The book has been translated into thirty languages and there are over three million copies in print worldwide. Ms. Esquivel lives in Mexico.